WINGS OF FIRE

THE LOST HEIR
THE GRAPHIC NOVEL

To Barry, Rachel, Mike, Maarta, and Phil —
thank you so much for understanding these dragons
and for all your graphic novel magic!
—T.T.S.

For Oscar — I can't wait to see how you draw.
—M.H.

Story and text copyright © 2019 by Tui T. Sutherland
Adaptation by Barry Deutsch
Map and border design © 2012 by Mike Schley
Art by Mike Holmes © 2019 by Scholastic Inc.

Library of Congress Control Number Available

ISBN 978-0-545-94221-8 (hardcover)
ISBN 978-0-545-94220-1 (paperback)

10 9   22 23

Printed in China   62
First edition, March 2019
Edited by Amanda Maciel
Lettering by John Green
Book design by Phil Falco
Creative Director: David Saylor

WINGS OF FIRE

OF FIRE

THE LOST HEIR
THE GRAPHIC NOVEL

BY TUI T. SUTHERLAND

ADAPTED BY BARRY DEUTSCH
ART BY MIKE HOLMES
COLOR BY MAARTA LAIHO

graphix
AN IMPRINT OF
■ SCHOLASTIC

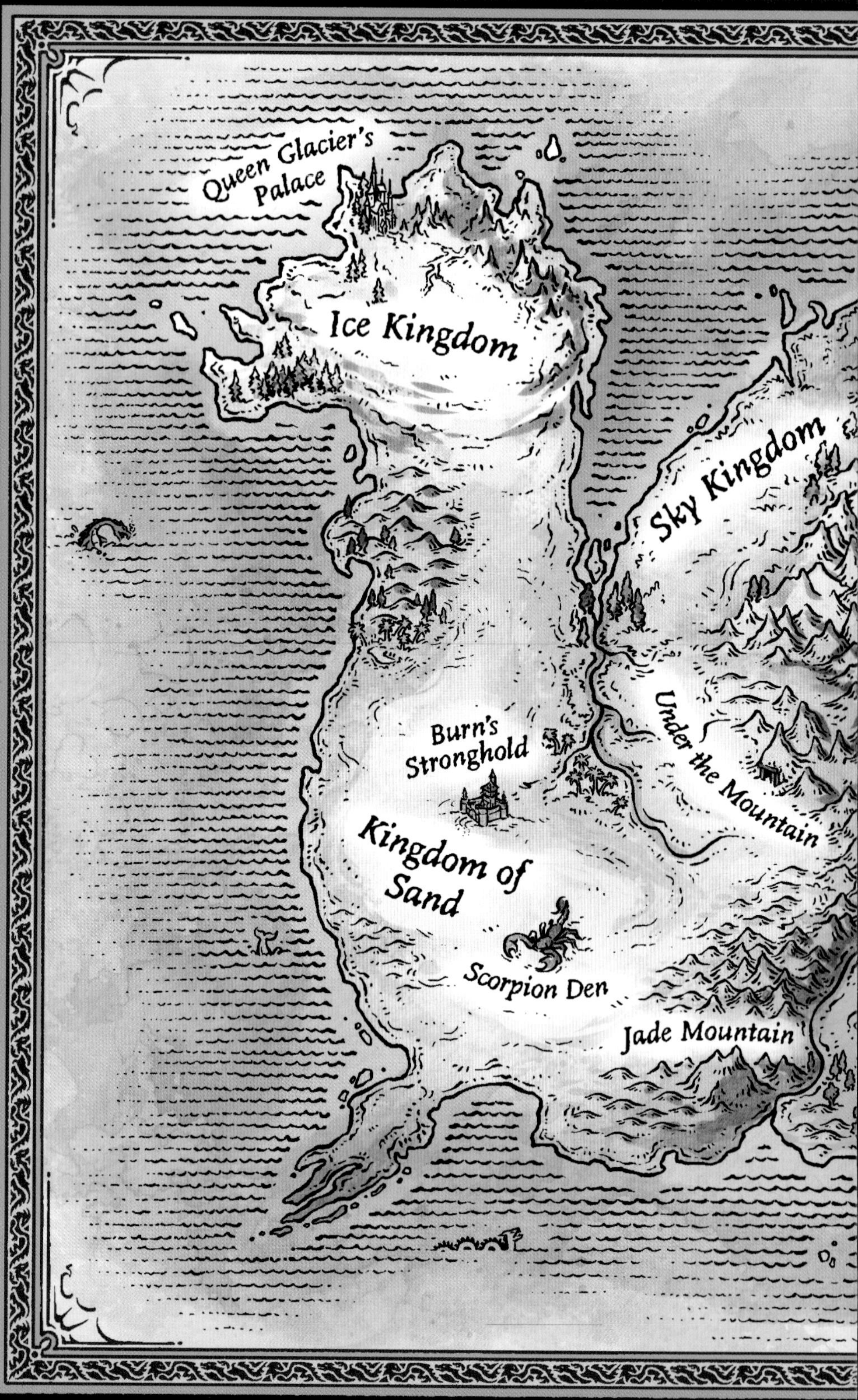
Queen Glacier's Palace
Ice Kingdom
Sky Kingdom
Burn's Stronghold
Under the Mountain
Kingdom of Sand
Scorpion Den
Jade Mountain

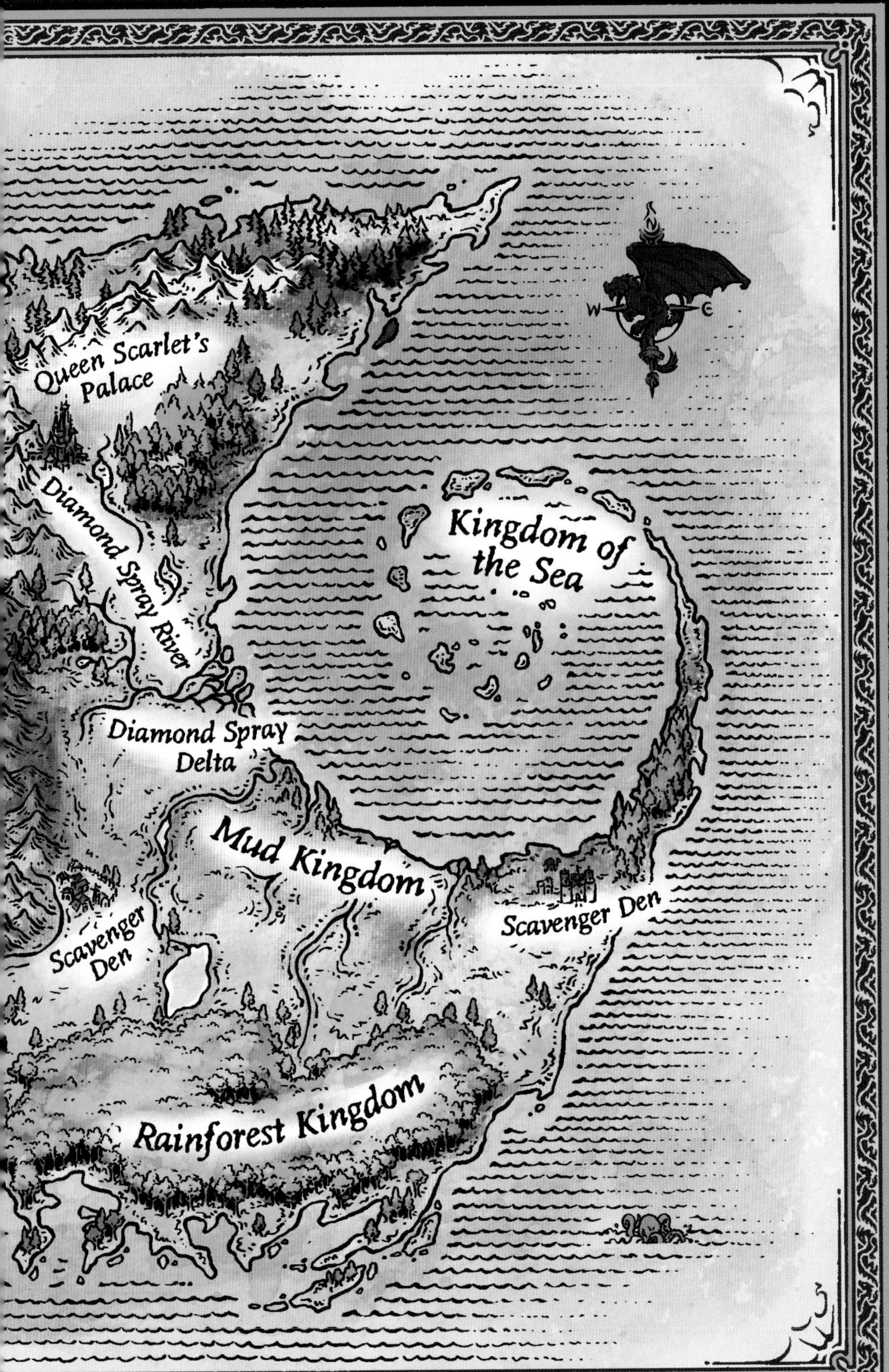

N
W
E
Queen Scarlet's Palace
Diamond Spray River
Kingdom of the Sea
Diamond Spray Delta
Mud Kingdom
Scavenger Den
Scavenger Den
Rainforest Kingdom

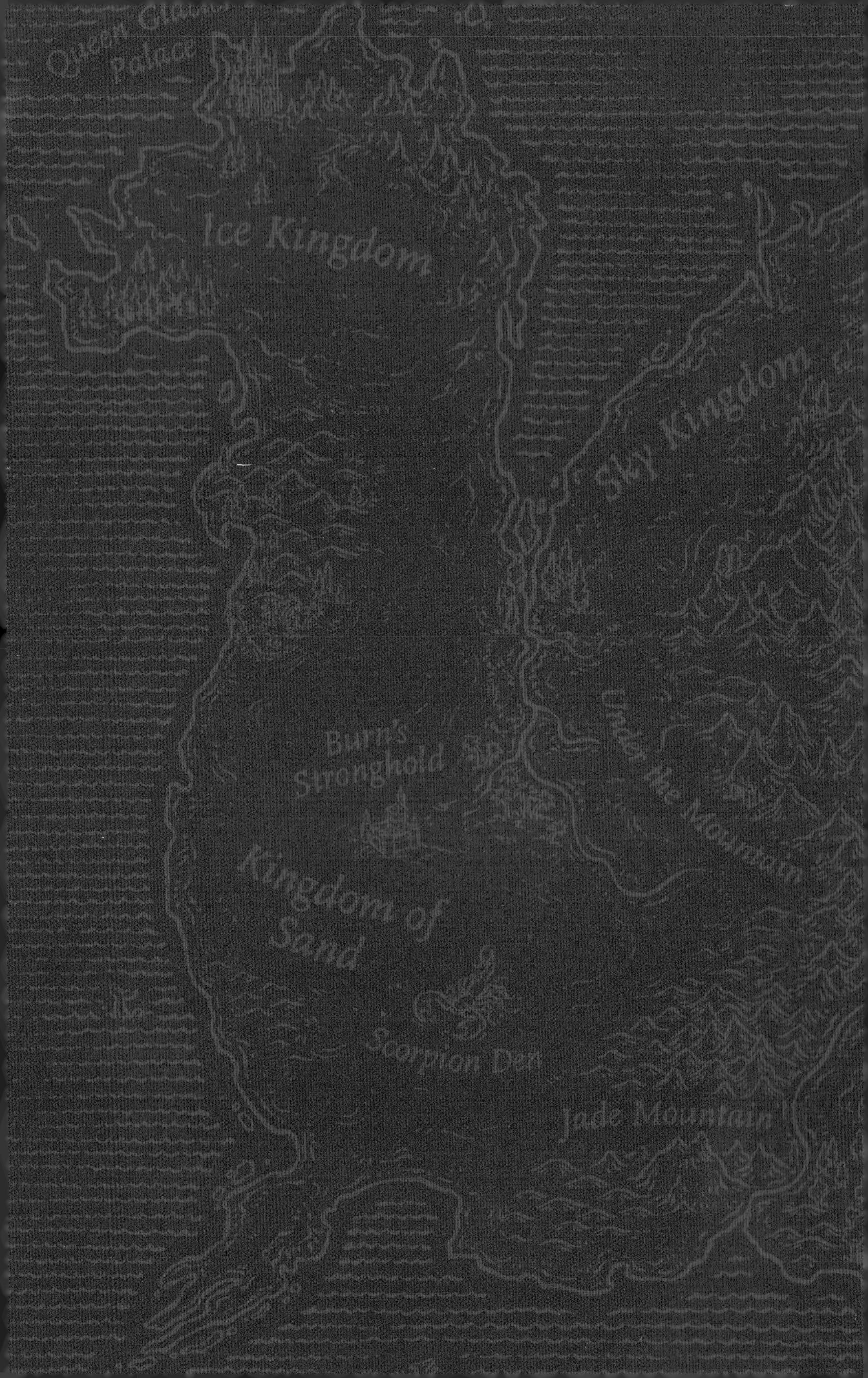
Queen Glacier's Palace
Ice Kingdom
Sky Kingdom
Burn's Stronghold
Kingdom of Sand
Under the Mountain
Scorpion Den
Jade Mountain

THE LOST HEIR

THE DRAGONET
PROPHECY

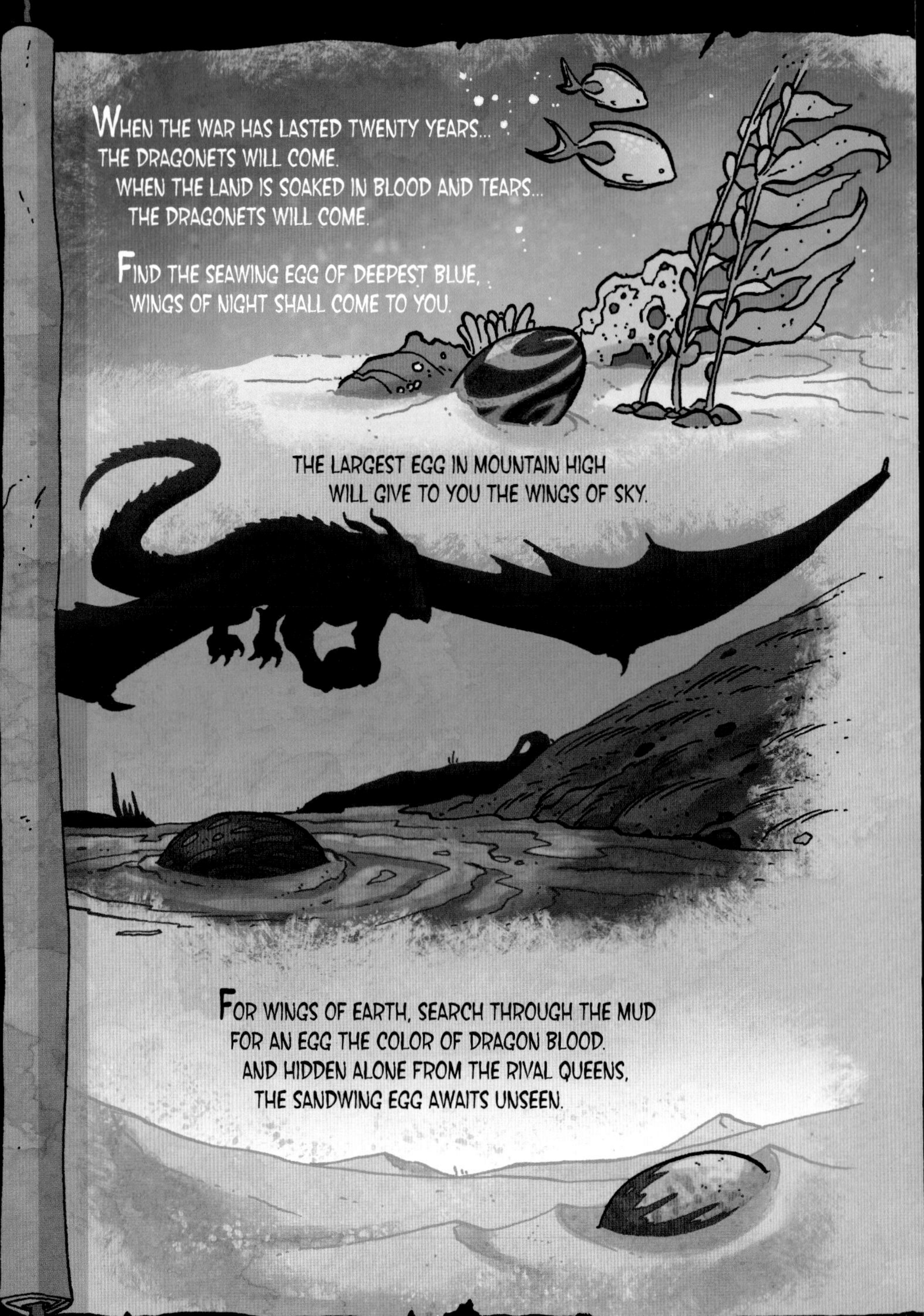
WHEN THE WAR HAS LASTED TWENTY YEARS...
THE DRAGONETS WILL COME.
WHEN THE LAND IS SOAKED IN BLOOD AND TEARS...
THE DRAGONETS WILL COME.
FIND THE SEAWING EGG OF DEEPEST BLUE,
WINGS OF NIGHT SHALL COME TO YOU.
THE LARGEST EGG IN MOUNTAIN HIGH
WILL GIVE TO YOU THE WINGS OF SKY.
FOR WINGS OF EARTH, SEARCH THROUGH THE MUD
FOR AN EGG THE COLOR OF DRAGON BLOOD.
AND HIDDEN ALONE FROM THE RIVAL QUEENS,
THE SANDWING EGG AWAITS UNSEEN.

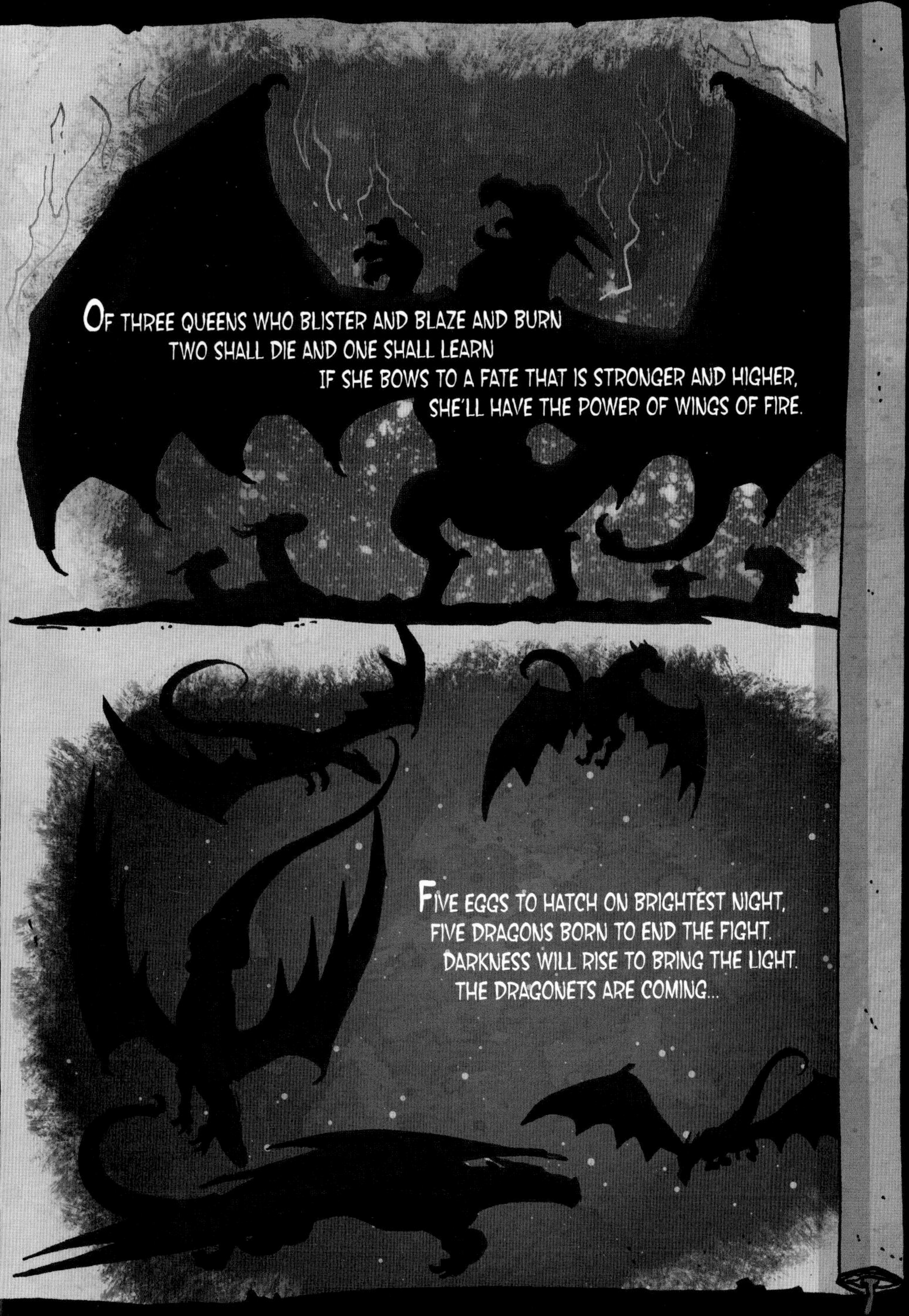
OF THREE QUEENS WHO BLISTER AND BLAZE AND BURN
TWO SHALL DIE AND ONE SHALL LEARN
IF SHE BOWS TO A FATE THAT IS STRONGER AND HIGHER,
SHE'LL HAVE THE POWER OF WINGS OF FIRE.
FIVE EGGS TO HATCH ON BRIGHTEST NIGHT,
FIVE DRAGONS BORN TO END THE FIGHT.
DARKNESS WILL RISE TO BRING THE LIGHT.
THE DRAGONETS ARE COMING...

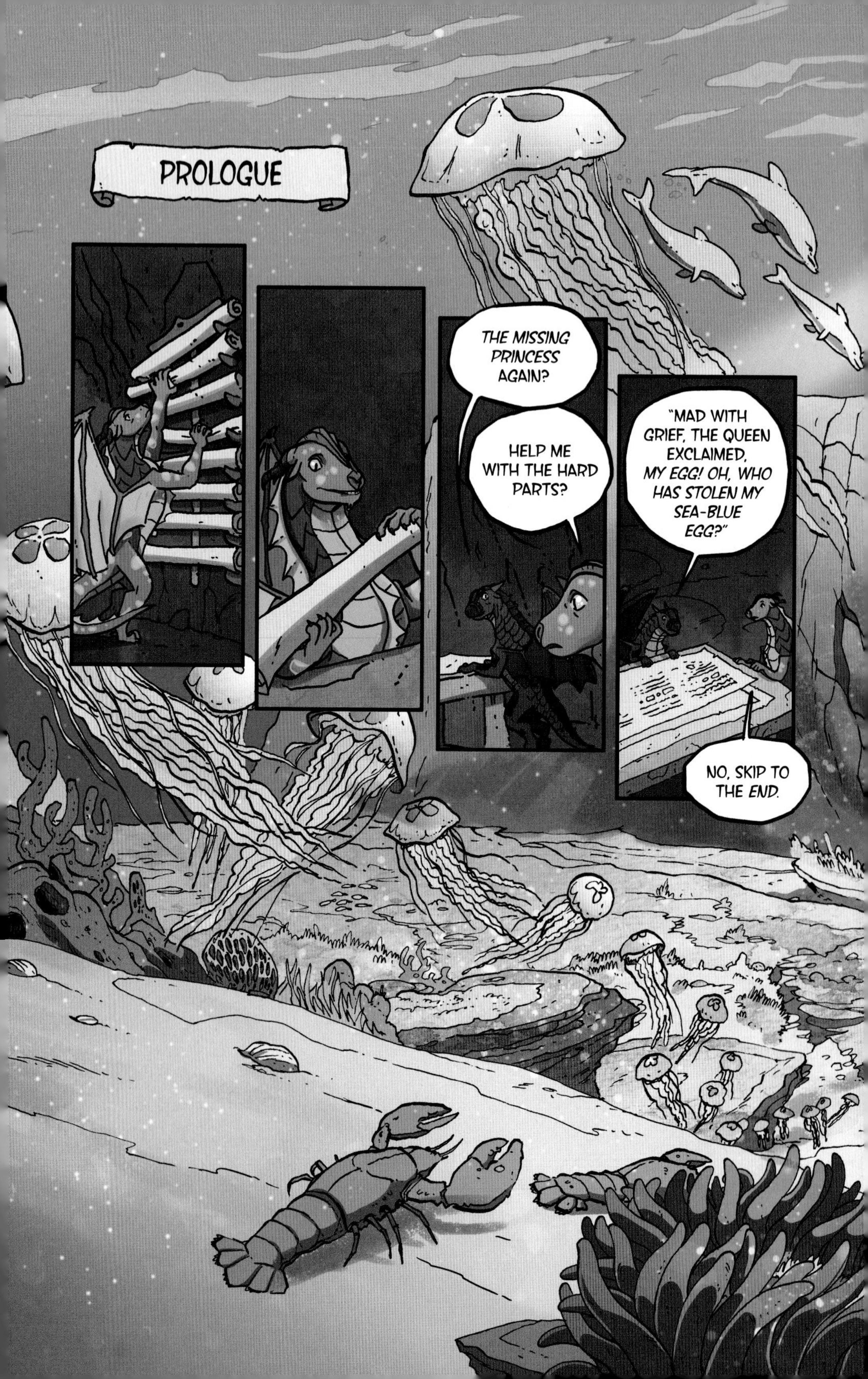
PROLOGUE
THE MISSING PRINCESS AGAIN?
HELP ME WITH THE HARD PARTS?
"MAD WITH GRIEF, THE QUEEN EXCLAIMED, *MY EGG! OH, WHO HAS STOLEN MY SEA-BLUE EGG?"*
NO, SKIP TO THE *END.*

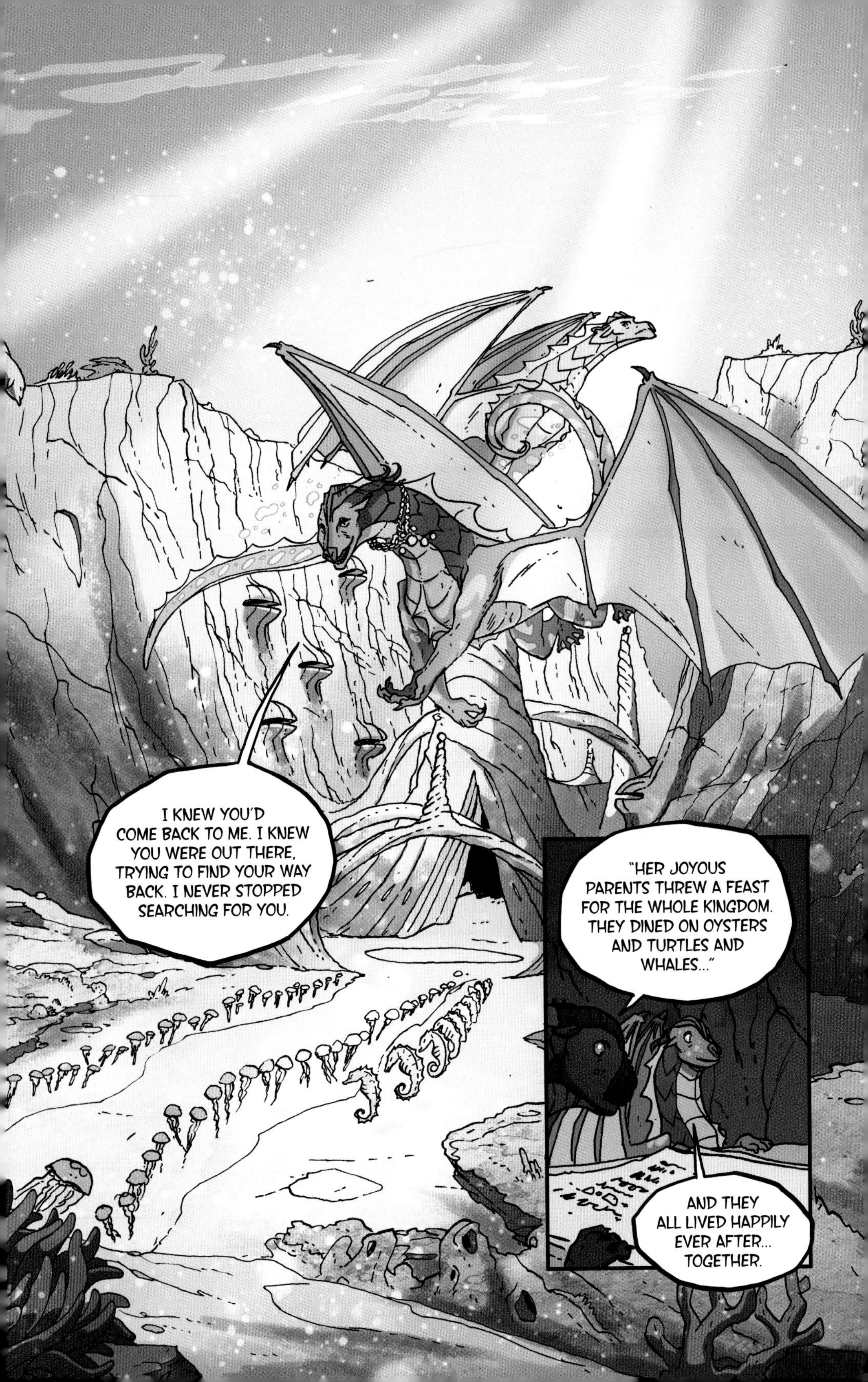
I KNEW YOU'D COME BACK TO ME. I KNEW YOU WERE OUT THERE, TRYING TO FIND YOUR WAY BACK. I NEVER STOPPED SEARCHING FOR YOU.
"HER JOYOUS PARENTS THREW A FEAST FOR THE WHOLE KINGDOM. THEY DINED ON OYSTERS AND TURTLES AND WHALES..."
AND THEY ALL LIVED HAPPILY EVER AFTER... TOGETHER.

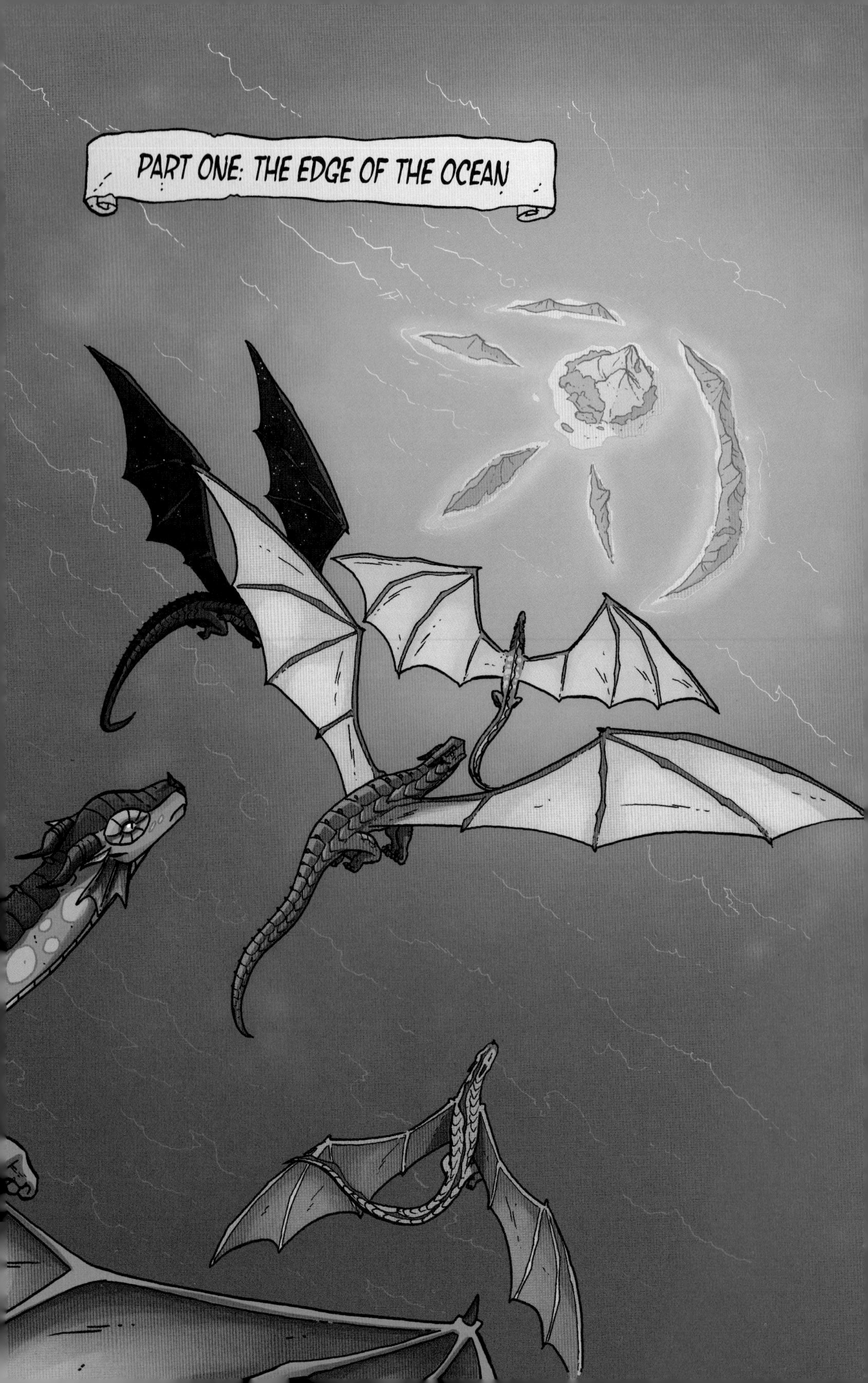
PART ONE: THE EDGE OF THE OCEAN

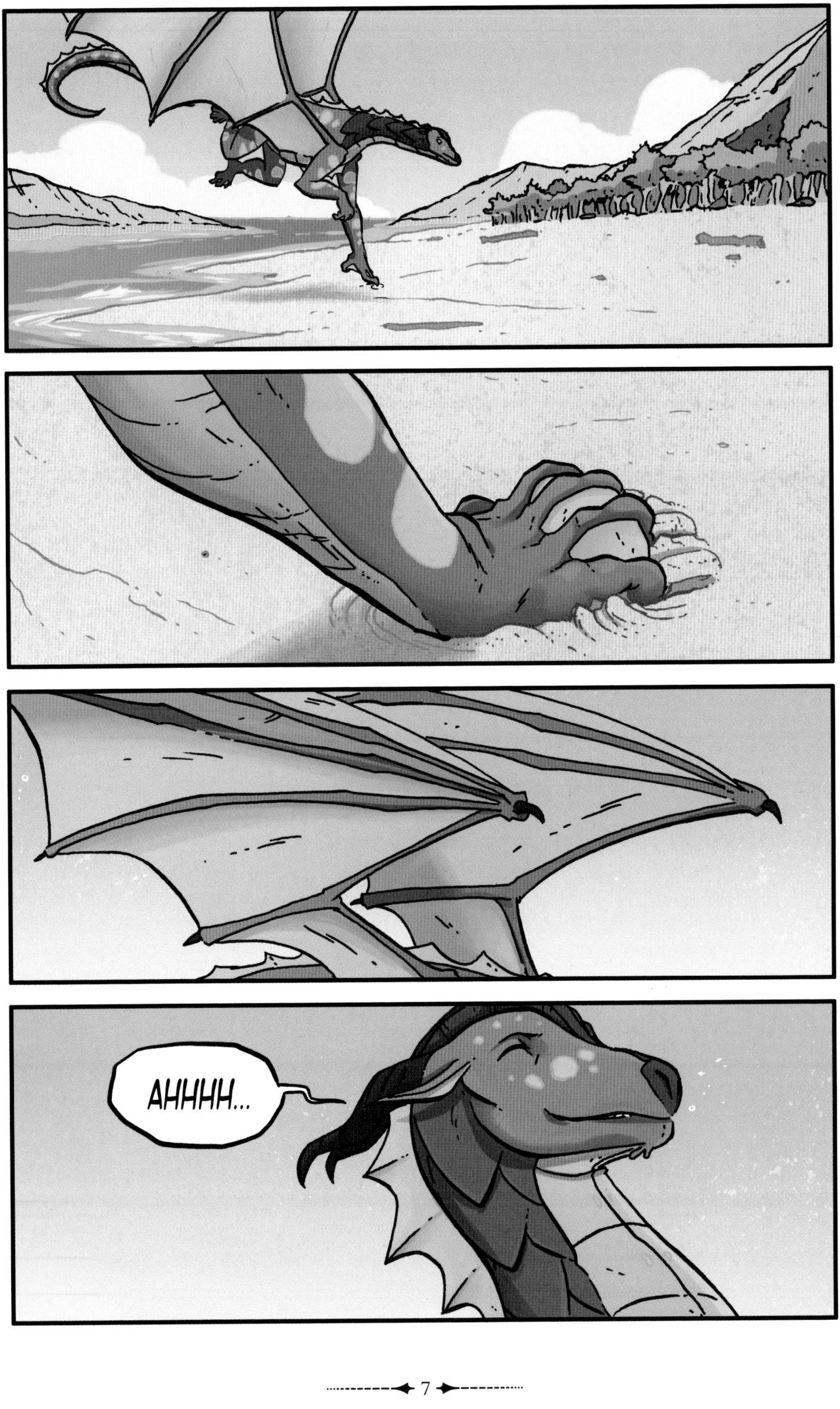
AHHHH...

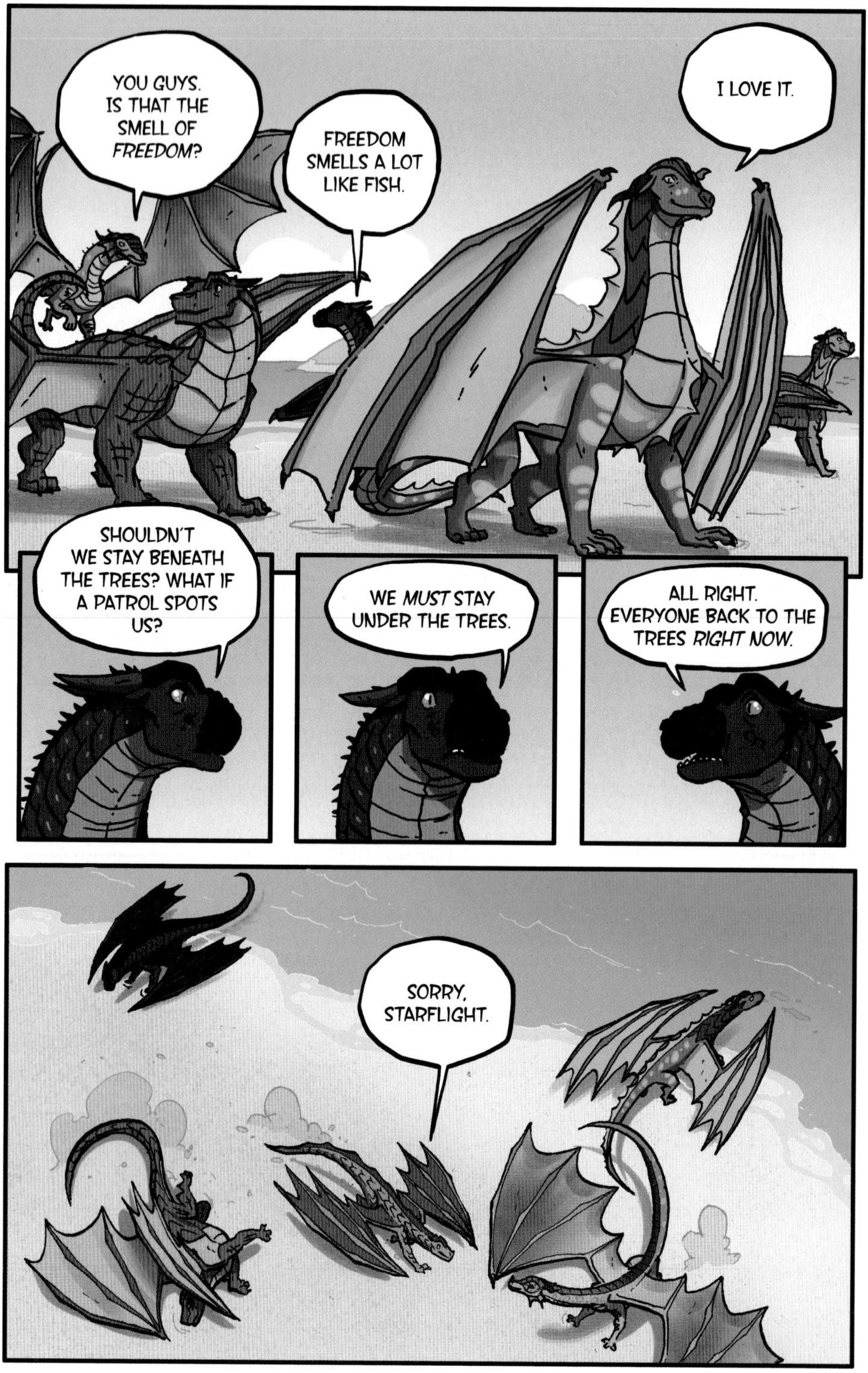
YOU GUYS. IS THAT THE SMELL OF *FREEDOM*?
FREEDOM SMELLS A LOT LIKE FISH.
I LOVE IT.
SHOULDN'T WE STAY BENEATH THE TREES? WHAT IF A PATROL SPOTS US?
WE *MUST* STAY UNDER THE TREES.
ALL RIGHT. EVERYONE BACK TO THE TREES *RIGHT NOW*.
SORRY, STARFLIGHT.

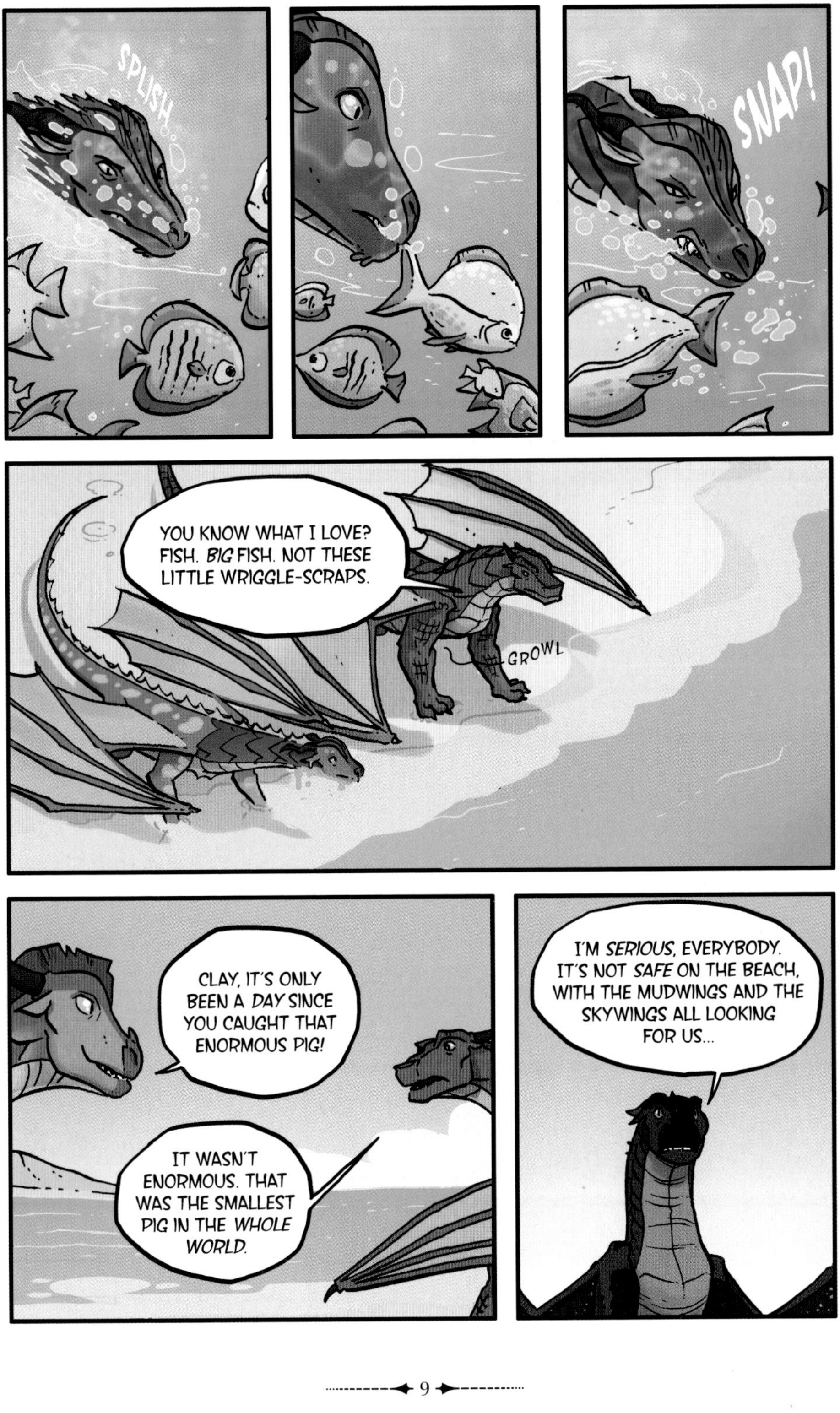
SPLISH
SNAP!
YOU KNOW WHAT I LOVE? FISH. BIG FISH. NOT THESE LITTLE WRIGGLE-SCRAPS.
GROWL
CLAY, IT'S ONLY BEEN A DAY SINCE YOU CAUGHT THAT ENORMOUS PIG!
IT WASN'T ENORMOUS. THAT WAS THE SMALLEST PIG IN THE WHOLE WORLD.
I'M SERIOUS, EVERYBODY. IT'S NOT SAFE ON THE BEACH, WITH THE MUDWINGS AND THE SKYWINGS ALL LOOKING FOR US...

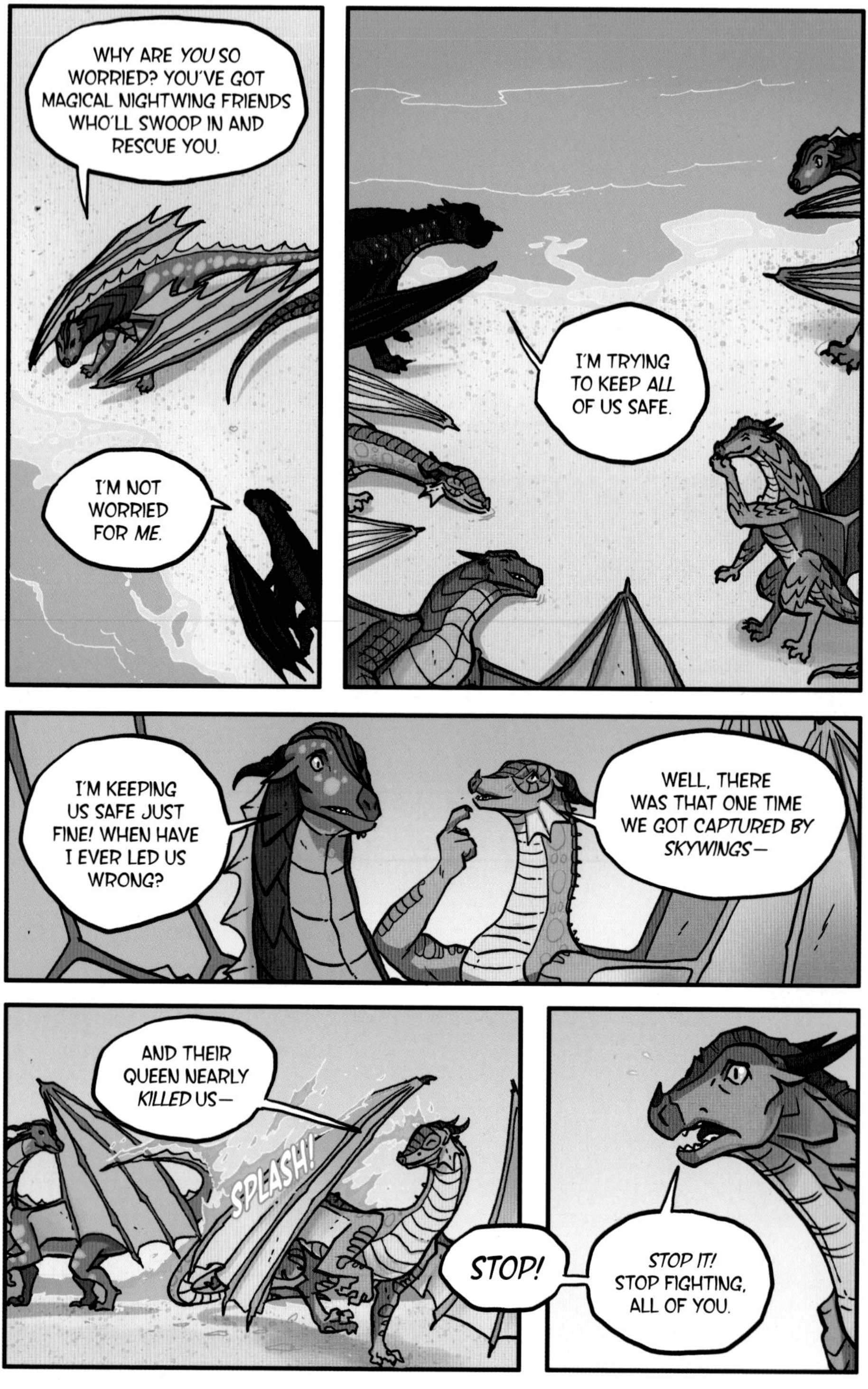
WHY ARE *YOU* SO WORRIED? YOU'VE GOT MAGICAL NIGHTWING FRIENDS WHO'LL SWOOP IN AND RESCUE YOU.
I'M NOT WORRIED FOR *ME*.
I'M TRYING TO KEEP *ALL* OF US SAFE.
I'M KEEPING US SAFE JUST FINE! WHEN HAVE I EVER LED US WRONG?
WELL, THERE WAS THAT ONE TIME WE GOT CAPTURED BY *SKYWINGS*—
AND THEIR QUEEN NEARLY *KILLED* US—
SPLASH!
STOP!
STOP IT! STOP FIGHTING, ALL OF YOU.

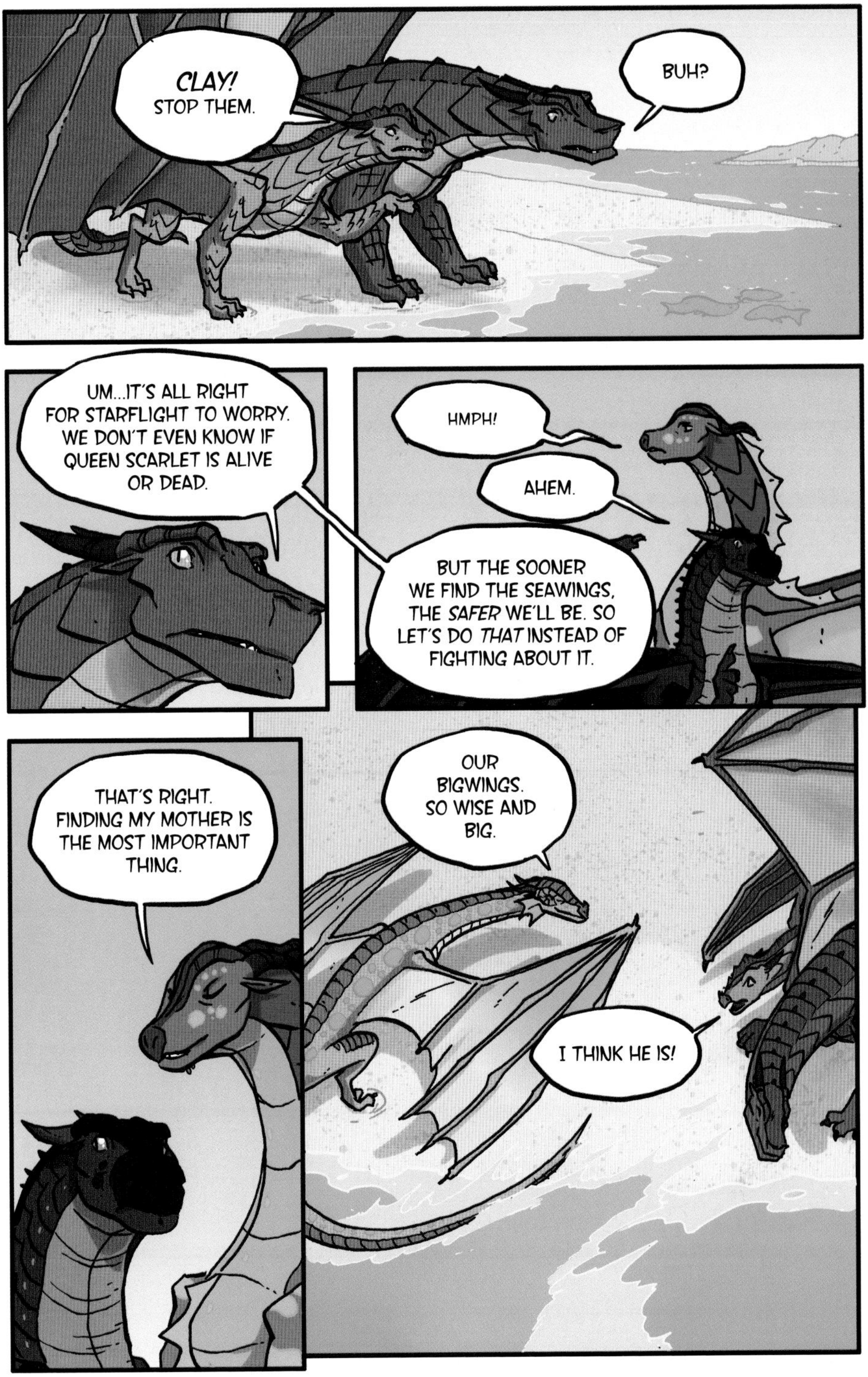
CLAY!
STOP THEM.
BUH?
UM...IT'S ALL RIGHT FOR STARFLIGHT TO WORRY. WE DON'T EVEN KNOW IF QUEEN SCARLET IS ALIVE OR DEAD.
HMPH!
AHEM.
BUT THE SOONER WE FIND THE SEAWINGS, THE *SAFER* WE'LL BE. SO LET'S DO *THAT* INSTEAD OF FIGHTING ABOUT IT.
THAT'S RIGHT. FINDING MY MOTHER IS THE MOST IMPORTANT THING.
OUR BIGWINGS. SO WISE AND BIG.
I THINK HE IS!

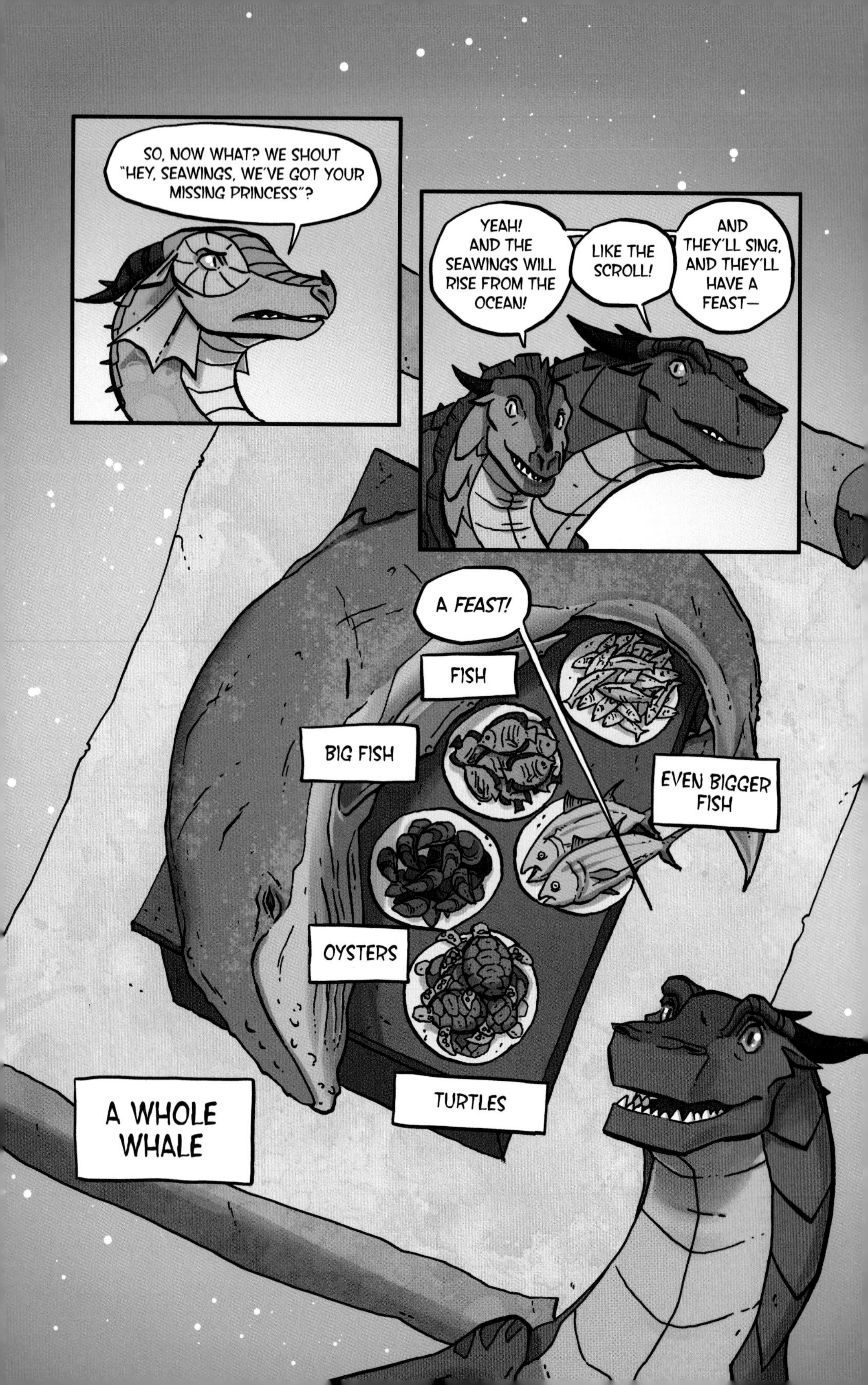
SO, NOW WHAT? WE SHOUT "HEY, SEAWINGS, WE'VE GOT YOUR MISSING PRINCESS"?
YEAH! AND THE SEAWINGS WILL RISE FROM THE OCEAN!
LIKE THE SCROLL!
AND THEY'LL SING, AND THEY'LL HAVE A FEAST—
A *FEAST!*
FISH
BIG FISH
EVEN BIGGER FISH
OYSTERS
TURTLES
A WHOLE WHALE

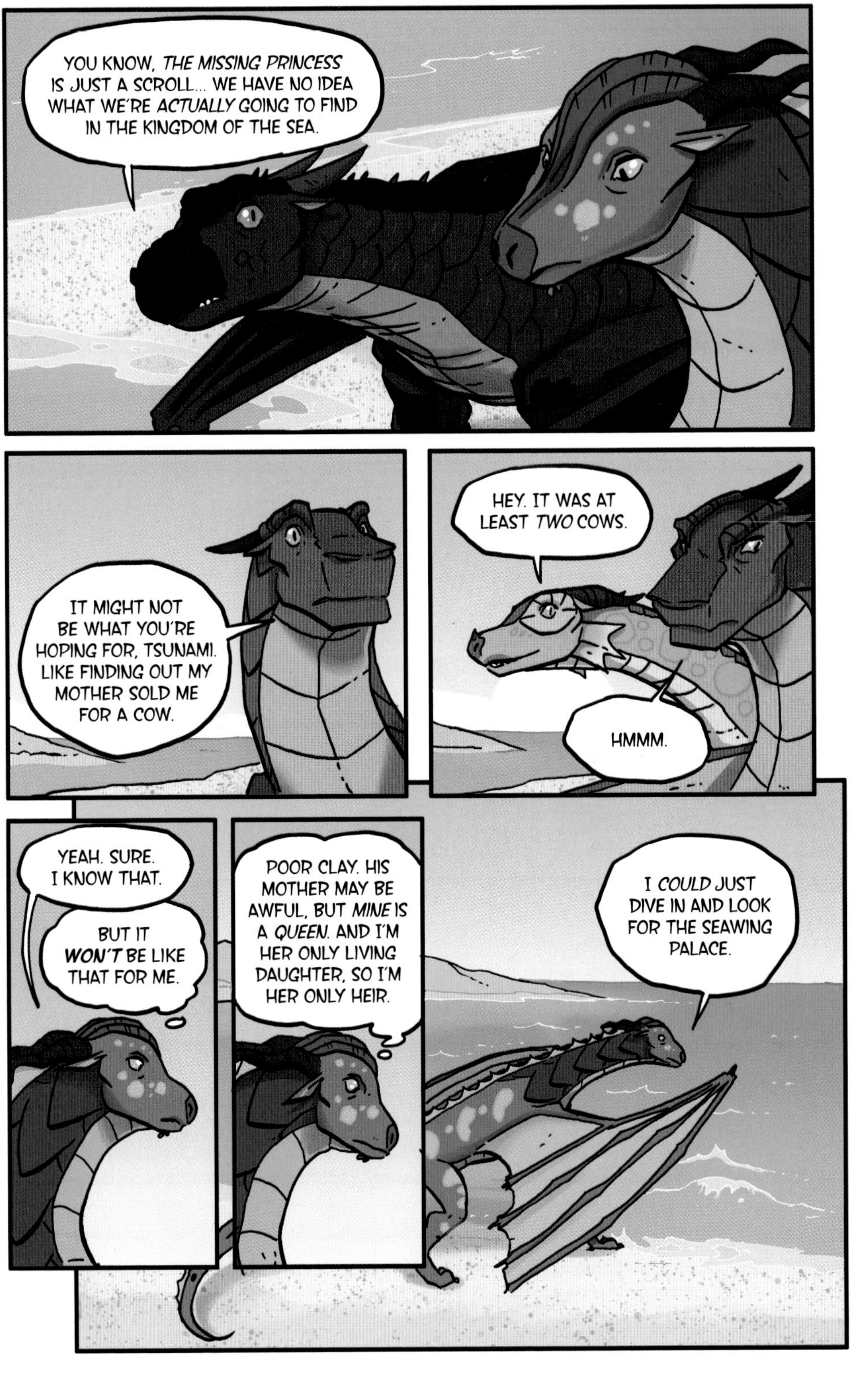
YOU KNOW, *THE MISSING PRINCESS* IS JUST A SCROLL... WE HAVE NO IDEA WHAT WE'RE *ACTUALLY* GOING TO FIND IN THE KINGDOM OF THE SEA.
IT MIGHT NOT BE WHAT YOU'RE HOPING FOR, TSUNAMI. LIKE FINDING OUT MY MOTHER SOLD ME FOR A COW.
HEY. IT WAS AT LEAST *TWO* COWS.
HMMM.
YEAH. SURE. I KNOW THAT.
BUT IT ***WON'T*** BE LIKE THAT FOR ME.
POOR CLAY. HIS MOTHER MAY BE AWFUL, BUT *MINE* IS A *QUEEN*. AND I'M HER ONLY LIVING DAUGHTER, SO I'M HER ONLY HEIR.
I *COULD* JUST DIVE IN AND LOOK FOR THE SEAWING PALACE.

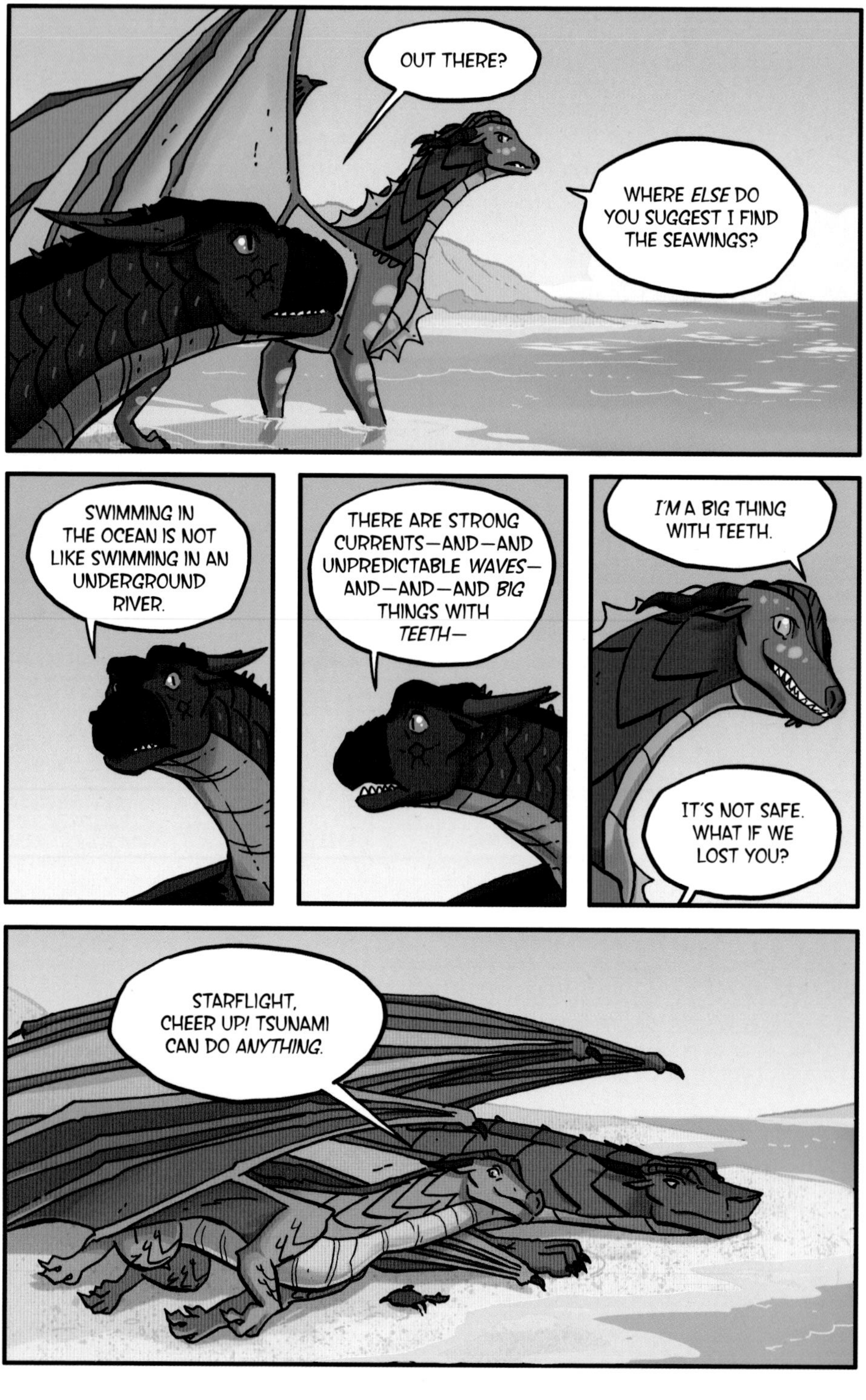
OUT THERE?
WHERE *ELSE* DO YOU SUGGEST I FIND THE SEAWINGS?
SWIMMING IN THE OCEAN IS NOT LIKE SWIMMING IN AN UNDERGROUND RIVER.
THERE ARE STRONG CURRENTS—AND—AND UNPREDICTABLE *WAVES*—AND—AND—AND *BIG* THINGS WITH *TEETH*—
I'M A BIG THING WITH TEETH.
IT'S NOT SAFE. WHAT IF WE LOST YOU?
STARFLIGHT, CHEER UP! TSUNAMI CAN DO *ANYTHING*.

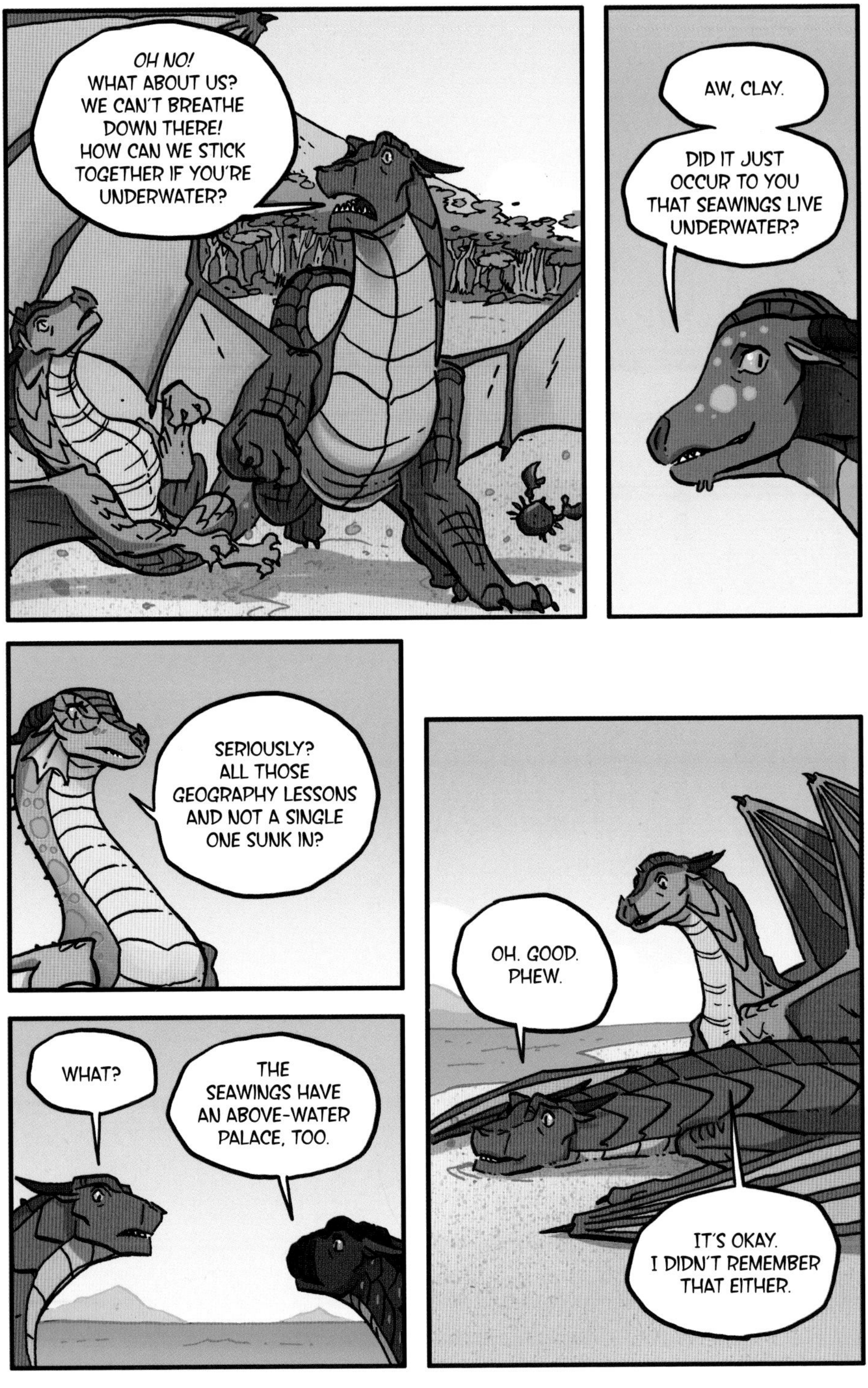
OH NO!
WHAT ABOUT US? WE CAN'T BREATHE DOWN THERE! HOW CAN WE STICK TOGETHER IF YOU'RE UNDERWATER?
AW, CLAY.
DID IT JUST OCCUR TO YOU THAT SEAWINGS LIVE UNDERWATER?
SERIOUSLY? ALL THOSE GEOGRAPHY LESSONS AND NOT A SINGLE ONE SUNK IN?
WHAT?
THE SEAWINGS HAVE AN ABOVE-WATER PALACE, TOO.
OH. GOOD. PHEW.
IT'S OKAY. I DIDN'T REMEMBER THAT EITHER.

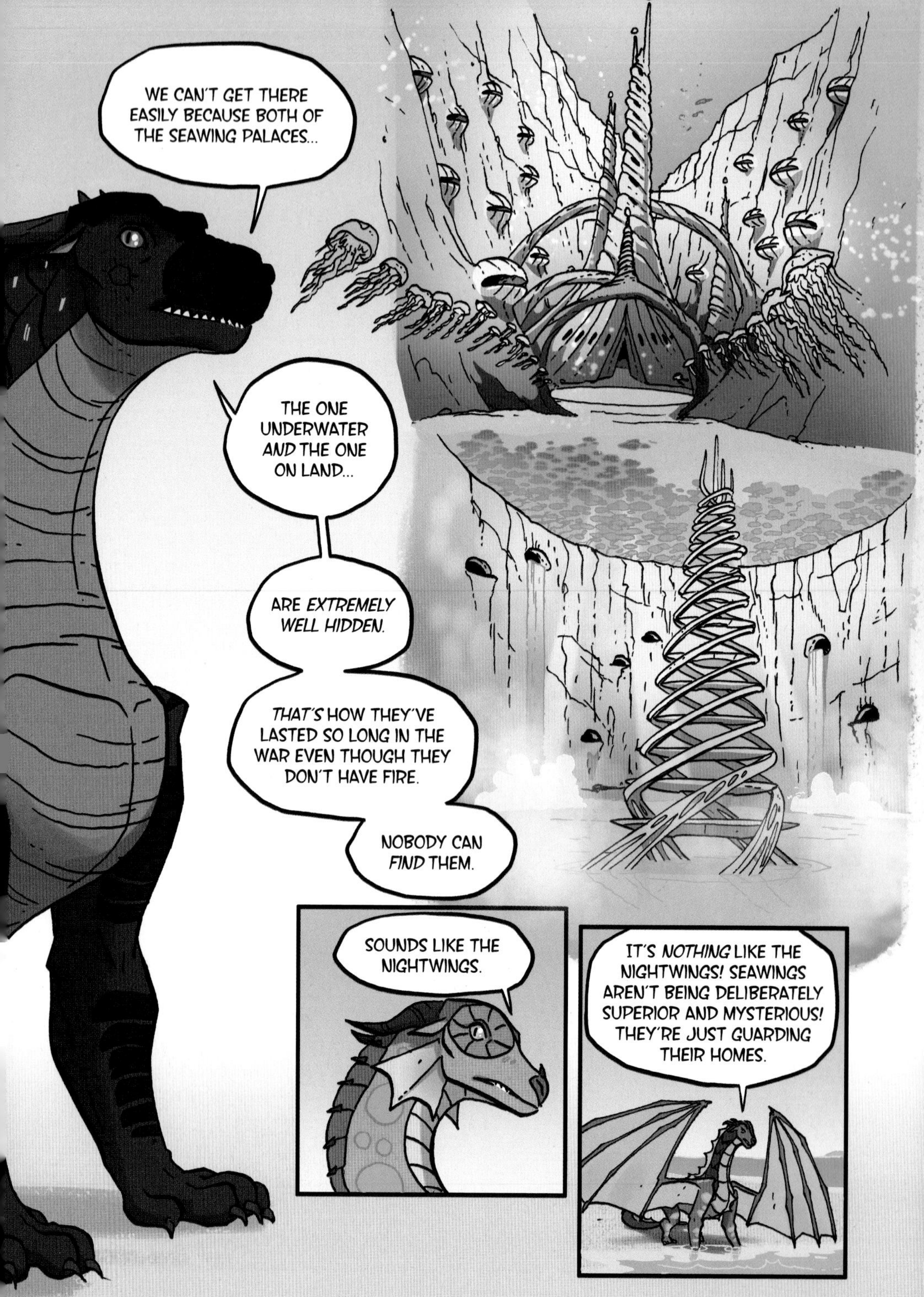

WE CAN'T GET THERE EASILY BECAUSE BOTH OF THE SEAWING PALACES...
THE ONE UNDERWATER AND THE ONE ON LAND...
ARE *EXTREMELY* WELL HIDDEN.
THAT'S HOW THEY'VE LASTED SO LONG IN THE WAR EVEN THOUGH THEY DON'T HAVE FIRE.
NOBODY CAN *FIND* THEM.
SOUNDS LIKE THE NIGHTWINGS.
IT'S *NOTHING* LIKE THE NIGHTWINGS! SEAWINGS AREN'T BEING DELIBERATELY SUPERIOR AND MYSTERIOUS! THEY'RE JUST GUARDING THEIR HOMES.

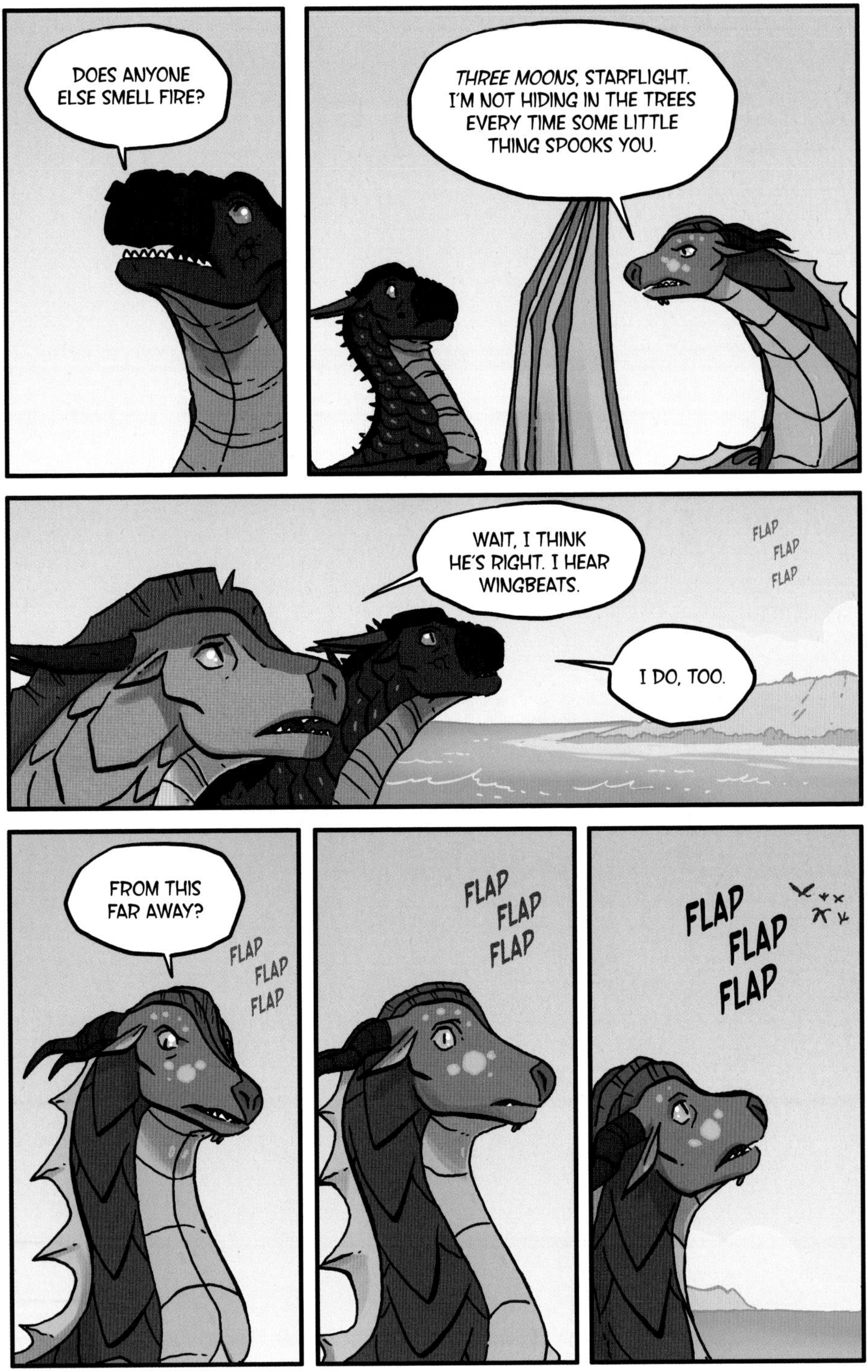
DOES ANYONE ELSE SMELL FIRE?
THREE MOONS, STARFLIGHT. I'M NOT HIDING IN THE TREES EVERY TIME SOME LITTLE THING SPOOKS YOU.
WAIT, I THINK HE'S RIGHT. I HEAR WINGBEATS.
FLAP FLAP FLAP
I DO, TOO.
FROM THIS FAR AWAY?
FLAP FLAP FLAP
FLAP FLAP FLAP
FLAP FLAP FLAP

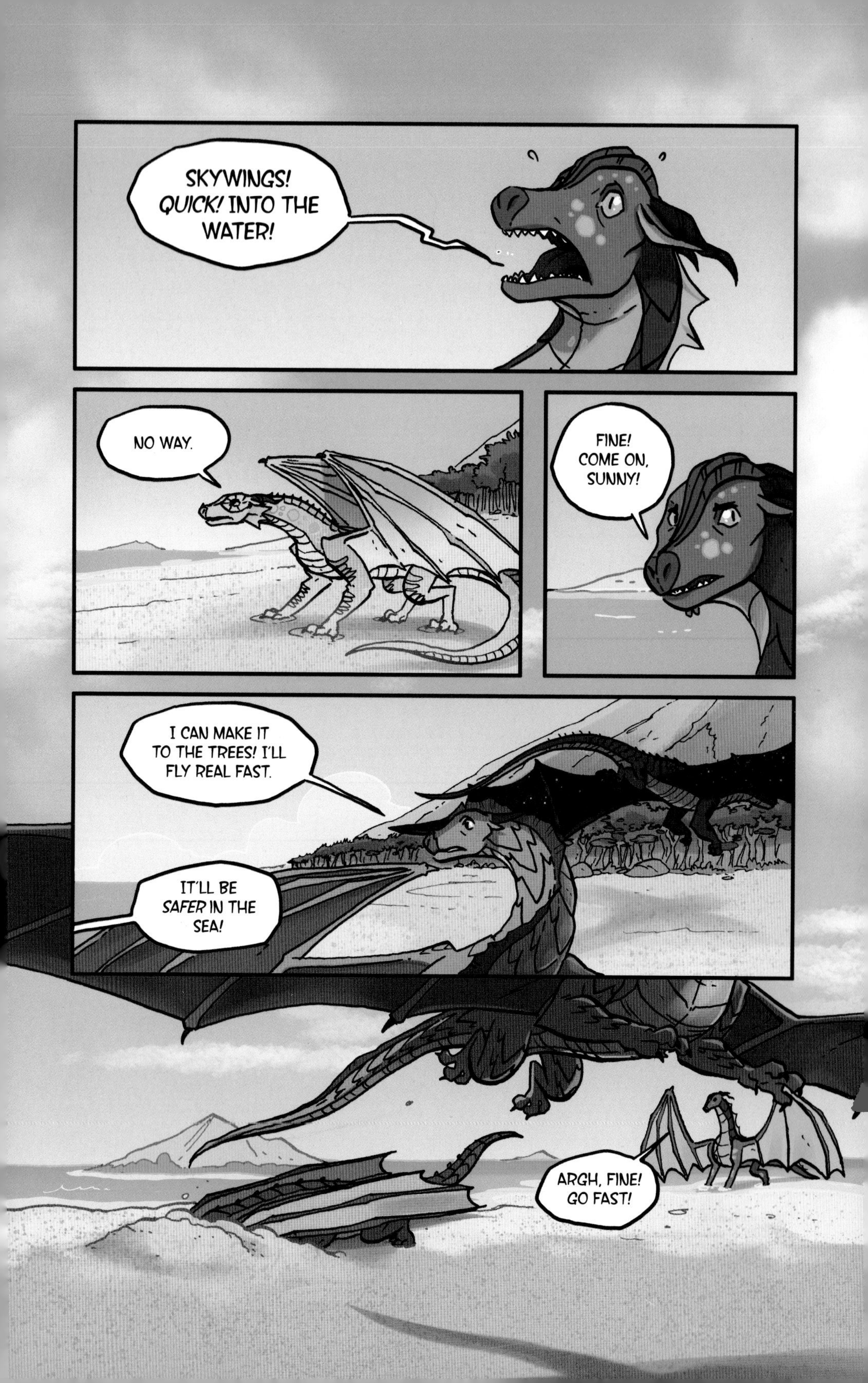
SKYWINGS! *QUICK!* INTO THE WATER!
NO WAY.
FINE! COME ON, SUNNY!
I CAN MAKE IT TO THE TREES! I'LL FLY REAL FAST.
IT'LL BE *SAFER* IN THE SEA!
ARGH, FINE! GO FAST!

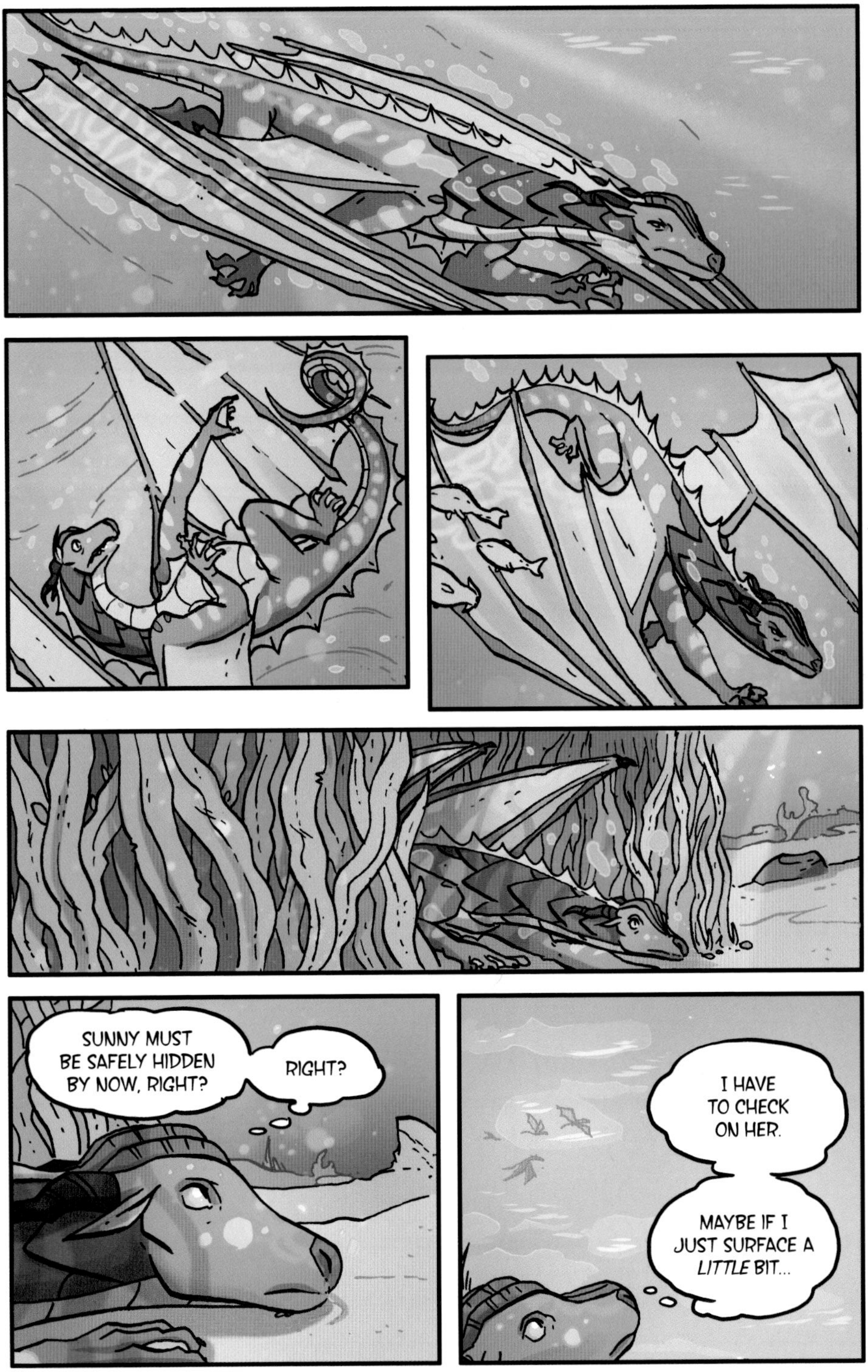
SUNNY MUST BE SAFELY HIDDEN BY NOW, RIGHT?
RIGHT?
I HAVE TO CHECK ON HER.
MAYBE IF I JUST SURFACE A *LITTLE* BIT...

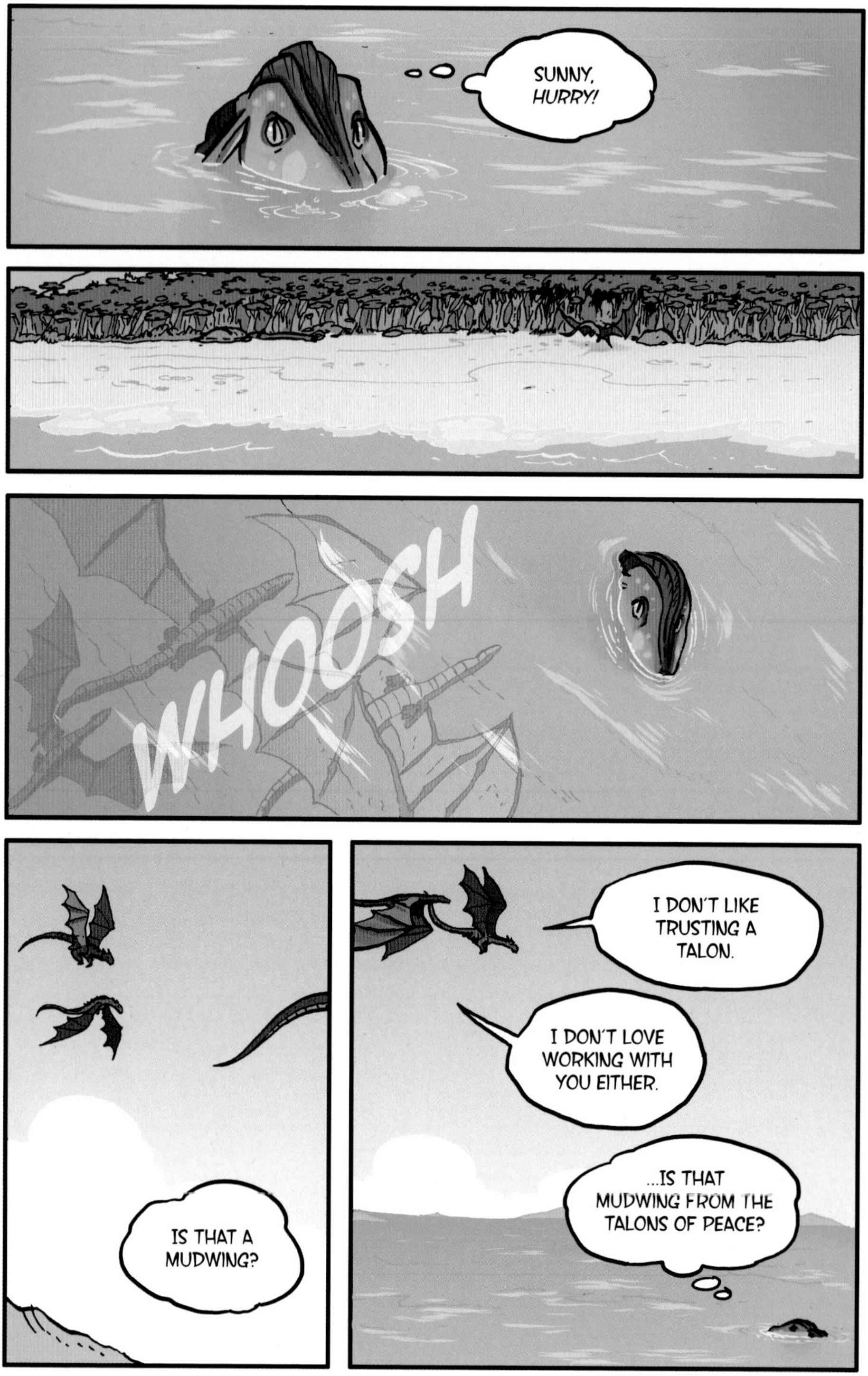
SUNNY, HURRY!
WHOOSH
I DON'T LIKE TRUSTING A TALON.
I DON'T LOVE WORKING WITH YOU EITHER.
IS THAT A MUDWING?
...IS THAT MUDWING FROM THE TALONS OF PEACE?

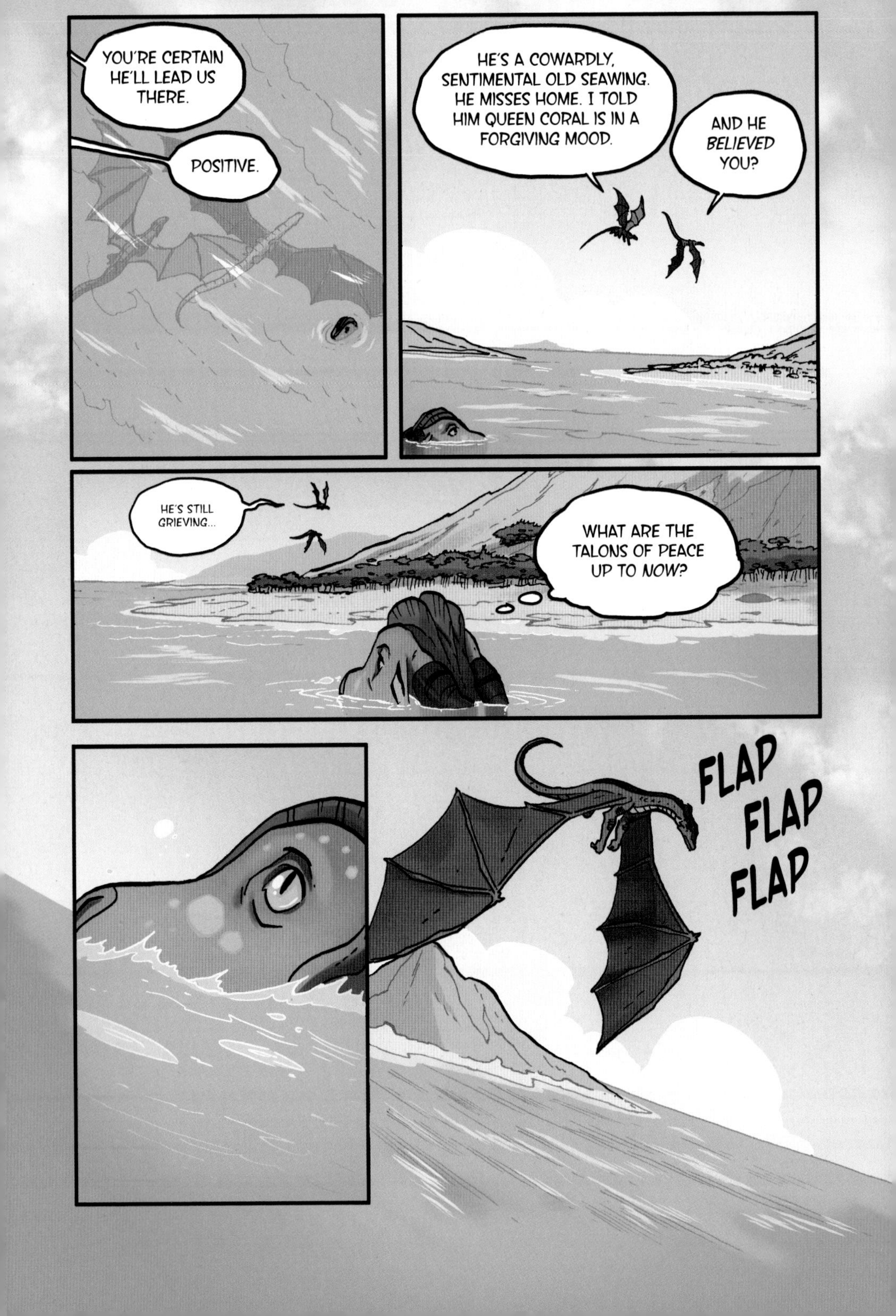

YOU'RE CERTAIN HE'LL LEAD US THERE.
POSITIVE.
HE'S A COWARDLY, SENTIMENTAL OLD SEAWING. HE MISSES HOME. I TOLD HIM QUEEN CORAL IS IN A FORGIVING MOOD.
AND HE *BELIEVED* YOU?
HE'S STILL GRIEVING...
WHAT ARE THE TALONS OF PEACE UP TO *NOW*?
FLAP
FLAP
FLAP

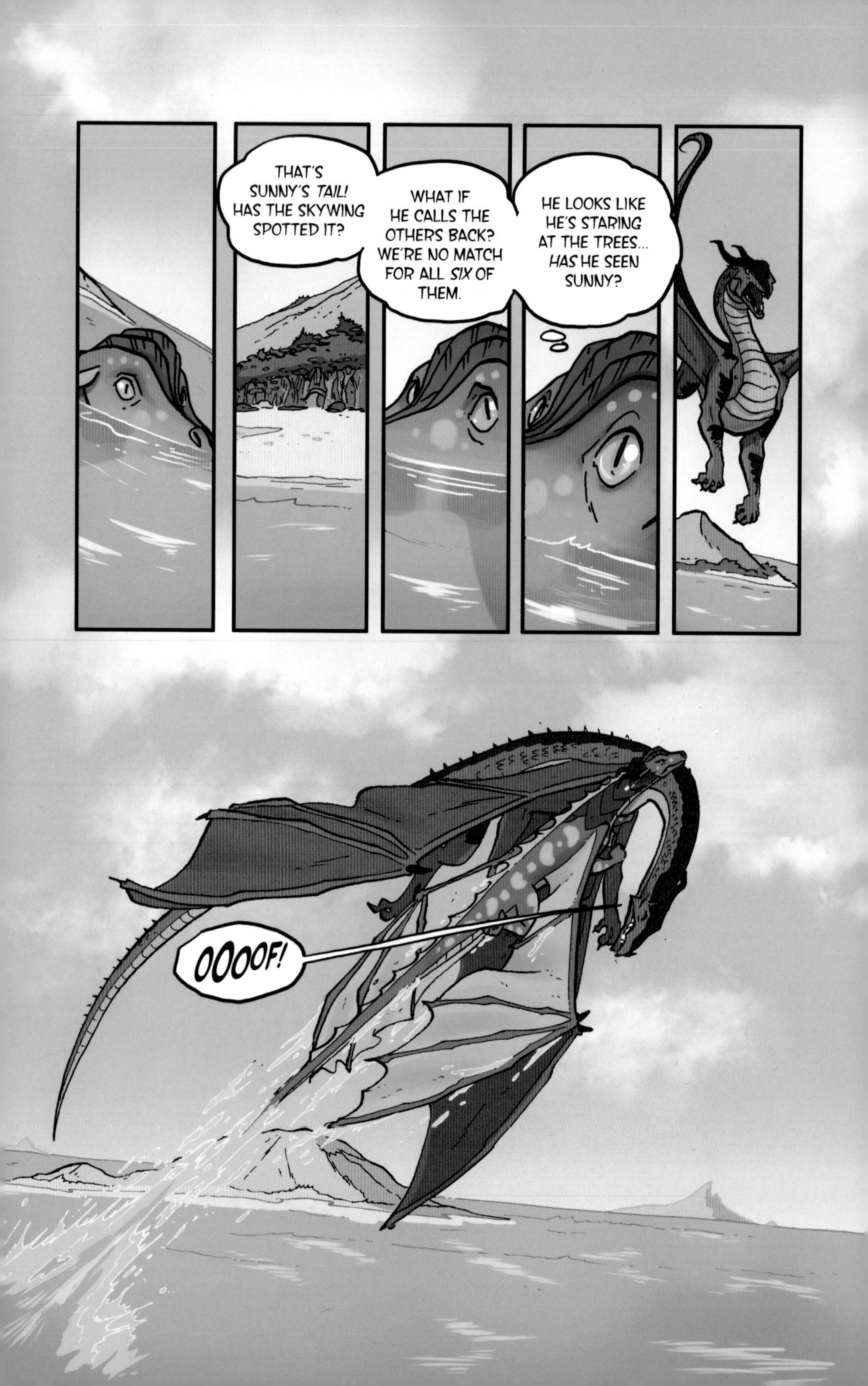
THAT'S SUNNY'S *TAIL!* HAS THE SKYWING SPOTTED IT?
WHAT IF HE CALLS THE OTHERS BACK? WE'RE NO MATCH FOR ALL *SIX* OF THEM.
HE LOOKS LIKE HE'S STARING AT THE TREES... *HAS* HE SEEN SUNNY?
OOOOF!

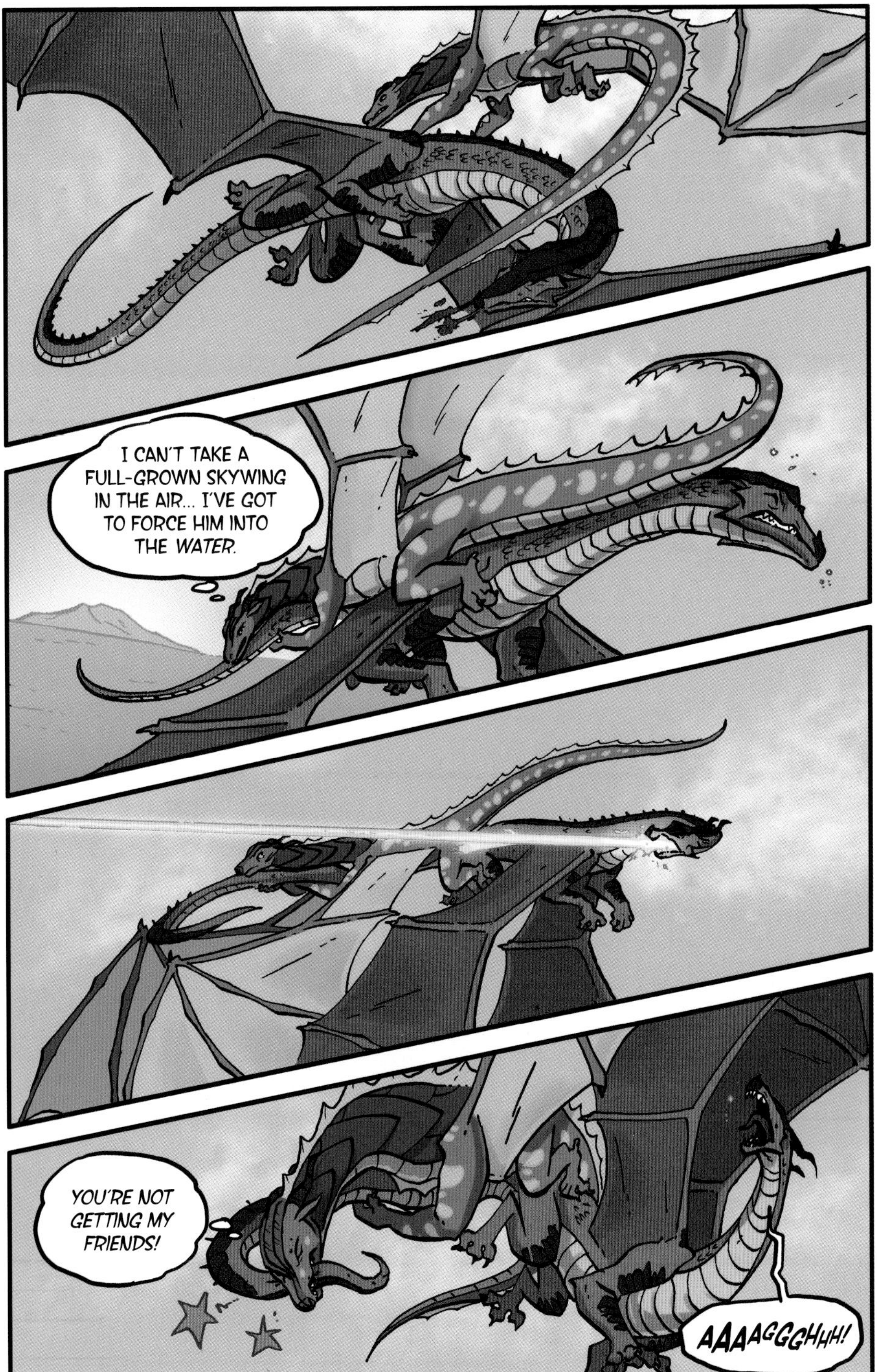
I CAN'T TAKE A FULL-GROWN SKYWING IN THE AIR... I'VE GOT TO FORCE HIM INTO THE *WATER*.
YOU'RE NOT GETTING MY FRIENDS!
AAAAGGGHHH!

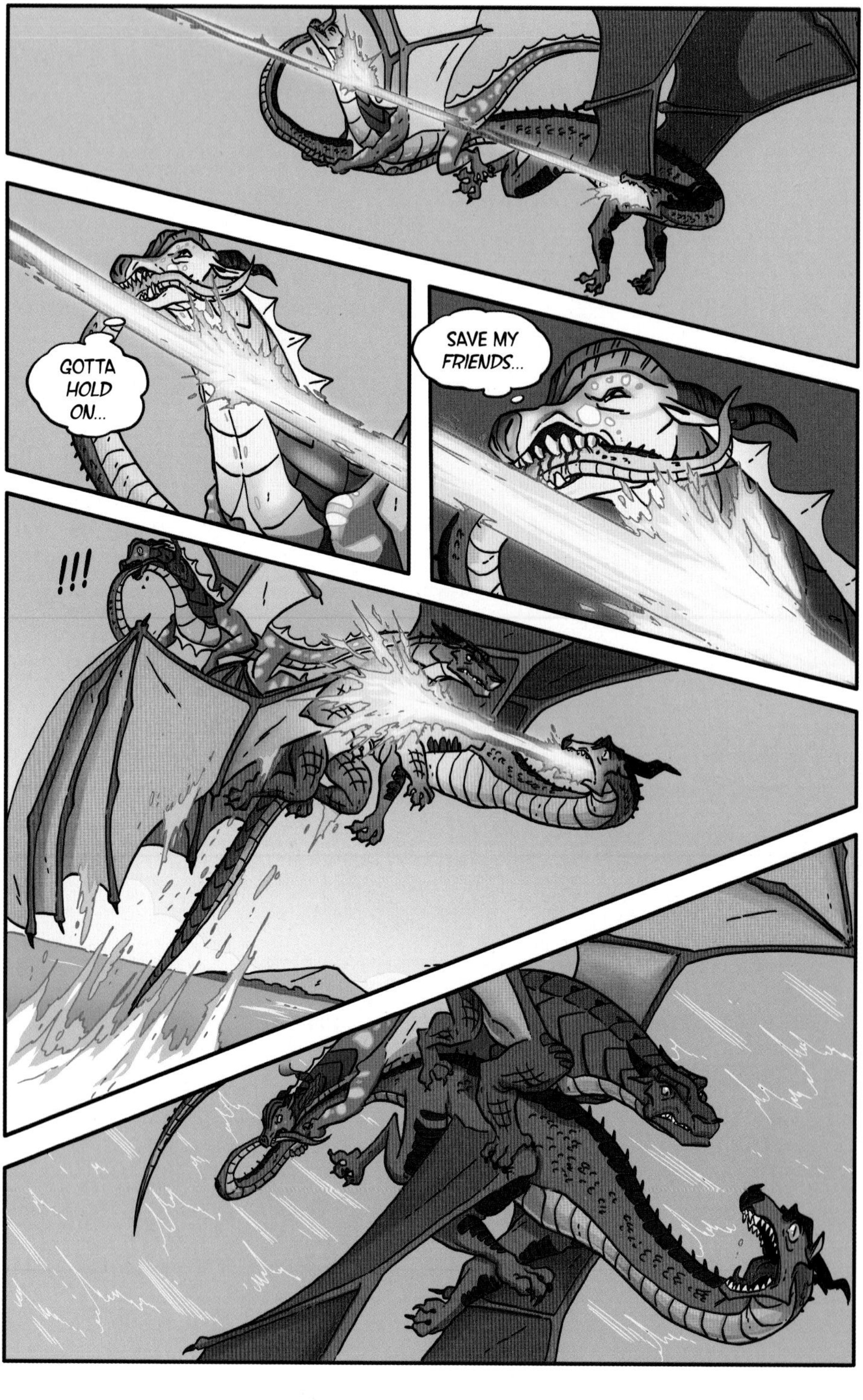
GOTTA HOLD ON...
SAVE MY FRIENDS...
!!!

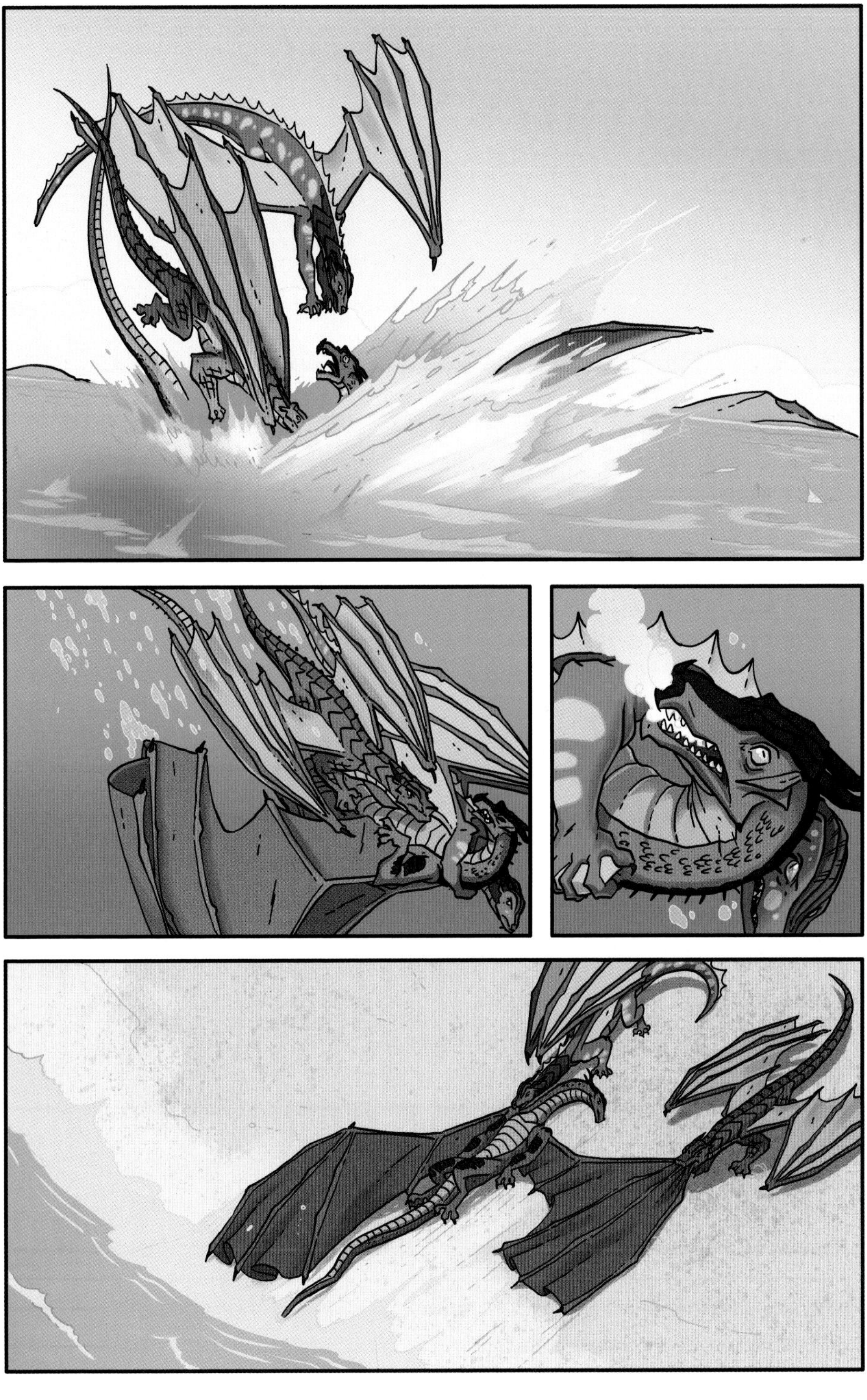

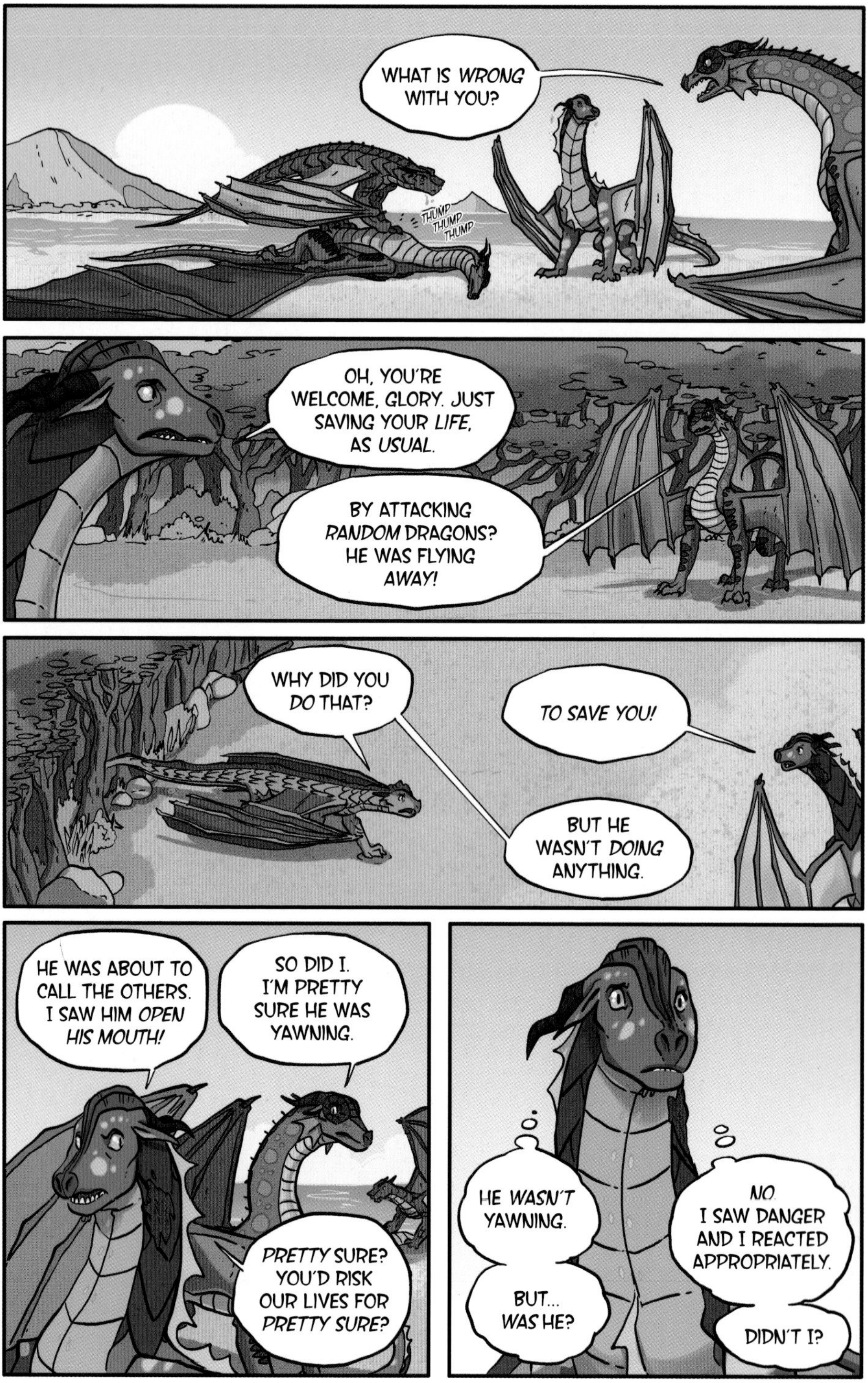
WHAT IS *WRONG* WITH YOU?
THUMP THUMP THUMP
OH, YOU'RE WELCOME, GLORY. JUST SAVING YOUR *LIFE*, AS *USUAL*.
BY ATTACKING *RANDOM* DRAGONS? HE WAS FLYING *AWAY!*
WHY DID YOU *DO* THAT?
TO SAVE YOU!
BUT HE WASN'T *DOING* ANYTHING.
HE WAS ABOUT TO CALL THE OTHERS. I SAW HIM *OPEN HIS MOUTH!*
SO DID I. I'M PRETTY SURE HE WAS YAWNING.
PRETTY SURE? YOU'D RISK OUR LIVES FOR *PRETTY SURE?*
HE *WASN'T* YAWNING.
BUT... WAS HE?
NO. I SAW DANGER AND I REACTED APPROPRIATELY.
DIDN'T I?

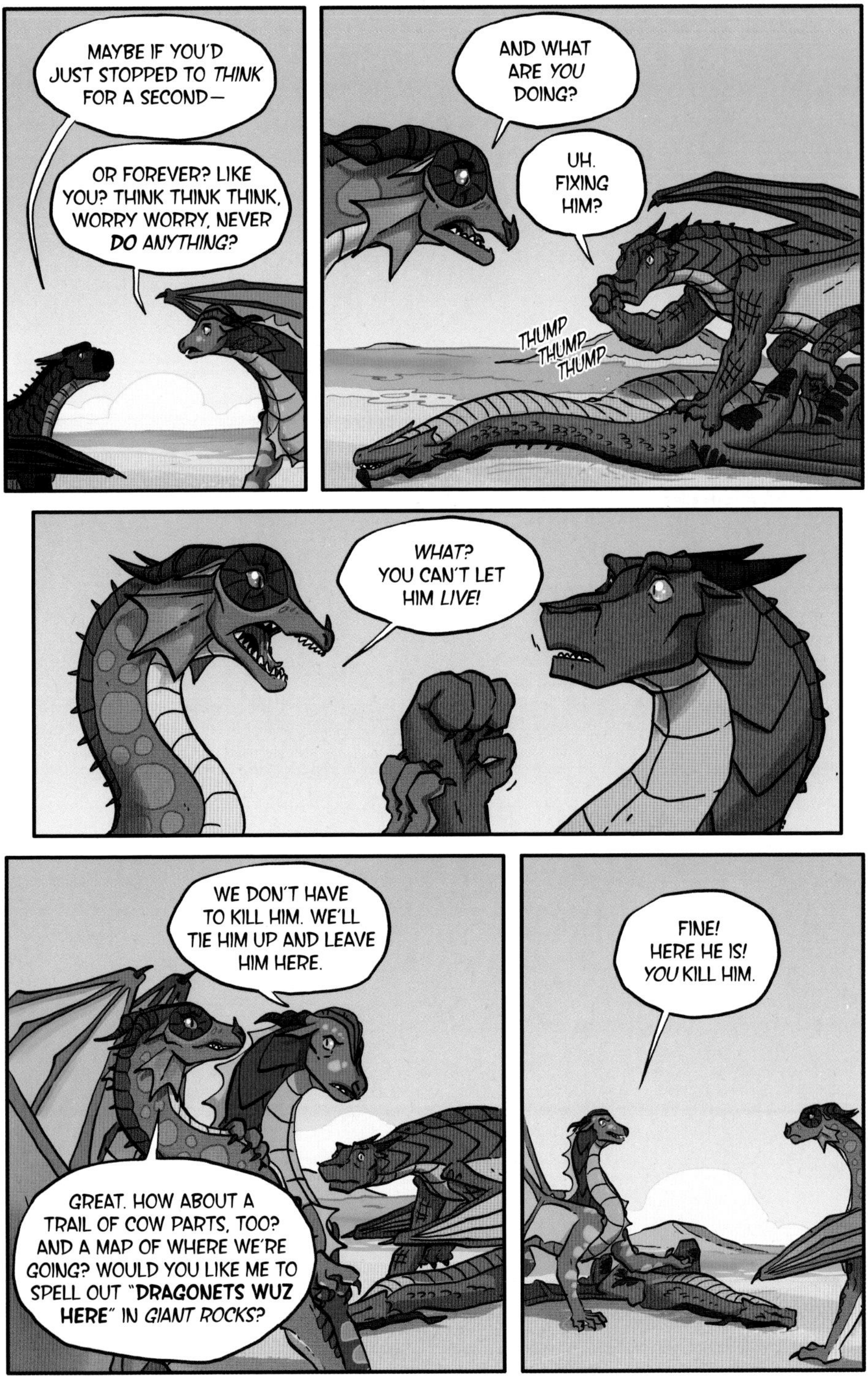
MAYBE IF YOU'D JUST STOPPED TO *THINK* FOR A SECOND—
OR FOREVER? LIKE YOU? THINK THINK THINK, WORRY WORRY, NEVER **DO** *ANYTHING?*
AND WHAT ARE *YOU* DOING?
UH. FIXING HIM?
THUMP THUMP THUMP
WHAT? YOU CAN'T LET HIM *LIVE!*
WE DON'T HAVE TO KILL HIM. WE'LL TIE HIM UP AND LEAVE HIM HERE.
GREAT. HOW ABOUT A TRAIL OF COW PARTS, TOO? AND A MAP OF WHERE WE'RE GOING? WOULD YOU LIKE ME TO SPELL OUT "**DRAGONETS WUZ HERE**" IN *GIANT ROCKS?*
FINE! HERE HE IS! *YOU* KILL HIM.

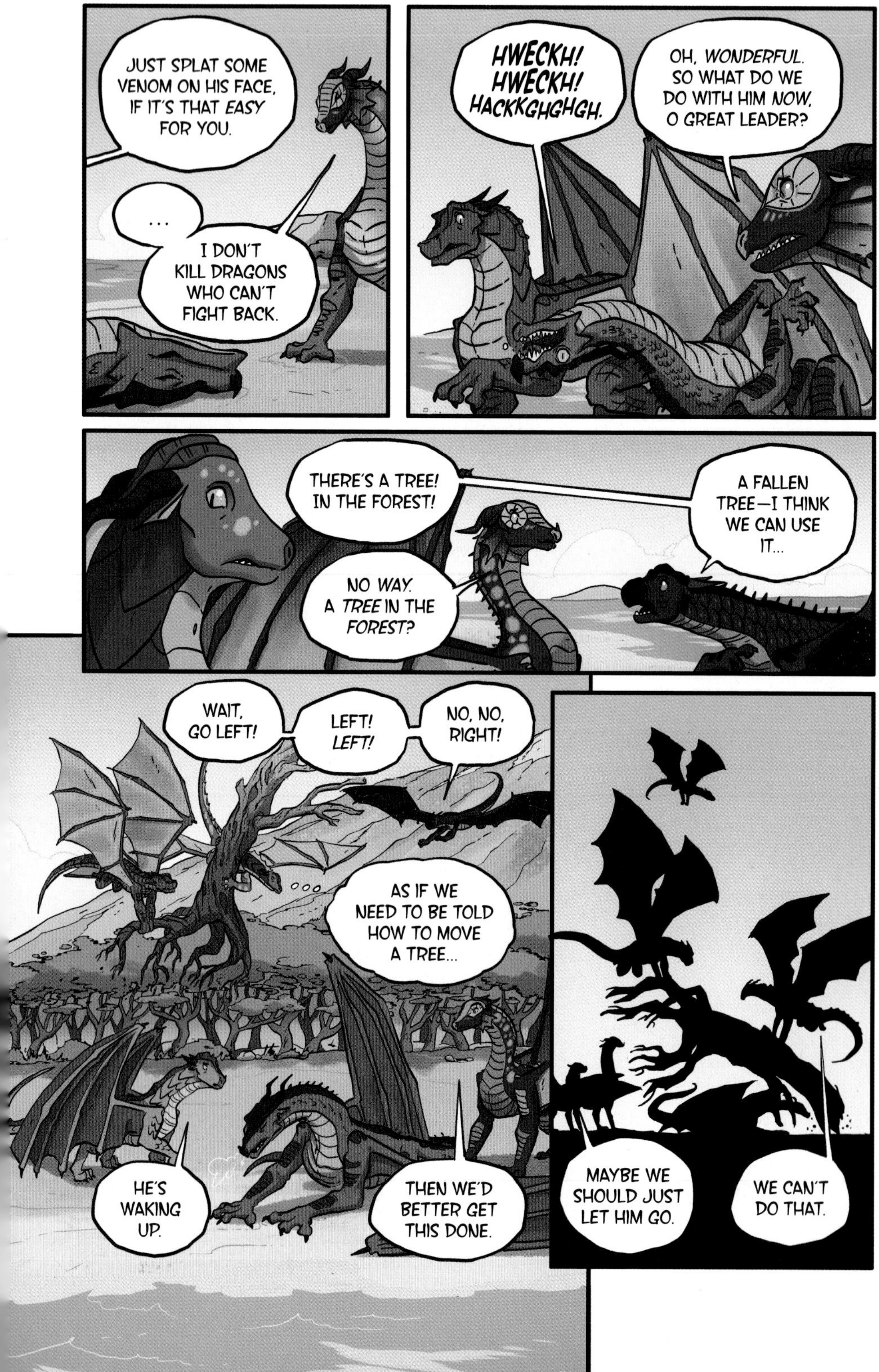
JUST SPLAT SOME VENOM ON HIS FACE, IF IT'S THAT *EASY* FOR YOU.
...
I DON'T KILL DRAGONS WHO CAN'T FIGHT BACK.
HWECKH! HWECKH! HACKKGHGHGH.
OH, *WONDERFUL*. SO WHAT DO WE DO WITH HIM *NOW*, O GREAT LEADER?
THERE'S A TREE! IN THE FOREST!
NO *WAY*. A *TREE* IN THE *FOREST*?
A FALLEN TREE—I THINK WE CAN USE IT...
WAIT, GO LEFT!
LEFT! LEFT!
NO, NO, RIGHT!
AS IF WE NEED TO BE TOLD HOW TO MOVE A TREE...
HE'S WAKING UP.
THEN WE'D BETTER GET THIS DONE.
MAYBE WE SHOULD JUST LET HIM GO.
WE CAN'T DO THAT.

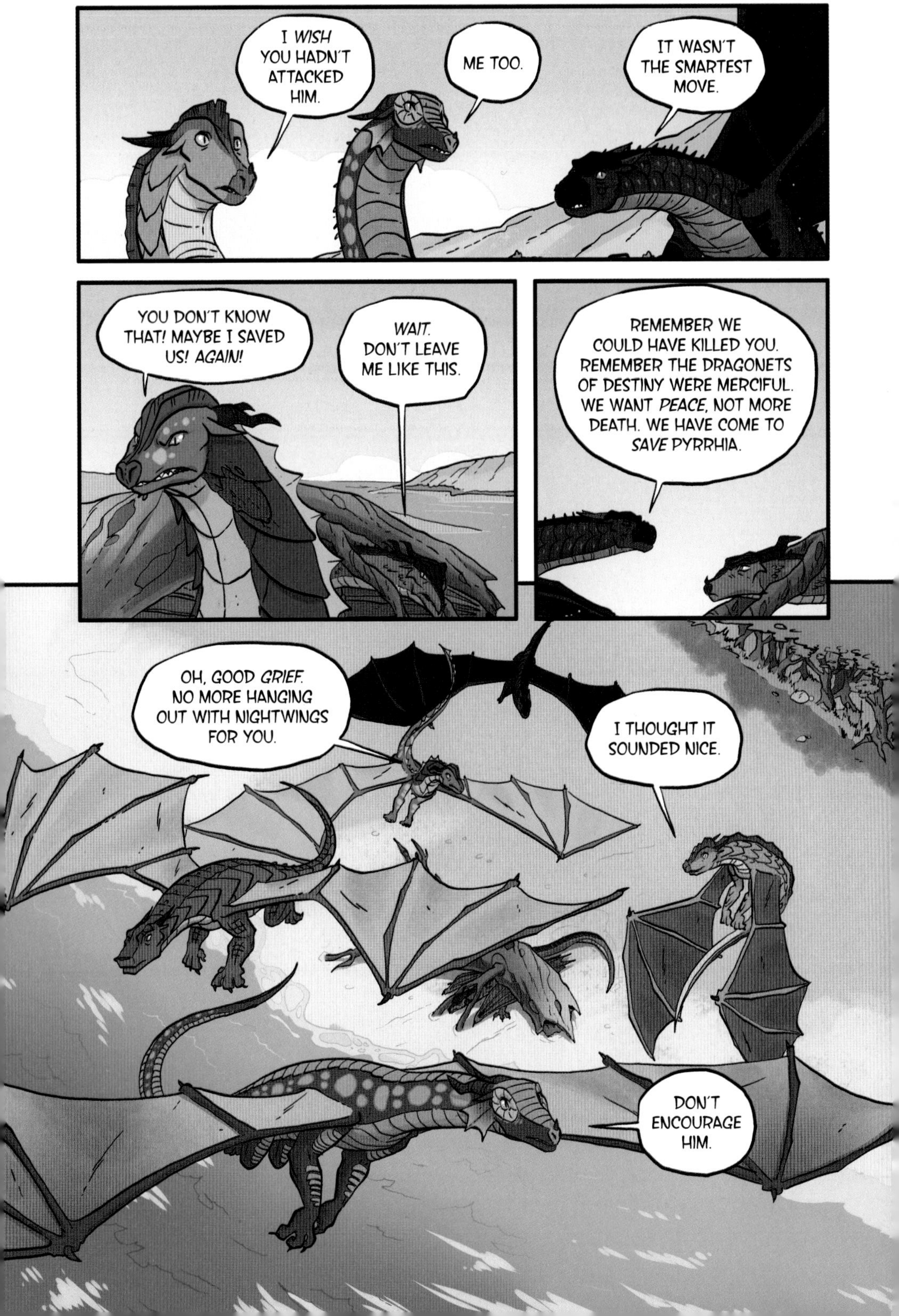
I *WISH* YOU HADN'T ATTACKED HIM.
ME TOO.
IT WASN'T THE SMARTEST MOVE.
YOU DON'T KNOW THAT! MAYBE I SAVED US! *AGAIN!*
WAIT. DON'T LEAVE ME LIKE THIS.
REMEMBER WE COULD HAVE KILLED YOU. REMEMBER THE DRAGONETS OF DESTINY WERE MERCIFUL. WE WANT *PEACE,* NOT MORE DEATH. WE HAVE COME TO *SAVE* PYRRHIA.
OH, GOOD *GRIEF.* NO MORE HANGING OUT WITH NIGHTWINGS FOR YOU.
I THOUGHT IT SOUNDED NICE.
DON'T ENCOURAGE HIM.

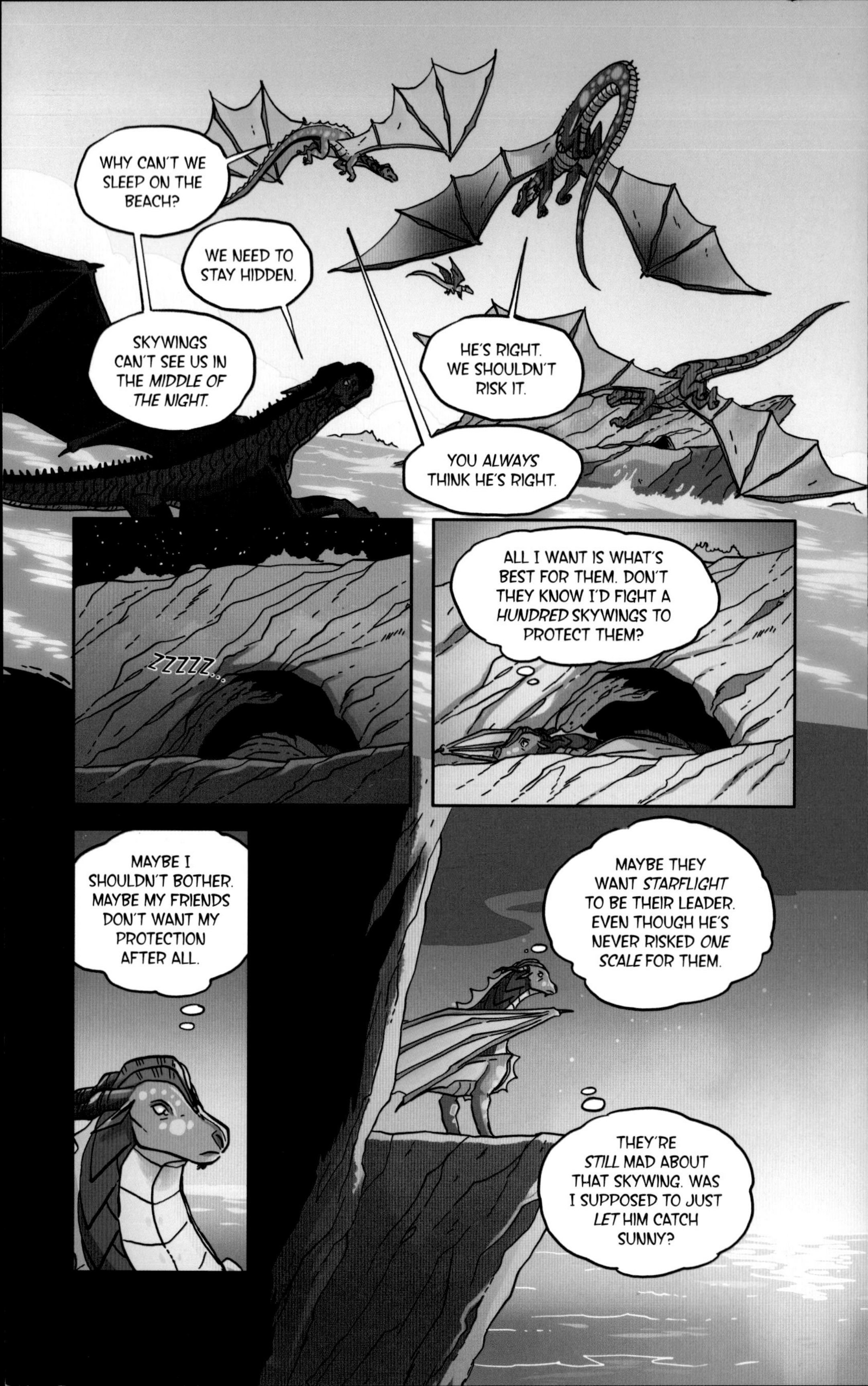
WHY CAN'T WE SLEEP ON THE BEACH?
WE NEED TO STAY HIDDEN.
SKYWINGS CAN'T SEE US IN THE *MIDDLE OF THE NIGHT.*
HE'S RIGHT. WE SHOULDN'T RISK IT.
YOU *ALWAYS* THINK HE'S RIGHT.
ZZZZZ...
ALL I WANT IS WHAT'S BEST FOR THEM. DON'T THEY KNOW I'D FIGHT A *HUNDRED* SKYWINGS TO PROTECT THEM?
MAYBE I SHOULDN'T BOTHER. MAYBE MY FRIENDS DON'T WANT MY PROTECTION AFTER ALL.
MAYBE THEY WANT *STARFLIGHT* TO BE THEIR LEADER. EVEN THOUGH HE'S NEVER RISKED *ONE SCALE* FOR THEM.
THEY'RE *STILL* MAD ABOUT THAT SKYWING. WAS I SUPPOSED TO JUST *LET* HIM CATCH SUNNY?

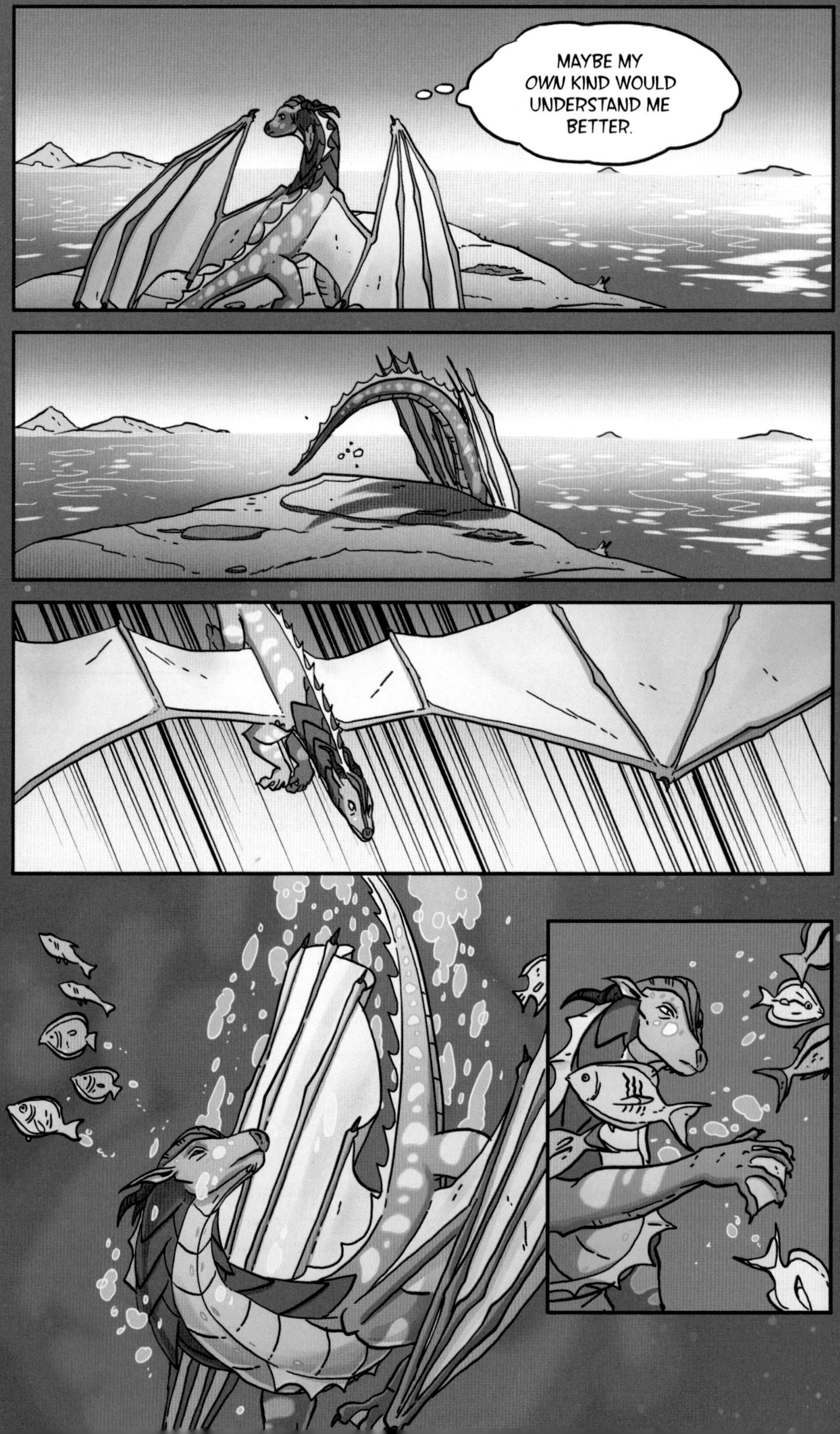
MAYBE MY OWN KIND WOULD UNDERSTAND ME BETTER.

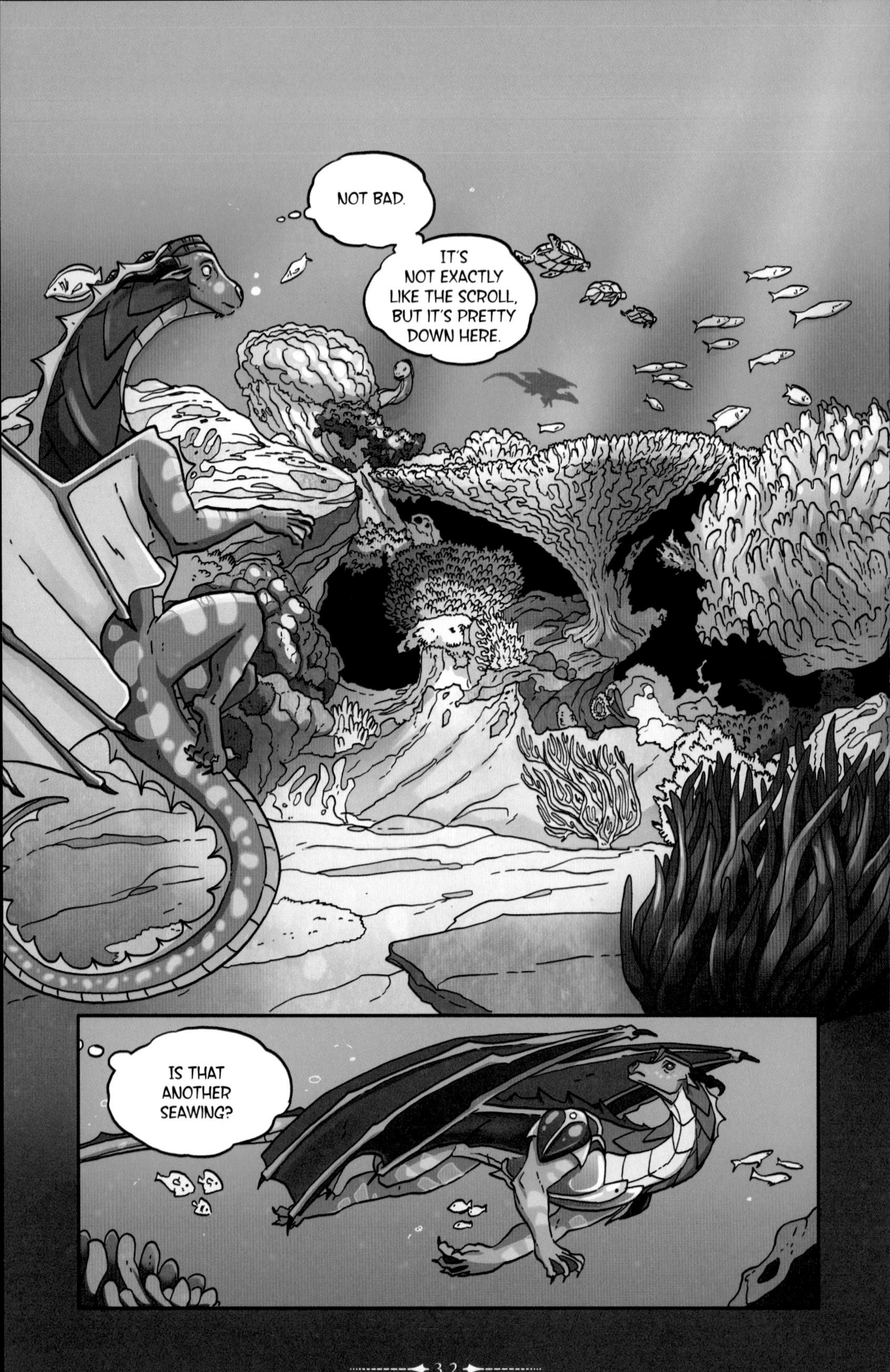
NOT BAD.
IT'S NOT EXACTLY LIKE THE SCROLL, BUT IT'S PRETTY DOWN HERE.
IS THAT ANOTHER SEAWING?

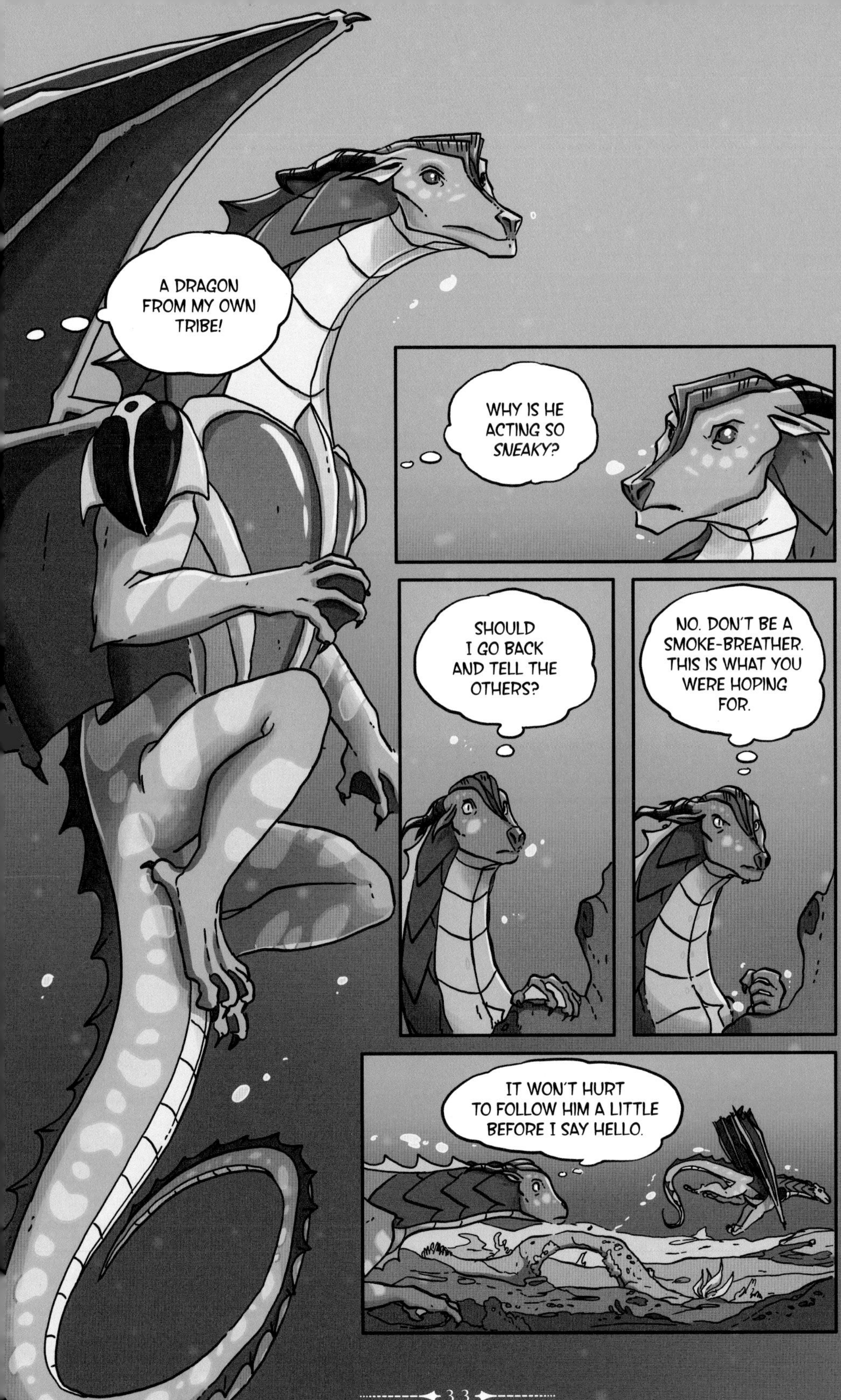
A DRAGON FROM MY OWN TRIBE!
WHY IS HE ACTING SO *SNEAKY*?
SHOULD I GO BACK AND TELL THE OTHERS?
NO. DON'T BE A SMOKE-BREATHER. THIS IS WHAT YOU WERE HOPING FOR.
IT WON'T HURT TO FOLLOW HIM A LITTLE BEFORE I SAY HELLO.

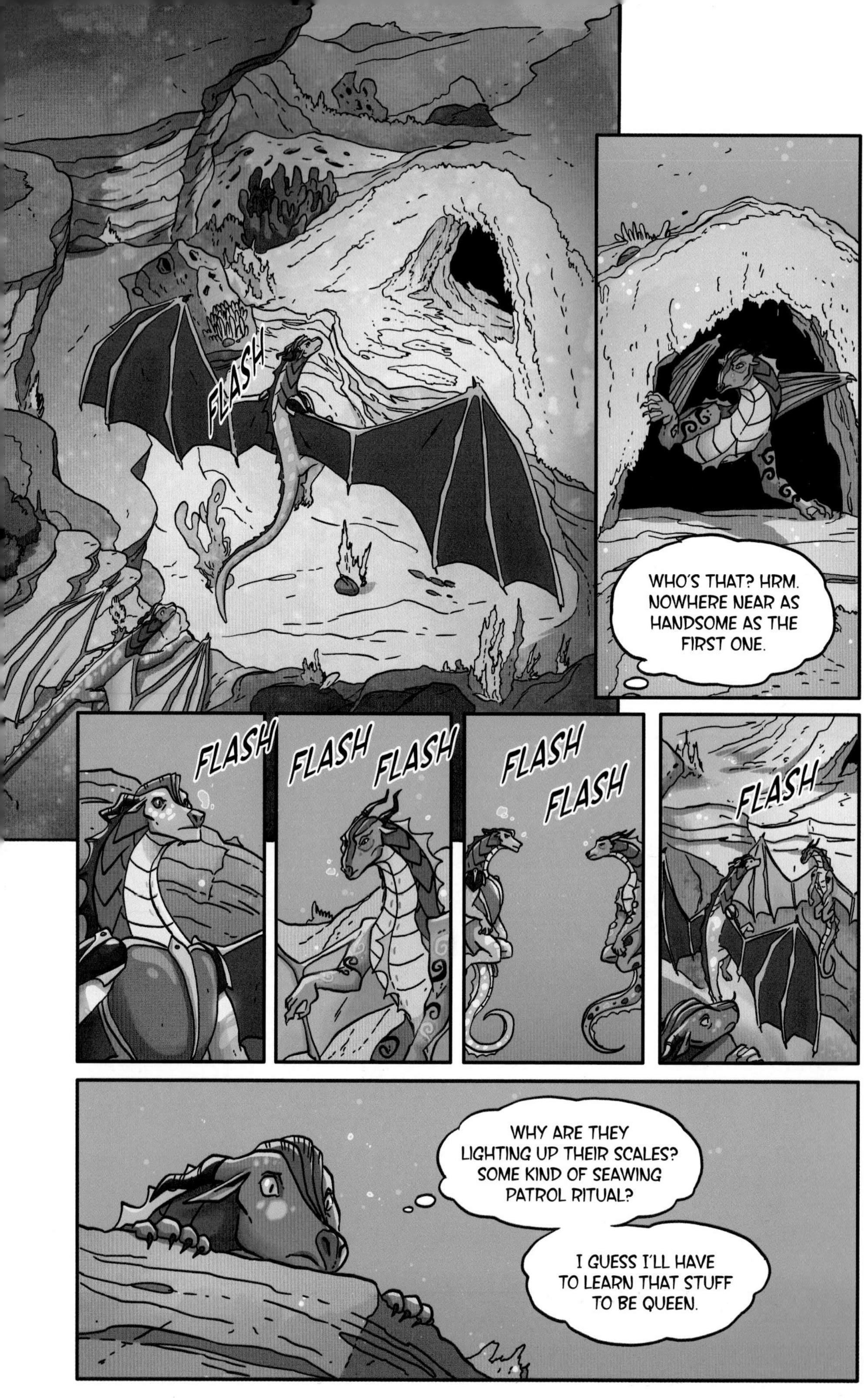
FLASH
WHO'S THAT? HRM. NOWHERE NEAR AS HANDSOME AS THE FIRST ONE.
FLASH
FLASH
FLASH
FLASH
FLASH
FLASH
WHY ARE THEY LIGHTING UP THEIR SCALES? SOME KIND OF SEAWING PATROL RITUAL?
I GUESS I'LL HAVE TO LEARN THAT STUFF TO BE QUEEN.

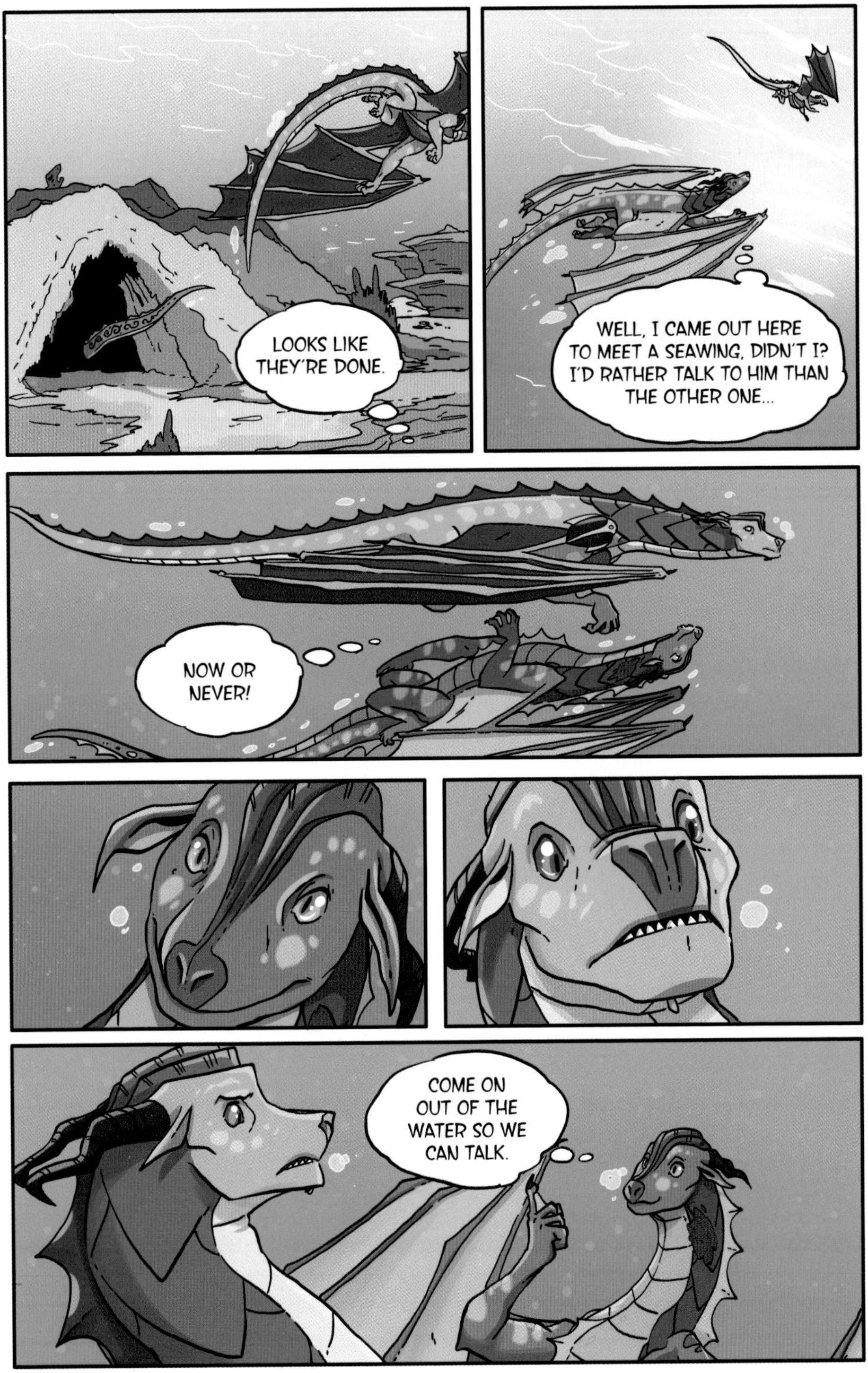
LOOKS LIKE THEY'RE DONE.
WELL, I CAME OUT HERE TO MEET A SEAWING, DIDN'T I? I'D RATHER TALK TO HIM THAN THE OTHER ONE...
NOW OR NEVER!
COME ON OUT OF THE WATER SO WE CAN TALK.

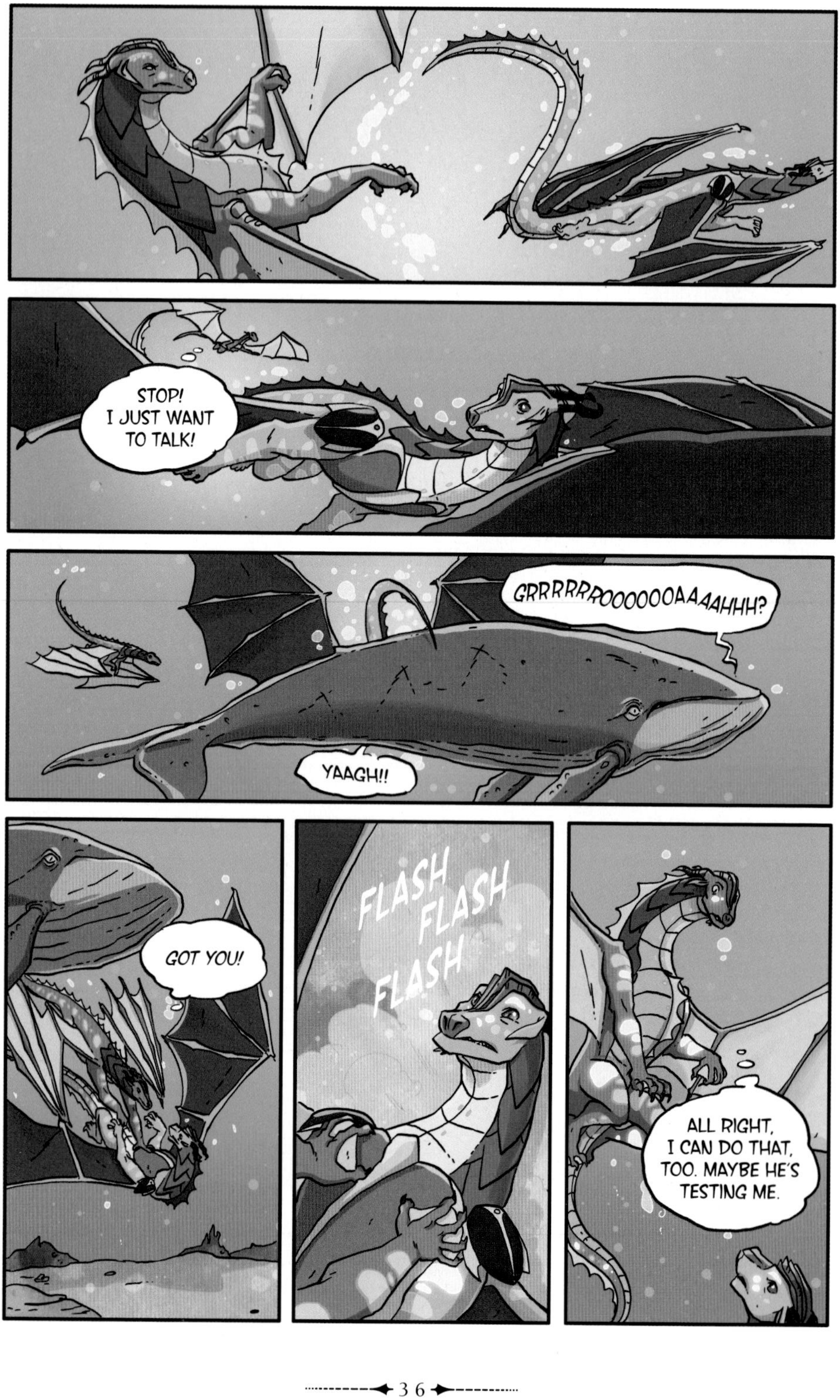

STOP! I JUST WANT TO TALK!
GRRRRRROOOOOOAAAAHHH?
YAAGH!!
GOT YOU!
FLASH FLASH FLASH
ALL RIGHT, I CAN DO THAT, TOO. MAYBE HE'S TESTING ME.

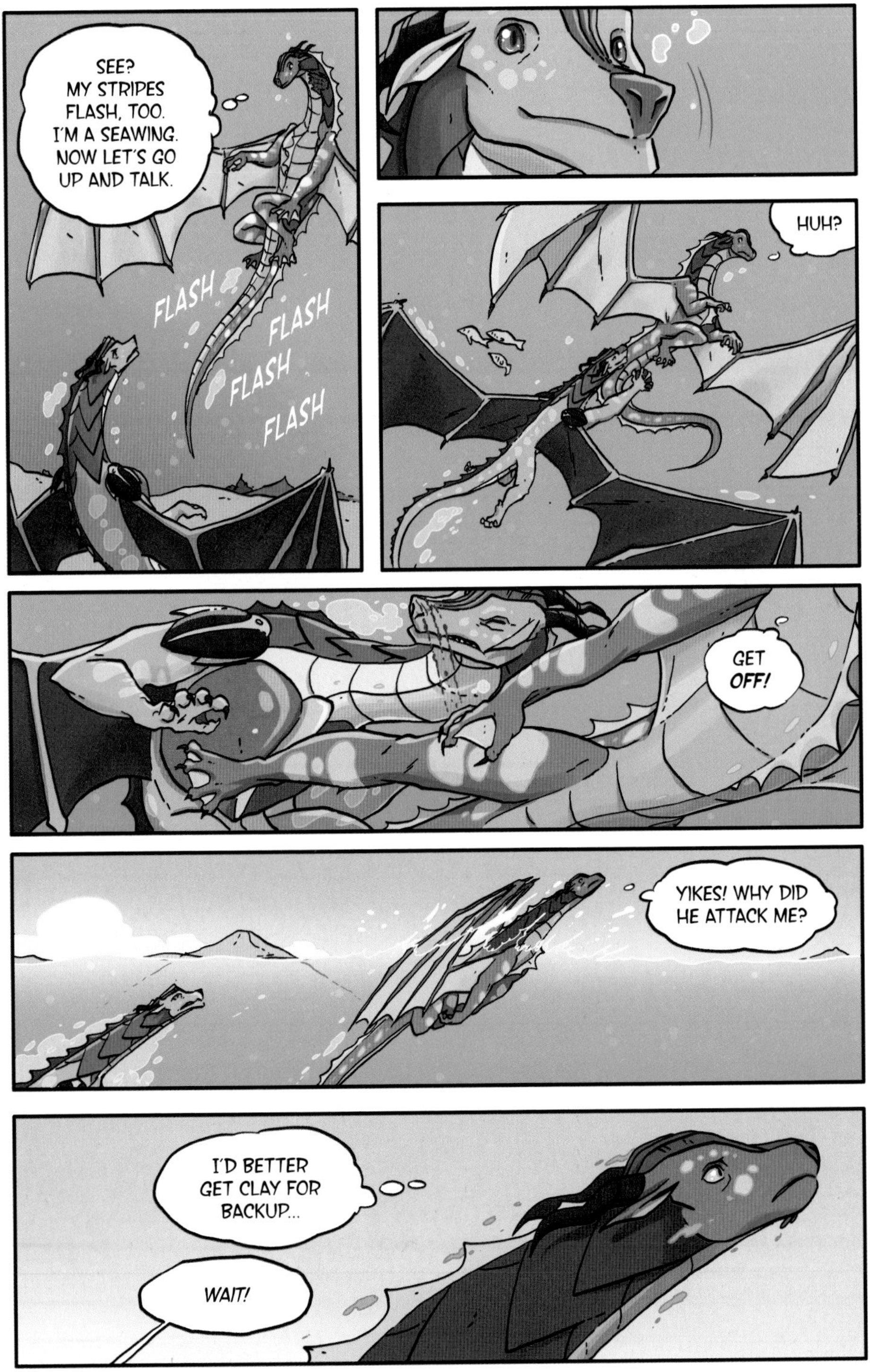
SEE? MY STRIPES FLASH, TOO. I'M A SEAWING. NOW LET'S GO UP AND TALK.
FLASH
FLASH
FLASH
FLASH
HUH?
GET OFF!
YIKES! WHY DID HE ATTACK ME?
I'D BETTER GET CLAY FOR BACKUP...
WAIT!

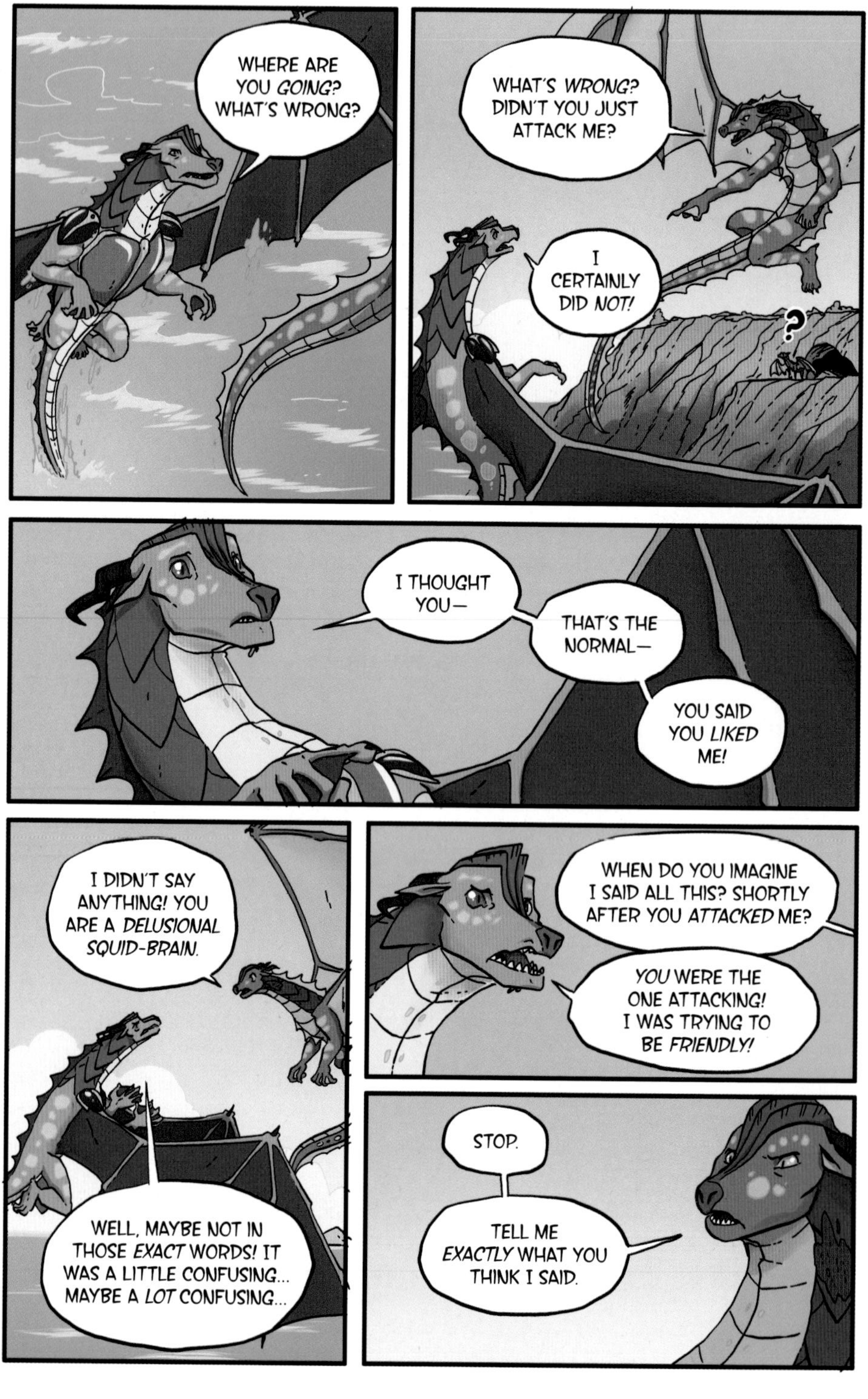
WHERE ARE YOU GOING? WHAT'S WRONG?
WHAT'S WRONG? DIDN'T YOU JUST ATTACK ME?
I CERTAINLY DID NOT!
?
I THOUGHT YOU—
THAT'S THE NORMAL—
YOU SAID YOU LIKED ME!
I DIDN'T SAY ANYTHING! YOU ARE A DELUSIONAL SQUID-BRAIN.
WELL, MAYBE NOT IN THOSE EXACT WORDS! IT WAS A LITTLE CONFUSING... MAYBE A LOT CONFUSING...
WHEN DO YOU IMAGINE I SAID ALL THIS? SHORTLY AFTER YOU ATTACKED ME?
YOU WERE THE ONE ATTACKING! I WAS TRYING TO BE FRIENDLY!
STOP.
TELL ME EXACTLY WHAT YOU THINK I SAID.

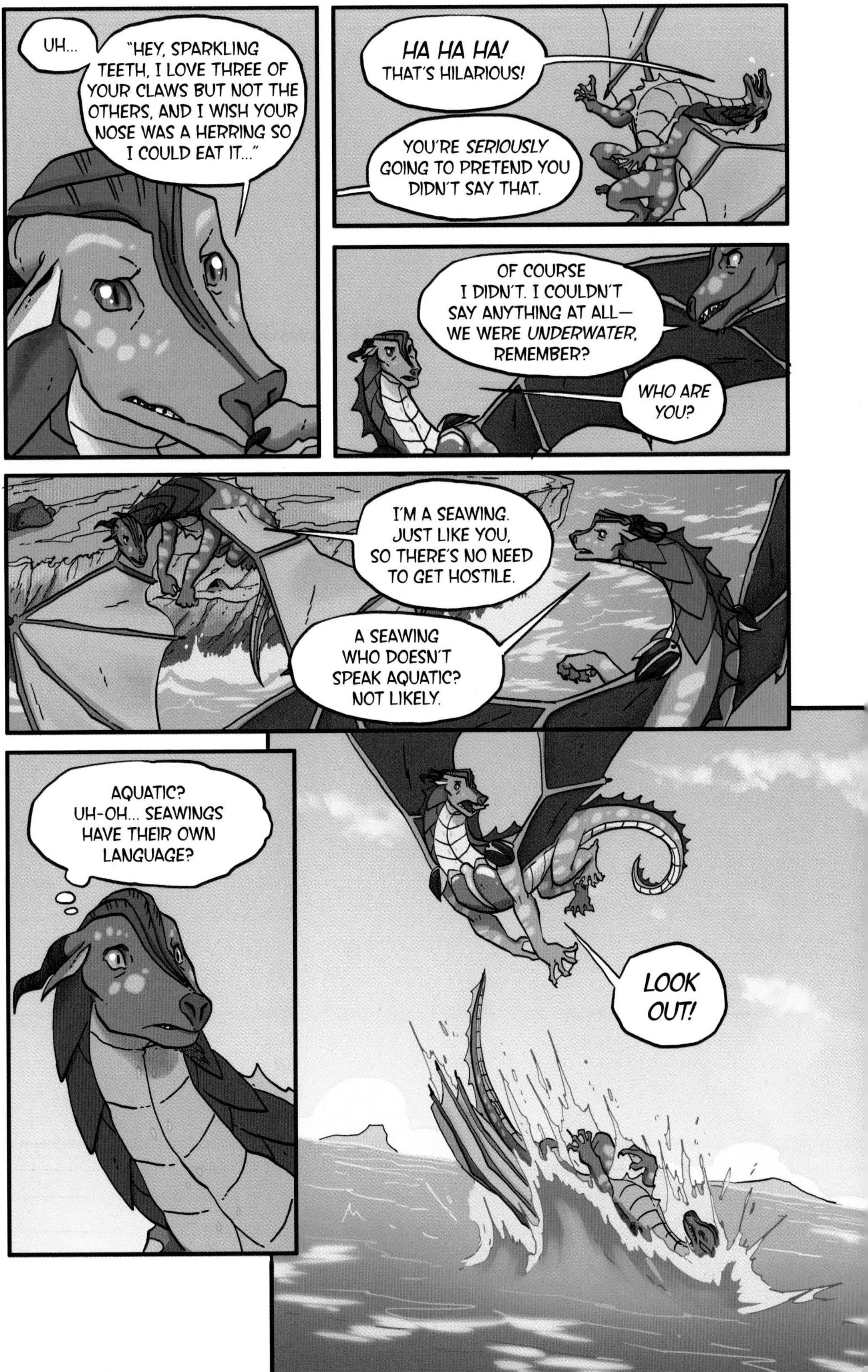
UH...
"HEY, SPARKLING TEETH, I LOVE THREE OF YOUR CLAWS BUT NOT THE OTHERS, AND I WISH YOUR NOSE WAS A HERRING SO I COULD EAT IT..."
HA HA HA! THAT'S HILARIOUS!
YOU'RE SERIOUSLY GOING TO PRETEND YOU DIDN'T SAY THAT.
OF COURSE I DIDN'T. I COULDN'T SAY ANYTHING AT ALL— WE WERE UNDERWATER, REMEMBER?
WHO ARE YOU?
I'M A SEAWING. JUST LIKE YOU, SO THERE'S NO NEED TO GET HOSTILE.
A SEAWING WHO DOESN'T SPEAK AQUATIC? NOT LIKELY.
AQUATIC? UH-OH... SEAWINGS HAVE THEIR OWN LANGUAGE?
LOOK OUT!

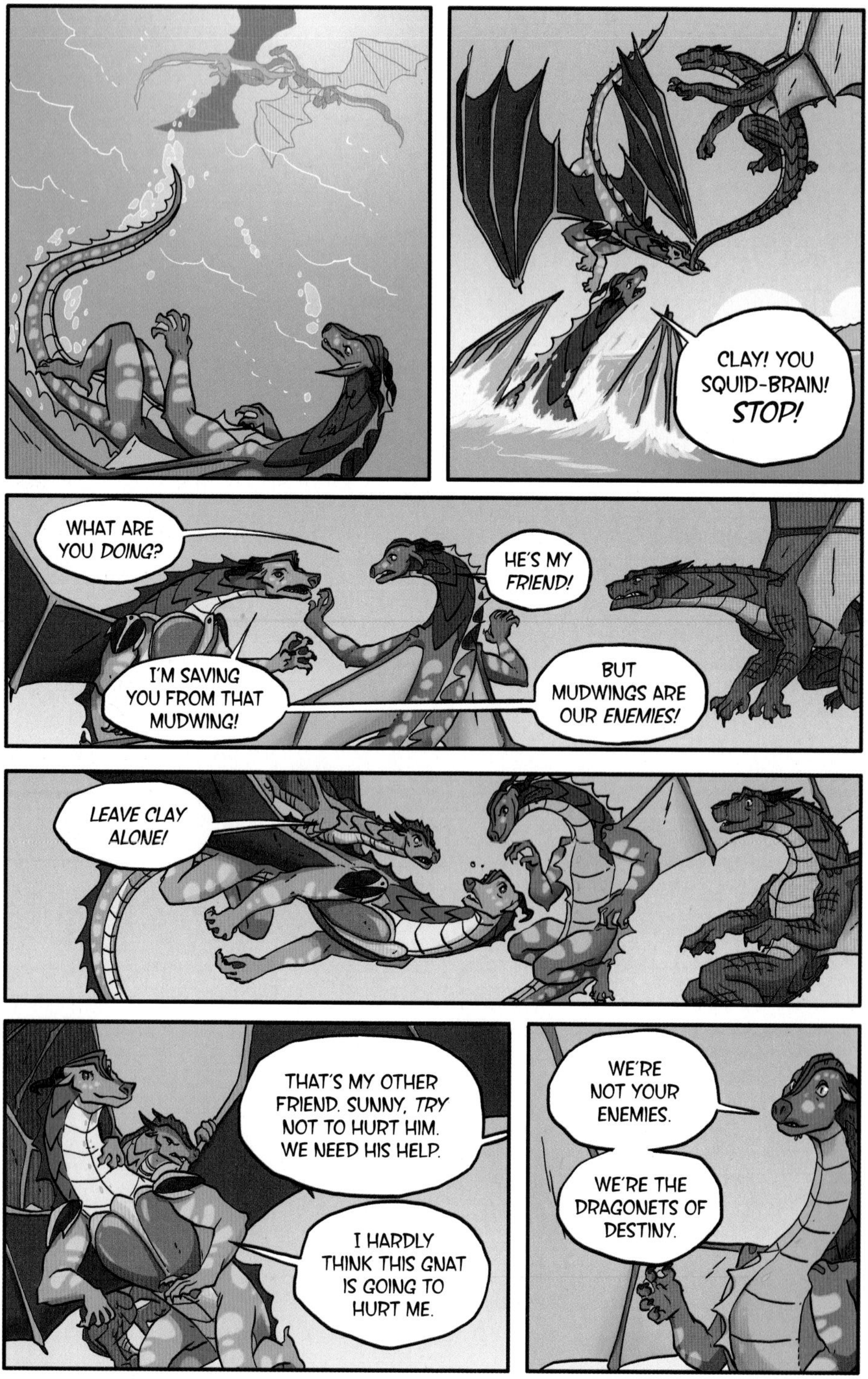
CLAY! YOU SQUID-BRAIN! STOP!
WHAT ARE YOU DOING?
I'M SAVING YOU FROM THAT MUDWING!
HE'S MY FRIEND!
BUT MUDWINGS ARE OUR ENEMIES!
LEAVE CLAY ALONE!
THAT'S MY OTHER FRIEND. SUNNY, TRY NOT TO HURT HIM. WE NEED HIS HELP.
I HARDLY THINK THIS GNAT IS GOING TO HURT ME.
WE'RE NOT YOUR ENEMIES.
WE'RE THE DRAGONETS OF DESTINY.

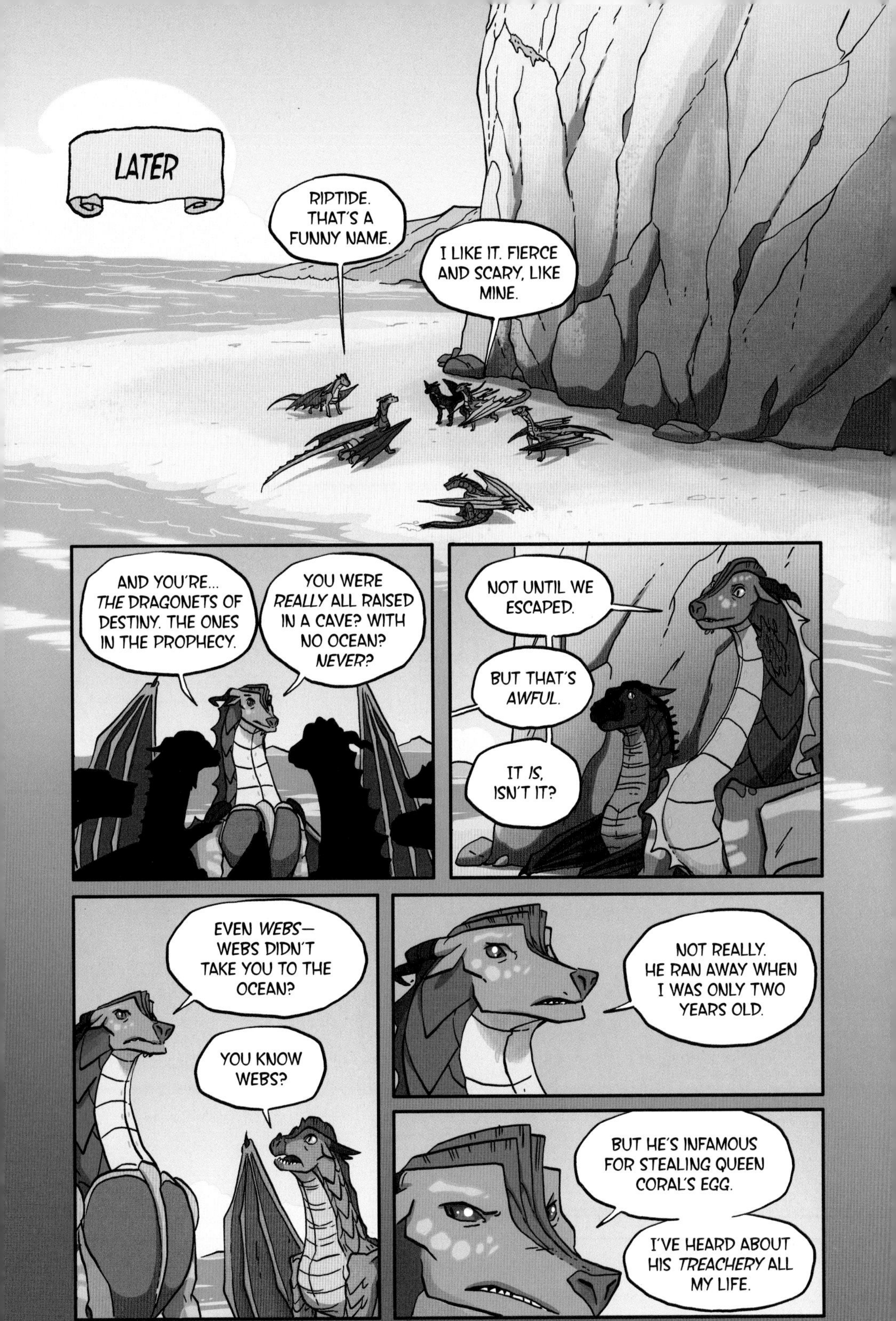
LATER
RIPTIDE. THAT'S A FUNNY NAME.
I LIKE IT. FIERCE AND SCARY, LIKE MINE.
AND YOU'RE... *THE* DRAGONETS OF DESTINY. THE ONES IN THE PROPHECY.
YOU WERE *REALLY* ALL RAISED IN A CAVE? WITH NO OCEAN? *NEVER?*
NOT UNTIL WE ESCAPED.
BUT THAT'S *AWFUL.*
IT *IS,* ISN'T IT?
EVEN *WEBS*— WEBS DIDN'T TAKE YOU TO THE OCEAN?
YOU KNOW WEBS?
NOT REALLY. HE RAN AWAY WHEN I WAS ONLY TWO YEARS OLD.
BUT HE'S INFAMOUS FOR STEALING QUEEN CORAL'S EGG.
I'VE HEARD ABOUT HIS *TREACHERY* ALL MY LIFE.

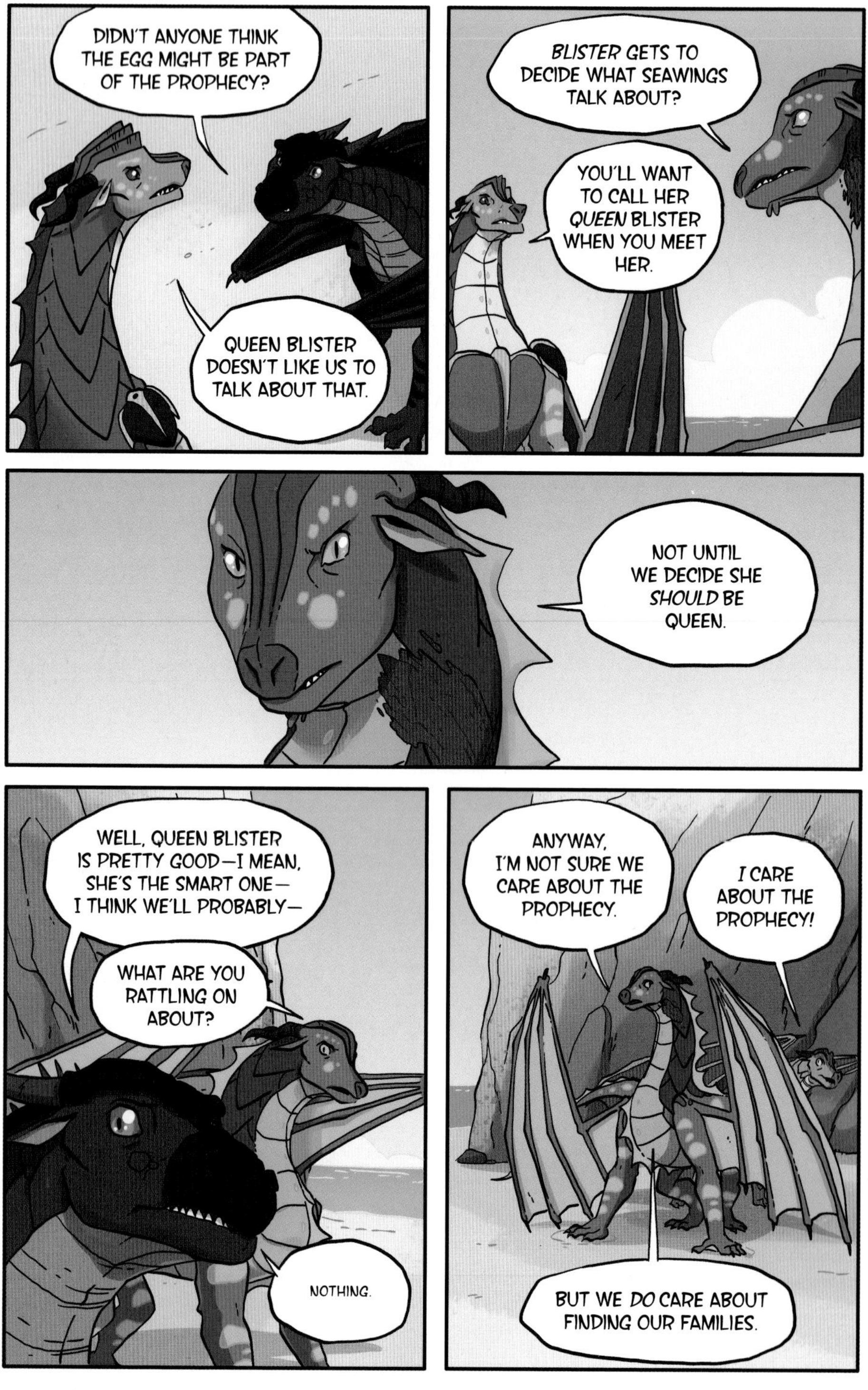
DIDN'T ANYONE THINK THE EGG MIGHT BE PART OF THE PROPHECY?
QUEEN BLISTER DOESN'T LIKE US TO TALK ABOUT THAT.
BLISTER GETS TO DECIDE WHAT SEAWINGS TALK ABOUT?
YOU'LL WANT TO CALL HER *QUEEN* BLISTER WHEN YOU MEET HER.
NOT UNTIL WE DECIDE SHE *SHOULD* BE QUEEN.
WELL, QUEEN BLISTER IS PRETTY GOOD—I MEAN, SHE'S THE SMART ONE— I THINK WE'LL PROBABLY—
WHAT ARE YOU RATTLING ON ABOUT?
NOTHING.
ANYWAY, I'M NOT SURE WE CARE ABOUT THE PROPHECY.
I CARE ABOUT THE PROPHECY!
BUT WE *DO* CARE ABOUT FINDING OUR FAMILIES.

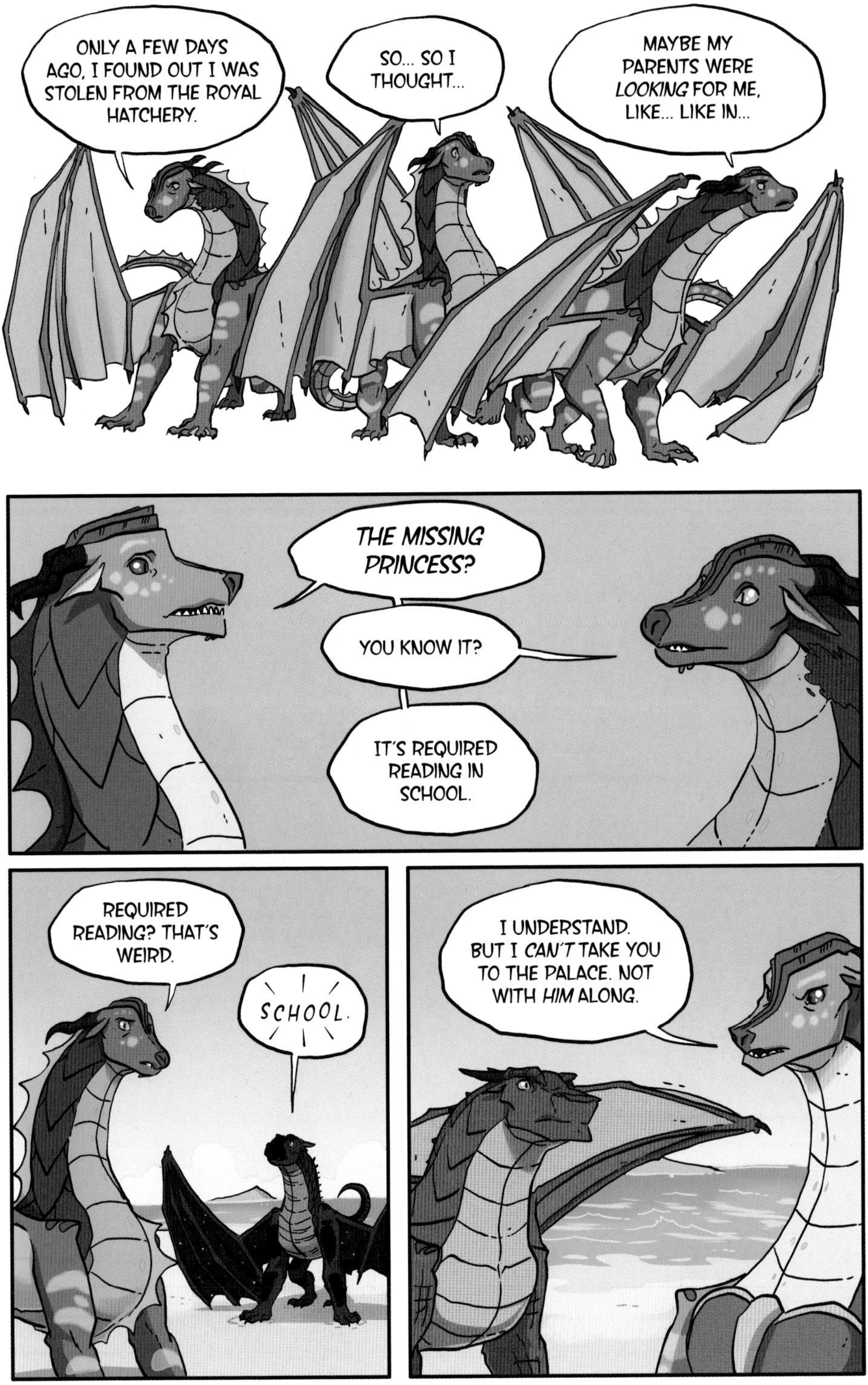
ONLY A FEW DAYS AGO, I FOUND OUT I WAS STOLEN FROM THE ROYAL HATCHERY.
SO... SO I THOUGHT...
MAYBE MY PARENTS WERE *LOOKING* FOR ME, LIKE... LIKE IN...
THE MISSING PRINCESS?
YOU KNOW IT?
IT'S REQUIRED READING IN SCHOOL.
REQUIRED READING? THAT'S WEIRD.
SCHOOL.
I UNDERSTAND. BUT I *CAN'T* TAKE YOU TO THE PALACE. NOT WITH *HIM* ALONG.

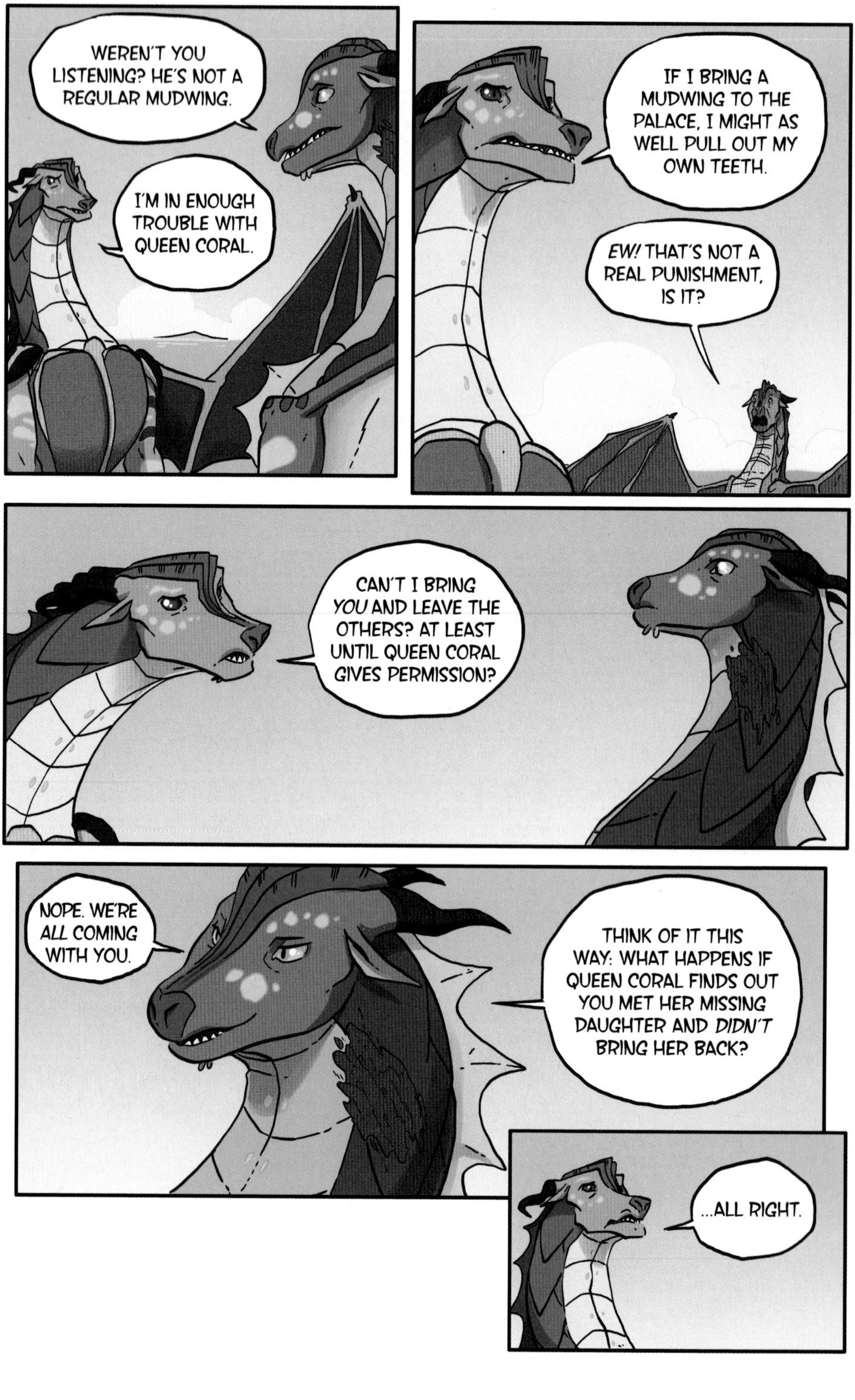
WEREN'T YOU LISTENING? HE'S NOT A REGULAR MUDWING.
I'M IN ENOUGH TROUBLE WITH QUEEN CORAL.
IF I BRING A MUDWING TO THE PALACE, I MIGHT AS WELL PULL OUT MY OWN TEETH.
EW! THAT'S NOT A REAL PUNISHMENT, IS IT?
CAN'T I BRING *YOU* AND LEAVE THE OTHERS? AT LEAST UNTIL QUEEN CORAL GIVES PERMISSION?
NOPE. WE'RE *ALL* COMING WITH YOU.
THINK OF IT THIS WAY: WHAT HAPPENS IF QUEEN CORAL FINDS OUT YOU MET HER MISSING DAUGHTER AND *DIDN'T* BRING HER BACK?
...ALL RIGHT.

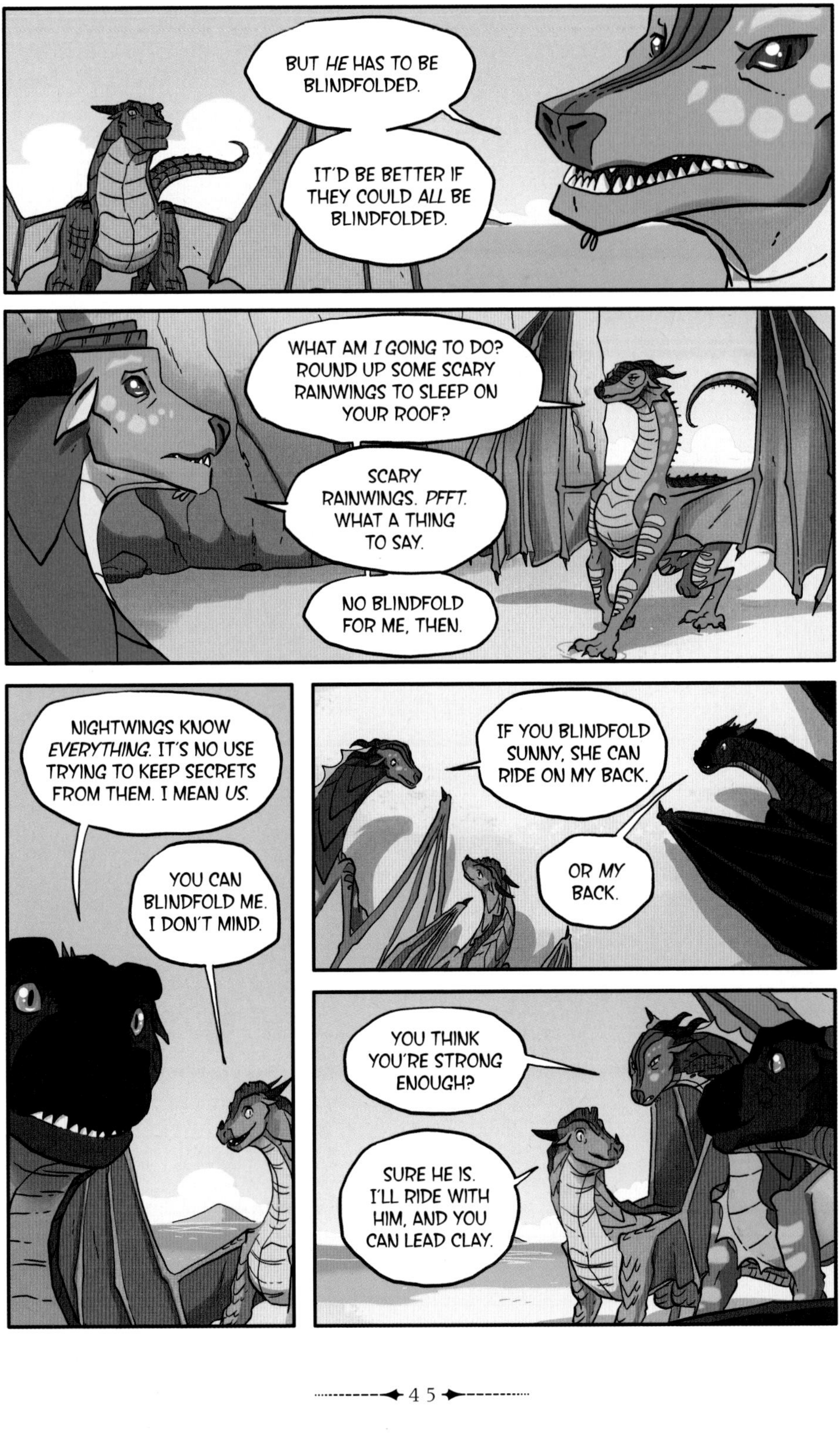
BUT *HE* HAS TO BE BLINDFOLDED.
IT'D BE BETTER IF THEY COULD *ALL* BE BLINDFOLDED.
WHAT AM *I* GOING TO DO? ROUND UP SOME SCARY RAINWINGS TO SLEEP ON YOUR ROOF?
SCARY RAINWINGS. *PFFT.* WHAT A THING TO SAY.
NO BLINDFOLD FOR ME, THEN.
NIGHTWINGS KNOW *EVERYTHING*. IT'S NO USE TRYING TO KEEP SECRETS FROM THEM. I MEAN *US*.
YOU CAN BLINDFOLD ME. I DON'T MIND.
IF YOU BLINDFOLD SUNNY, SHE CAN RIDE ON MY BACK.
OR *MY* BACK.
YOU THINK YOU'RE STRONG ENOUGH?
SURE HE IS. I'LL RIDE WITH HIM, AND YOU CAN LEAD CLAY.

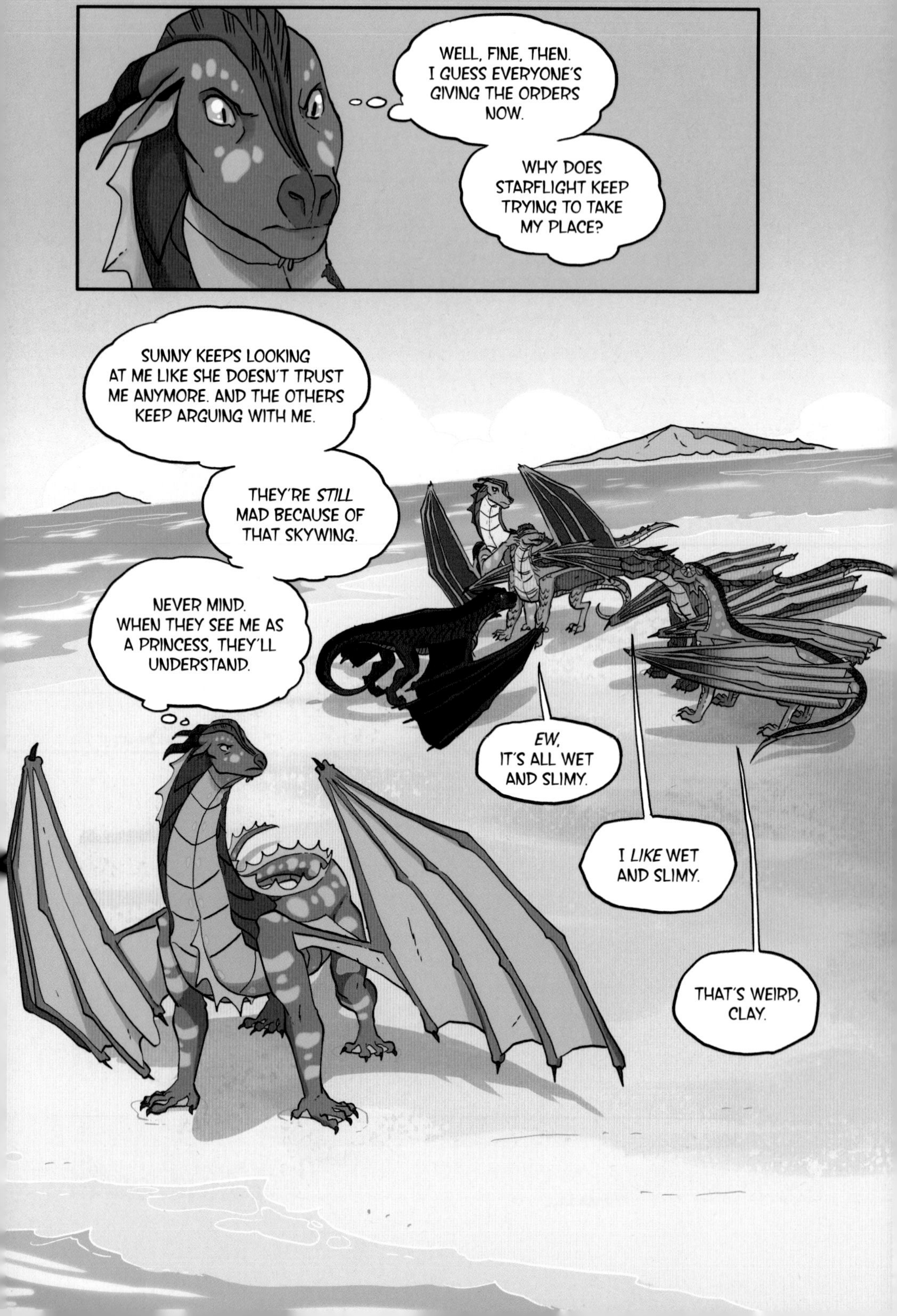
WELL, FINE, THEN. I GUESS EVERYONE'S GIVING THE ORDERS NOW.
WHY DOES STARFLIGHT KEEP TRYING TO TAKE MY PLACE?
SUNNY KEEPS LOOKING AT ME LIKE SHE DOESN'T TRUST ME ANYMORE. AND THE OTHERS KEEP ARGUING WITH ME.
THEY'RE *STILL* MAD BECAUSE OF THAT SKYWING.
NEVER MIND. WHEN THEY SEE ME AS A PRINCESS, THEY'LL UNDERSTAND.
EW, IT'S ALL WET AND SLIMY.
I *LIKE* WET AND SLIMY.
THAT'S WEIRD, CLAY.

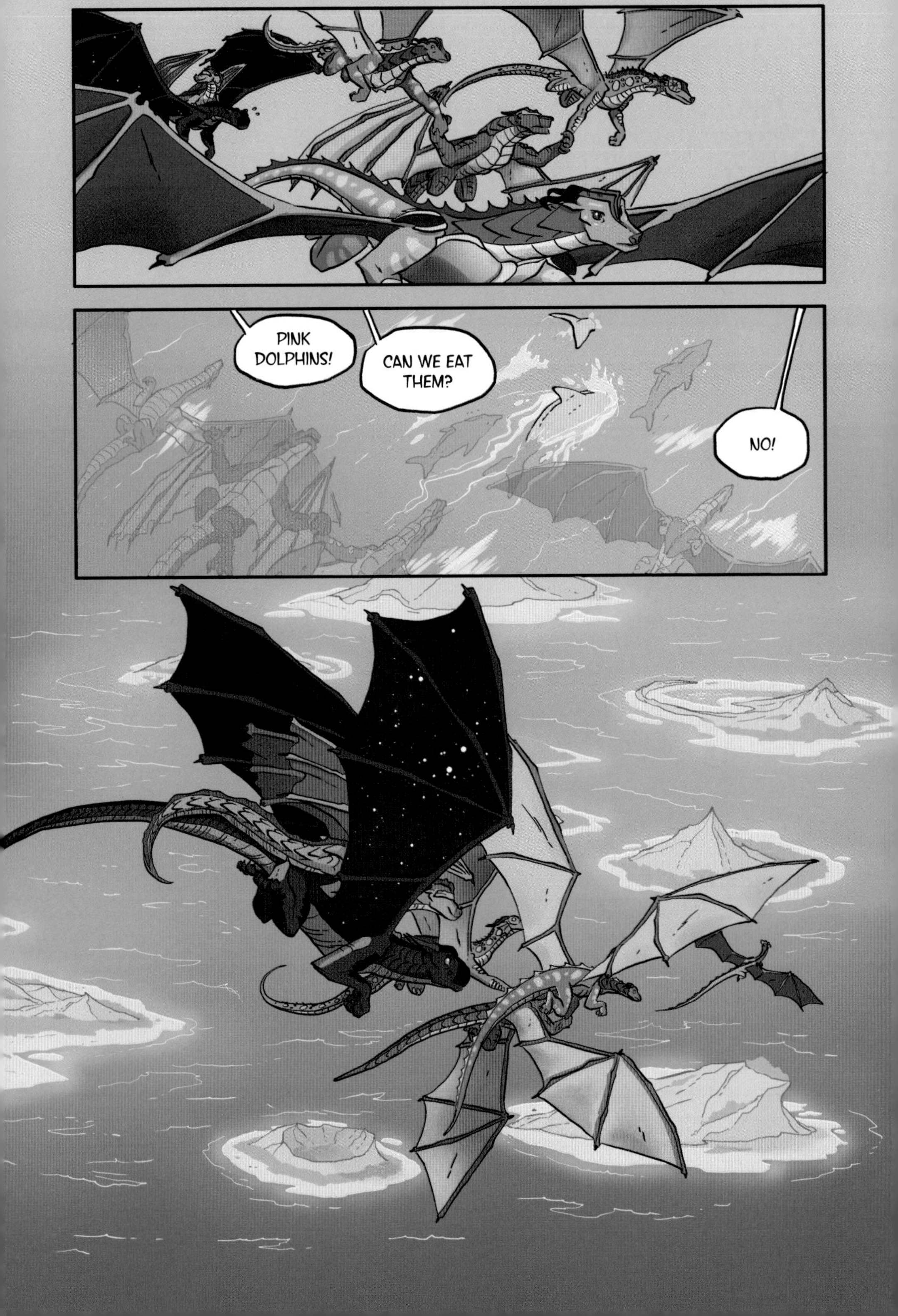
PINK DOLPHINS!
CAN WE EAT THEM?
NO!

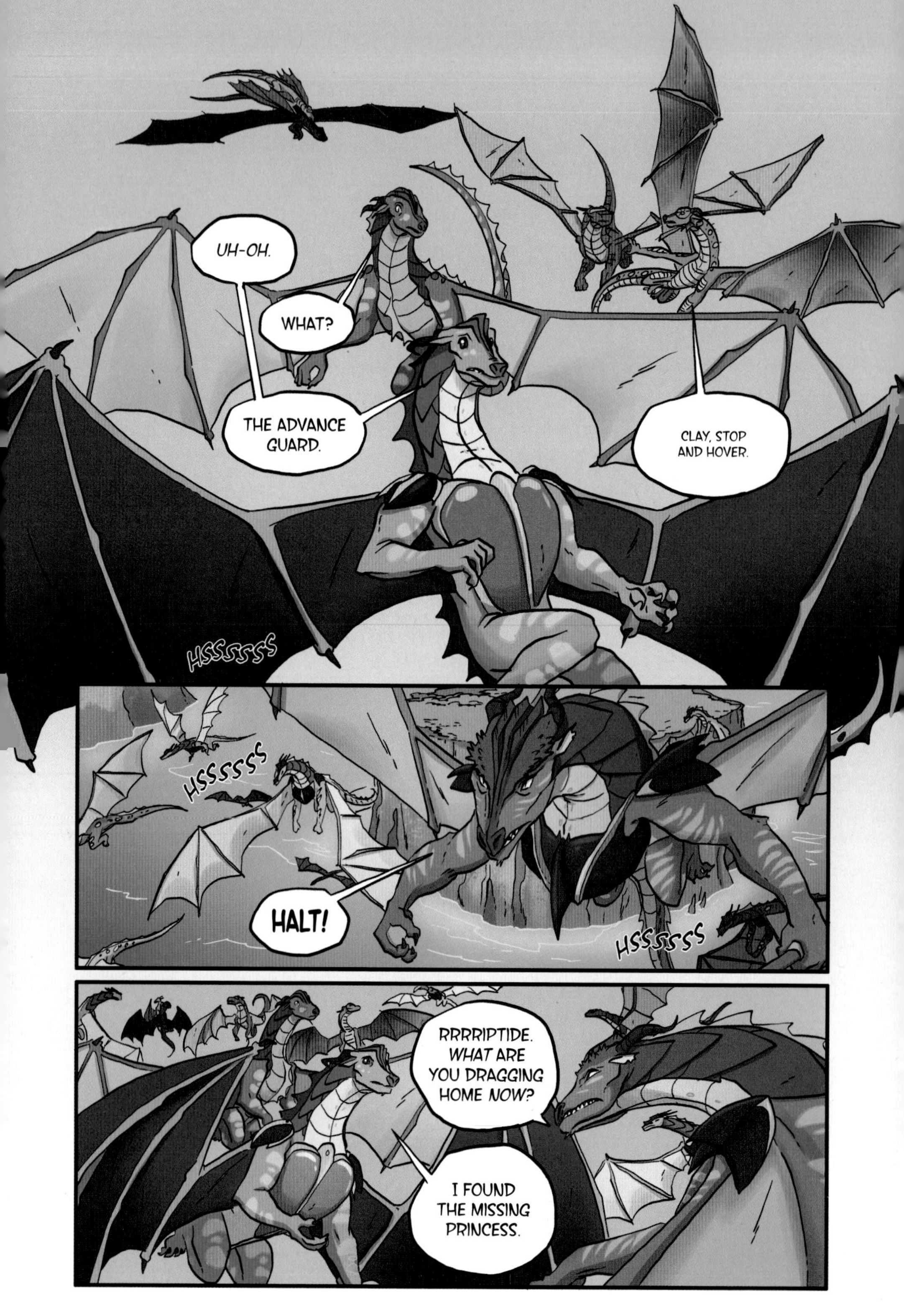
UH-OH.
WHAT?
THE ADVANCE GUARD.
CLAY, STOP AND HOVER.
HSSSSSS
HSSSSSS
HALT!
HSSSSSS
RRRRIPTIDE. WHAT ARE YOU DRAGGING HOME NOW?
I FOUND THE MISSING PRINCESS.

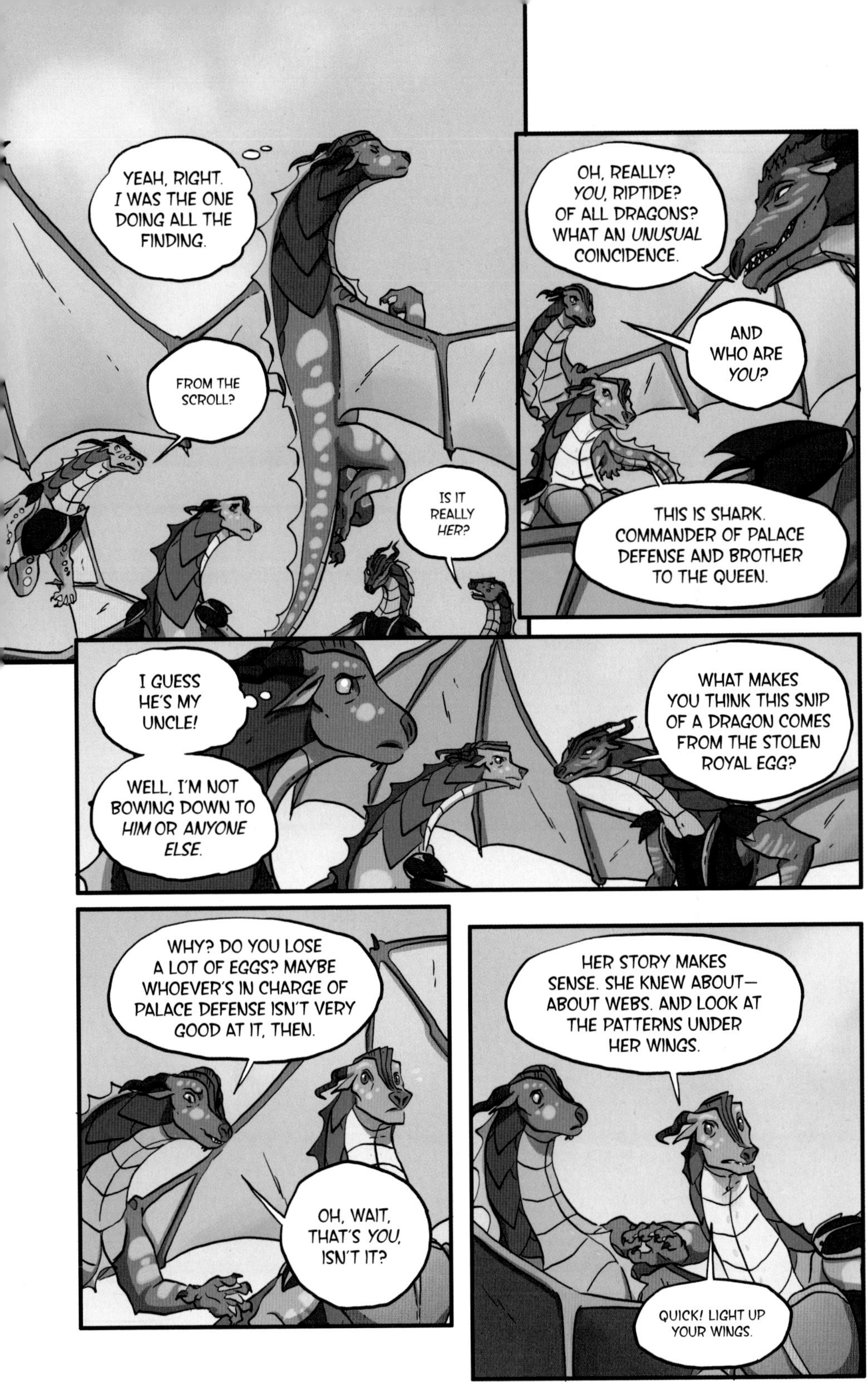
YEAH, RIGHT. I WAS THE ONE DOING ALL THE FINDING.
FROM THE SCROLL?
IS IT REALLY HER?
OH, REALLY? YOU, RIPTIDE? OF ALL DRAGONS? WHAT AN UNUSUAL COINCIDENCE.
AND WHO ARE YOU?
THIS IS SHARK. COMMANDER OF PALACE DEFENSE AND BROTHER TO THE QUEEN.
I GUESS HE'S MY UNCLE!
WELL, I'M NOT BOWING DOWN TO HIM OR ANYONE ELSE.
WHAT MAKES YOU THINK THIS SNIP OF A DRAGON COMES FROM THE STOLEN ROYAL EGG?
WHY? DO YOU LOSE A LOT OF EGGS? MAYBE WHOEVER'S IN CHARGE OF PALACE DEFENSE ISN'T VERY GOOD AT IT, THEN.
OH, WAIT, THAT'S YOU, ISN'T IT?
HER STORY MAKES SENSE. SHE KNEW ABOUT— ABOUT WEBS. AND LOOK AT THE PATTERNS UNDER HER WINGS.
QUICK! LIGHT UP YOUR WINGS.

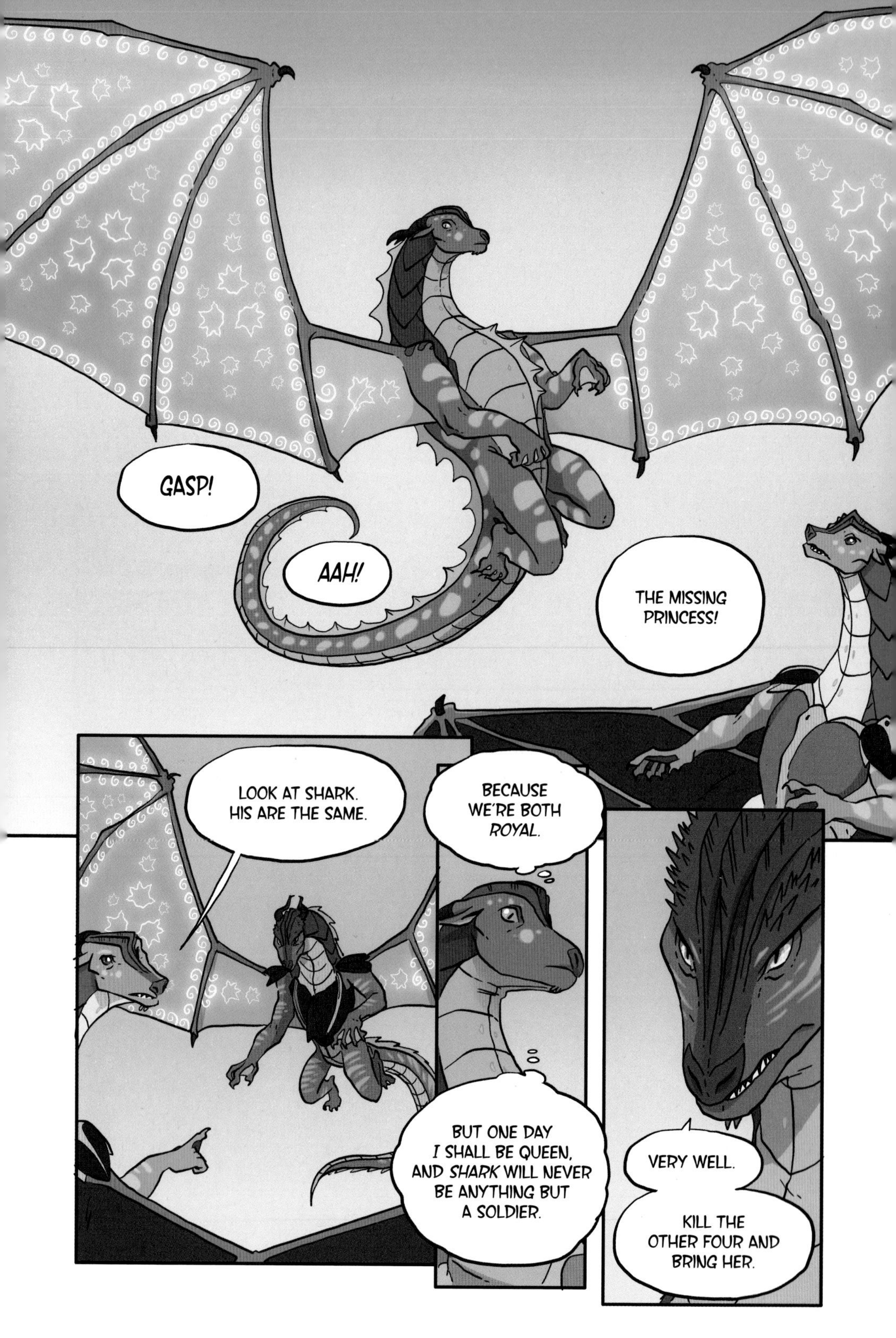
GASP!
AAH!
THE MISSING PRINCESS!
LOOK AT SHARK. HIS ARE THE SAME.
BECAUSE WE'RE BOTH *ROYAL.*
BUT ONE DAY I SHALL BE QUEEN, AND *SHARK* WILL NEVER BE ANYTHING BUT A SOLDIER.
VERY WELL.
KILL THE OTHER FOUR AND BRING HER.

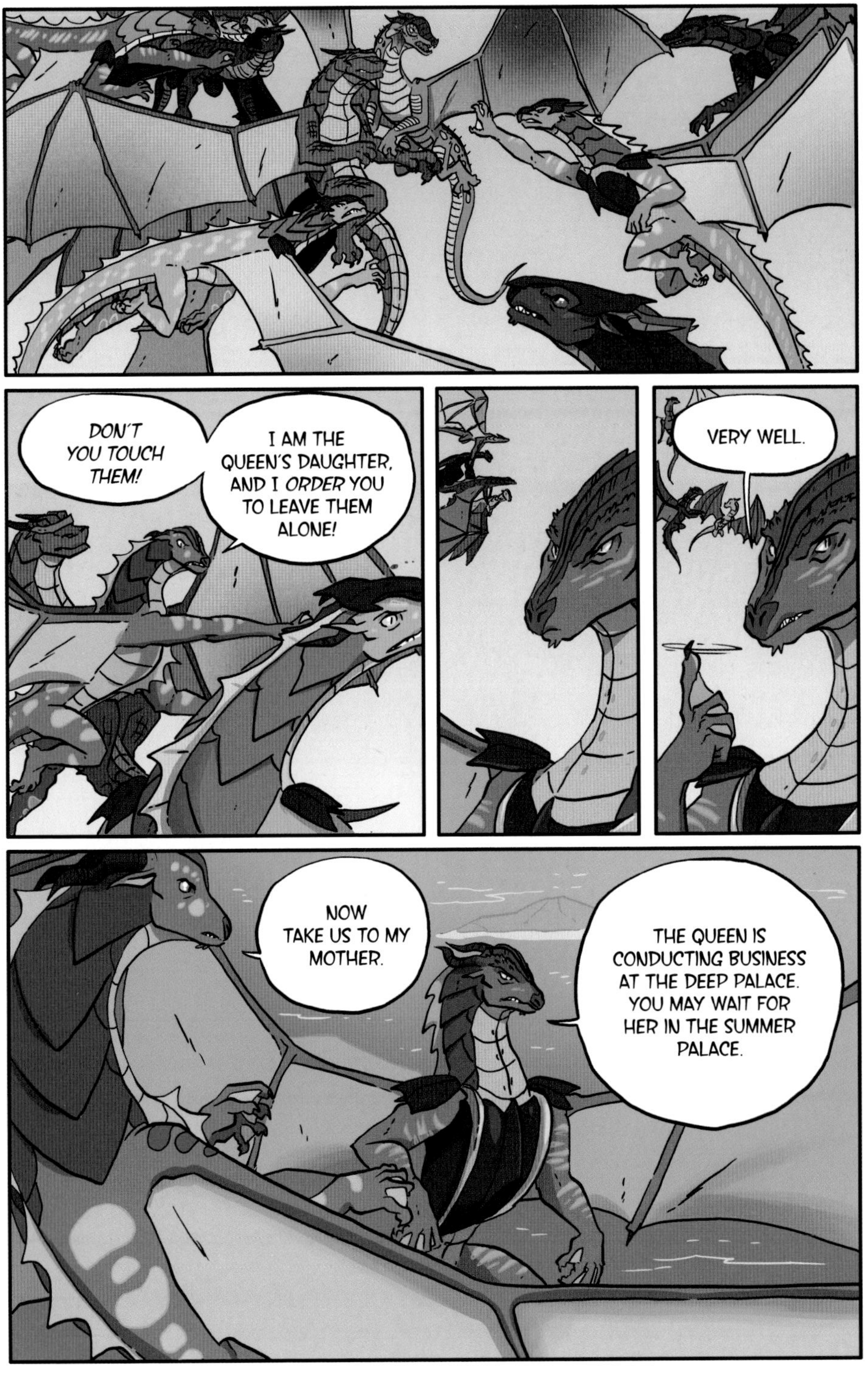
DON'T YOU TOUCH THEM!
I AM THE QUEEN'S DAUGHTER, AND I *ORDER* YOU TO LEAVE THEM ALONE!
VERY WELL.
NOW TAKE US TO MY MOTHER.
THE QUEEN IS CONDUCTING BUSINESS AT THE DEEP PALACE. YOU MAY WAIT FOR HER IN THE SUMMER PALACE.

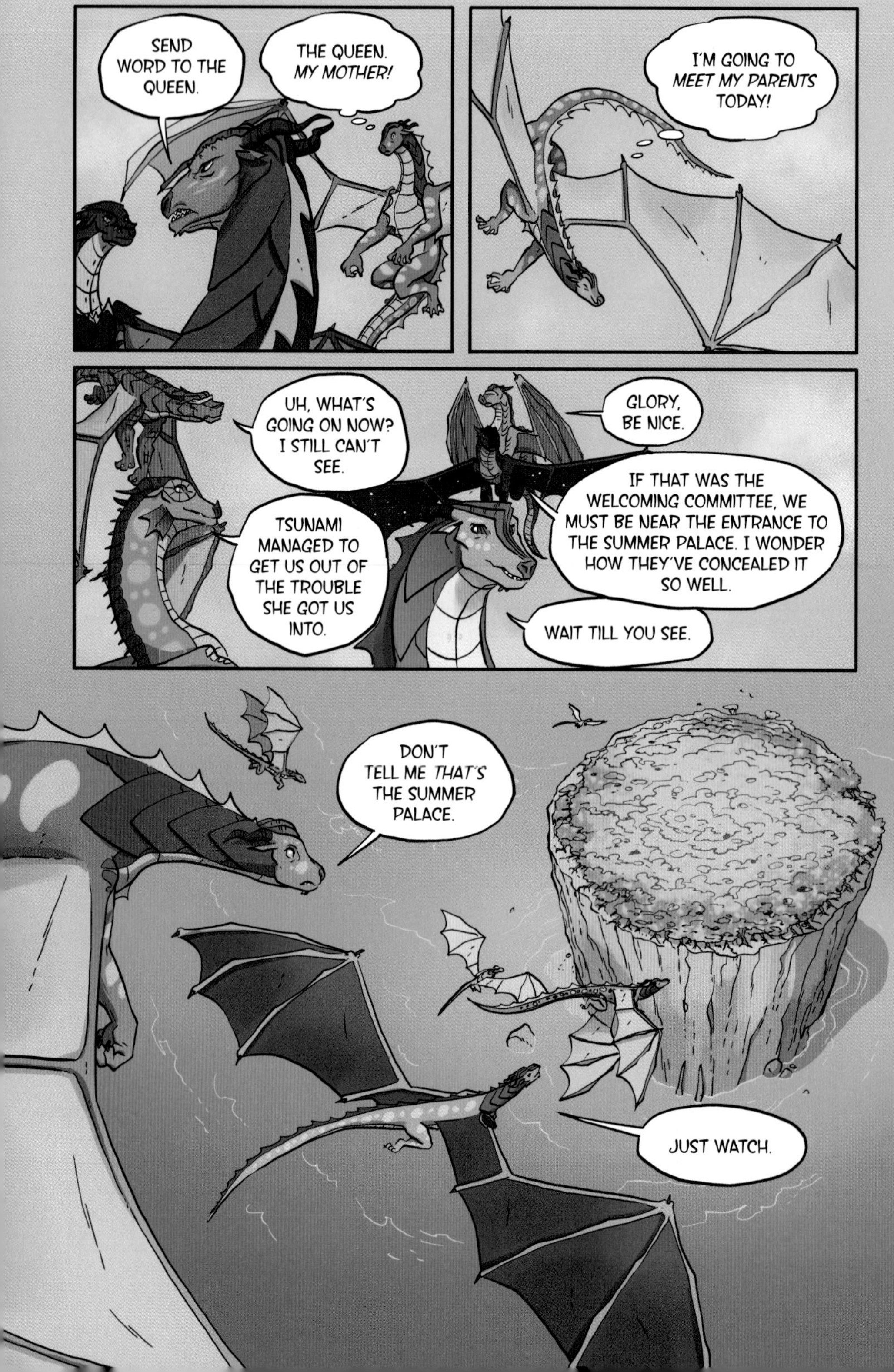
SEND WORD TO THE QUEEN.
THE QUEEN. *MY MOTHER!*
I'M GOING TO *MEET MY PARENTS* TODAY!
UH, WHAT'S GOING ON NOW? I STILL CAN'T SEE.
GLORY, BE NICE.
TSUNAMI MANAGED TO GET US OUT OF THE TROUBLE SHE GOT US INTO.
IF THAT WAS THE WELCOMING COMMITTEE, WE MUST BE NEAR THE ENTRANCE TO THE SUMMER PALACE. I WONDER HOW THEY'VE CONCEALED IT SO WELL.
WAIT TILL YOU SEE.
DON'T TELL ME *THAT'S* THE SUMMER PALACE.
JUST WATCH.

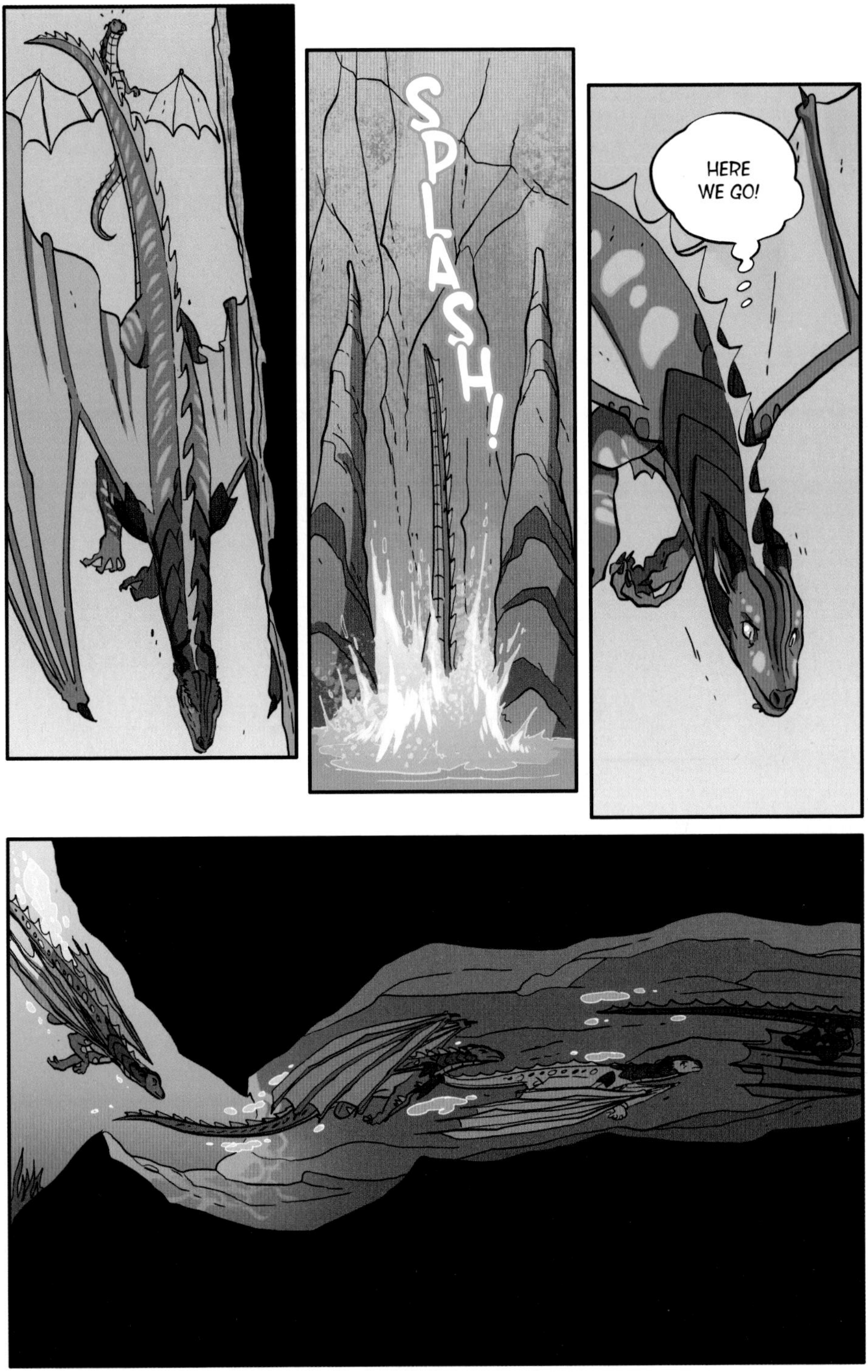
SPLASH!
HERE WE GO!

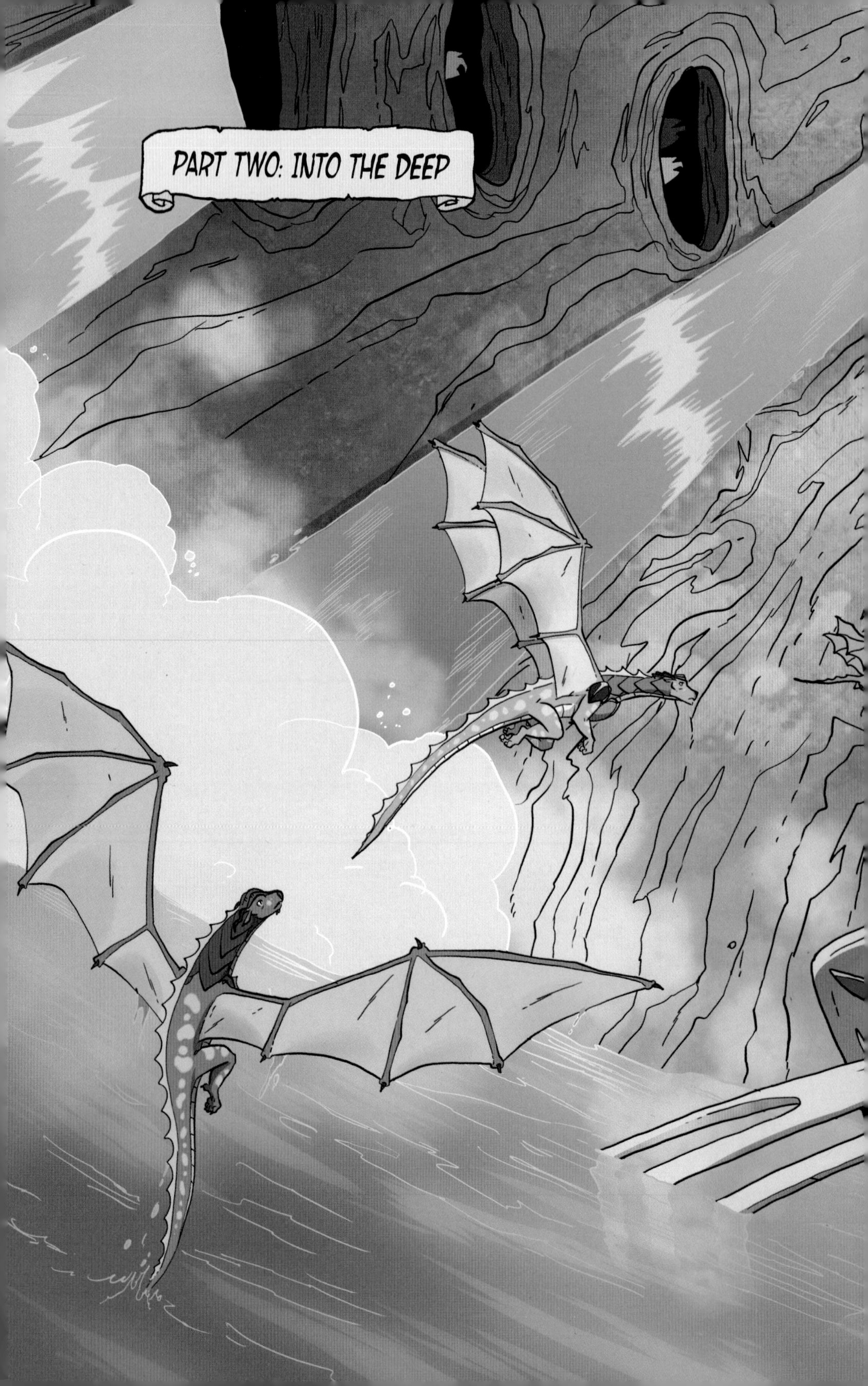
PART TWO: INTO THE DEEP

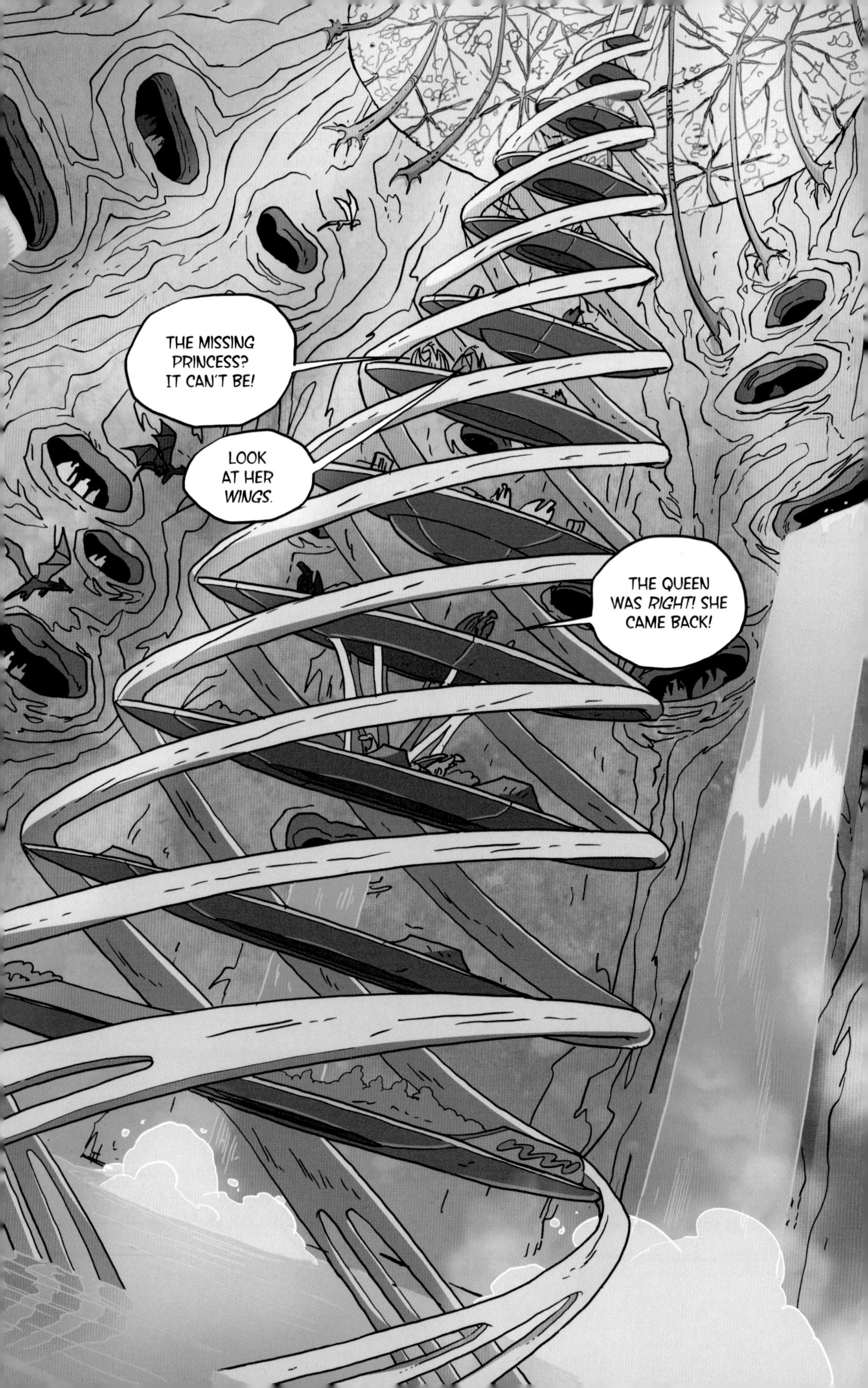
THE MISSING PRINCESS? IT CAN'T BE!
LOOK AT HER *WINGS*.
THE QUEEN WAS *RIGHT*! SHE CAME BACK!

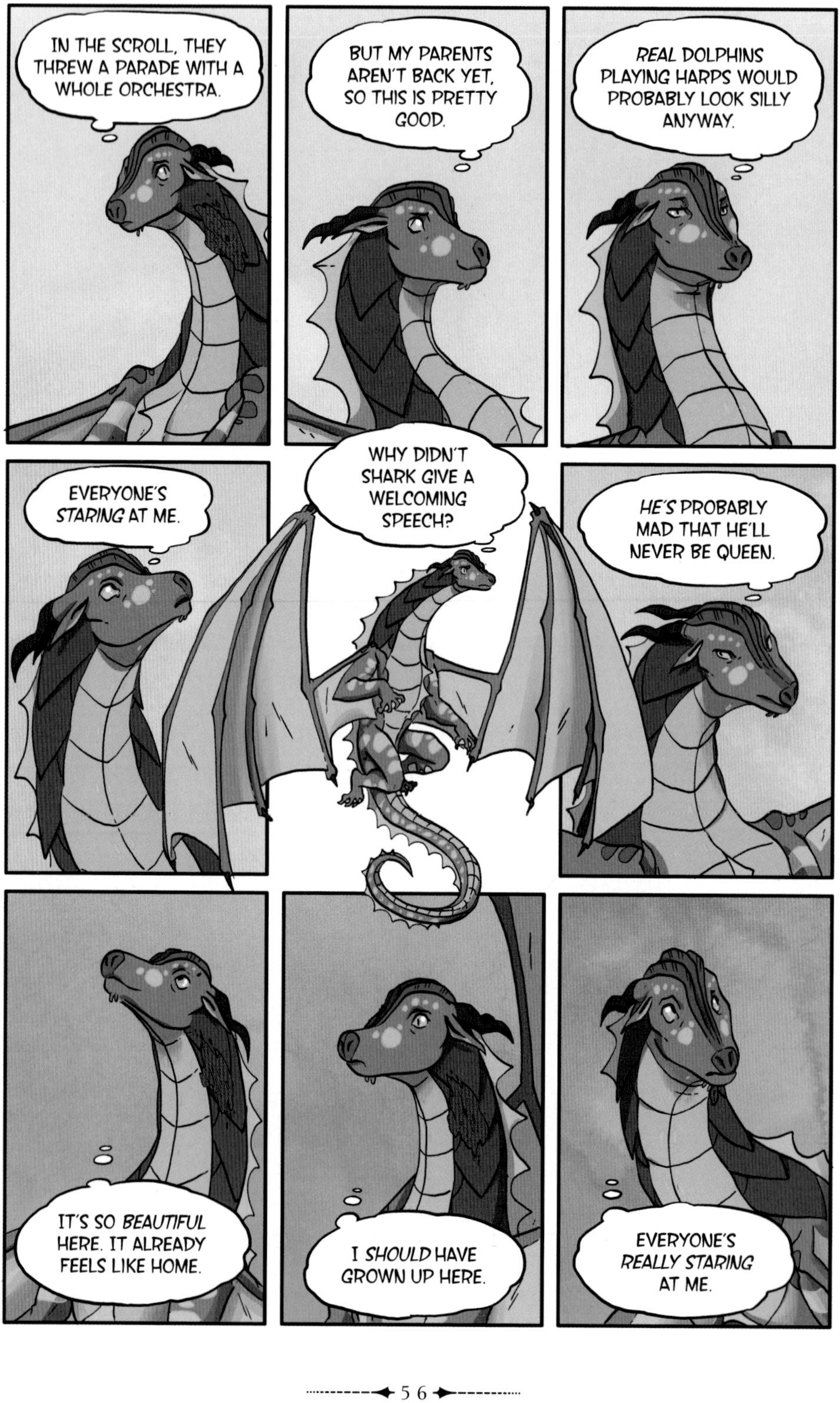
IN THE SCROLL, THEY THREW A PARADE WITH A WHOLE ORCHESTRA.
BUT MY PARENTS AREN'T BACK YET, SO THIS IS PRETTY GOOD.
REAL DOLPHINS PLAYING HARPS WOULD PROBABLY LOOK SILLY ANYWAY.
EVERYONE'S *STARING* AT ME.
WHY DIDN'T SHARK GIVE A WELCOMING SPEECH?
HE'S PROBABLY MAD THAT HE'LL NEVER BE QUEEN.
IT'S SO *BEAUTIFUL* HERE. IT ALREADY FEELS LIKE HOME.
I *SHOULD* HAVE GROWN UP HERE.
EVERYONE'S *REALLY STARING* AT ME.

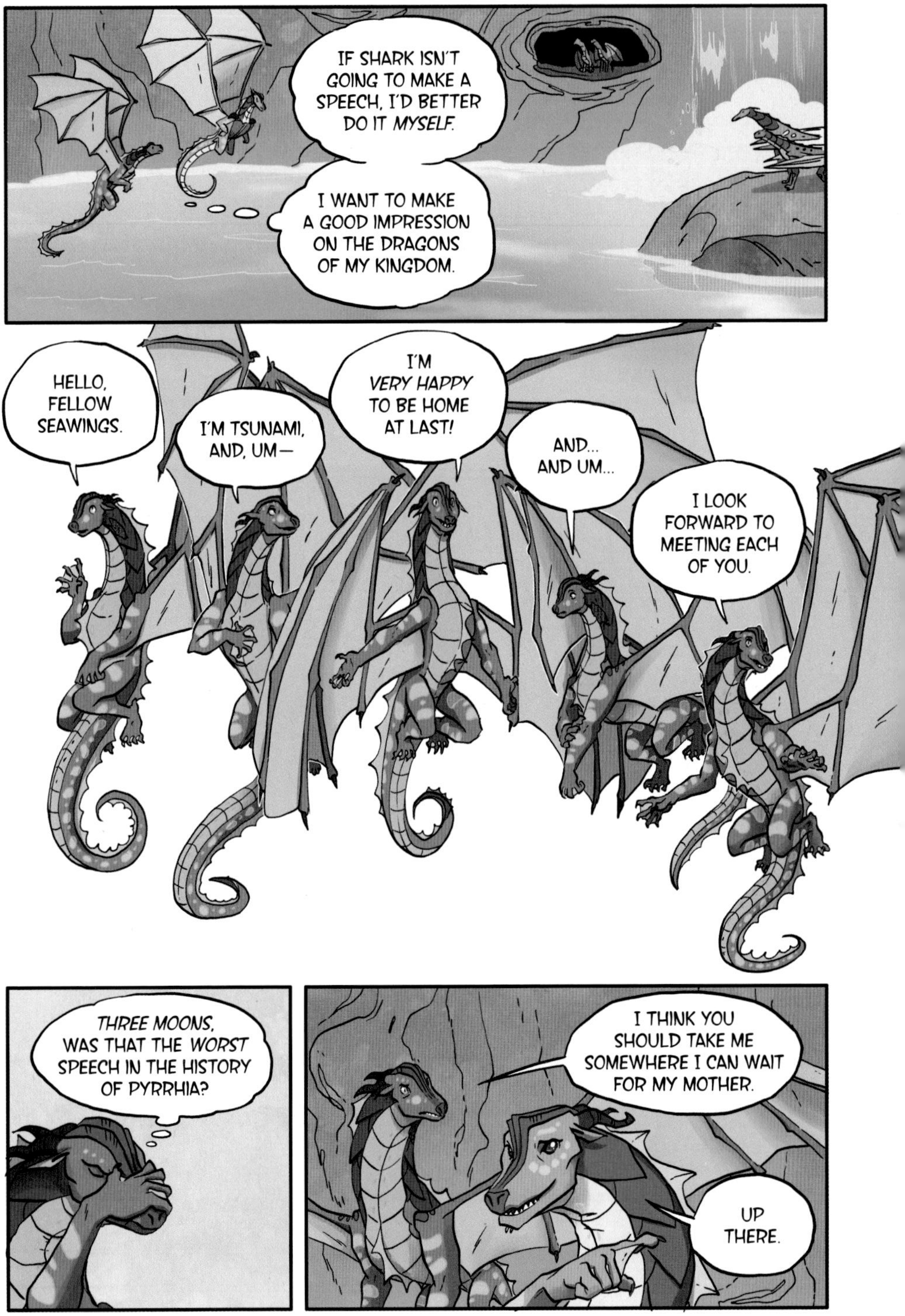
IF SHARK ISN'T GOING TO MAKE A SPEECH, I'D BETTER DO IT *MYSELF*.
I WANT TO MAKE A GOOD IMPRESSION ON THE DRAGONS OF MY KINGDOM.
HELLO, FELLOW SEAWINGS.
I'M TSUNAMI, AND, UM—
I'M *VERY HAPPY* TO BE HOME AT LAST!
AND... AND UM...
I LOOK FORWARD TO MEETING EACH OF YOU.
THREE MOONS, WAS THAT THE *WORST* SPEECH IN THE HISTORY OF PYRRHIA?
I THINK YOU SHOULD TAKE ME SOMEWHERE I CAN WAIT FOR MY MOTHER.
UP THERE.

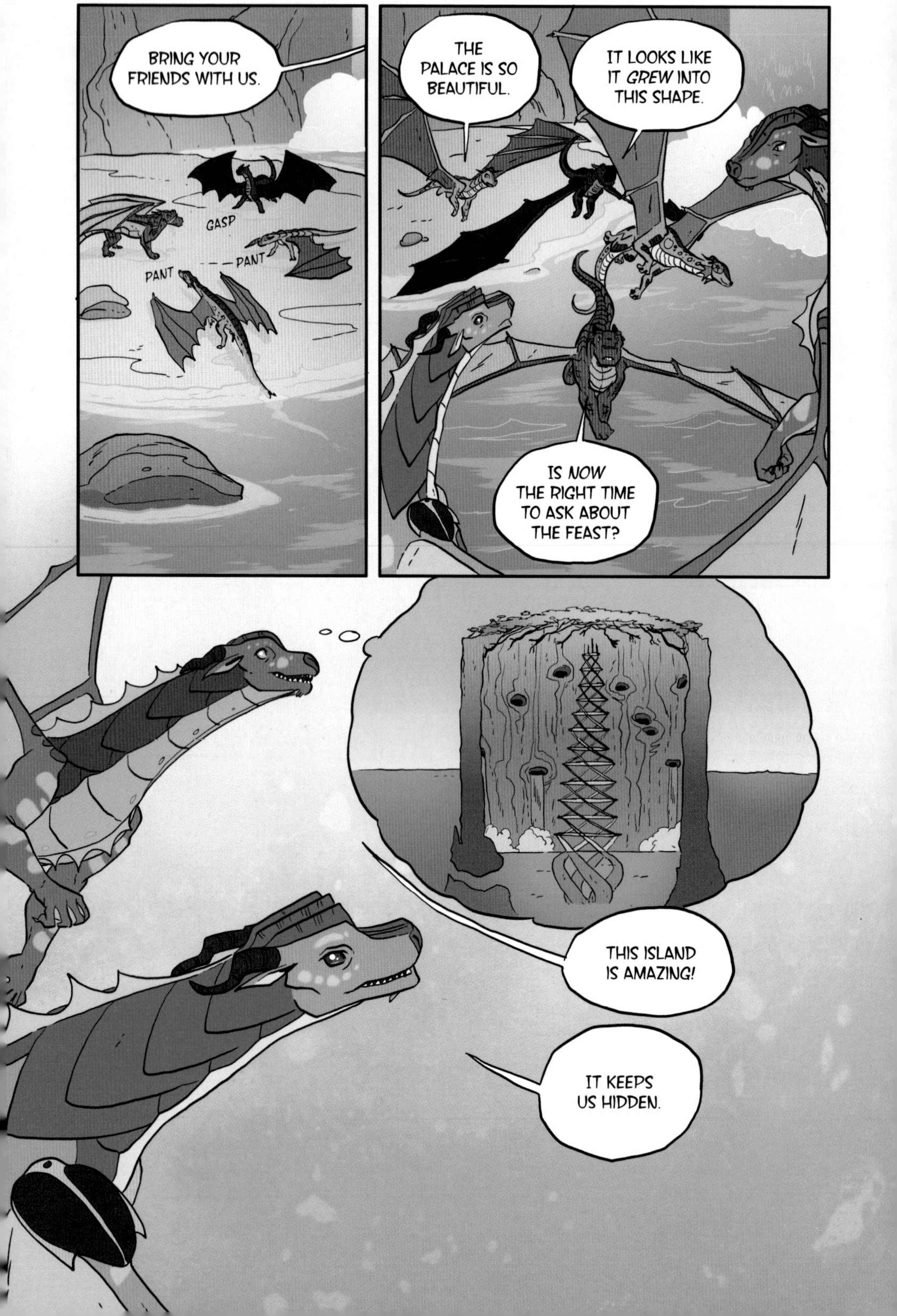
BRING YOUR FRIENDS WITH US.
GASP
PANT
PANT
THE PALACE IS SO BEAUTIFUL.
IT LOOKS LIKE IT *GREW* INTO THIS SHAPE.
IS *NOW* THE RIGHT TIME TO ASK ABOUT THE FEAST?
THIS ISLAND IS AMAZING!
IT KEEPS US HIDDEN.

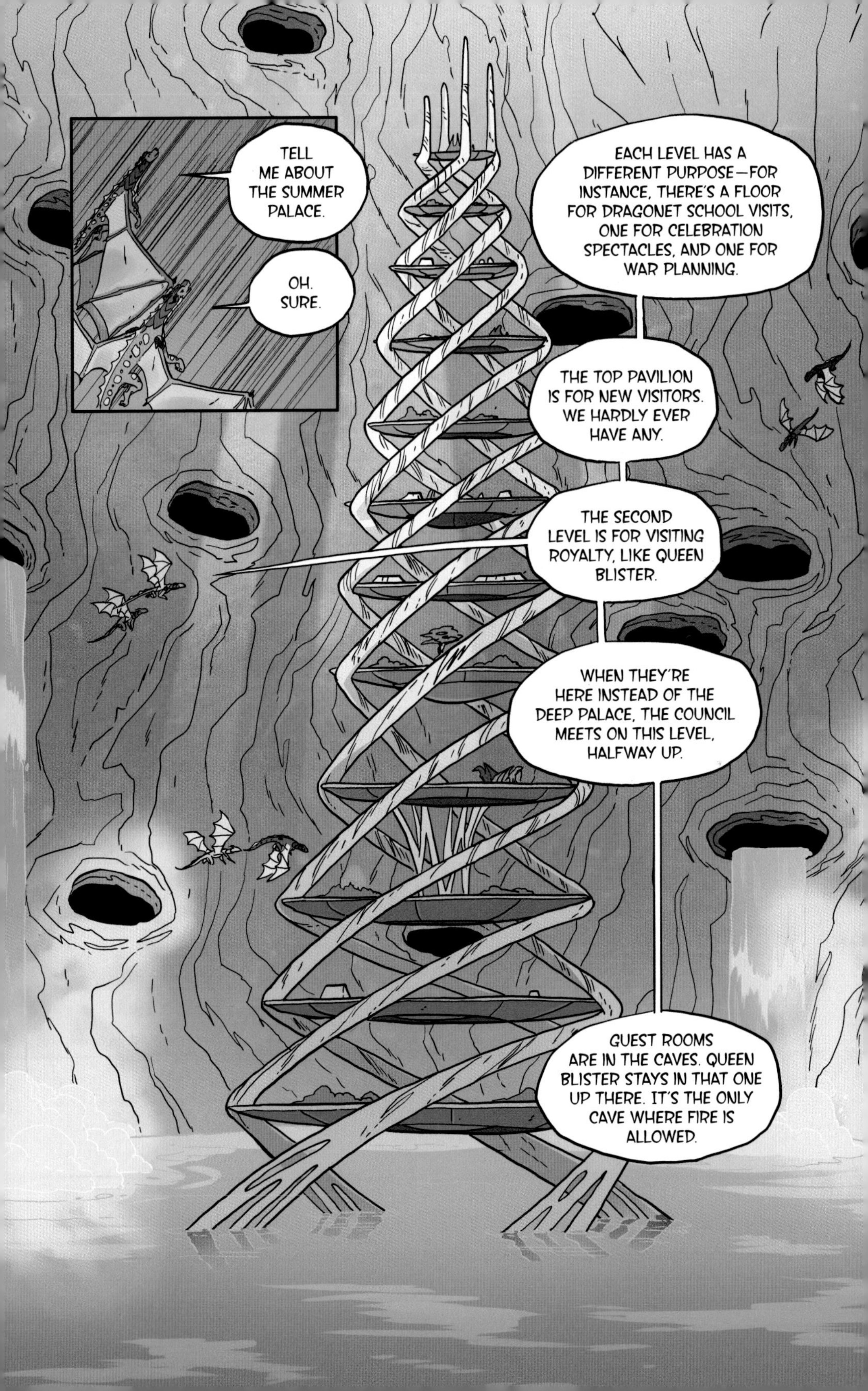
TELL ME ABOUT THE SUMMER PALACE.
OH. SURE.
EACH LEVEL HAS A DIFFERENT PURPOSE—FOR INSTANCE, THERE'S A FLOOR FOR DRAGONET SCHOOL VISITS, ONE FOR CELEBRATION SPECTACLES, AND ONE FOR WAR PLANNING.
THE TOP PAVILION IS FOR NEW VISITORS. WE HARDLY EVER HAVE ANY.
THE SECOND LEVEL IS FOR VISITING ROYALTY, LIKE QUEEN BLISTER.
WHEN THEY'RE HERE INSTEAD OF THE DEEP PALACE, THE COUNCIL MEETS ON THIS LEVEL, HALFWAY UP.
GUEST ROOMS ARE IN THE CAVES. QUEEN BLISTER STAYS IN THAT ONE UP THERE. IT'S THE ONLY CAVE WHERE FIRE IS ALLOWED.

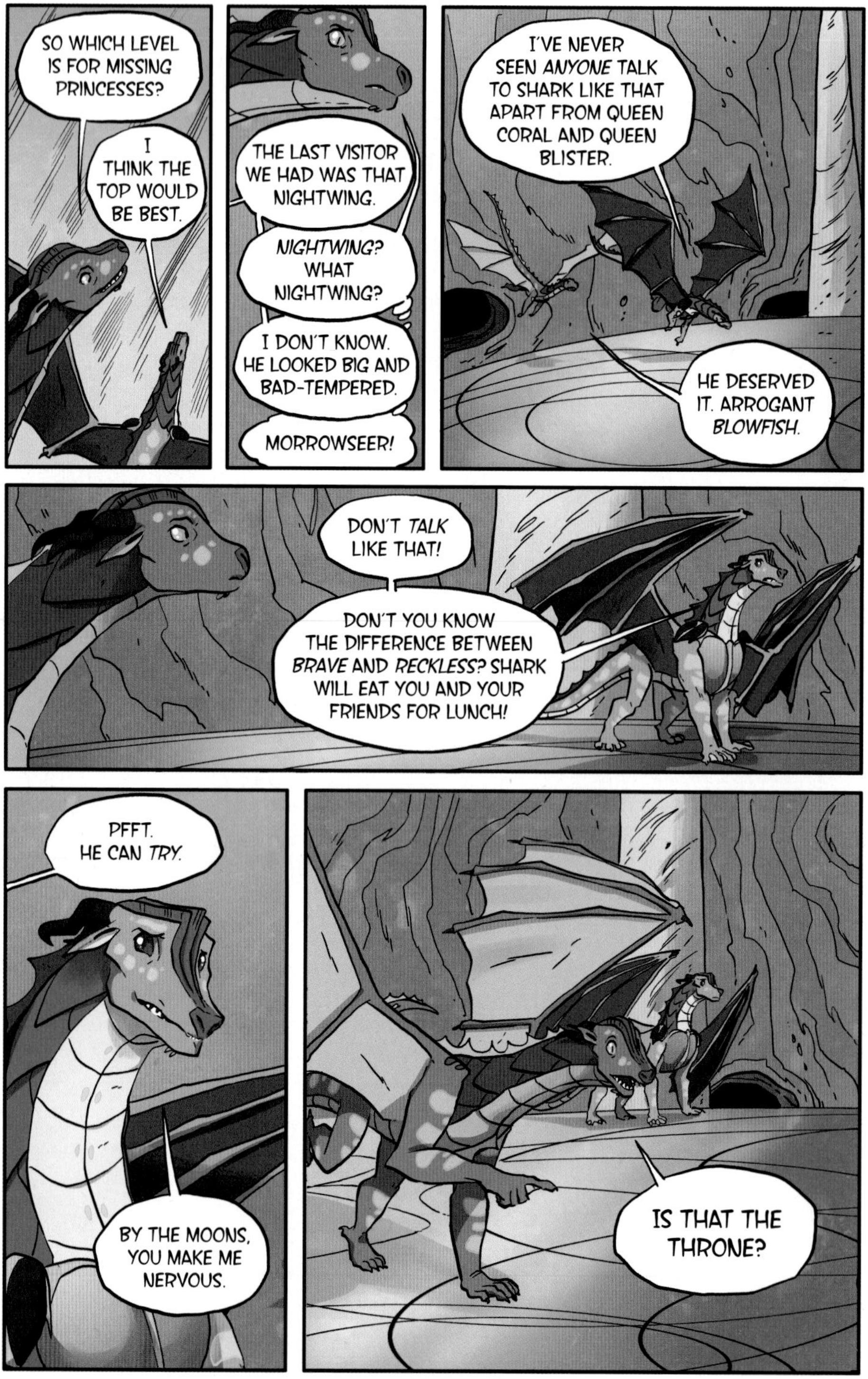
SO WHICH LEVEL IS FOR MISSING PRINCESSES?
I THINK THE TOP WOULD BE BEST.
THE LAST VISITOR WE HAD WAS THAT NIGHTWING.
NIGHTWING? WHAT NIGHTWING?
I DON'T KNOW. HE LOOKED BIG AND BAD-TEMPERED.
MORROWSEER!
I'VE NEVER SEEN *ANYONE* TALK TO SHARK LIKE THAT APART FROM QUEEN CORAL AND QUEEN BLISTER.
HE DESERVED IT. ARROGANT *BLOWFISH.*
DON'T *TALK* LIKE THAT!
DON'T YOU KNOW THE DIFFERENCE BETWEEN *BRAVE* AND *RECKLESS?* SHARK WILL EAT YOU AND YOUR FRIENDS FOR LUNCH!
PFFT. HE CAN *TRY.*
BY THE MOONS, YOU MAKE ME NERVOUS.
IS THAT THE THRONE?

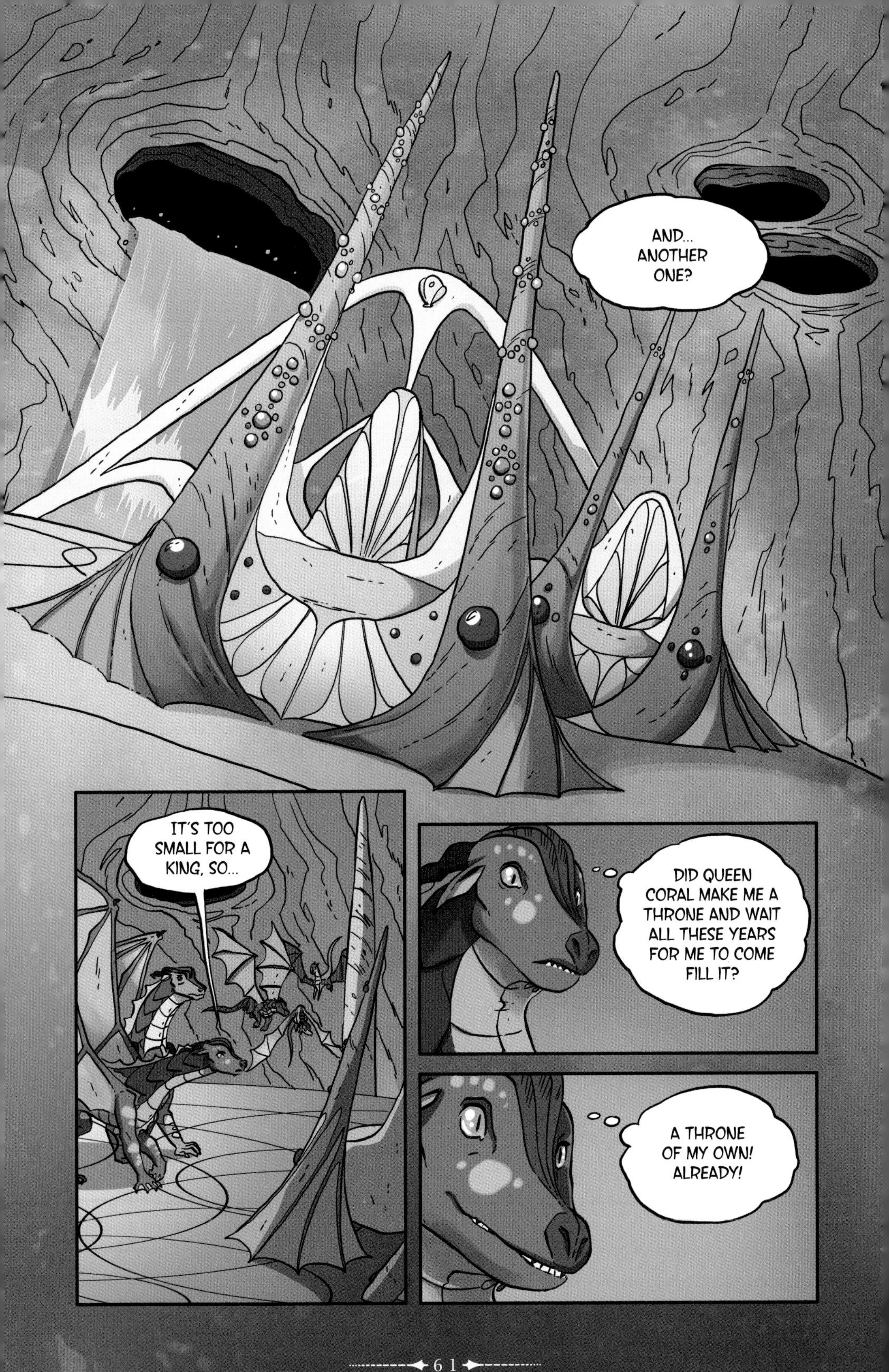
AND... ANOTHER ONE?
IT'S TOO SMALL FOR A KING, SO...
DID QUEEN CORAL MAKE ME A THRONE AND WAIT ALL THESE YEARS FOR ME TO COME FILL IT?
A THRONE OF MY OWN! ALREADY!

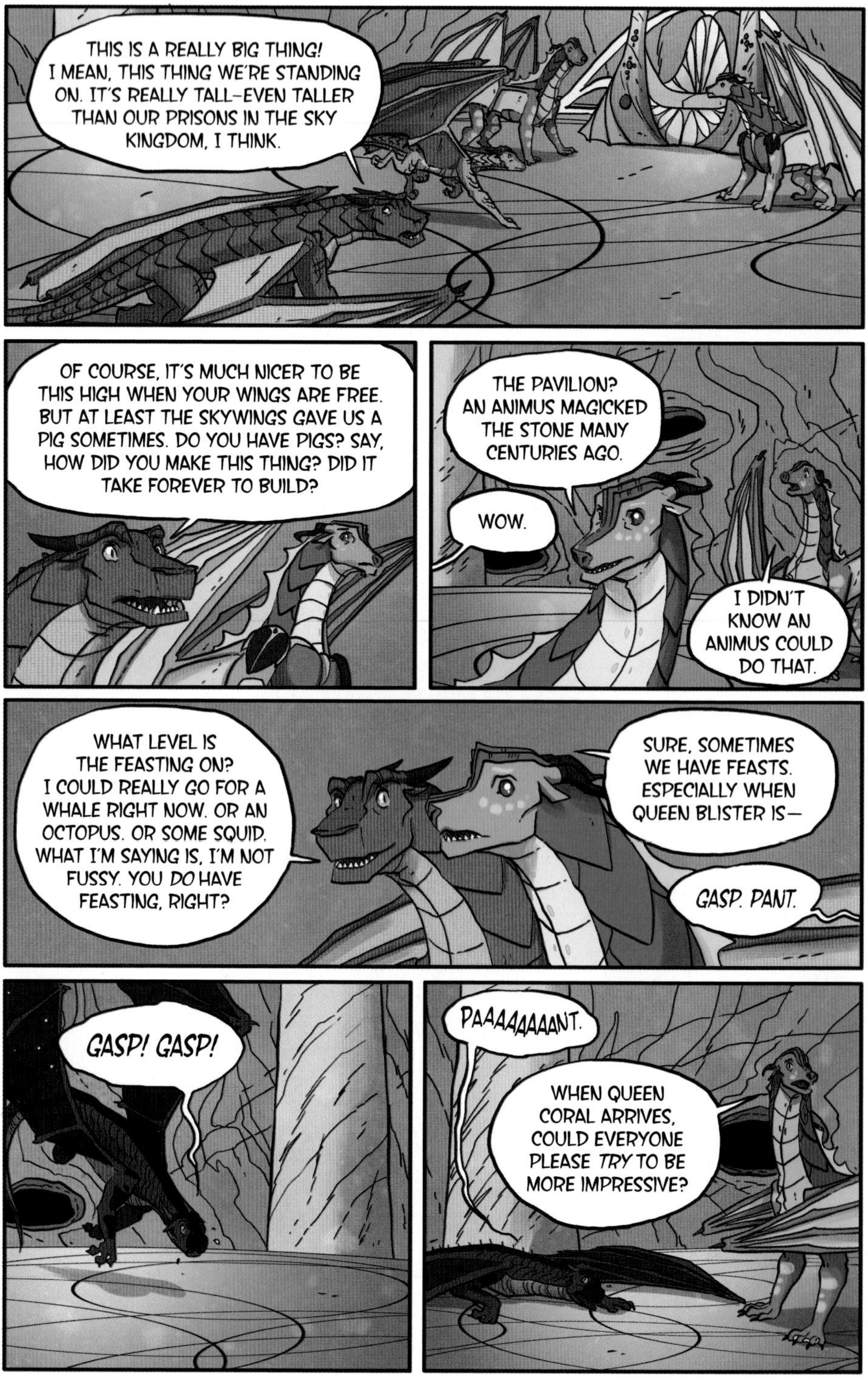
THIS IS A REALLY BIG THING! I MEAN, THIS THING WE'RE STANDING ON. IT'S REALLY TALL–EVEN TALLER THAN OUR PRISONS IN THE SKY KINGDOM, I THINK.
OF COURSE, IT'S MUCH NICER TO BE THIS HIGH WHEN YOUR WINGS ARE FREE. BUT AT LEAST THE SKYWINGS GAVE US A PIG SOMETIMES. DO YOU HAVE PIGS? SAY, HOW DID YOU MAKE THIS THING? DID IT TAKE FOREVER TO BUILD?
THE PAVILION? AN ANIMUS MAGICKED THE STONE MANY CENTURIES AGO.
WOW.
I DIDN'T KNOW AN ANIMUS COULD DO THAT.
WHAT LEVEL IS THE FEASTING ON? I COULD REALLY GO FOR A WHALE RIGHT NOW. OR AN OCTOPUS. OR SOME SQUID. WHAT I'M SAYING IS, I'M NOT FUSSY. YOU *DO* HAVE FEASTING, RIGHT?
SURE, SOMETIMES WE HAVE FEASTS. ESPECIALLY WHEN QUEEN BLISTER IS—
GASP. PANT.
GASP! GASP!
PAAAAAAAANT.
WHEN QUEEN CORAL ARRIVES, COULD EVERYONE PLEASE *TRY* TO BE MORE IMPRESSIVE?

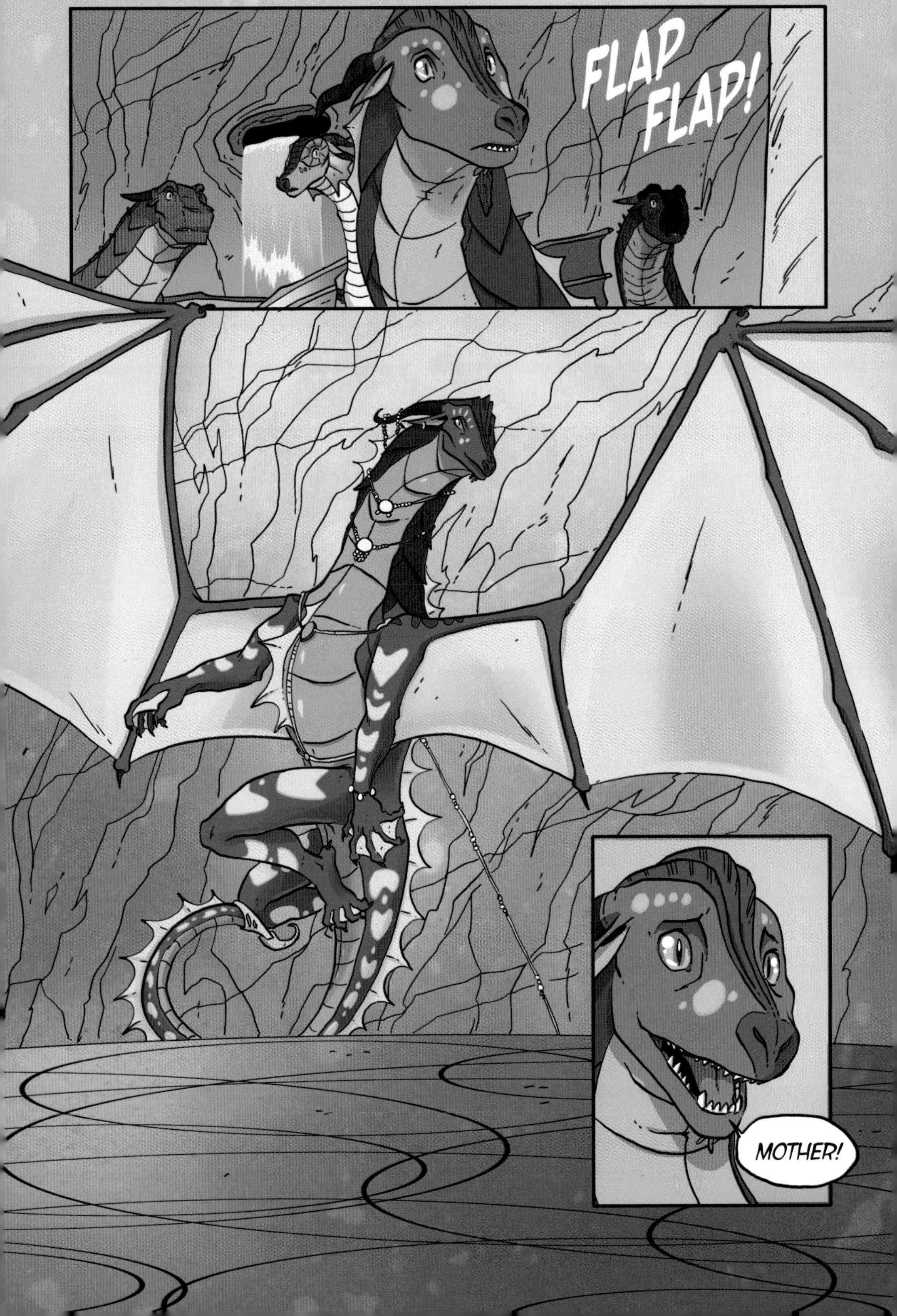
FLAP FLAP!
MOTHER!

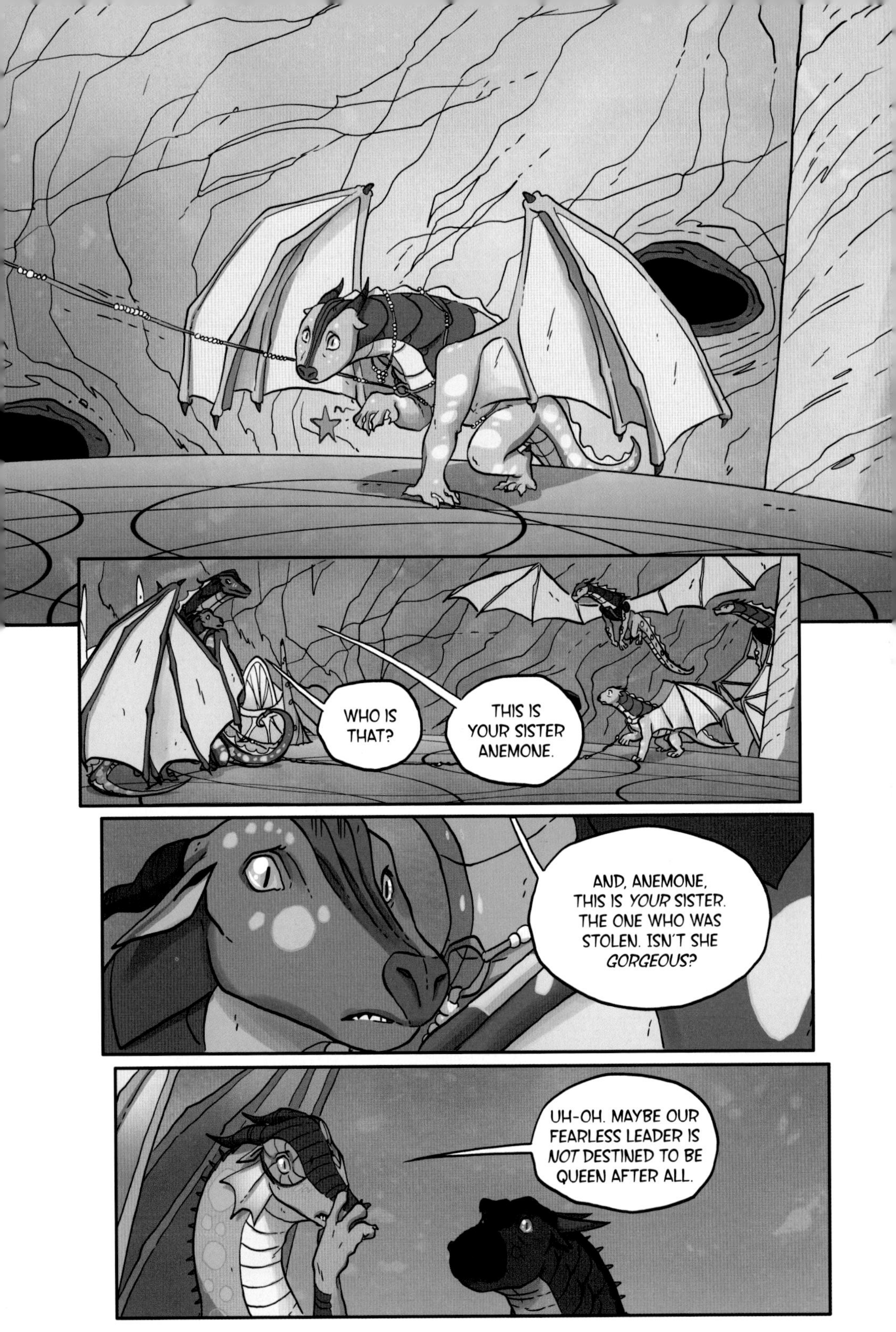
WHO IS THAT?
THIS IS YOUR SISTER ANEMONE.
AND, ANEMONE, THIS IS *YOUR* SISTER. THE ONE WHO WAS STOLEN. ISN'T SHE *GORGEOUS*?
UH-OH. MAYBE OUR FEARLESS LEADER IS *NOT* DESTINED TO BE QUEEN AFTER ALL.

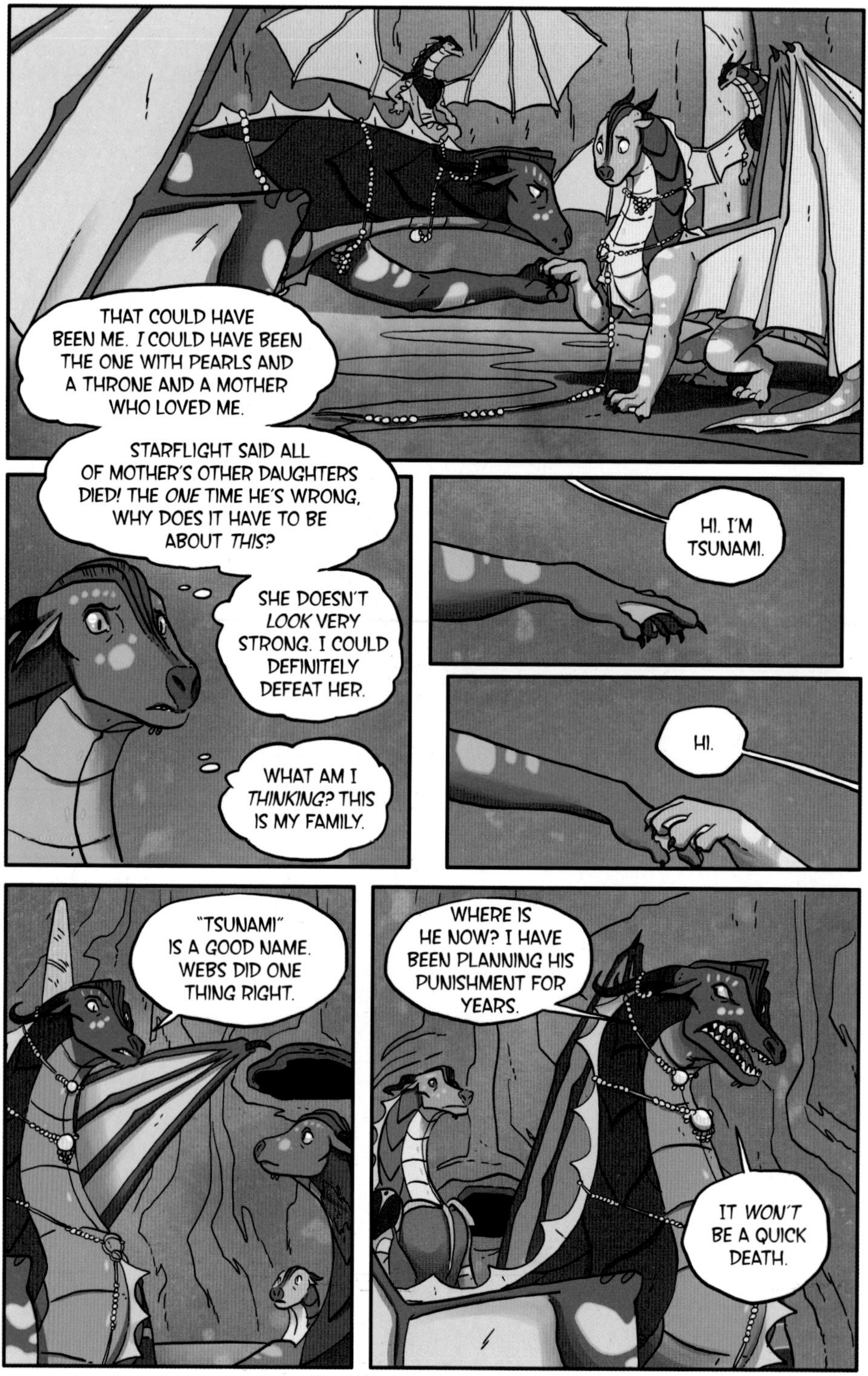
THAT COULD HAVE BEEN ME. *I* COULD HAVE BEEN THE ONE WITH PEARLS AND A THRONE AND A MOTHER WHO LOVED ME.
STARFLIGHT SAID ALL OF MOTHER'S OTHER DAUGHTERS DIED! THE *ONE* TIME HE'S WRONG, WHY DOES IT HAVE TO BE ABOUT *THIS*?
SHE DOESN'T *LOOK* VERY STRONG. I COULD DEFINITELY DEFEAT HER.
WHAT AM I *THINKING*? THIS IS MY FAMILY.
HI. I'M TSUNAMI.
HI.
"TSUNAMI" IS A GOOD NAME. WEBS DID ONE THING RIGHT.
WHERE IS HE NOW? I HAVE BEEN PLANNING HIS PUNISHMENT FOR YEARS.
IT *WON'T* BE A QUICK DEATH.

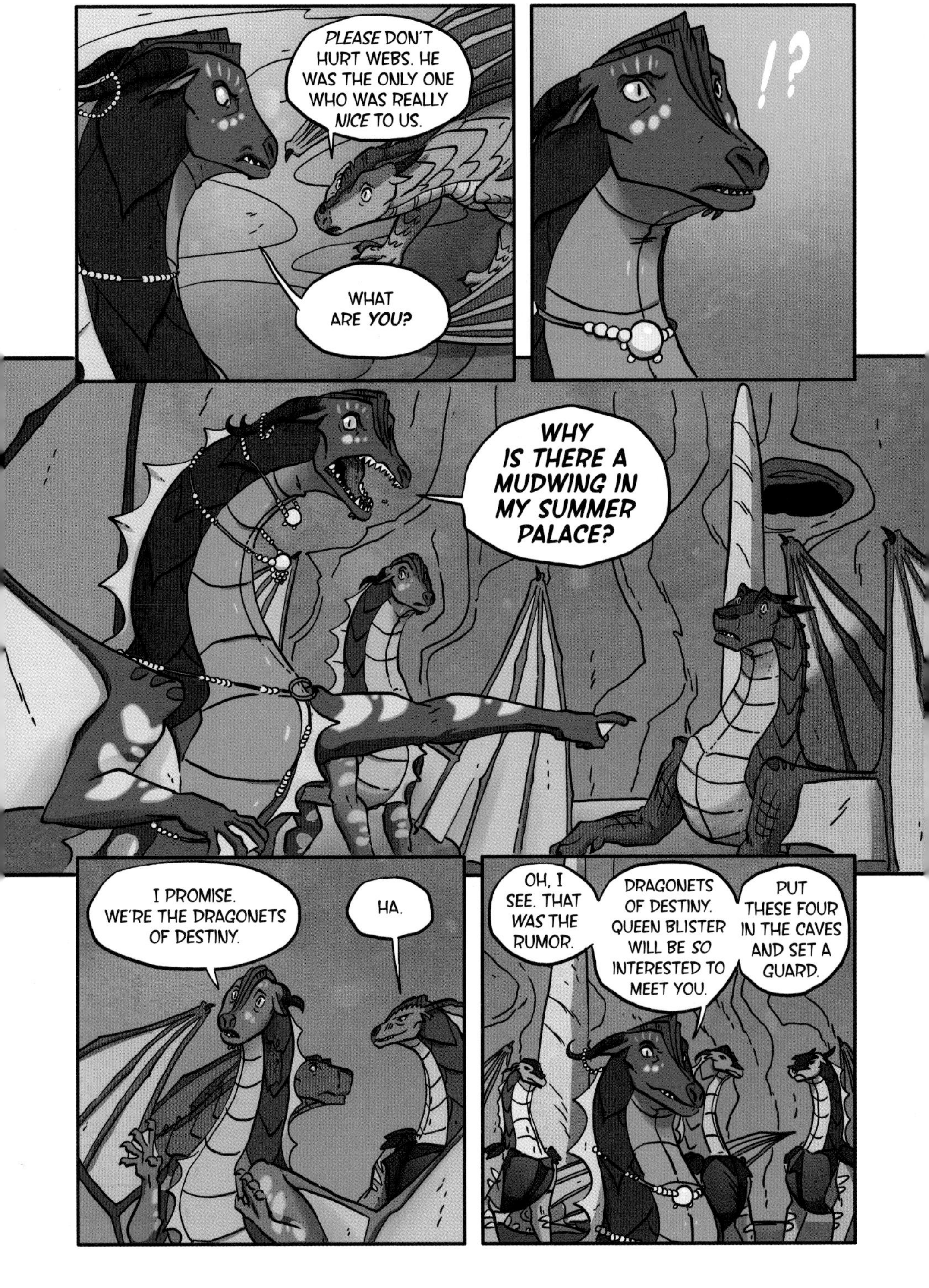
PLEASE DON'T HURT WEBS. HE WAS THE ONLY ONE WHO WAS REALLY NICE TO US.
WHAT ARE YOU?
!?
WHY IS THERE A MUDWING IN MY SUMMER PALACE?
I PROMISE. WE'RE THE DRAGONETS OF DESTINY.
HA.
OH, I SEE. THAT WAS THE RUMOR.
DRAGONETS OF DESTINY. QUEEN BLISTER WILL BE SO INTERESTED TO MEET YOU.
PUT THESE FOUR IN THE CAVES AND SET A GUARD.

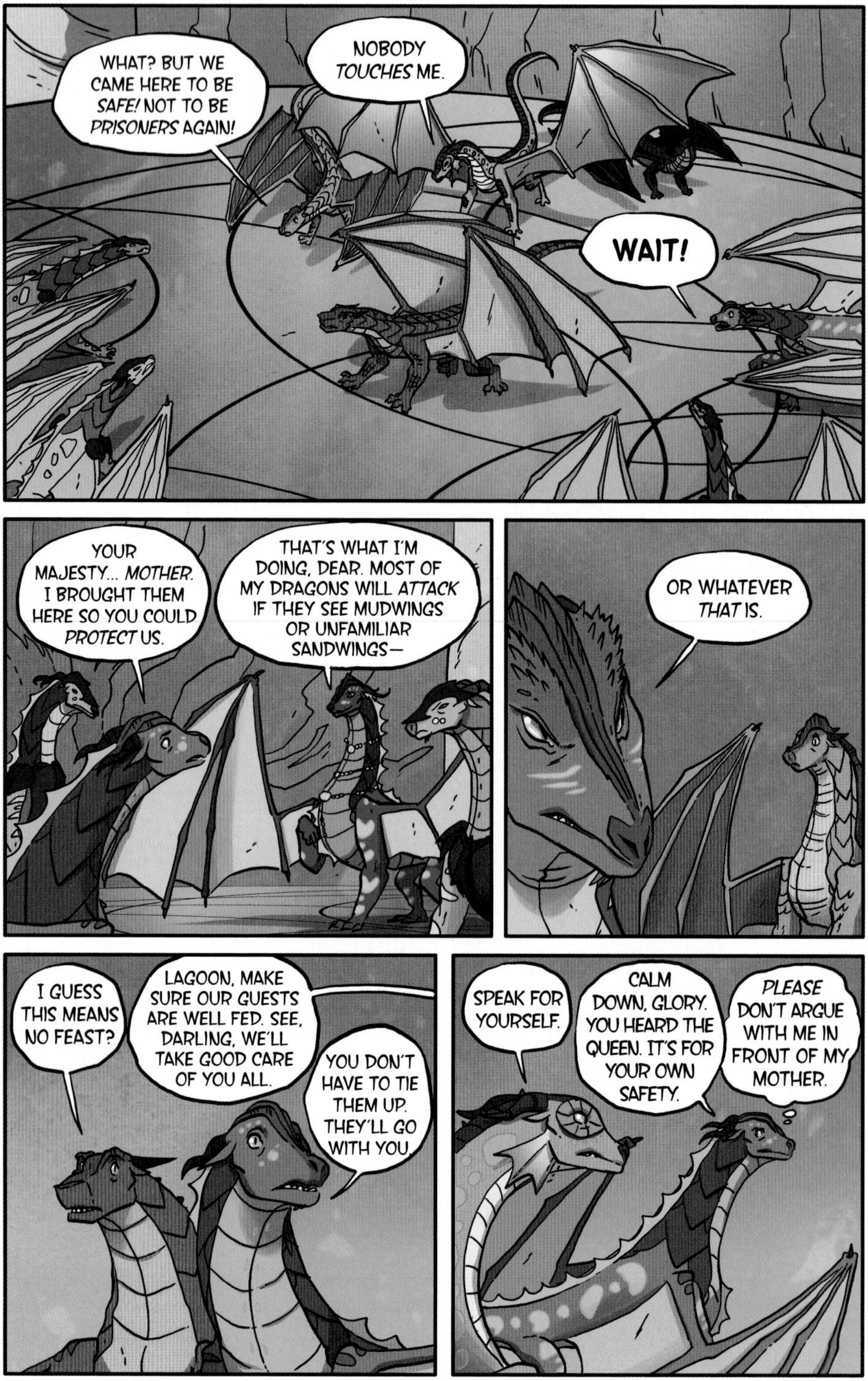
WHAT? BUT WE CAME HERE TO BE *SAFE!* NOT TO BE *PRISONERS* AGAIN!
NOBODY *TOUCHES* ME.
WAIT!
YOUR MAJESTY... *MOTHER.* I BROUGHT THEM HERE SO YOU COULD *PROTECT* US.
THAT'S WHAT I'M DOING, DEAR. MOST OF MY DRAGONS WILL *ATTACK* IF THEY SEE MUDWINGS OR UNFAMILIAR SANDWINGS—
OR WHATEVER *THAT* IS.
I GUESS THIS MEANS NO FEAST?
LAGOON, MAKE SURE OUR GUESTS ARE WELL FED. SEE, DARLING, WE'LL TAKE GOOD CARE OF YOU ALL.
YOU DON'T HAVE TO TIE THEM UP. THEY'LL GO WITH YOU.
SPEAK FOR YOURSELF.
CALM DOWN, GLORY. YOU HEARD THE QUEEN. IT'S FOR YOUR OWN SAFETY.
PLEASE DON'T ARGUE WITH ME IN FRONT OF MY MOTHER.

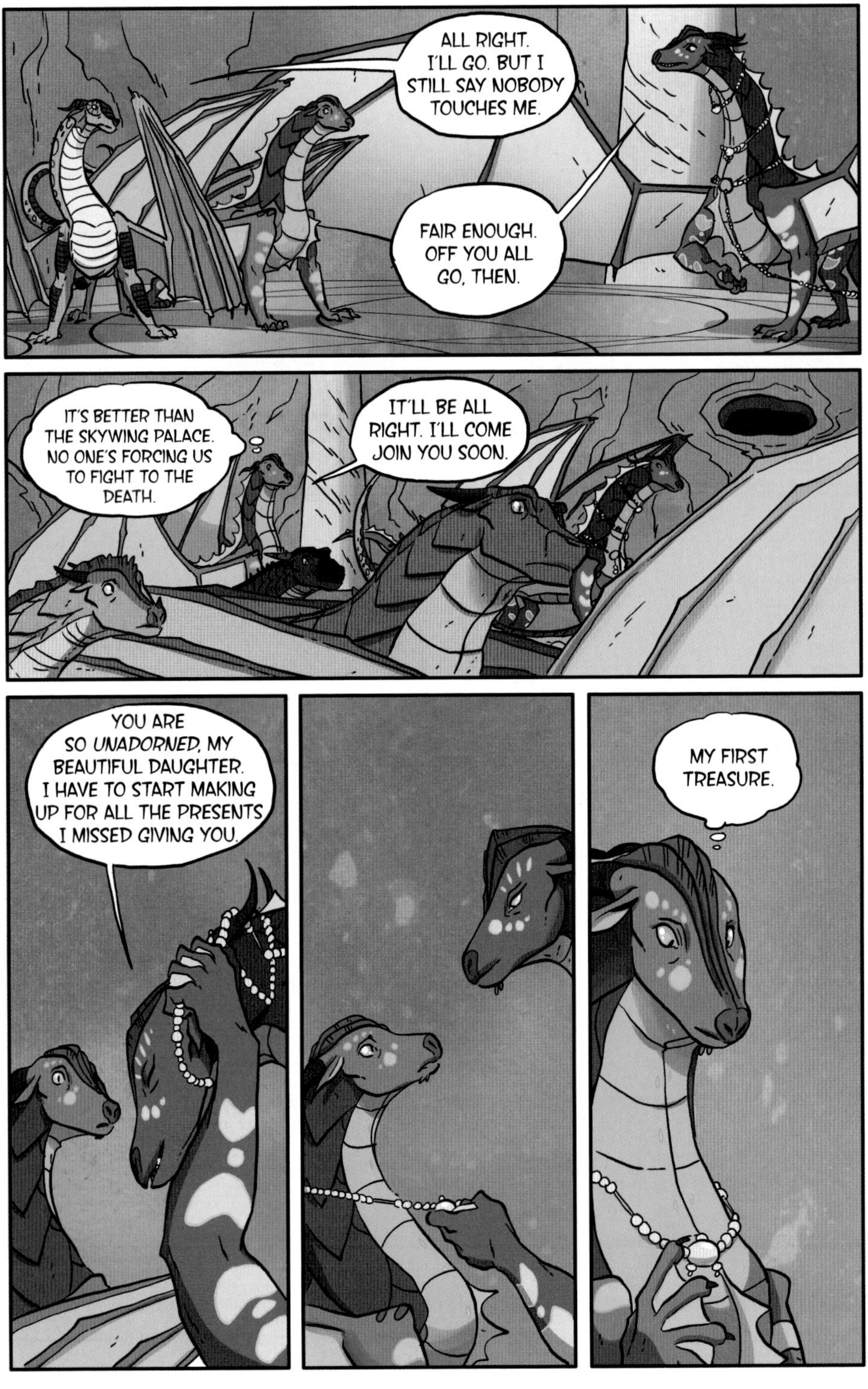
ALL RIGHT. I'LL GO. BUT I STILL SAY NOBODY TOUCHES ME.
FAIR ENOUGH. OFF YOU ALL GO, THEN.
IT'S BETTER THAN THE SKYWING PALACE. NO ONE'S FORCING US TO FIGHT TO THE DEATH.
IT'LL BE ALL RIGHT. I'LL COME JOIN YOU SOON.
YOU ARE SO *UNADORNED*, MY BEAUTIFUL DAUGHTER. I HAVE TO START MAKING UP FOR ALL THE PRESENTS I MISSED GIVING YOU.
MY FIRST TREASURE.

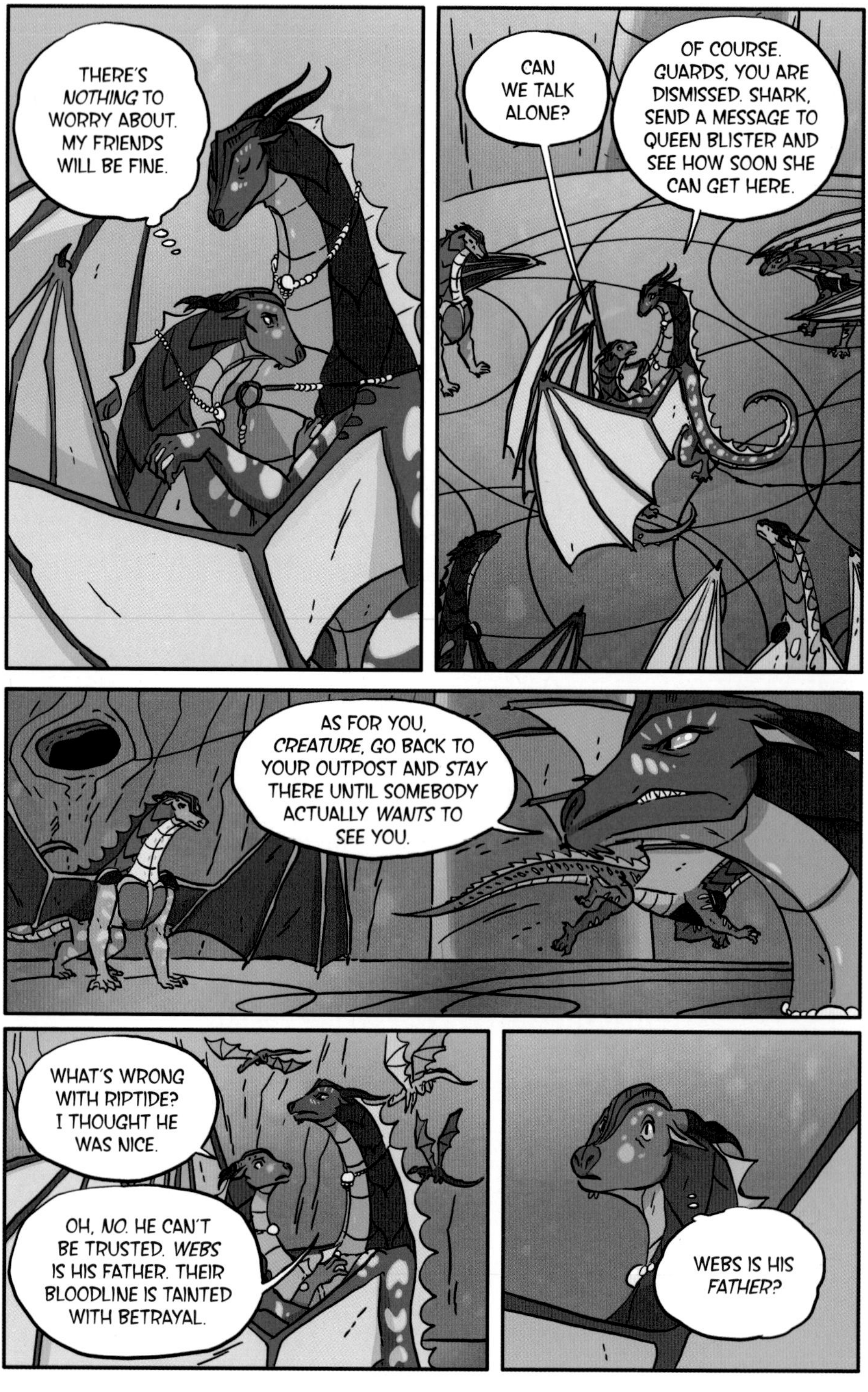
THERE'S *NOTHING* TO WORRY ABOUT. MY FRIENDS WILL BE FINE.
CAN WE TALK ALONE?
OF COURSE. GUARDS, YOU ARE DISMISSED. SHARK, SEND A MESSAGE TO QUEEN BLISTER AND SEE HOW SOON SHE CAN GET HERE.
AS FOR YOU, *CREATURE*, GO BACK TO YOUR OUTPOST AND *STAY* THERE UNTIL SOMEBODY ACTUALLY *WANTS* TO SEE YOU.
WHAT'S WRONG WITH RIPTIDE? I THOUGHT HE WAS NICE.
OH, *NO*. HE CAN'T BE TRUSTED. *WEBS* IS HIS FATHER. THEIR BLOODLINE IS TAINTED WITH BETRAYAL.
WEBS IS HIS *FATHER*?

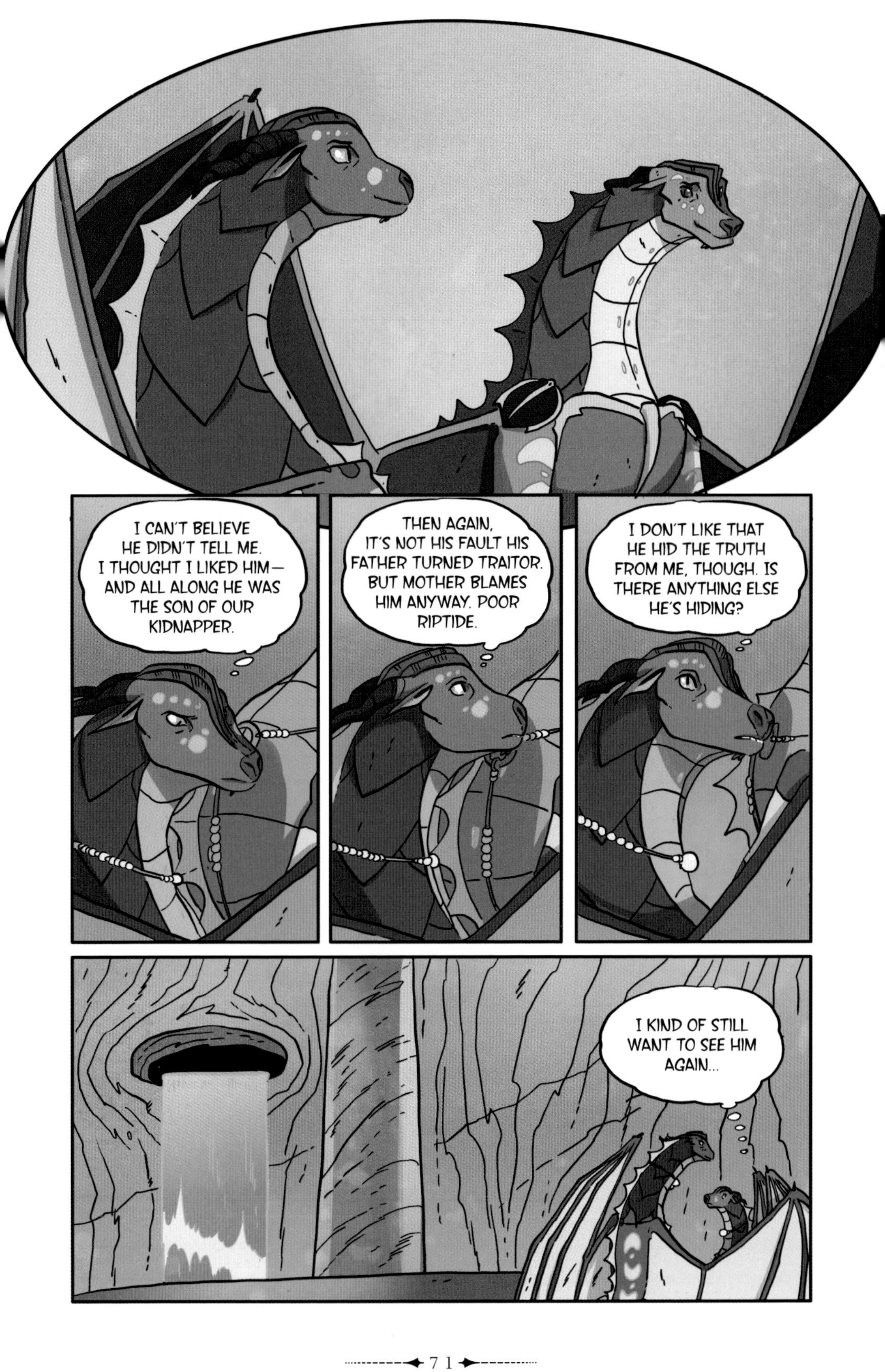
I CAN'T BELIEVE HE DIDN'T TELL ME. I THOUGHT I LIKED HIM— AND ALL ALONG HE WAS THE SON OF OUR KIDNAPPER.
THEN AGAIN, IT'S NOT HIS FAULT HIS FATHER TURNED TRAITOR. BUT MOTHER BLAMES HIM ANYWAY. POOR RIPTIDE.
I DON'T LIKE THAT HE HID THE TRUTH FROM ME, THOUGH. IS THERE ANYTHING ELSE HE'S HIDING?
I KIND OF STILL WANT TO SEE HIM AGAIN...

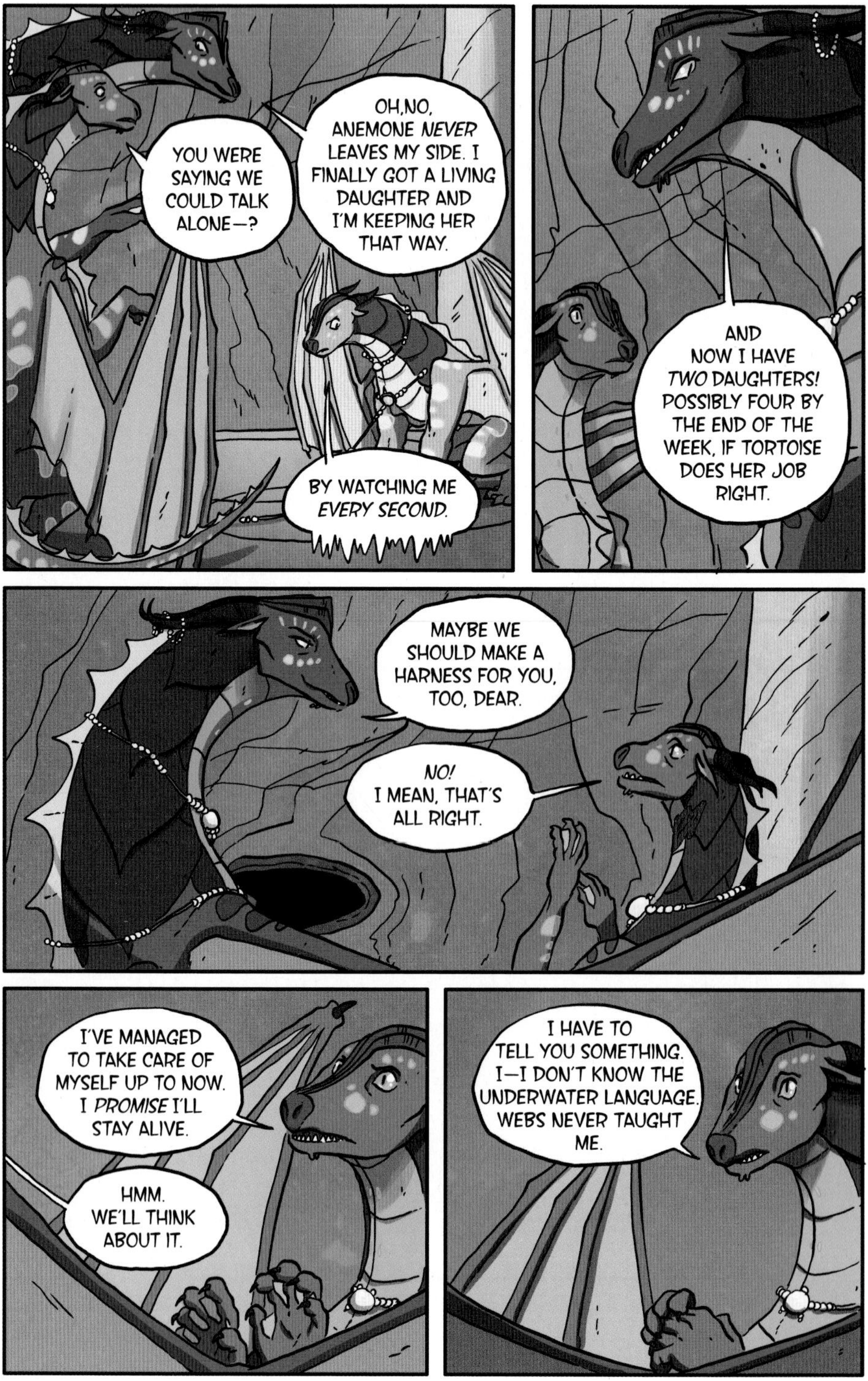
YOU WERE SAYING WE COULD TALK ALONE—?
OH,NO, ANEMONE *NEVER* LEAVES MY SIDE. I FINALLY GOT A LIVING DAUGHTER AND I'M KEEPING HER THAT WAY.
BY WATCHING ME *EVERY SECOND.*
AND NOW I HAVE *TWO* DAUGHTERS! POSSIBLY FOUR BY THE END OF THE WEEK, IF TORTOISE DOES HER JOB RIGHT.
MAYBE WE SHOULD MAKE A HARNESS FOR YOU, TOO, DEAR.
NO! I MEAN, THAT'S ALL RIGHT.
I'VE MANAGED TO TAKE CARE OF MYSELF UP TO NOW. I *PROMISE* I'LL STAY ALIVE.
HMM. WE'LL THINK ABOUT IT.
I HAVE TO TELL YOU SOMETHING. I—I DON'T KNOW THE UNDERWATER LANGUAGE. WEBS NEVER TAUGHT ME.

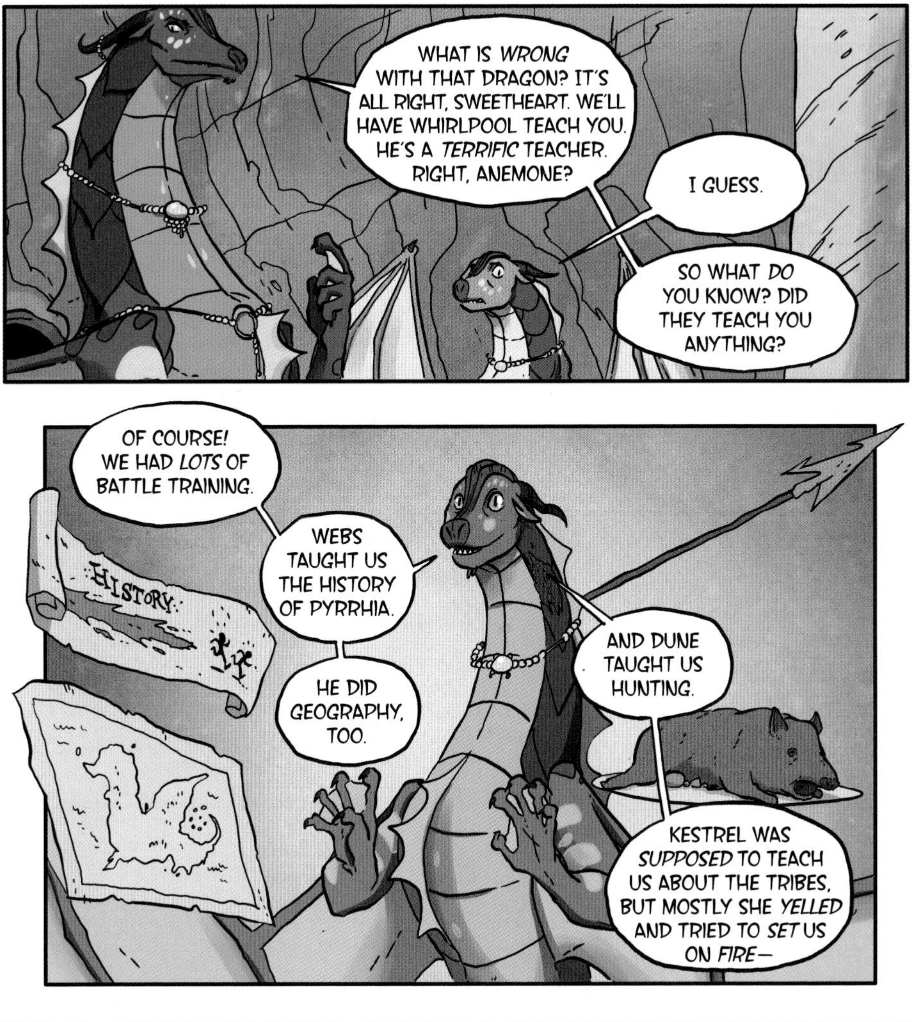
WHAT IS *WRONG* WITH THAT DRAGON? IT'S ALL RIGHT, SWEETHEART. WE'LL HAVE WHIRLPOOL TEACH YOU. HE'S A *TERRIFIC* TEACHER. RIGHT, ANEMONE?
I GUESS.
SO WHAT *DO* YOU KNOW? DID THEY TEACH YOU ANYTHING?
OF COURSE! WE HAD *LOTS* OF BATTLE TRAINING.
HISTORY
WEBS TAUGHT US THE HISTORY OF PYRRHIA.
HE DID GEOGRAPHY, TOO.
AND DUNE TAUGHT US HUNTING.
KESTREL WAS *SUPPOSED* TO TEACH US ABOUT THE TRIBES, BUT MOSTLY SHE *YELLED* AND TRIED TO *SET* US ON *FIRE*—
WHY DON'T *I* GET TO LEARN THOSE THINGS, MOTHER?
YOU *WILL*, DEAR. WHEN I THINK YOU'RE READY.

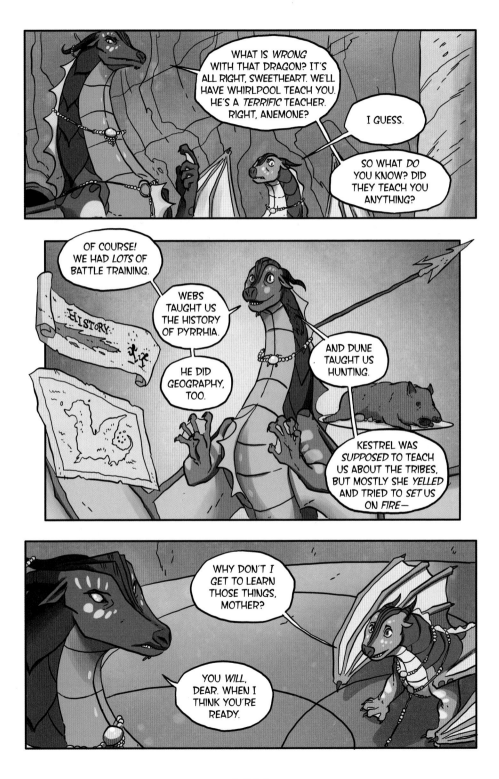

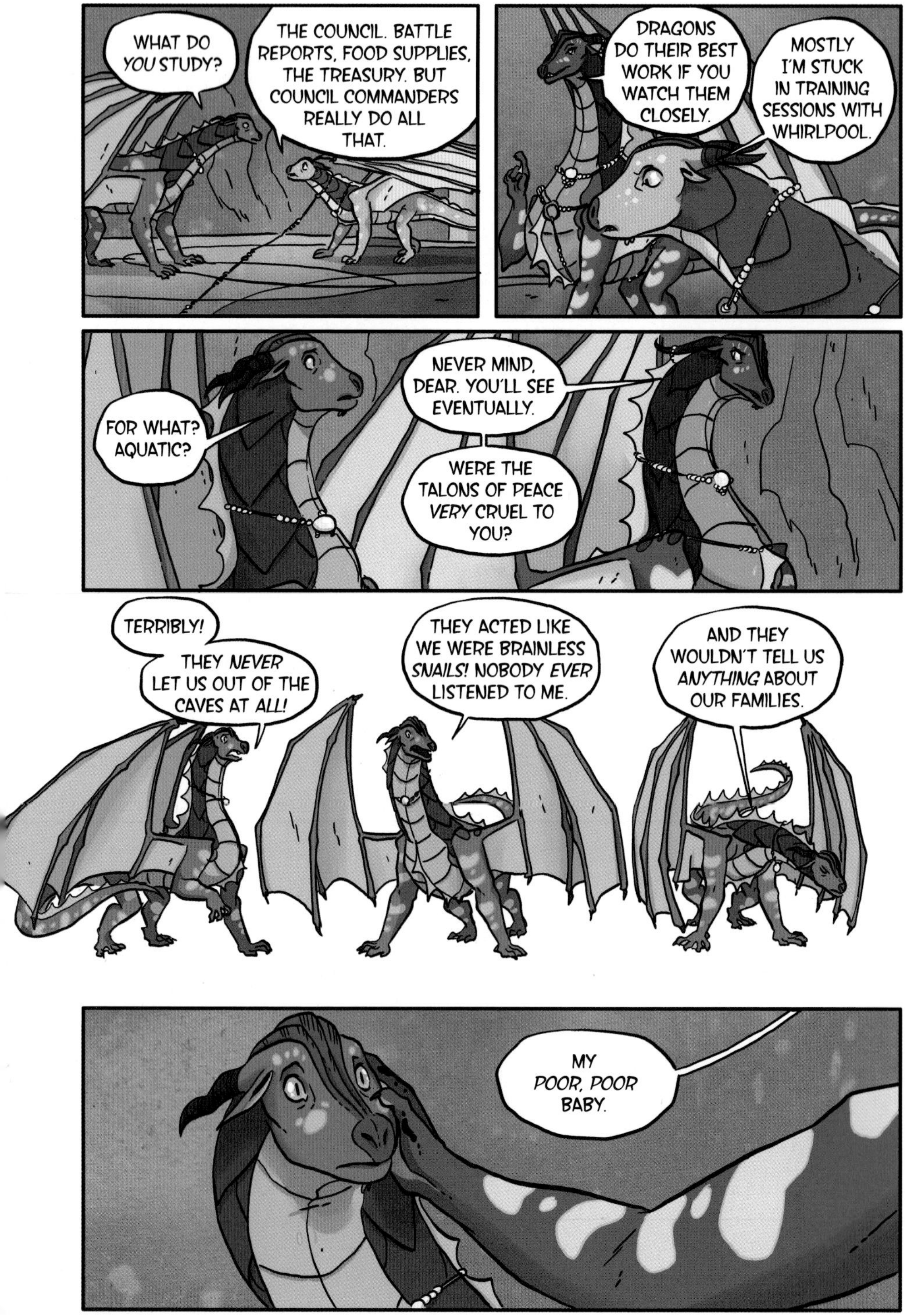
WHAT DO *YOU* STUDY?
THE COUNCIL. BATTLE REPORTS, FOOD SUPPLIES, THE TREASURY. BUT COUNCIL COMMANDERS REALLY DO ALL THAT.
DRAGONS DO THEIR BEST WORK IF YOU WATCH THEM CLOSELY.
MOSTLY I'M STUCK IN TRAINING SESSIONS WITH WHIRLPOOL.
FOR WHAT? AQUATIC?
NEVER MIND, DEAR. YOU'LL SEE EVENTUALLY.
WERE THE TALONS OF PEACE *VERY* CRUEL TO YOU?
TERRIBLY!
THEY *NEVER* LET US OUT OF THE CAVES AT *ALL!*
THEY ACTED LIKE WE WERE BRAINLESS *SNAILS!* NOBODY *EVER* LISTENED TO ME.
AND THEY WOULDN'T TELL US *ANYTHING* ABOUT OUR FAMILIES.
MY *POOR, POOR* BABY.

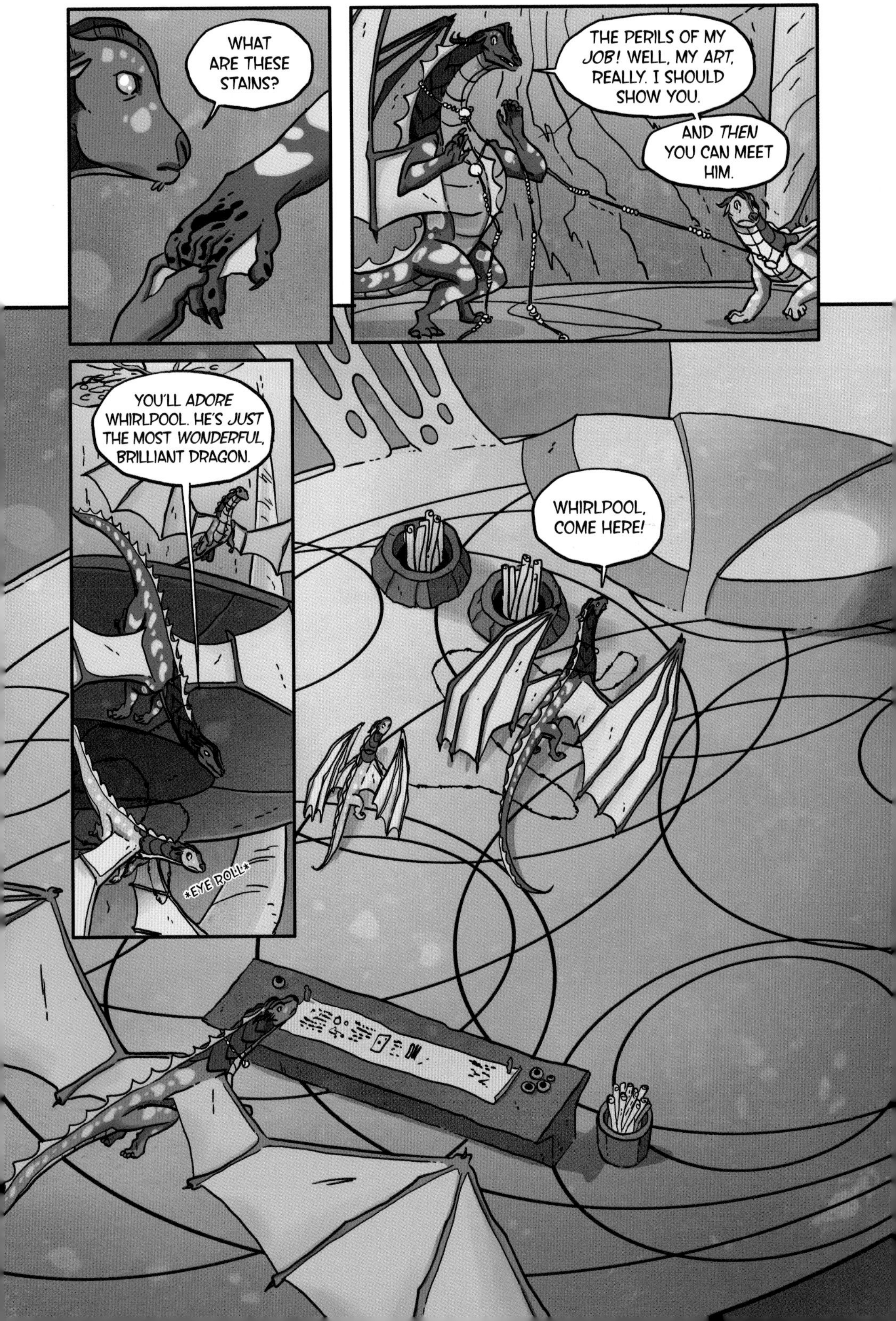
WHAT ARE THESE STAINS?
THE PERILS OF MY *JOB*! WELL, MY *ART*, REALLY. I SHOULD SHOW YOU.
AND *THEN* YOU CAN MEET HIM.
YOU'LL *ADORE* WHIRLPOOL. HE'S *JUST* THE MOST *WONDERFUL*, BRILLIANT DRAGON.
EYE ROLL
WHIRLPOOL, COME HERE!

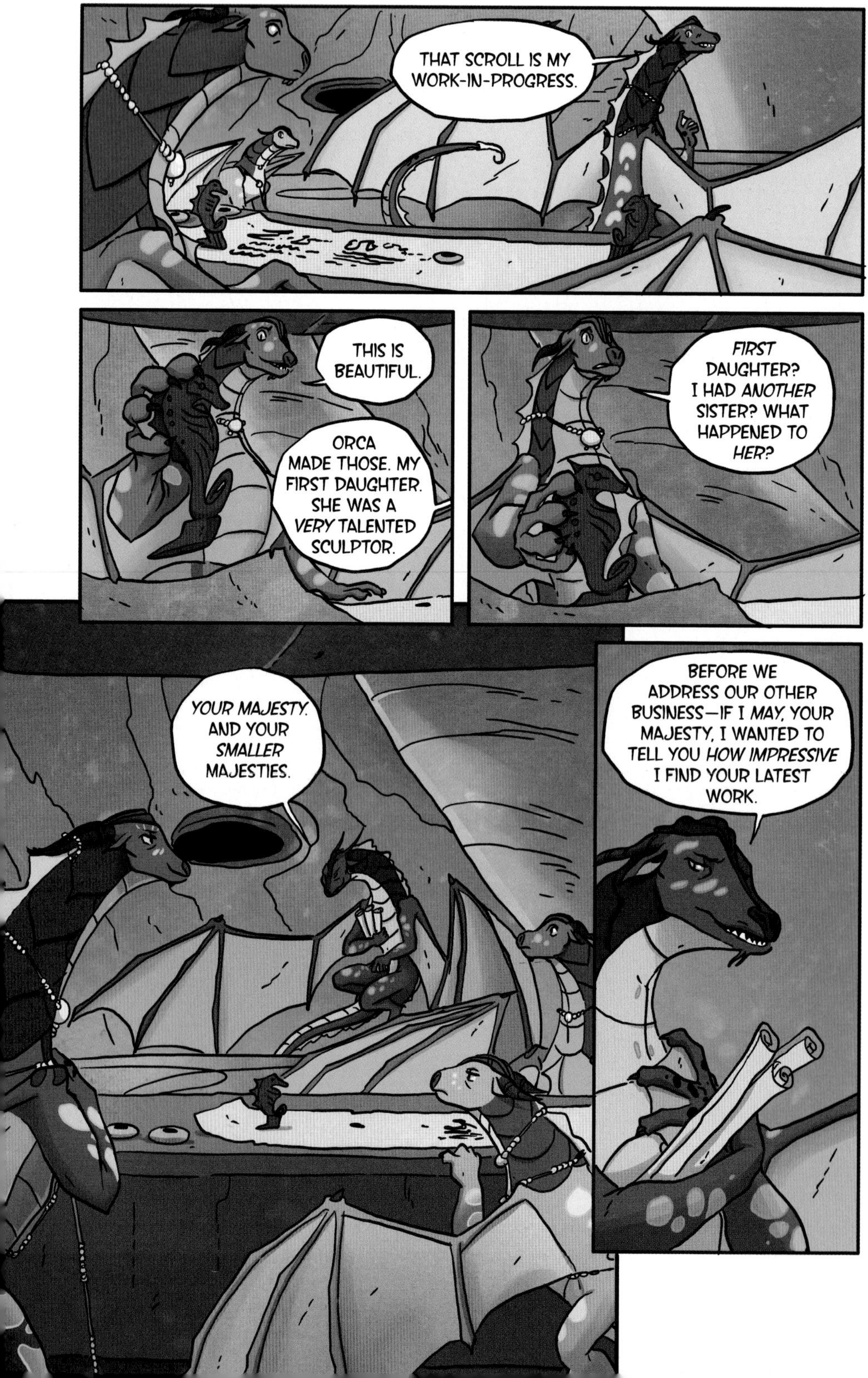
THAT SCROLL IS MY WORK-IN-PROGRESS.
THIS IS BEAUTIFUL.
ORCA MADE THOSE. MY FIRST DAUGHTER. SHE WAS A *VERY* TALENTED SCULPTOR.
FIRST DAUGHTER? I HAD *ANOTHER* SISTER? WHAT HAPPENED TO *HER*?
YOUR MAJESTY. AND YOUR *SMALLER* MAJESTIES.
BEFORE WE ADDRESS OUR OTHER BUSINESS—IF I *MAY*, YOUR MAJESTY, I WANTED TO TELL YOU *HOW IMPRESSIVE* I FIND YOUR LATEST WORK.

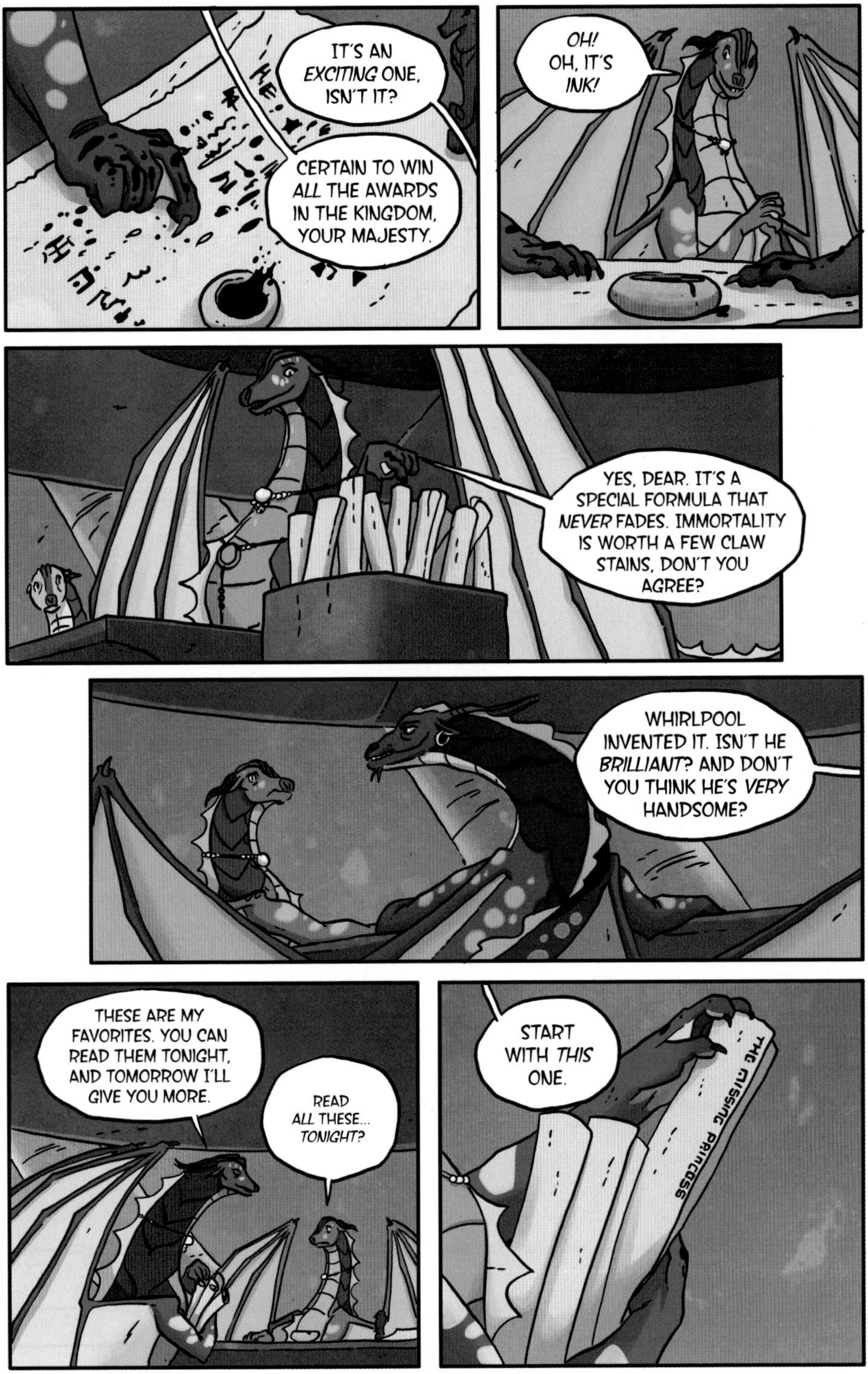
IT'S AN EXCITING ONE, ISN'T IT?
CERTAIN TO WIN ALL THE AWARDS IN THE KINGDOM, YOUR MAJESTY.
OH! OH, IT'S INK!
YES, DEAR. IT'S A SPECIAL FORMULA THAT NEVER FADES. IMMORTALITY IS WORTH A FEW CLAW STAINS, DON'T YOU AGREE?
WHIRLPOOL INVENTED IT. ISN'T HE BRILLIANT? AND DON'T YOU THINK HE'S VERY HANDSOME?
THESE ARE MY FAVORITES. YOU CAN READ THEM TONIGHT, AND TOMORROW I'LL GIVE YOU MORE.
READ ALL THESE... TONIGHT?
START WITH THIS ONE.
THE MISSING PRINCESS

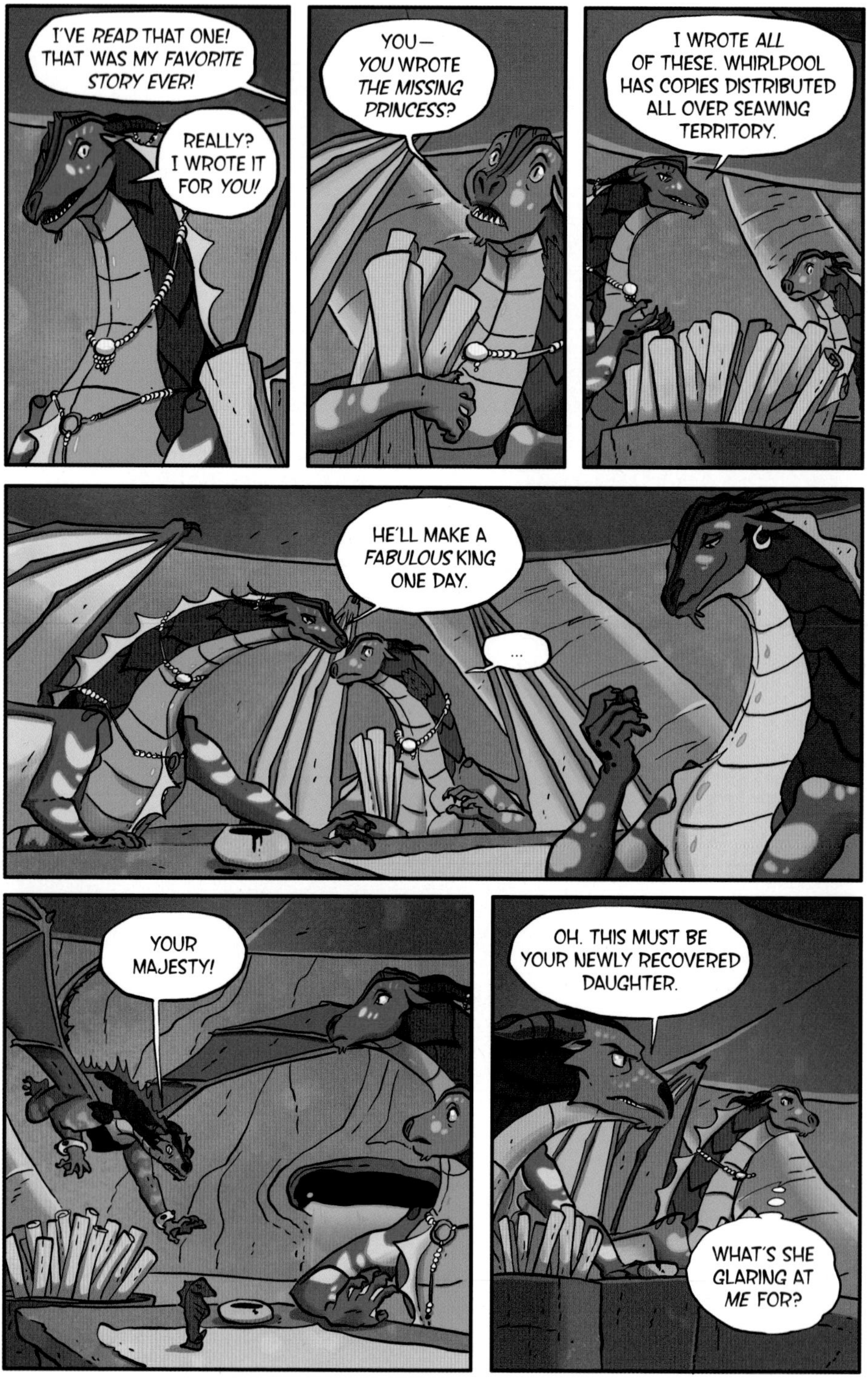
I'VE *READ* THAT ONE! THAT WAS MY *FAVORITE* STORY EVER!
REALLY? I WROTE IT FOR *YOU!*
YOU— *YOU* WROTE *THE MISSING PRINCESS?*
I WROTE *ALL* OF THESE. WHIRLPOOL HAS COPIES DISTRIBUTED ALL OVER SEAWING TERRITORY.
HE'LL MAKE A *FABULOUS* KING ONE DAY.
...
YOUR MAJESTY!
OH. THIS MUST BE YOUR NEWLY RECOVERED DAUGHTER.
WHAT'S SHE GLARING AT *ME* FOR?

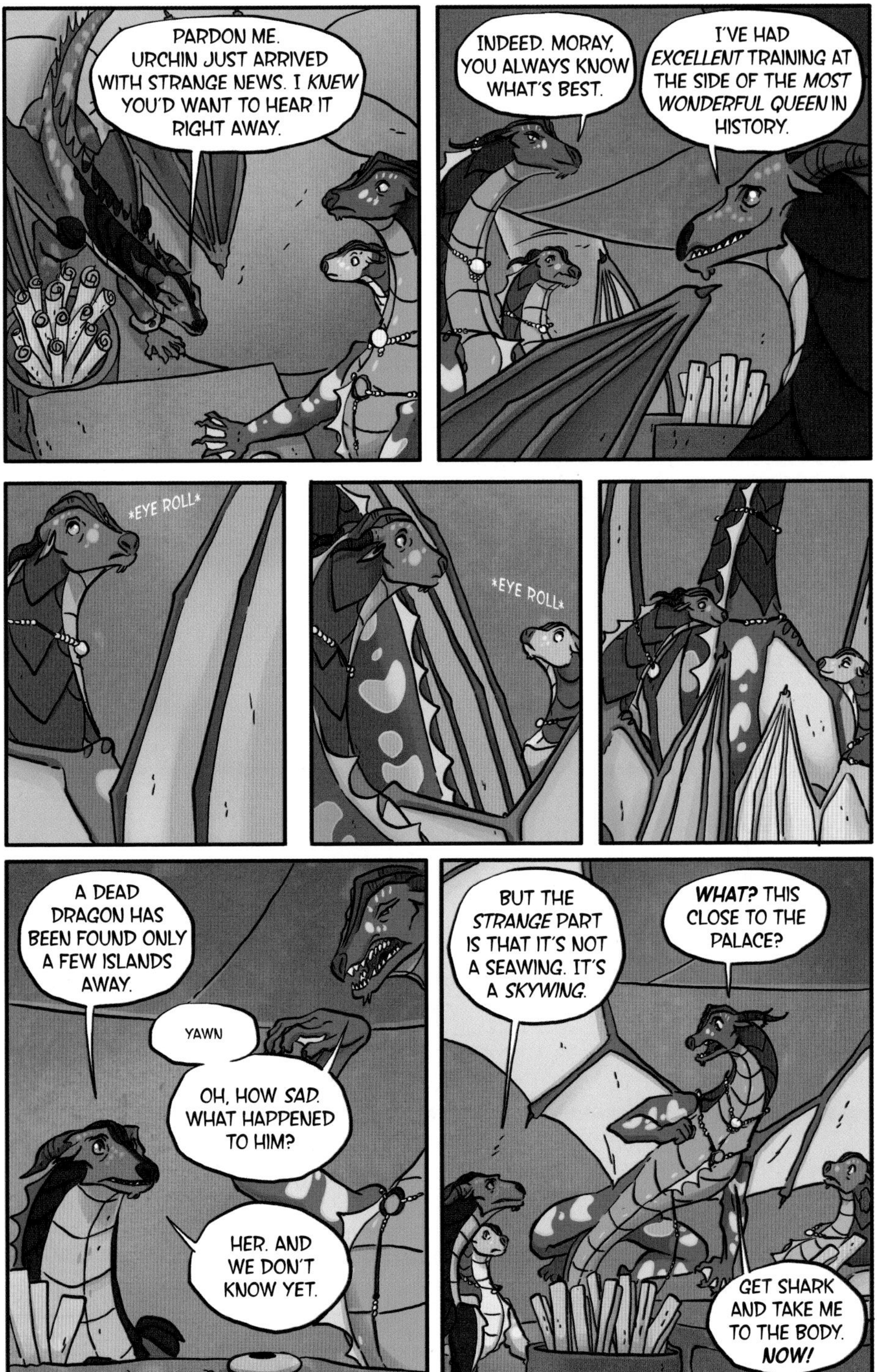
PARDON ME. URCHIN JUST ARRIVED WITH STRANGE NEWS. I *KNEW* YOU'D WANT TO HEAR IT RIGHT AWAY.
INDEED. MORAY, YOU ALWAYS KNOW WHAT'S BEST.
I'VE HAD *EXCELLENT* TRAINING AT THE SIDE OF THE *MOST WONDERFUL QUEEN* IN HISTORY.
EYE ROLL
EYE ROLL
A DEAD DRAGON HAS BEEN FOUND ONLY A FEW ISLANDS AWAY.
YAWN
OH, HOW *SAD*. WHAT HAPPENED TO HIM?
HER. AND WE DON'T KNOW YET.
BUT THE *STRANGE* PART IS THAT IT'S NOT A SEAWING. IT'S A *SKYWING*.
WHAT? THIS CLOSE TO THE PALACE?
GET SHARK AND TAKE ME TO THE BODY. ***NOW!***

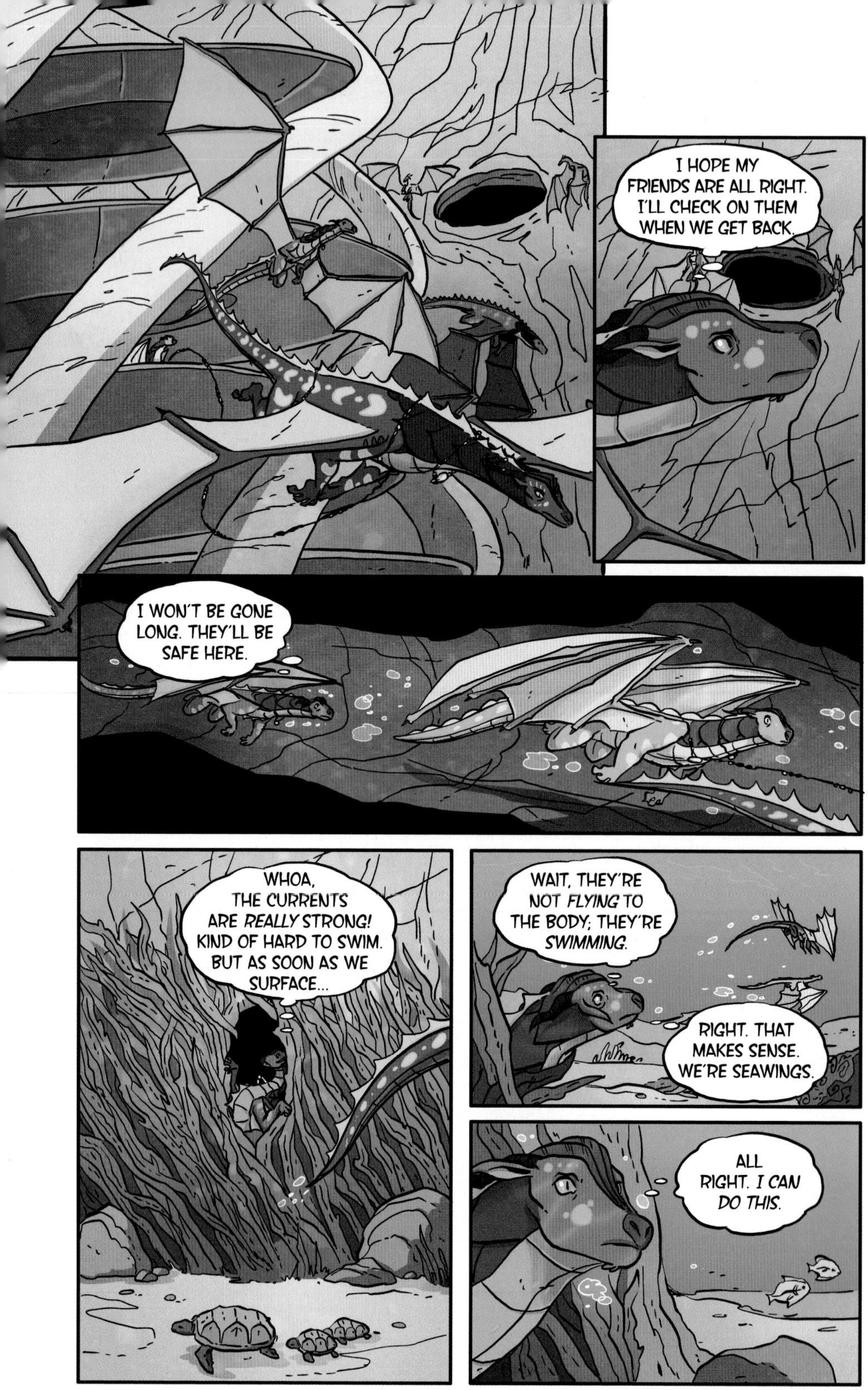
I HOPE MY FRIENDS ARE ALL RIGHT. I'LL CHECK ON THEM WHEN WE GET BACK.
I WON'T BE GONE LONG. THEY'LL BE SAFE HERE.
WHOA, THE CURRENTS ARE *REALLY* STRONG! KIND OF HARD TO SWIM. BUT AS SOON AS WE SURFACE...
WAIT, THEY'RE NOT *FLYING* TO THE BODY; THEY'RE *SWIMMING*.
RIGHT. THAT MAKES SENSE. WE'RE SEAWINGS.
ALL RIGHT. *I CAN DO THIS.*

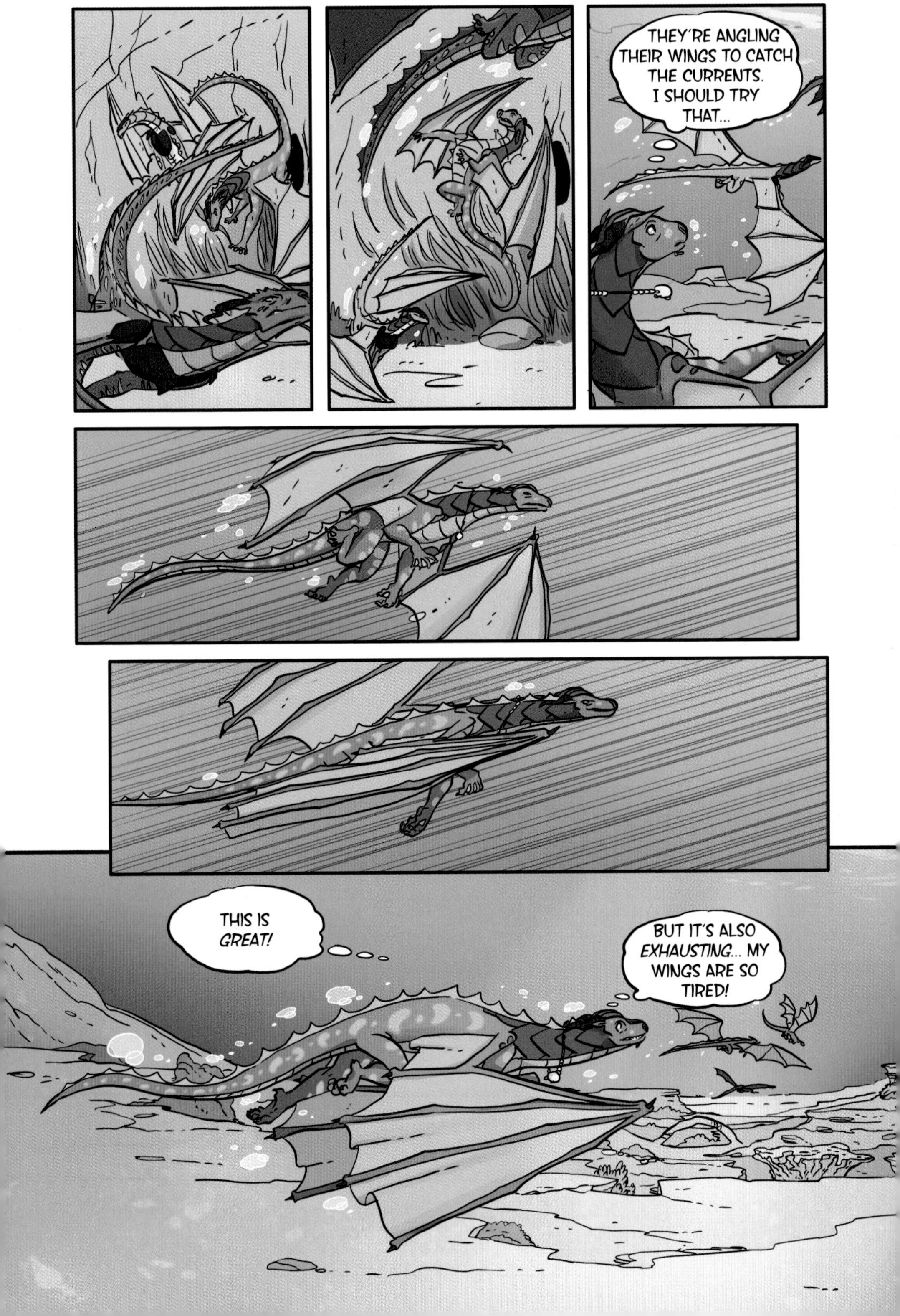
THEY'RE ANGLING THEIR WINGS TO CATCH THE CURRENTS. I SHOULD TRY THAT...
THIS IS *GREAT!*
BUT IT'S ALSO *EXHAUSTING*... MY WINGS ARE SO TIRED!

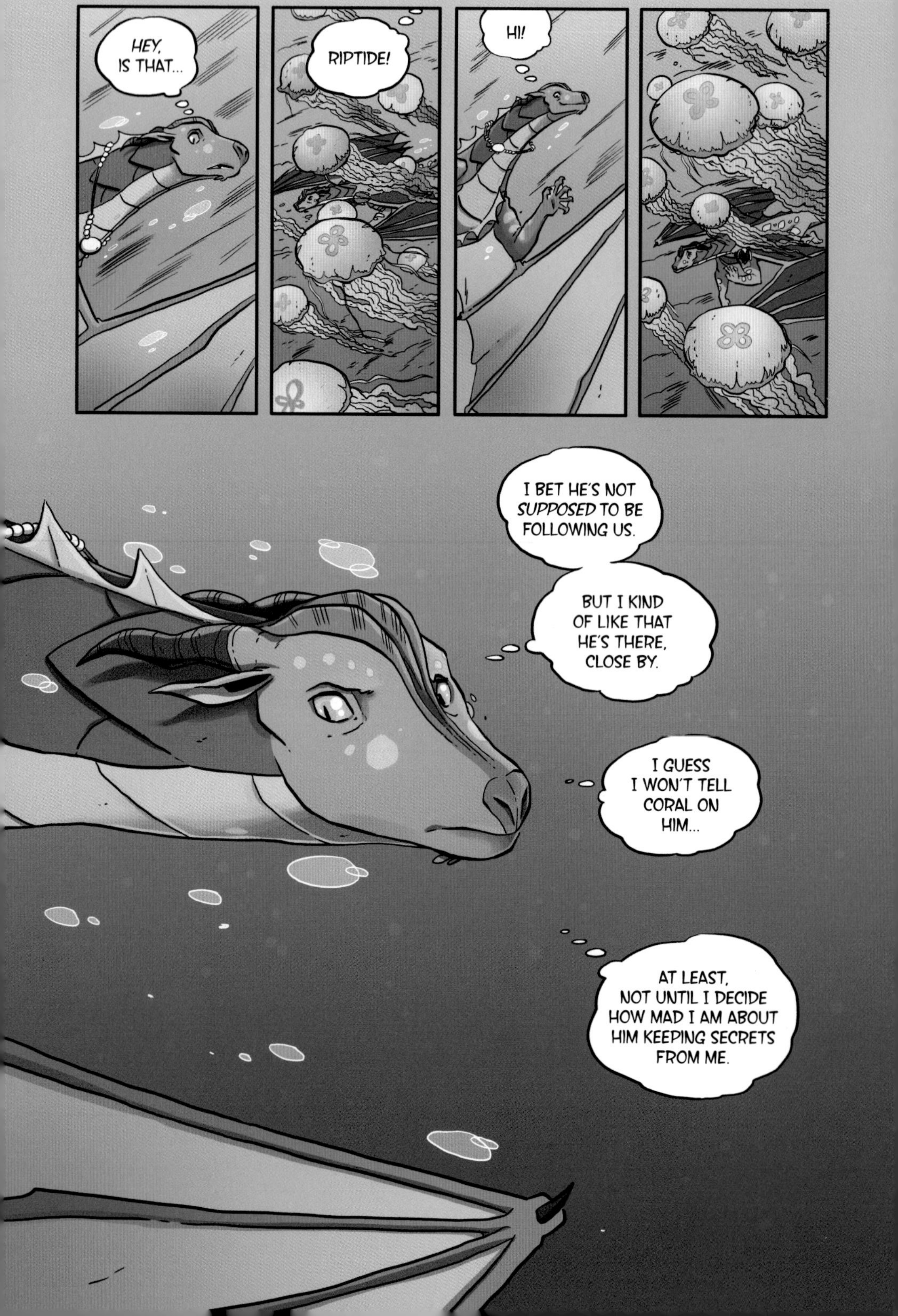
HEY, IS THAT...
RIPTIDE!
HI!
I BET HE'S NOT *SUPPOSED* TO BE FOLLOWING US.
BUT I KIND OF LIKE THAT HE'S THERE, CLOSE BY.
I GUESS I WON'T TELL CORAL ON HIM...
AT LEAST, NOT UNTIL I DECIDE HOW MAD I AM ABOUT HIM KEEPING SECRETS FROM ME.

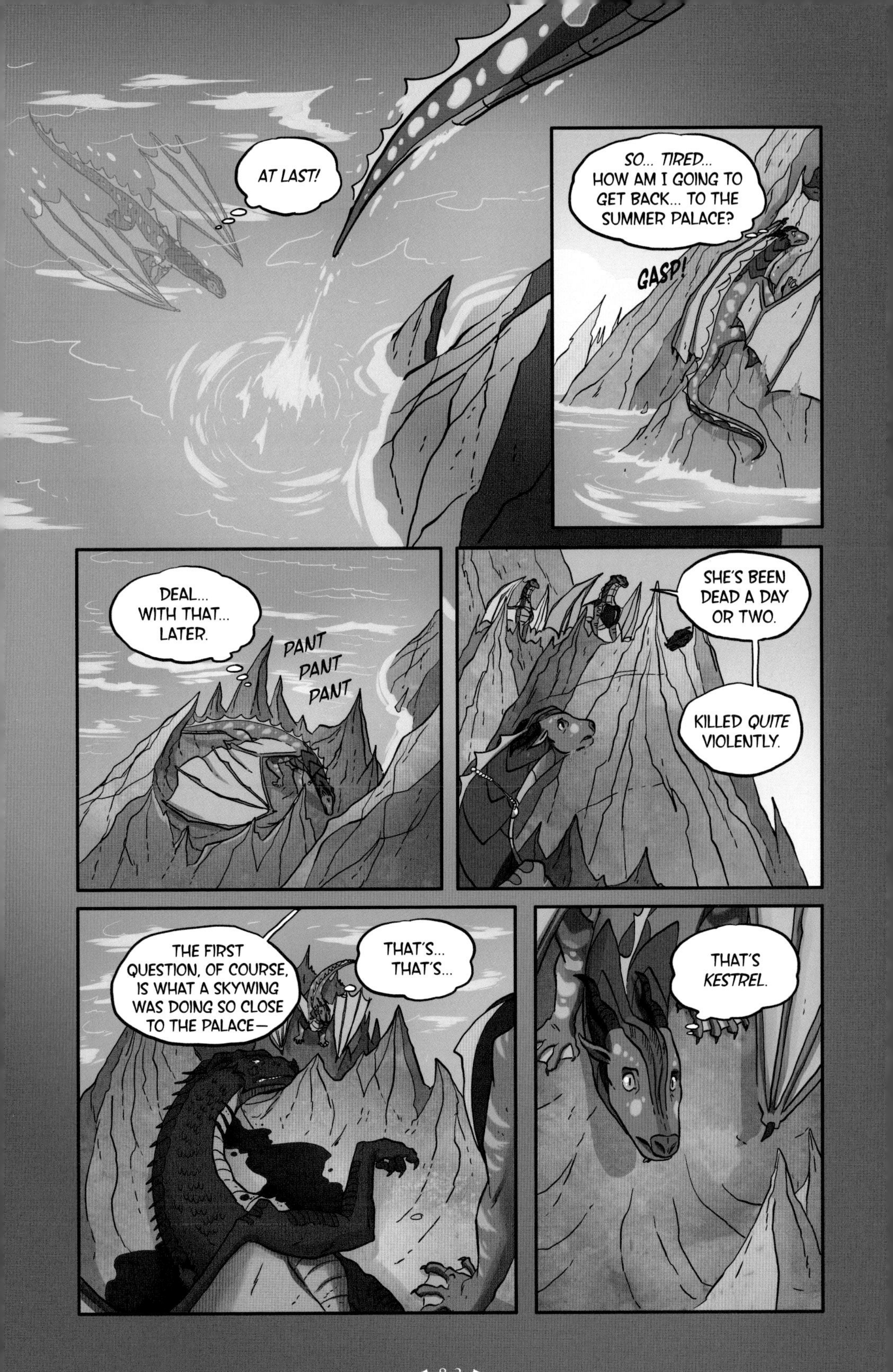
AT LAST!
SO... TIRED... HOW AM I GOING TO GET BACK... TO THE SUMMER PALACE?
GASP!
DEAL... WITH THAT... LATER.
PANT PANT PANT
SHE'S BEEN DEAD A DAY OR TWO.
KILLED *QUITE* VIOLENTLY.
THE FIRST QUESTION, OF COURSE, IS WHAT A SKYWING WAS DOING SO CLOSE TO THE PALACE—
THAT'S... THAT'S...
THAT'S *KESTREL*.

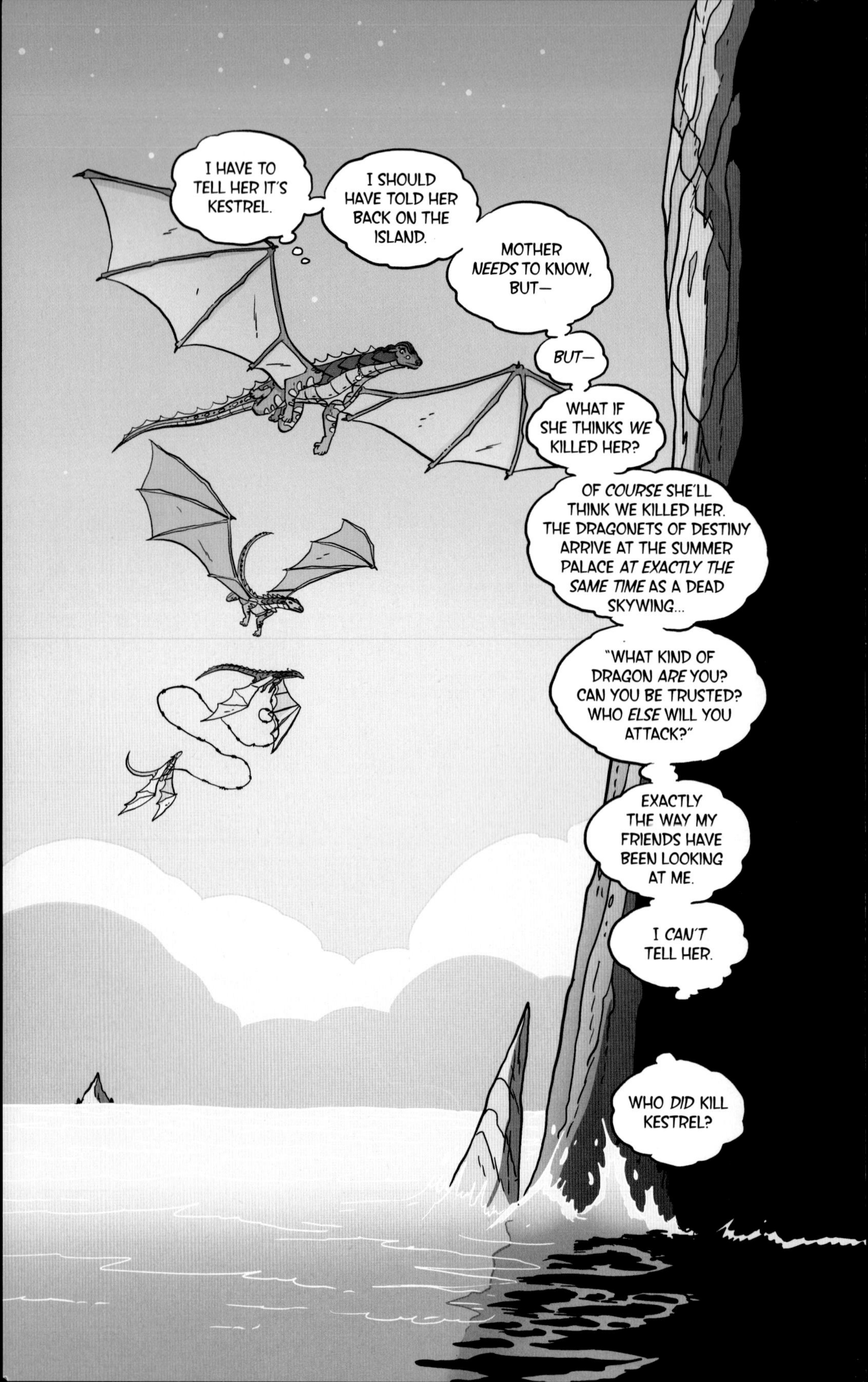
I HAVE TO TELL HER IT'S KESTREL.
I SHOULD HAVE TOLD HER BACK ON THE ISLAND.
MOTHER *NEEDS* TO KNOW, BUT—
BUT—
WHAT IF SHE THINKS *WE* KILLED HER?
OF *COURSE* SHE'LL THINK WE KILLED HER. THE DRAGONETS OF DESTINY ARRIVE AT THE SUMMER PALACE *AT EXACTLY THE SAME TIME* AS A DEAD SKYWING...
"WHAT KIND OF DRAGON *ARE* YOU? CAN YOU BE TRUSTED? WHO *ELSE* WILL YOU ATTACK?"
EXACTLY THE WAY MY FRIENDS HAVE BEEN LOOKING AT ME.
I *CAN'T* TELL HER.
WHO *DID* KILL KESTREL?

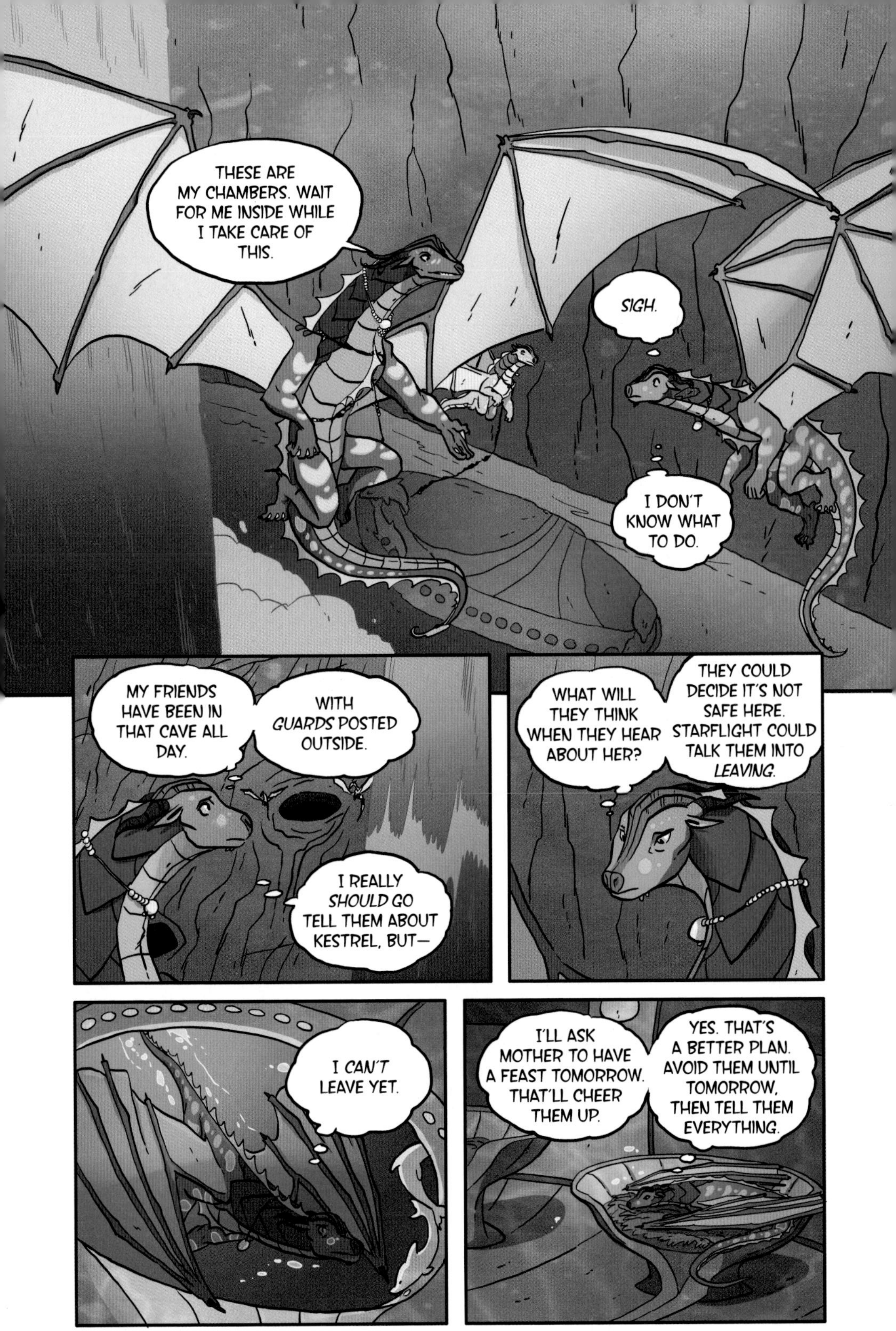
THESE ARE MY CHAMBERS. WAIT FOR ME INSIDE WHILE I TAKE CARE OF THIS.
SIGH.
I DON'T KNOW WHAT TO DO.
MY FRIENDS HAVE BEEN IN THAT CAVE ALL DAY.
WITH *GUARDS* POSTED OUTSIDE.
I REALLY *SHOULD* GO TELL THEM ABOUT KESTREL, BUT—
WHAT WILL THEY THINK WHEN THEY HEAR ABOUT HER?
THEY COULD DECIDE IT'S NOT SAFE HERE. STARFLIGHT COULD TALK THEM INTO *LEAVING*.
I *CAN'T* LEAVE YET.
I'LL ASK MOTHER TO HAVE A FEAST TOMORROW. THAT'LL CHEER THEM UP.
YES. THAT'S A BETTER PLAN. AVOID THEM UNTIL TOMORROW, THEN TELL THEM EVERYTHING.

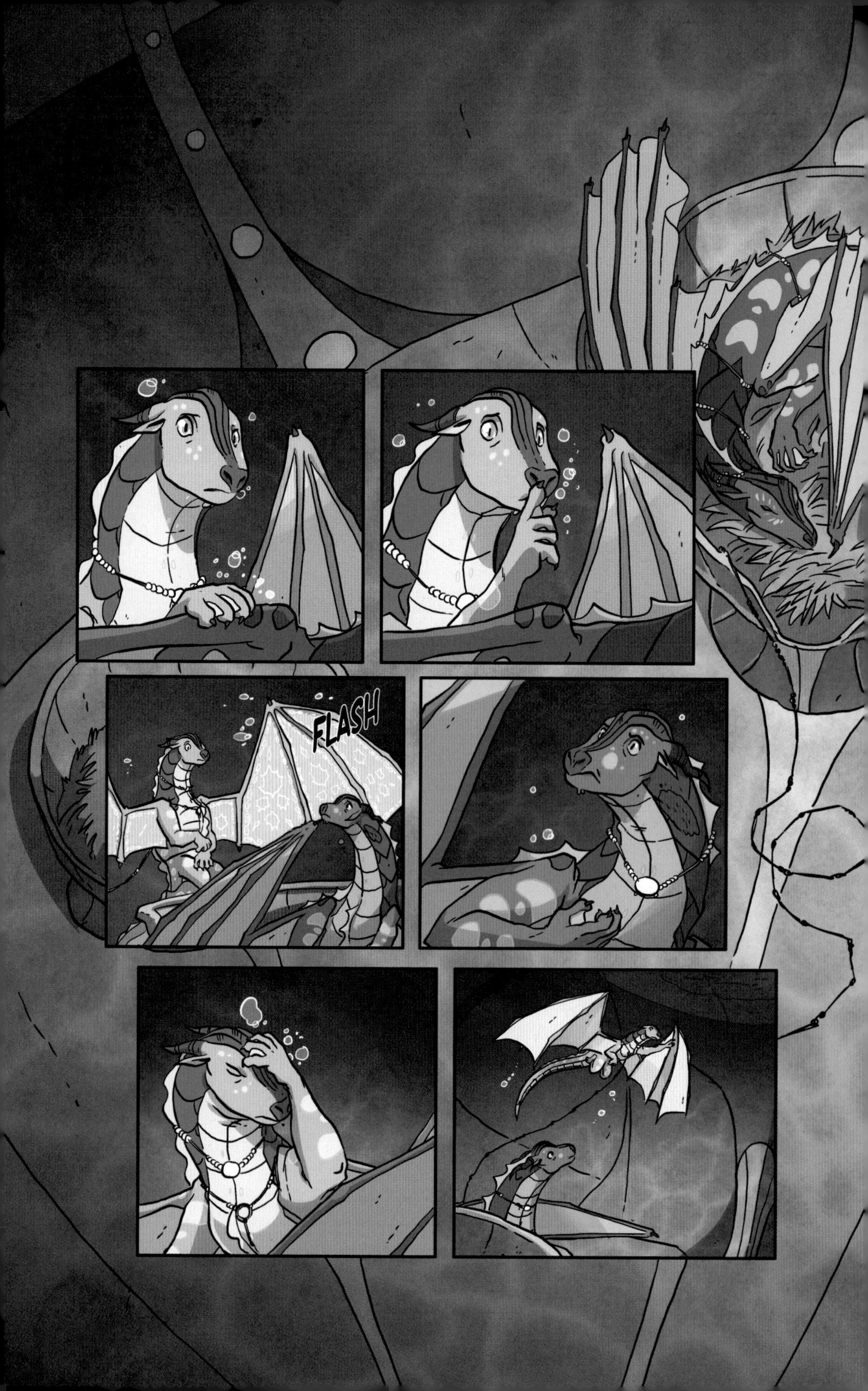
FLASH

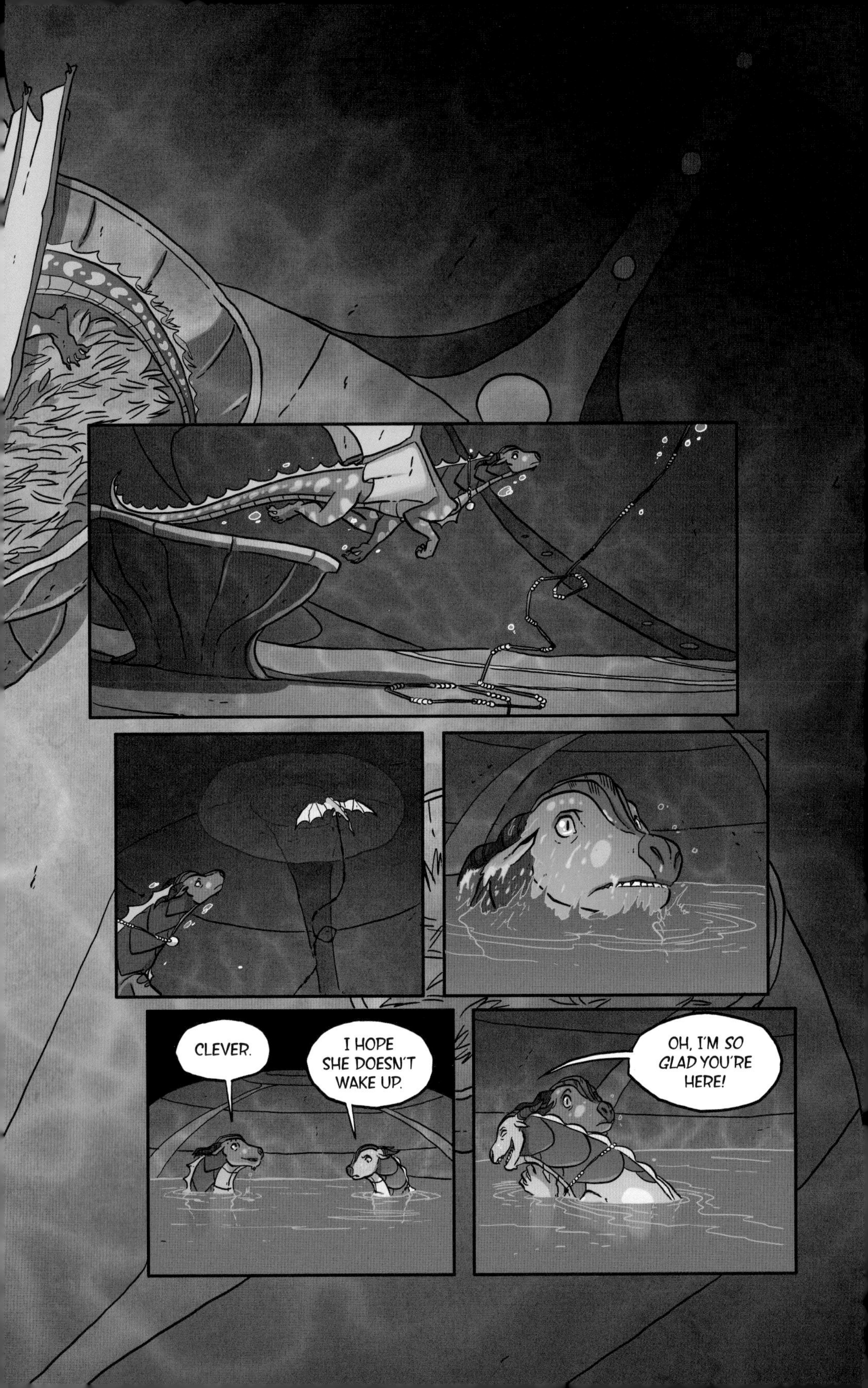
CLEVER.
I HOPE SHE DOESN'T WAKE UP.
OH, I'M SO GLAD YOU'RE HERE!

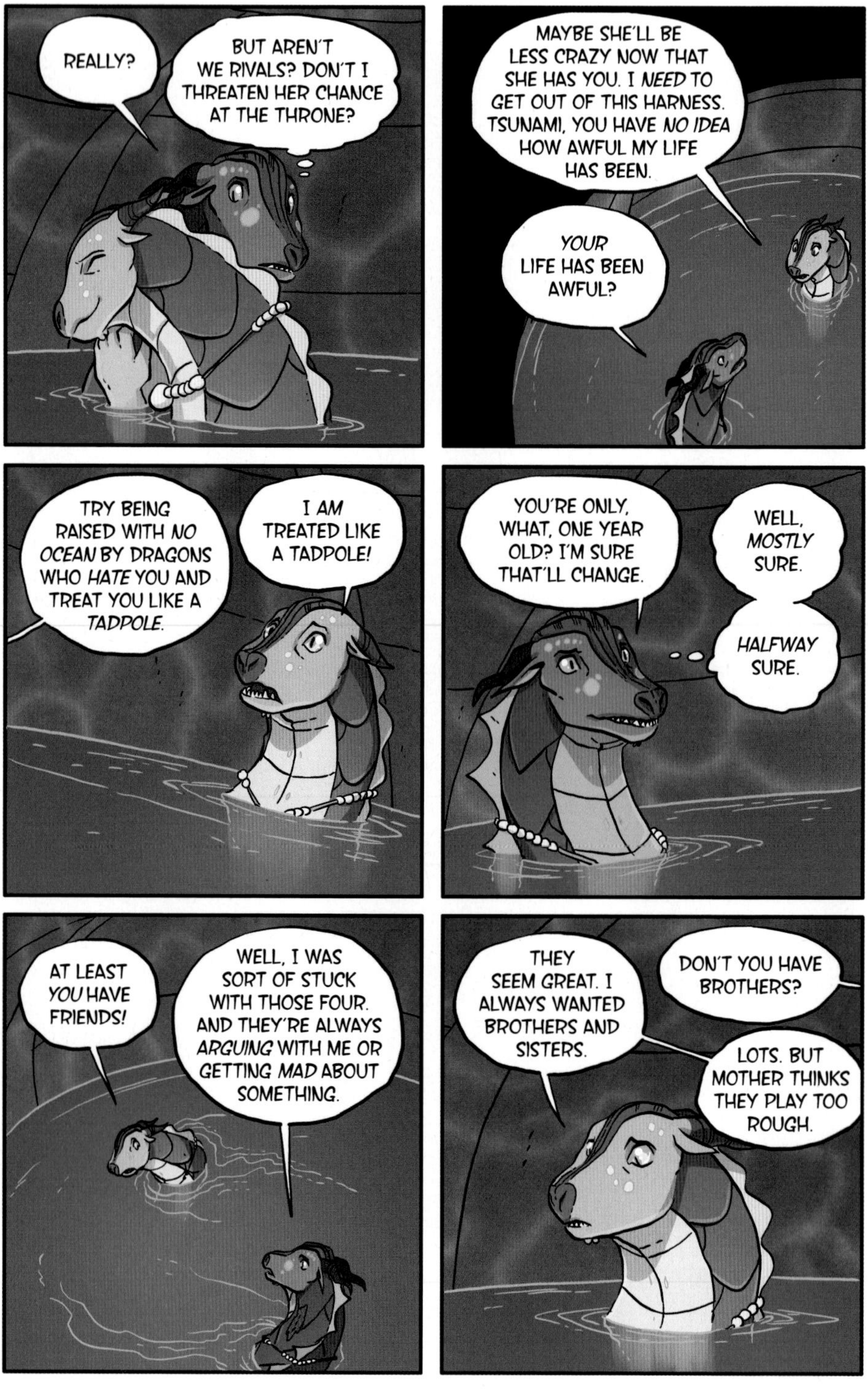
REALLY?
BUT AREN'T WE RIVALS? DON'T I THREATEN HER CHANCE AT THE THRONE?
MAYBE SHE'LL BE LESS CRAZY NOW THAT SHE HAS YOU. I *NEED* TO GET OUT OF THIS HARNESS. TSUNAMI, YOU HAVE *NO IDEA* HOW AWFUL MY LIFE HAS BEEN.
YOUR LIFE HAS BEEN AWFUL?
TRY BEING RAISED WITH *NO OCEAN* BY DRAGONS WHO *HATE* YOU AND TREAT YOU LIKE A *TADPOLE*.
I *AM* TREATED LIKE A TADPOLE!
YOU'RE ONLY, WHAT, ONE YEAR OLD? I'M SURE THAT'LL CHANGE.
WELL, *MOSTLY* SURE.
HALFWAY SURE.
AT LEAST *YOU* HAVE FRIENDS!
WELL, I WAS SORT OF STUCK WITH THOSE FOUR. AND THEY'RE ALWAYS *ARGUING* WITH ME OR GETTING *MAD* ABOUT SOMETHING.
THEY SEEM GREAT. I ALWAYS WANTED BROTHERS AND SISTERS.
DON'T YOU HAVE BROTHERS?
LOTS. BUT MOTHER THINKS THEY PLAY TOO ROUGH.

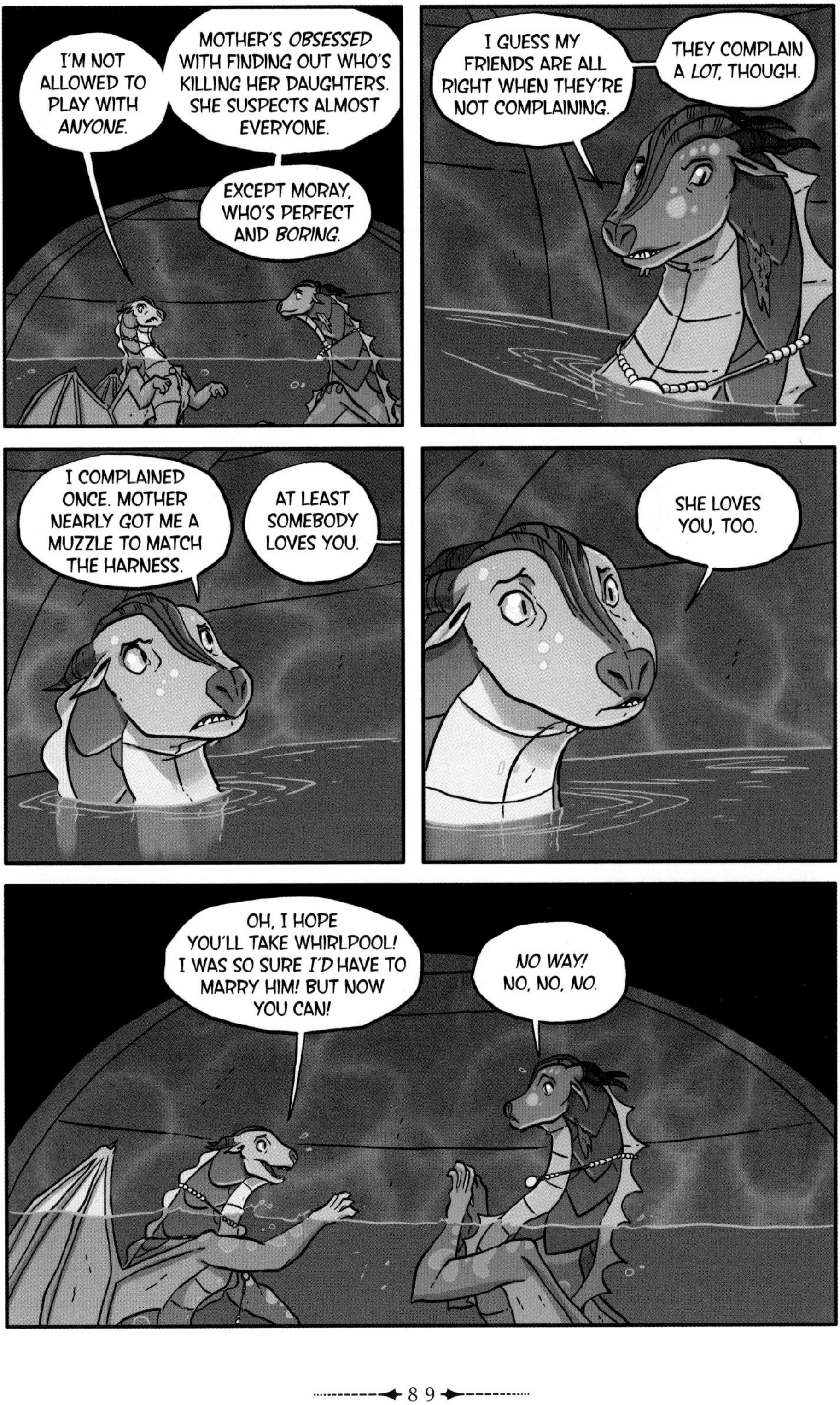
I'M NOT ALLOWED TO PLAY WITH *ANYONE*.
MOTHER'S *OBSESSED* WITH FINDING OUT WHO'S KILLING HER DAUGHTERS. SHE SUSPECTS ALMOST EVERYONE.
EXCEPT MORAY, WHO'S PERFECT AND *BORING*.
I GUESS MY FRIENDS ARE ALL RIGHT WHEN THEY'RE NOT COMPLAINING.
THEY COMPLAIN A *LOT*, THOUGH.
I COMPLAINED ONCE. MOTHER NEARLY GOT ME A MUZZLE TO MATCH THE HARNESS.
AT LEAST SOMEBODY LOVES YOU.
SHE LOVES YOU, TOO.
OH, I HOPE YOU'LL TAKE WHIRLPOOL! I WAS SO SURE *I'D* HAVE TO MARRY HIM! BUT NOW YOU CAN!
NO WAY! NO, NO, *NO*.

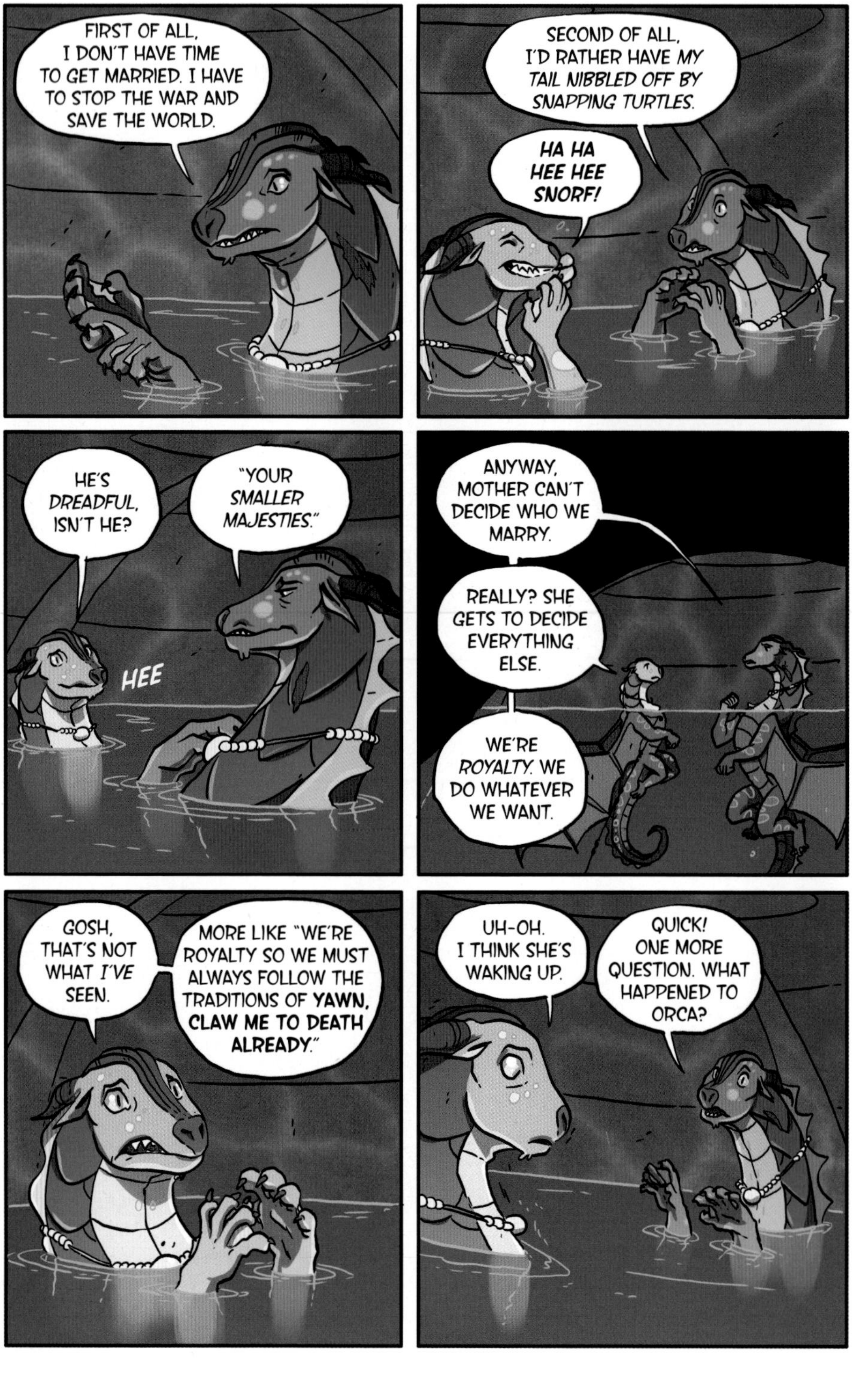
FIRST OF ALL, I DON'T HAVE TIME TO GET MARRIED. I HAVE TO STOP THE WAR AND SAVE THE WORLD.
SECOND OF ALL, I'D RATHER HAVE *MY TAIL NIBBLED OFF BY SNAPPING TURTLES.*
HA HA HEE HEE SNORF!
HE'S *DREADFUL,* ISN'T HE?
"YOUR *SMALLER MAJESTIES.*"
HEE
ANYWAY, MOTHER CAN'T DECIDE WHO WE MARRY.
REALLY? SHE GETS TO DECIDE EVERYTHING ELSE.
WE'RE *ROYALTY.* WE DO WHATEVER WE WANT.
GOSH, THAT'S NOT WHAT *I'VE* SEEN.
MORE LIKE "WE'RE ROYALTY SO WE MUST ALWAYS FOLLOW THE TRADITIONS OF **YAWN, CLAW ME TO DEATH ALREADY.**"
UH-OH. I THINK SHE'S WAKING UP.
QUICK! ONE MORE QUESTION. WHAT HAPPENED TO ORCA?

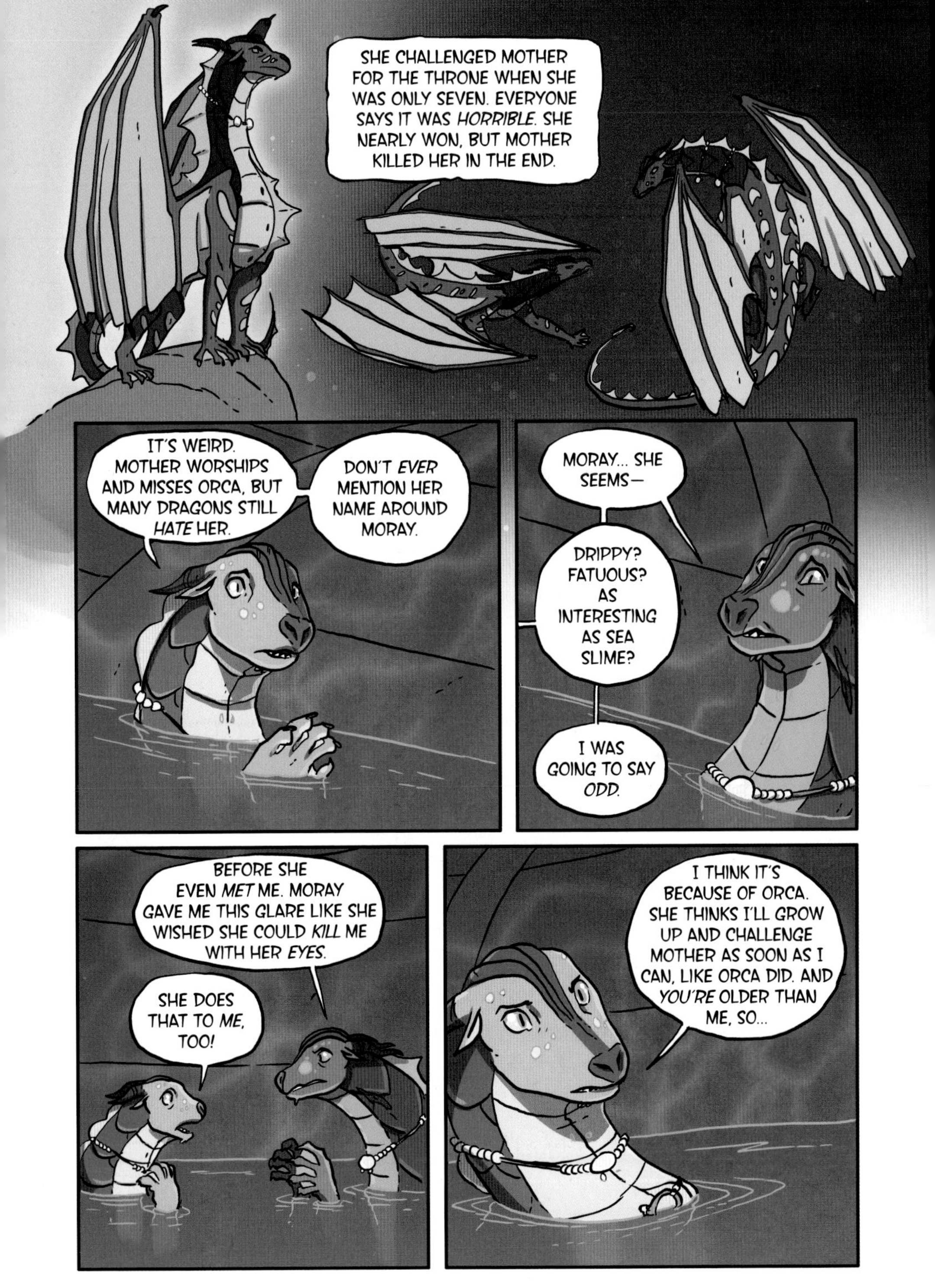
SHE CHALLENGED MOTHER FOR THE THRONE WHEN SHE WAS ONLY SEVEN. EVERYONE SAYS IT WAS *HORRIBLE*. SHE NEARLY WON, BUT MOTHER KILLED HER IN THE END.
IT'S WEIRD. MOTHER WORSHIPS AND MISSES ORCA, BUT MANY DRAGONS STILL *HATE* HER.
DON'T *EVER* MENTION HER NAME AROUND MORAY.
MORAY... SHE SEEMS—
DRIPPY? FATUOUS? AS INTERESTING AS SEA SLIME?
I WAS GOING TO SAY *ODD*.
BEFORE SHE EVEN *MET* ME. MORAY GAVE ME THIS GLARE LIKE SHE WISHED SHE COULD *KILL* ME WITH HER *EYES*.
SHE DOES THAT TO *ME*, TOO!
I THINK IT'S BECAUSE OF ORCA. SHE THINKS I'LL GROW UP AND CHALLENGE MOTHER AS SOON AS I CAN, LIKE ORCA DID. AND *YOU'RE* OLDER THAN ME, SO...

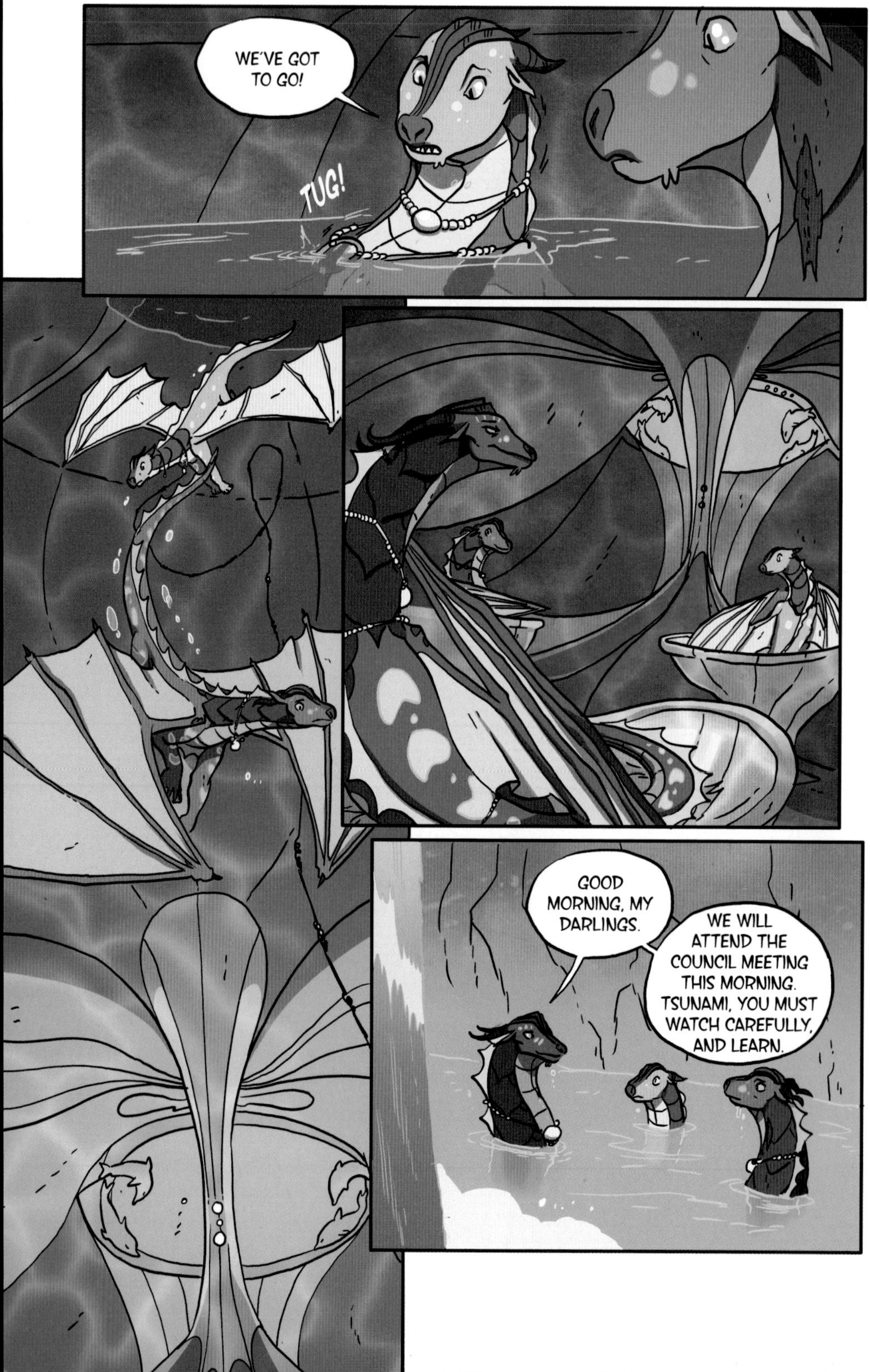

WE'VE GOT TO GO!
TUG!
GOOD MORNING, MY DARLINGS.
WE WILL ATTEND THE COUNCIL MEETING THIS MORNING. TSUNAMI, YOU MUST WATCH CAREFULLY, AND LEARN.

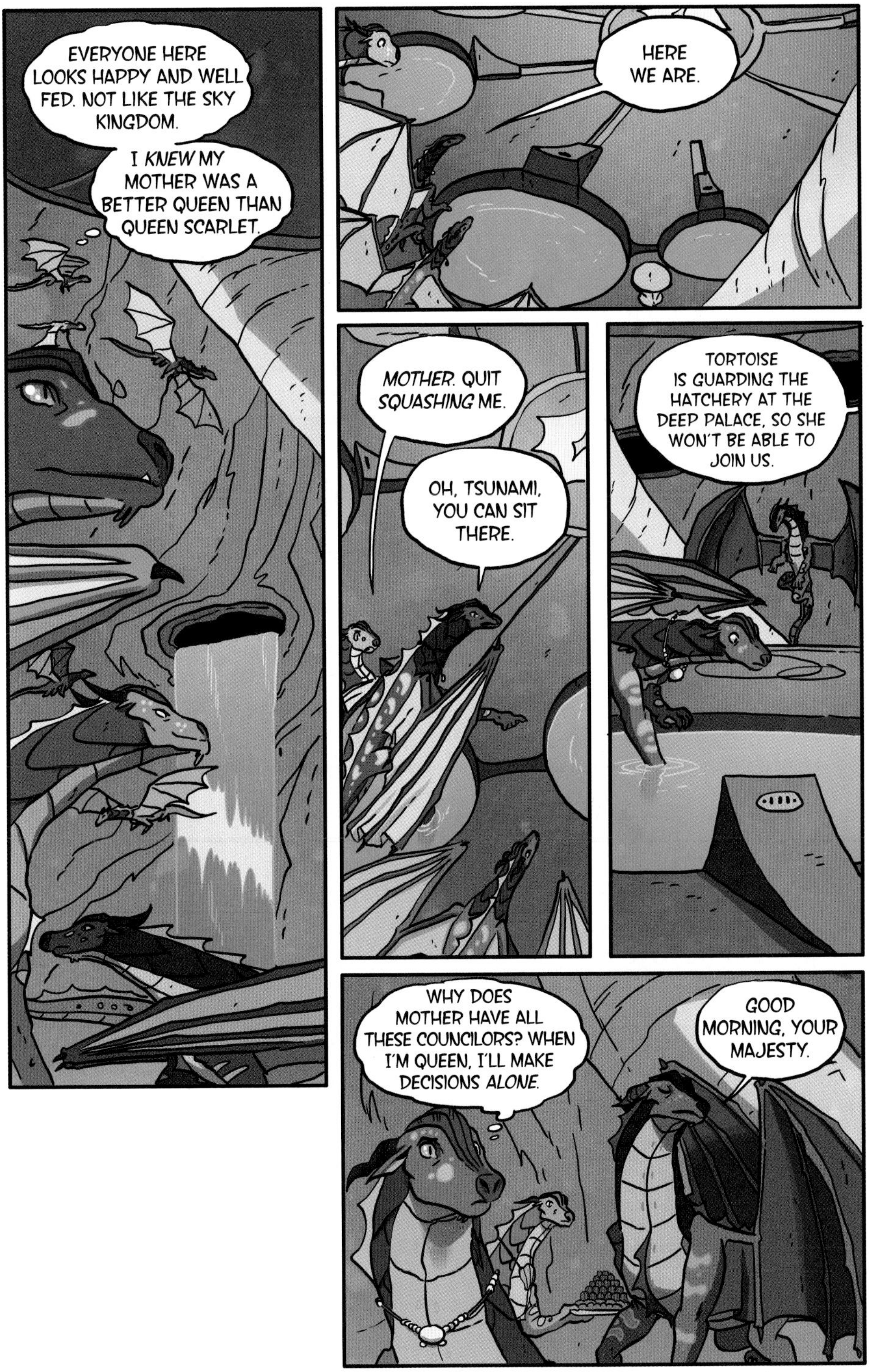
EVERYONE HERE LOOKS HAPPY AND WELL FED. NOT LIKE THE SKY KINGDOM.
I *KNEW* MY MOTHER WAS A BETTER QUEEN THAN QUEEN SCARLET.
HERE WE ARE.
MOTHER. QUIT *SQUASHING* ME.
OH, TSUNAMI, YOU CAN SIT THERE.
TORTOISE IS GUARDING THE HATCHERY AT THE DEEP PALACE, SO SHE WON'T BE ABLE TO JOIN US.
WHY DOES MOTHER HAVE ALL THESE COUNCILORS? WHEN I'M QUEEN, I'LL MAKE DECISIONS *ALONE.*
GOOD MORNING, YOUR MAJESTY.

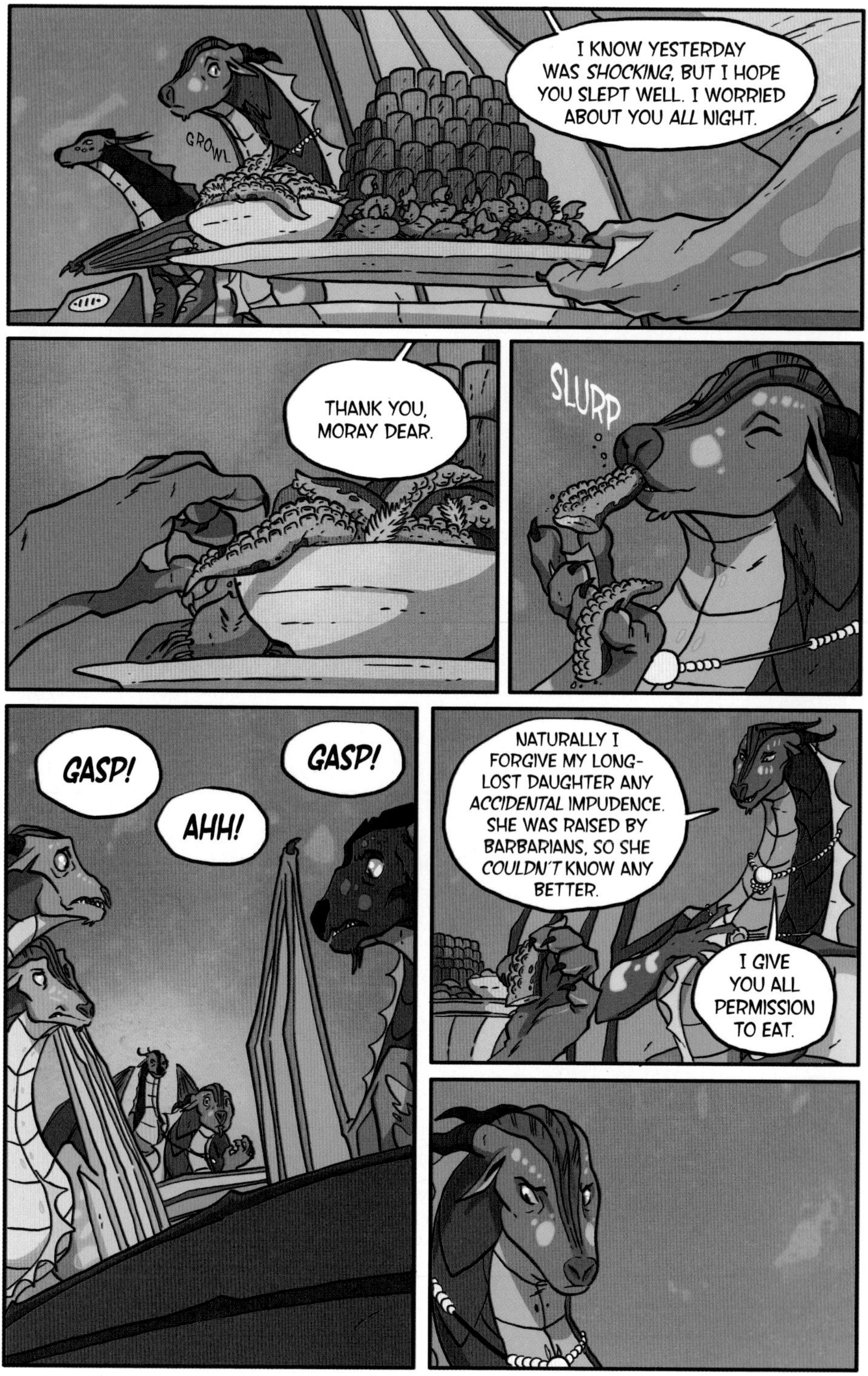
GROWL
I KNOW YESTERDAY WAS SHOCKING, BUT I HOPE YOU SLEPT WELL. I WORRIED ABOUT YOU ALL NIGHT.
THANK YOU, MORAY DEAR.
SLURP
GASP!
AHH!
GASP!
NATURALLY I FORGIVE MY LONG-LOST DAUGHTER ANY ACCIDENTAL IMPUDENCE. SHE WAS RAISED BY BARBARIANS, SO SHE COULDN'T KNOW ANY BETTER.
I GIVE YOU ALL PERMISSION TO EAT.

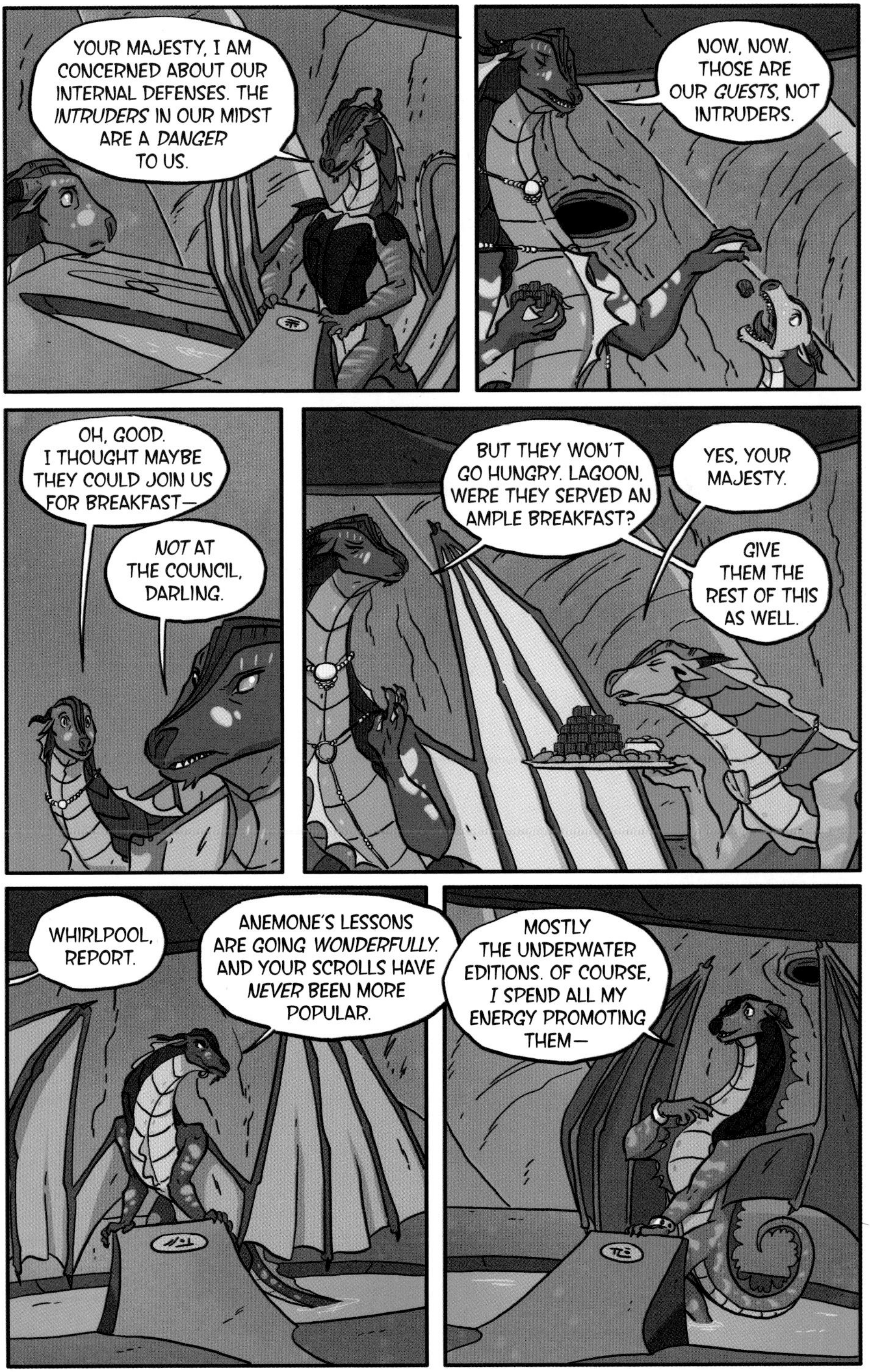
YOUR MAJESTY, I AM CONCERNED ABOUT OUR INTERNAL DEFENSES. THE *INTRUDERS* IN OUR MIDST ARE A *DANGER* TO US.
NOW, NOW. THOSE ARE OUR *GUESTS*, NOT INTRUDERS.
OH, GOOD. I THOUGHT MAYBE THEY COULD JOIN US FOR BREAKFAST—
NOT AT THE COUNCIL, DARLING.
BUT THEY WON'T GO HUNGRY. LAGOON, WERE THEY SERVED AN AMPLE BREAKFAST?
YES, YOUR MAJESTY.
GIVE THEM THE REST OF THIS AS WELL.
WHIRLPOOL, REPORT.
ANEMONE'S LESSONS ARE GOING *WONDERFULLY*. AND YOUR SCROLLS HAVE *NEVER* BEEN MORE POPULAR.
MOSTLY THE UNDERWATER EDITIONS. OF COURSE, I SPEND ALL MY ENERGY PROMOTING THEM—

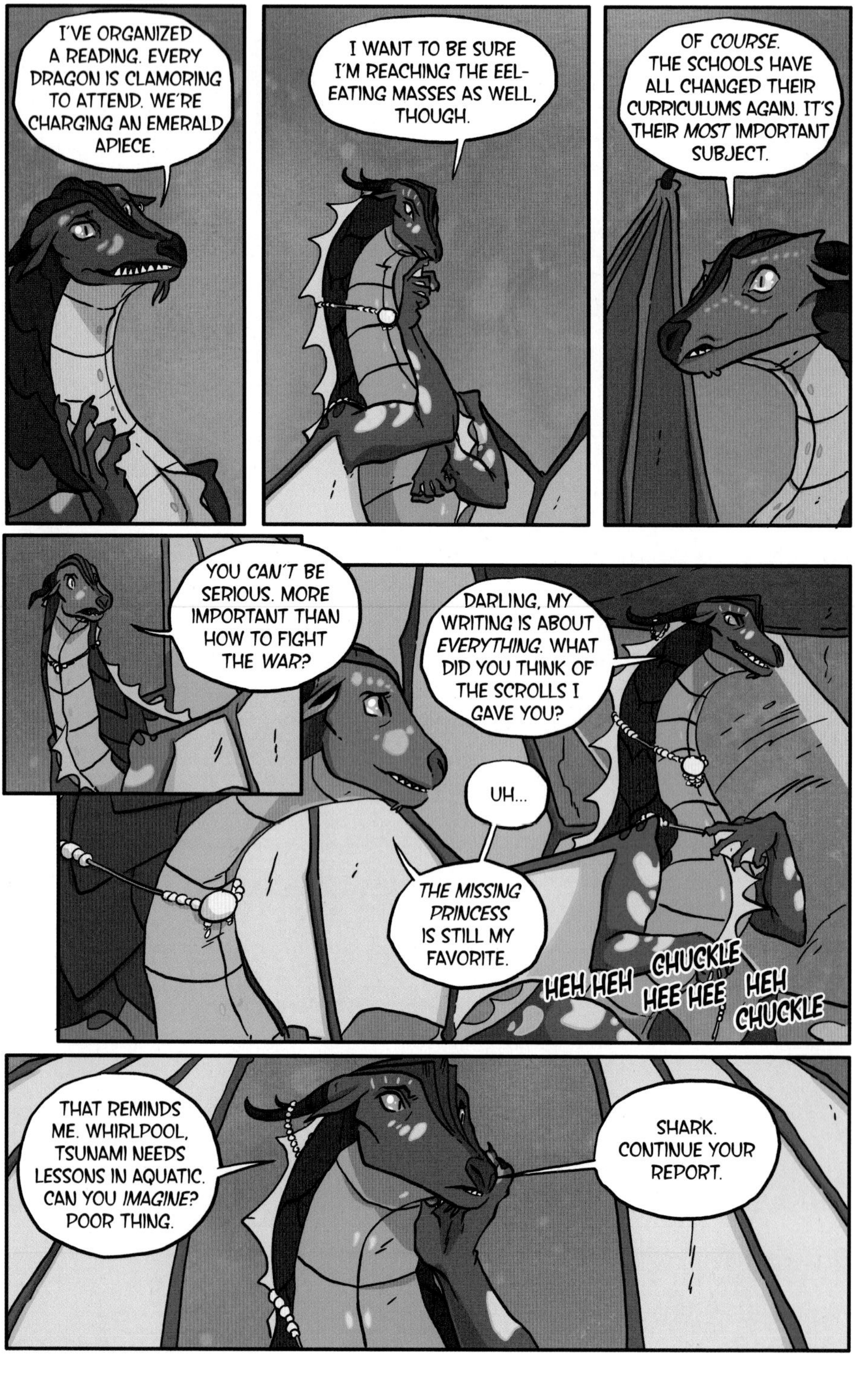
I'VE ORGANIZED A READING. EVERY DRAGON IS CLAMORING TO ATTEND. WE'RE CHARGING AN EMERALD APIECE.
I WANT TO BE SURE I'M REACHING THE EEL-EATING MASSES AS WELL, THOUGH.
OF *COURSE*. THE SCHOOLS HAVE ALL CHANGED THEIR CURRICULUMS AGAIN. IT'S THEIR *MOST* IMPORTANT SUBJECT.
YOU *CAN'T* BE SERIOUS. MORE IMPORTANT THAN HOW TO FIGHT THE *WAR*?
DARLING, MY WRITING IS ABOUT *EVERYTHING*. WHAT DID YOU THINK OF THE SCROLLS I GAVE YOU?
UH...
THE MISSING PRINCESS IS STILL MY FAVORITE.
HEH HEH
CHUCKLE
HEE HEE
HEH
CHUCKLE
THAT REMINDS ME. WHIRLPOOL, TSUNAMI NEEDS LESSONS IN AQUATIC. CAN YOU *IMAGINE*? POOR THING.
SHARK. CONTINUE YOUR REPORT.

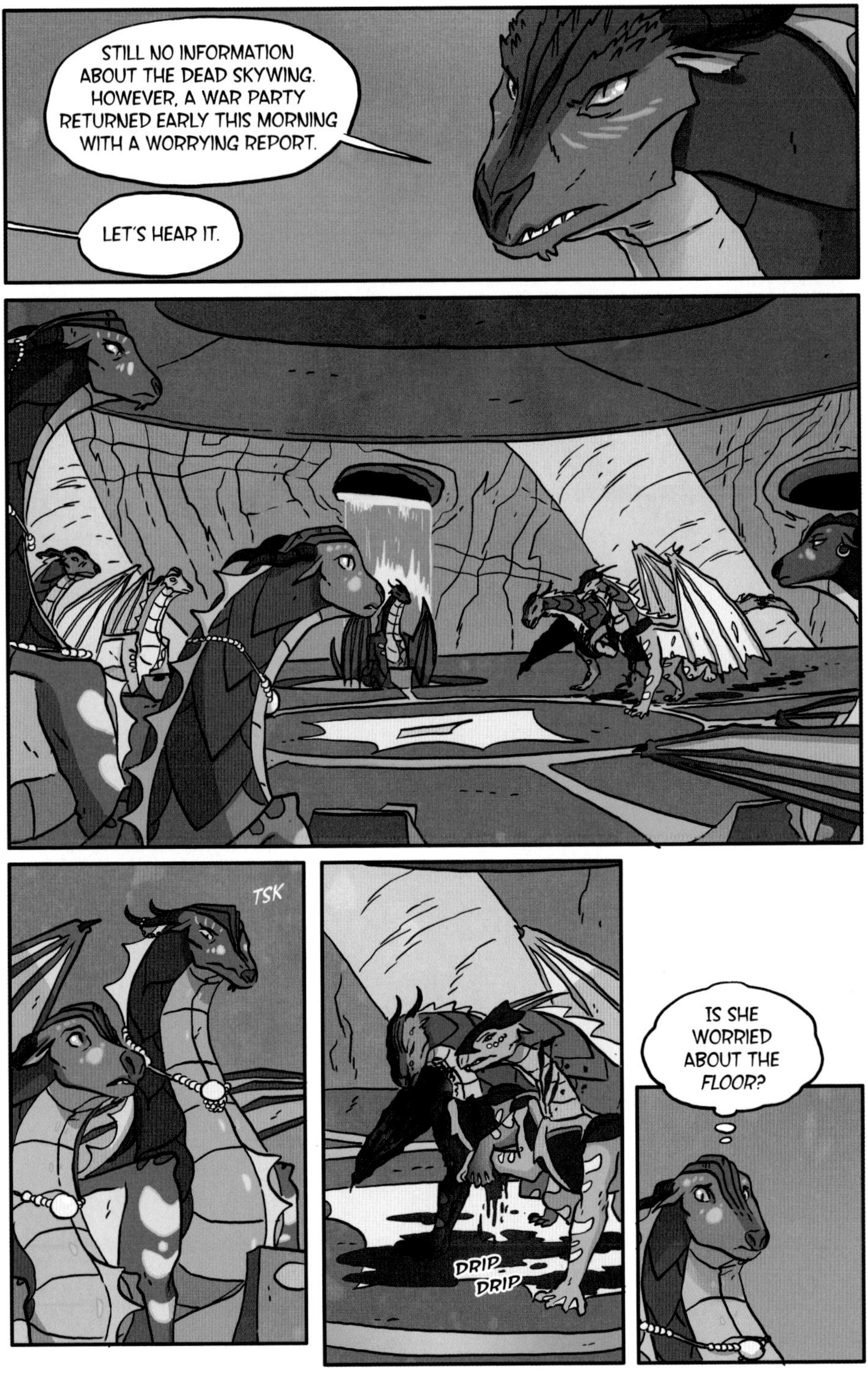
STILL NO INFORMATION ABOUT THE DEAD SKYWING. HOWEVER, A WAR PARTY RETURNED EARLY THIS MORNING WITH A WORRYING REPORT.
LET'S HEAR IT.
TSK
DRIP DRIP
IS SHE WORRIED ABOUT THE *FLOOR?*

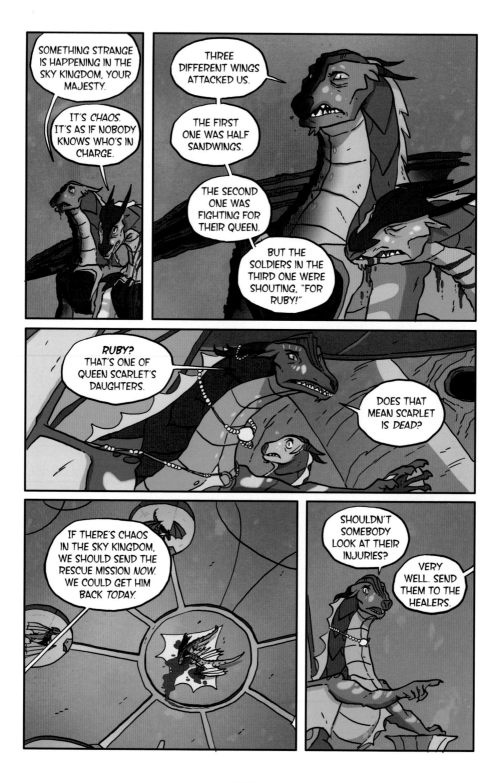

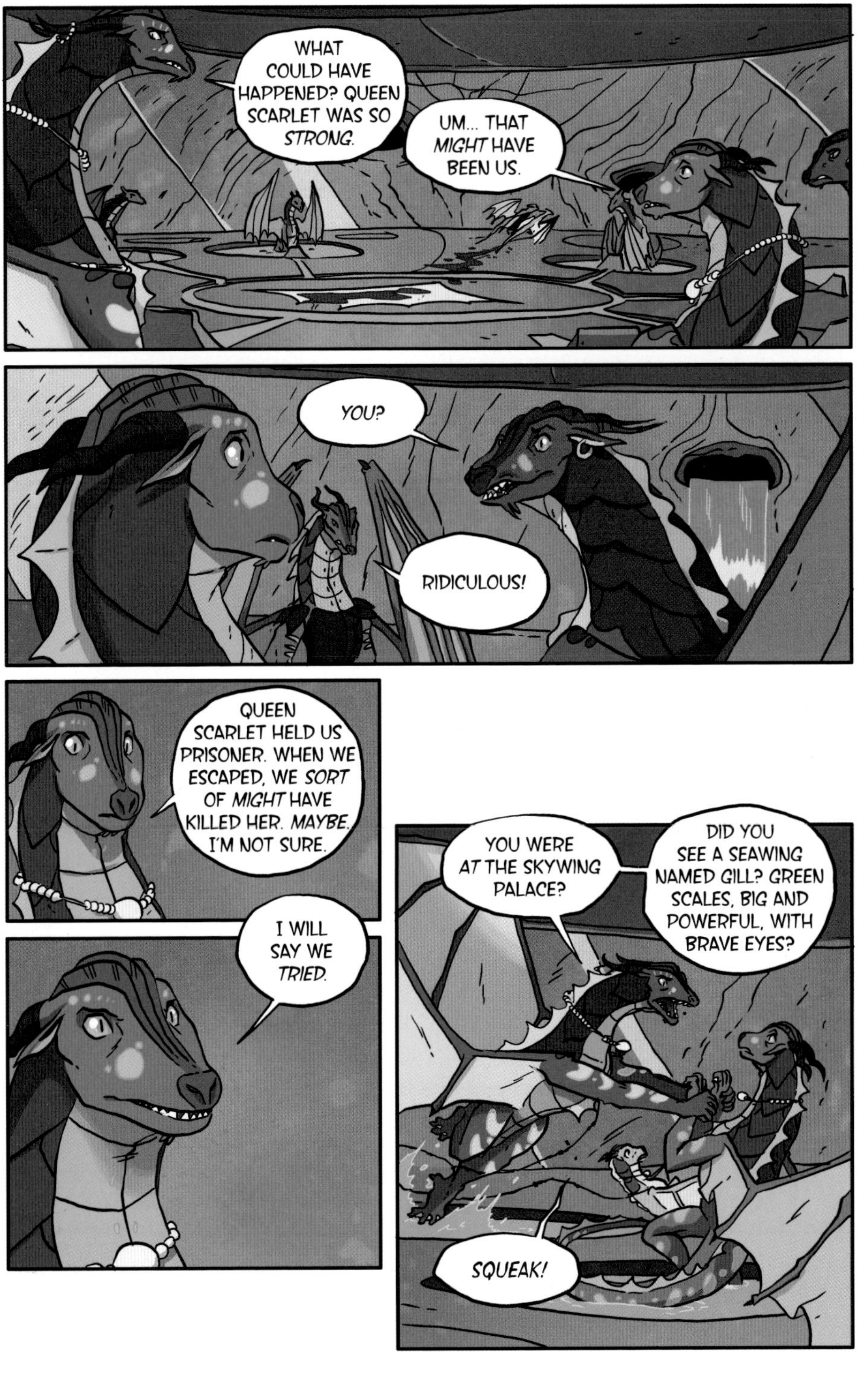
WHAT COULD HAVE HAPPENED? QUEEN SCARLET WAS SO *STRONG*.
UM... THAT *MIGHT* HAVE BEEN US.
YOU?
RIDICULOUS!
QUEEN SCARLET HELD US PRISONER. WHEN WE ESCAPED, WE *SORT* OF *MIGHT* HAVE KILLED HER. *MAYBE*. I'M NOT SURE.
I WILL SAY WE *TRIED*.
YOU WERE AT THE SKYWING PALACE?
DID YOU SEE A SEAWING NAMED GILL? GREEN SCALES, BIG AND POWERFUL, WITH BRAVE EYES?
SQUEAK!

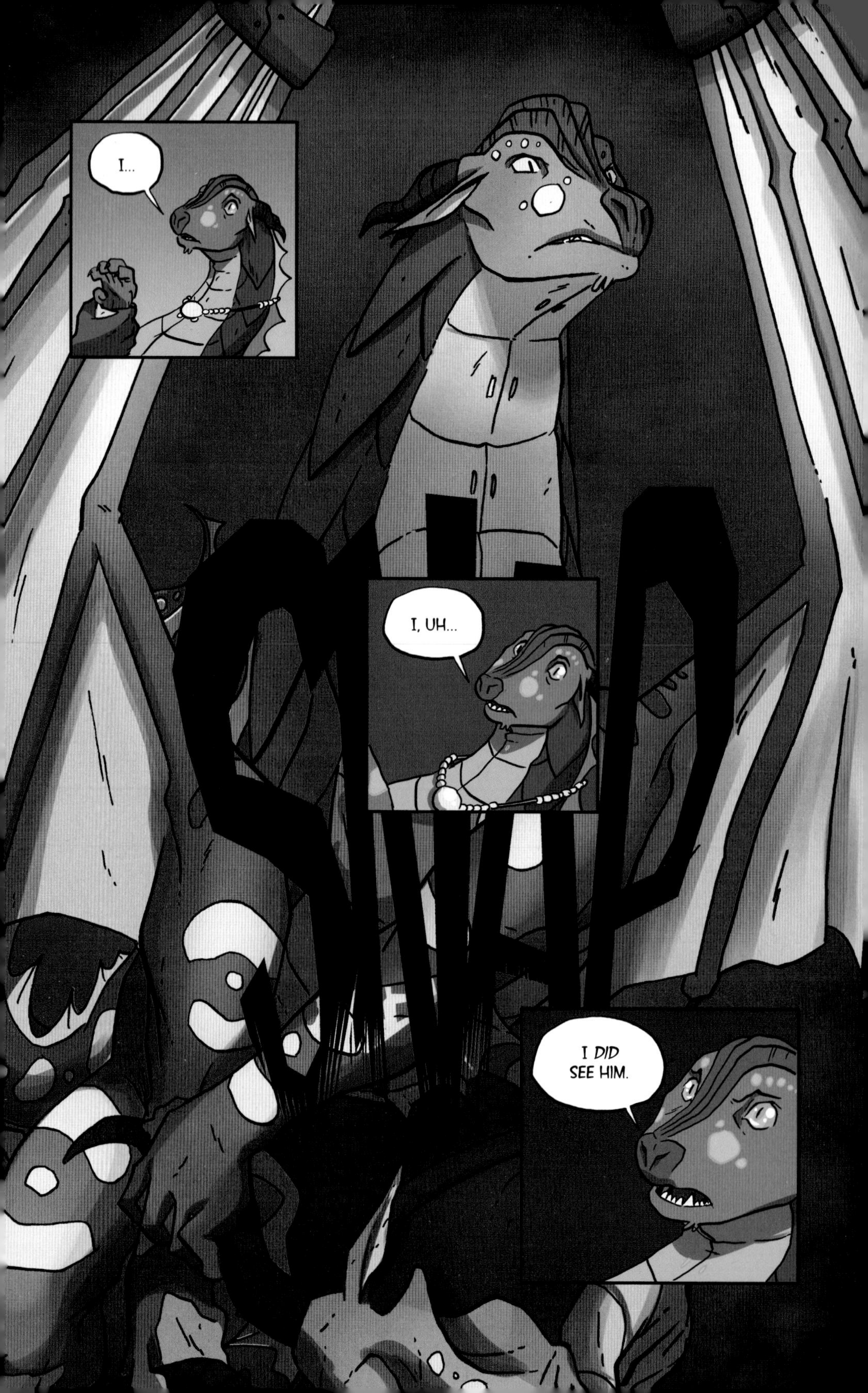
I...
I, UH...
I DID SEE HIM.

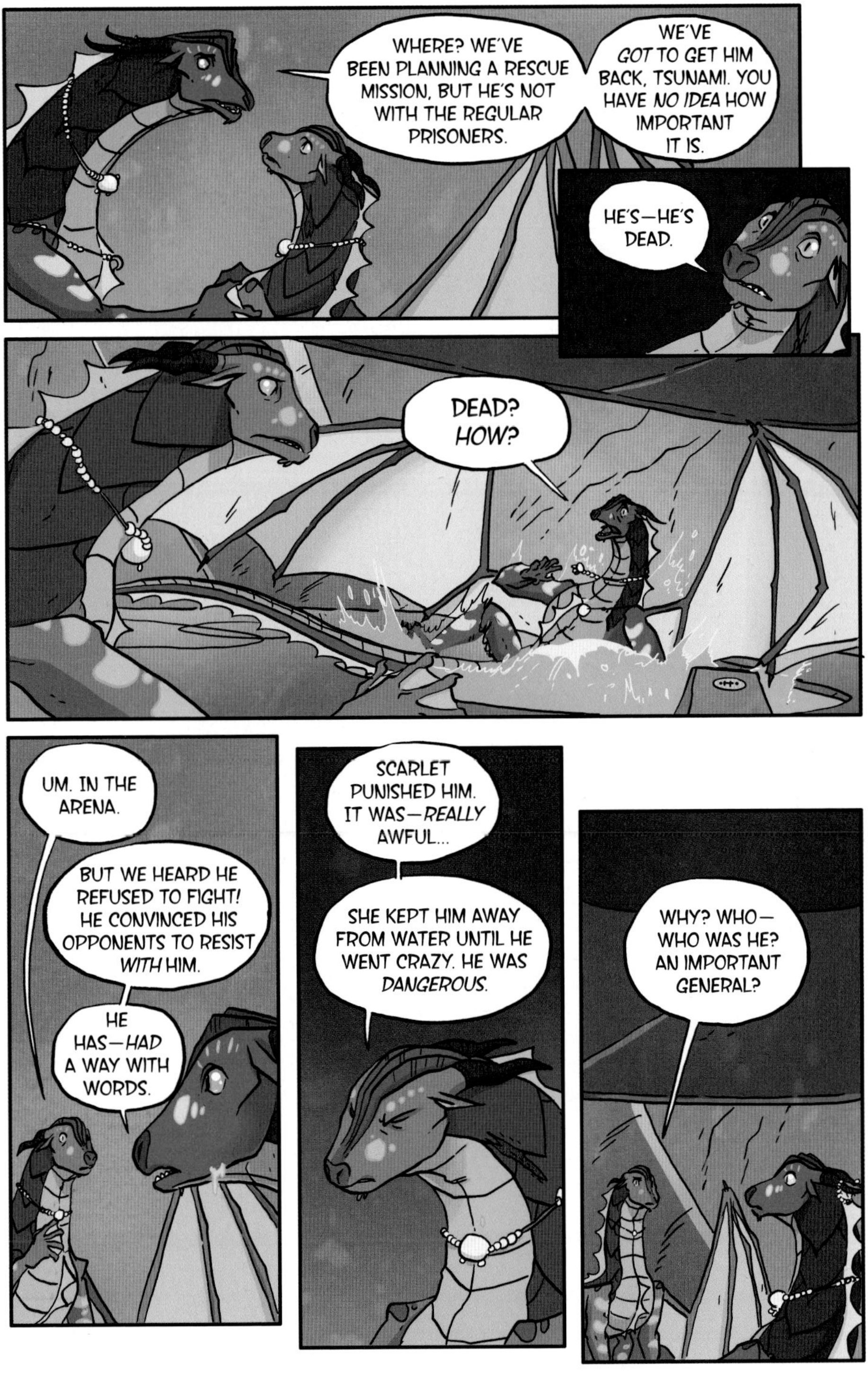
WHERE? WE'VE BEEN PLANNING A RESCUE MISSION, BUT HE'S NOT WITH THE REGULAR PRISONERS.
WE'VE *GOT* TO GET HIM BACK, TSUNAMI. YOU HAVE *NO IDEA* HOW IMPORTANT IT IS.
HE'S—HE'S DEAD.
DEAD? *HOW?*
UM. IN THE ARENA.
BUT WE HEARD HE REFUSED TO FIGHT! HE CONVINCED HIS OPPONENTS TO RESIST *WITH* HIM.
HE HAS—*HAD* A WAY WITH WORDS.
SCARLET PUNISHED HIM. IT WAS—*REALLY* AWFUL...
SHE KEPT HIM AWAY FROM WATER UNTIL HE WENT CRAZY. HE WAS *DANGEROUS*.
WHY? WHO—WHO WAS HE? AN IMPORTANT GENERAL?

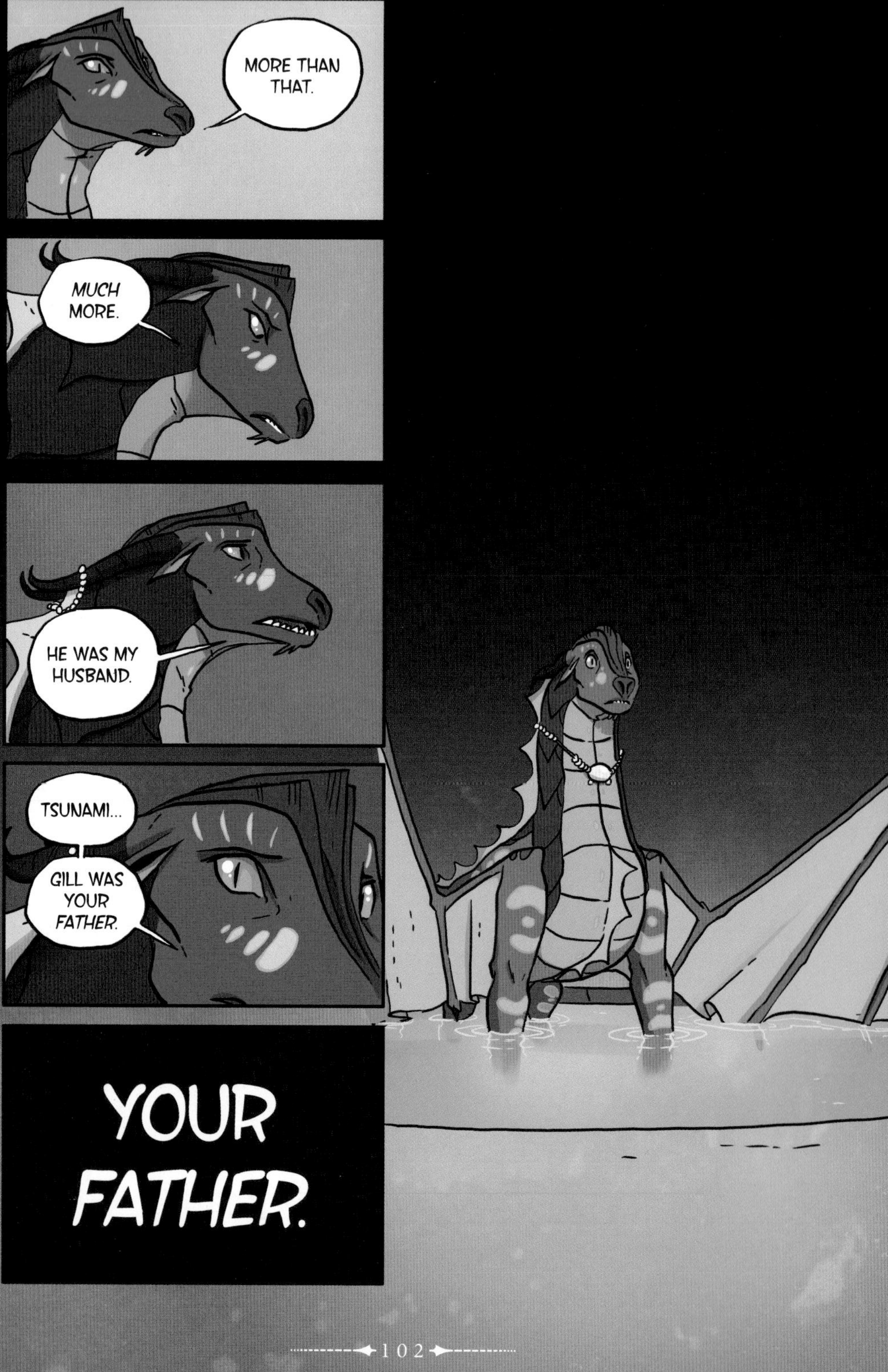
MORE THAN THAT.
MUCH MORE.
HE WAS MY HUSBAND.
TSUNAMI...
GILL WAS YOUR FATHER.
YOUR FATHER.

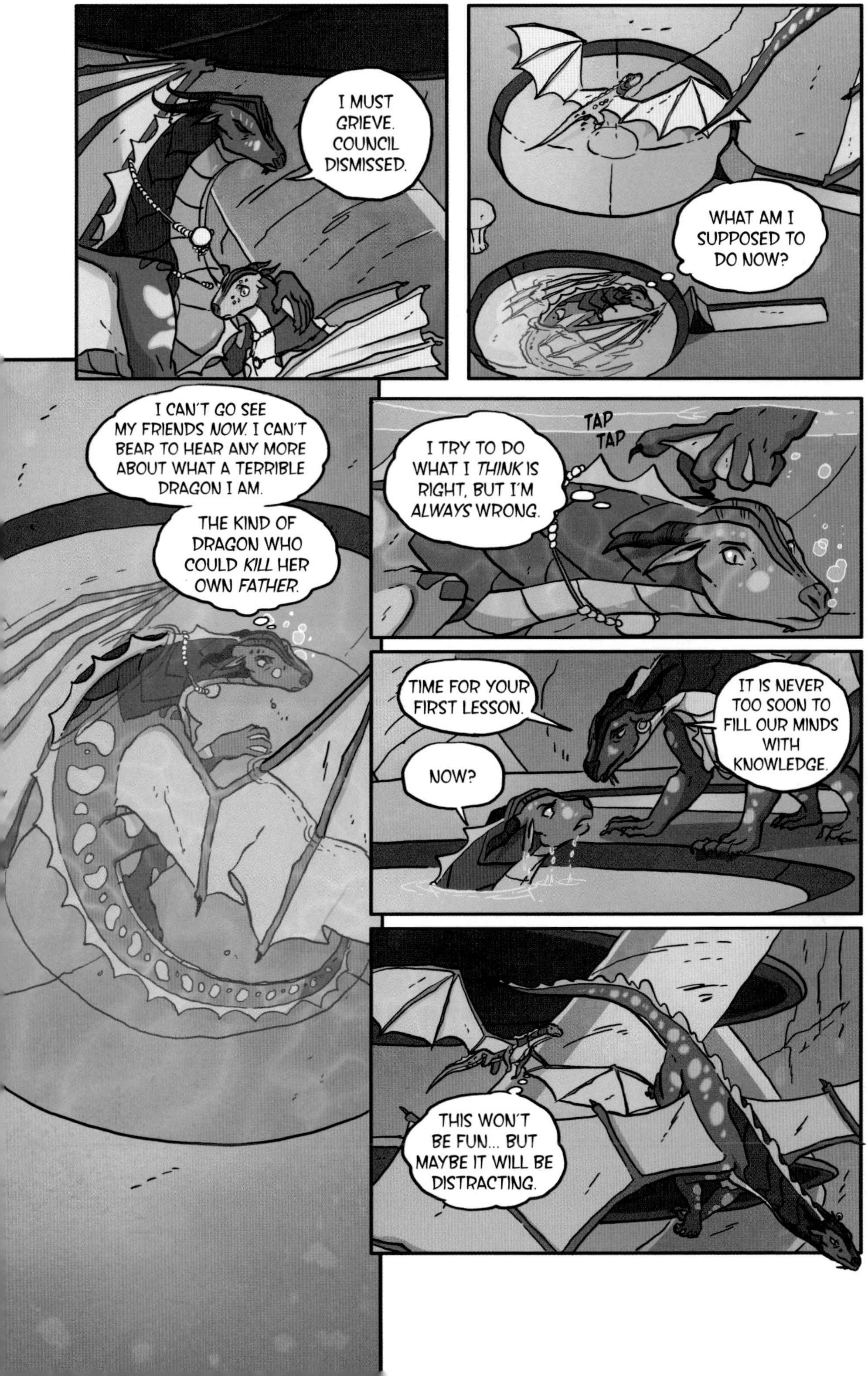
I MUST GRIEVE. COUNCIL DISMISSED.
WHAT AM I SUPPOSED TO DO NOW?
I CAN'T GO SEE MY FRIENDS *NOW.* I CAN'T BEAR TO HEAR ANY MORE ABOUT WHAT A TERRIBLE DRAGON I AM.
THE KIND OF DRAGON WHO COULD *KILL* HER OWN *FATHER.*
TAP TAP
I TRY TO DO WHAT I *THINK* IS RIGHT, BUT I'M *ALWAYS* WRONG.
TIME FOR YOUR FIRST LESSON.
NOW?
IT IS NEVER TOO SOON TO FILL OUR MINDS WITH KNOWLEDGE.
THIS WON'T BE FUN... BUT MAYBE IT WILL BE DISTRACTING.

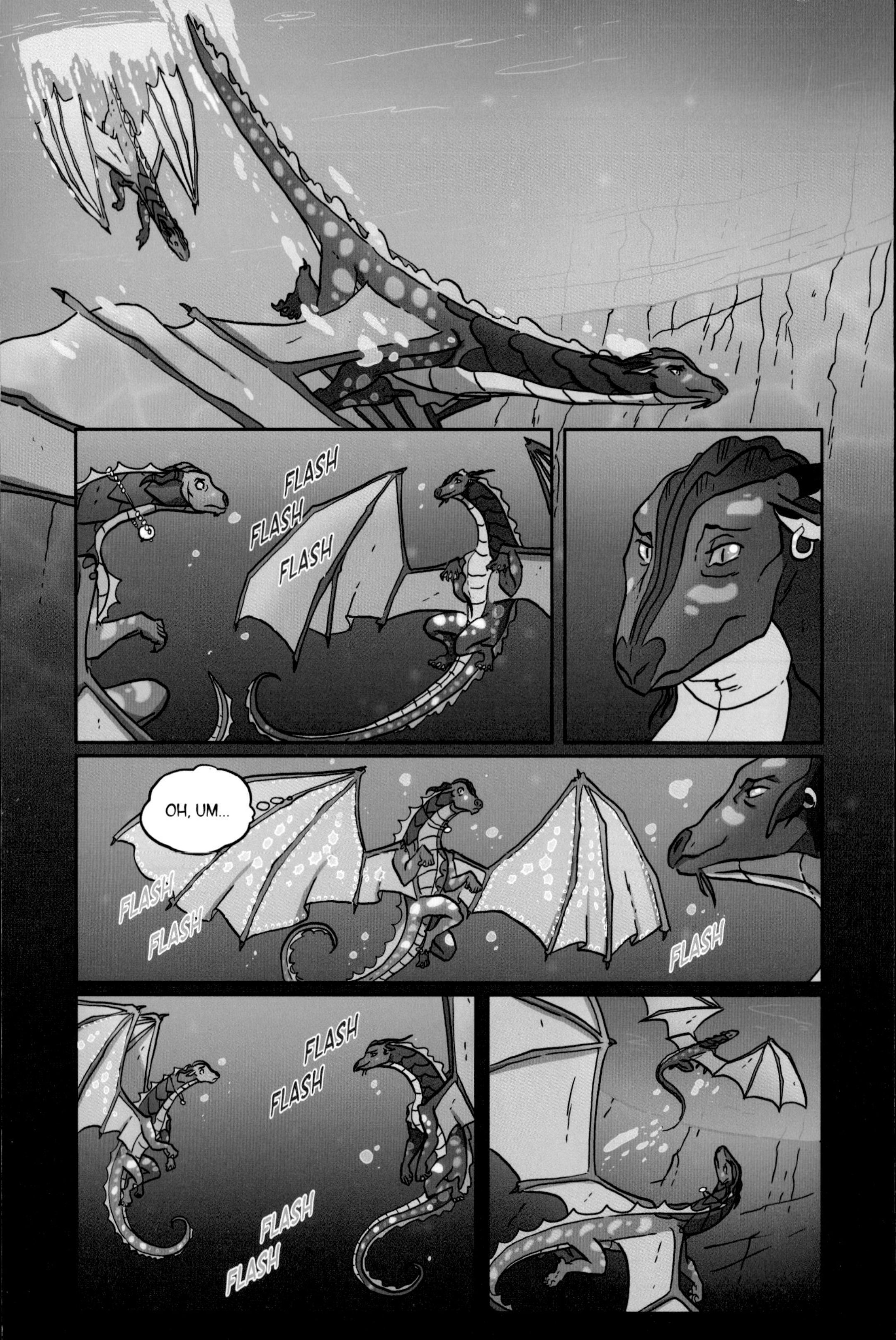
FLASH
FLASH
FLASH
OH, UM...
FLASH
FLASH
FLASH
FLASH
FLASH
FLASH
FLASH

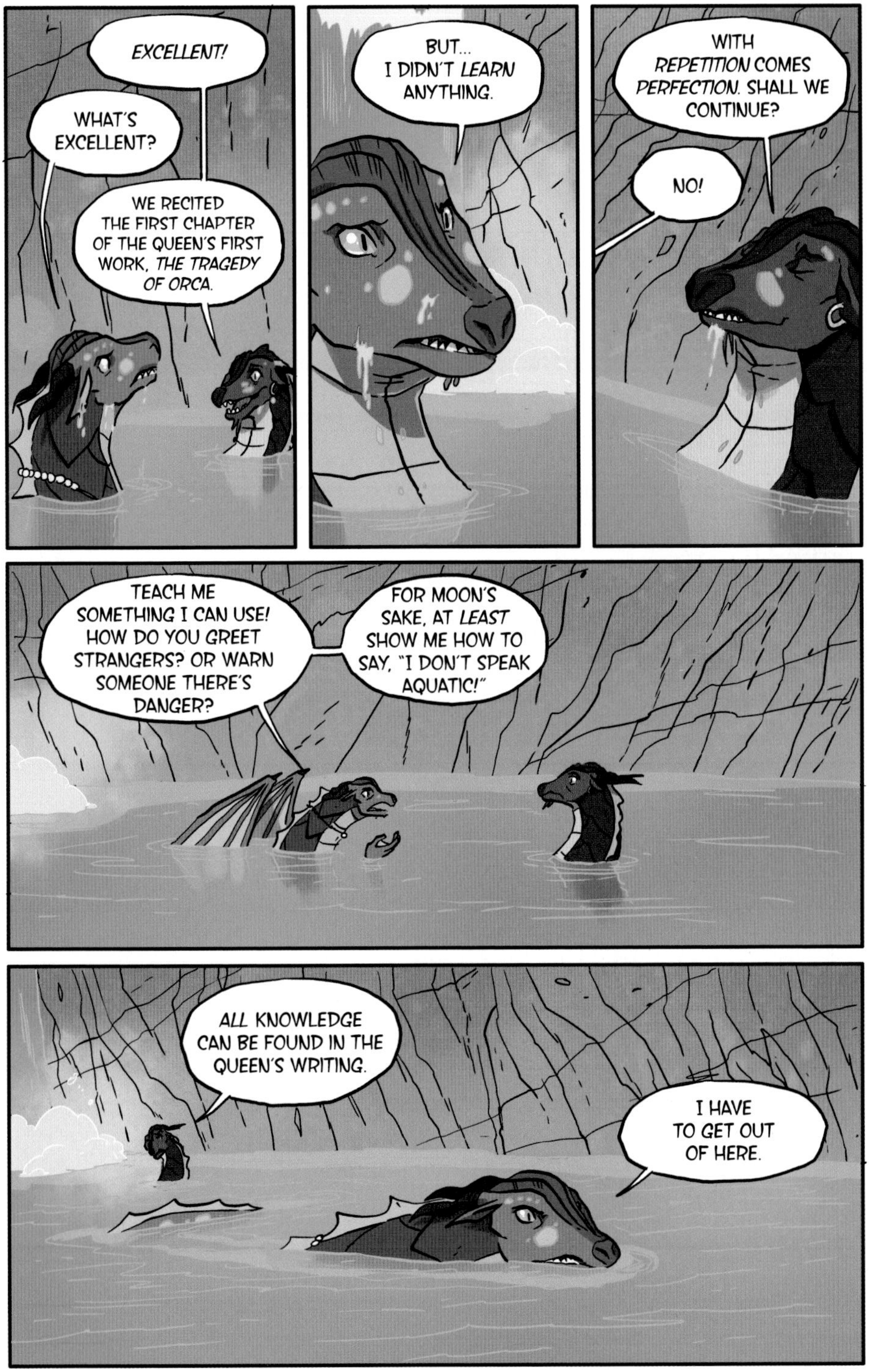
EXCELLENT!
WHAT'S EXCELLENT?
WE RECITED THE FIRST CHAPTER OF THE QUEEN'S FIRST WORK, *THE TRAGEDY OF ORCA*.
BUT... I DIDN'T *LEARN* ANYTHING.
WITH *REPETITION* COMES *PERFECTION*. SHALL WE CONTINUE?
NO!
TEACH ME SOMETHING I CAN USE! HOW DO YOU GREET STRANGERS? OR WARN SOMEONE THERE'S DANGER?
FOR MOON'S SAKE, AT *LEAST* SHOW ME HOW TO SAY, "I DON'T SPEAK AQUATIC!"
ALL KNOWLEDGE CAN BE FOUND IN THE QUEEN'S WRITING.
I HAVE TO GET OUT OF HERE.

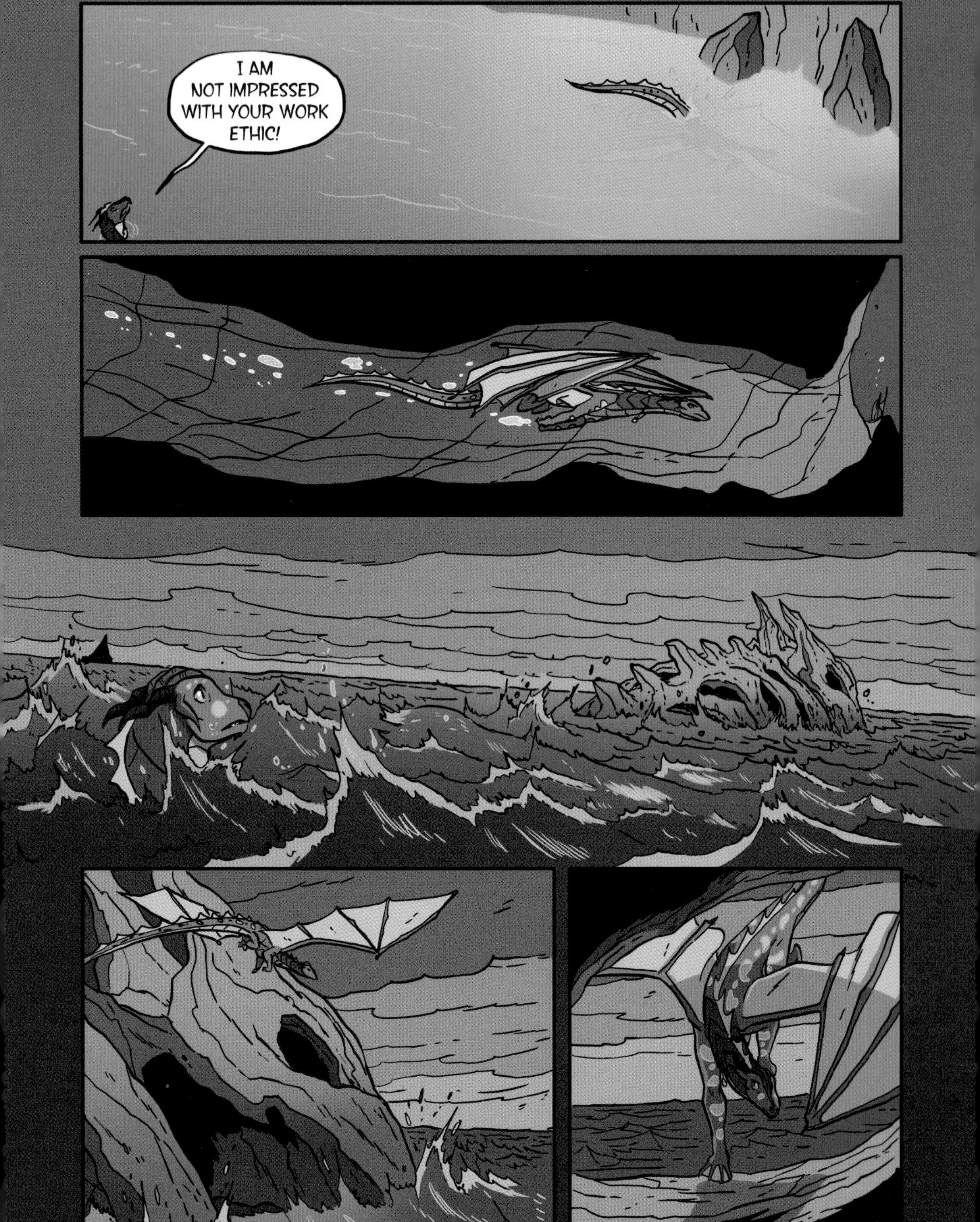
I AM NOT IMPRESSED WITH YOUR WORK ETHIC!

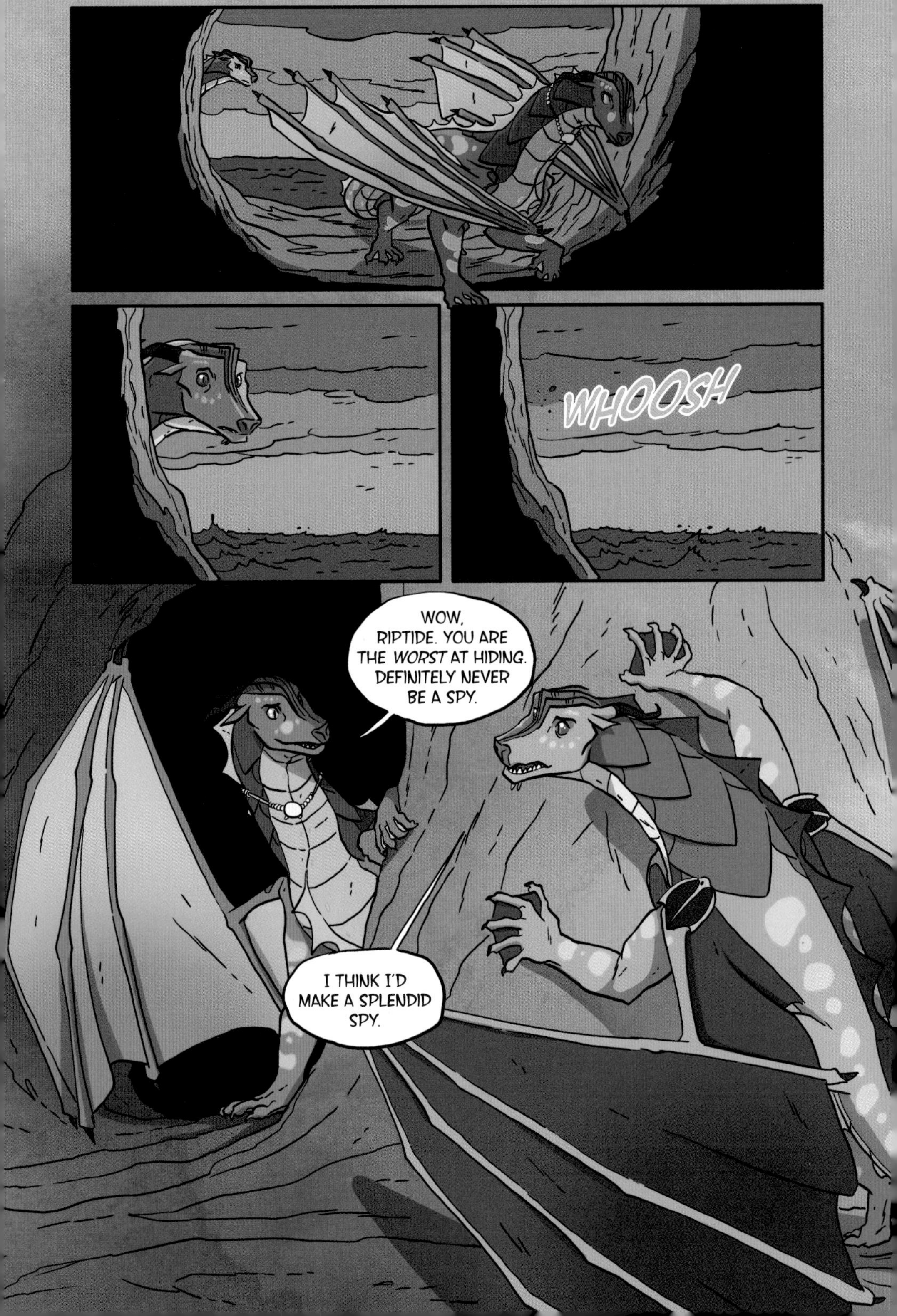
WHOOSH
WOW, RIPTIDE. YOU ARE THE *WORST* AT HIDING. DEFINITELY NEVER BE A SPY.
I THINK I'D MAKE A SPLENDID SPY.

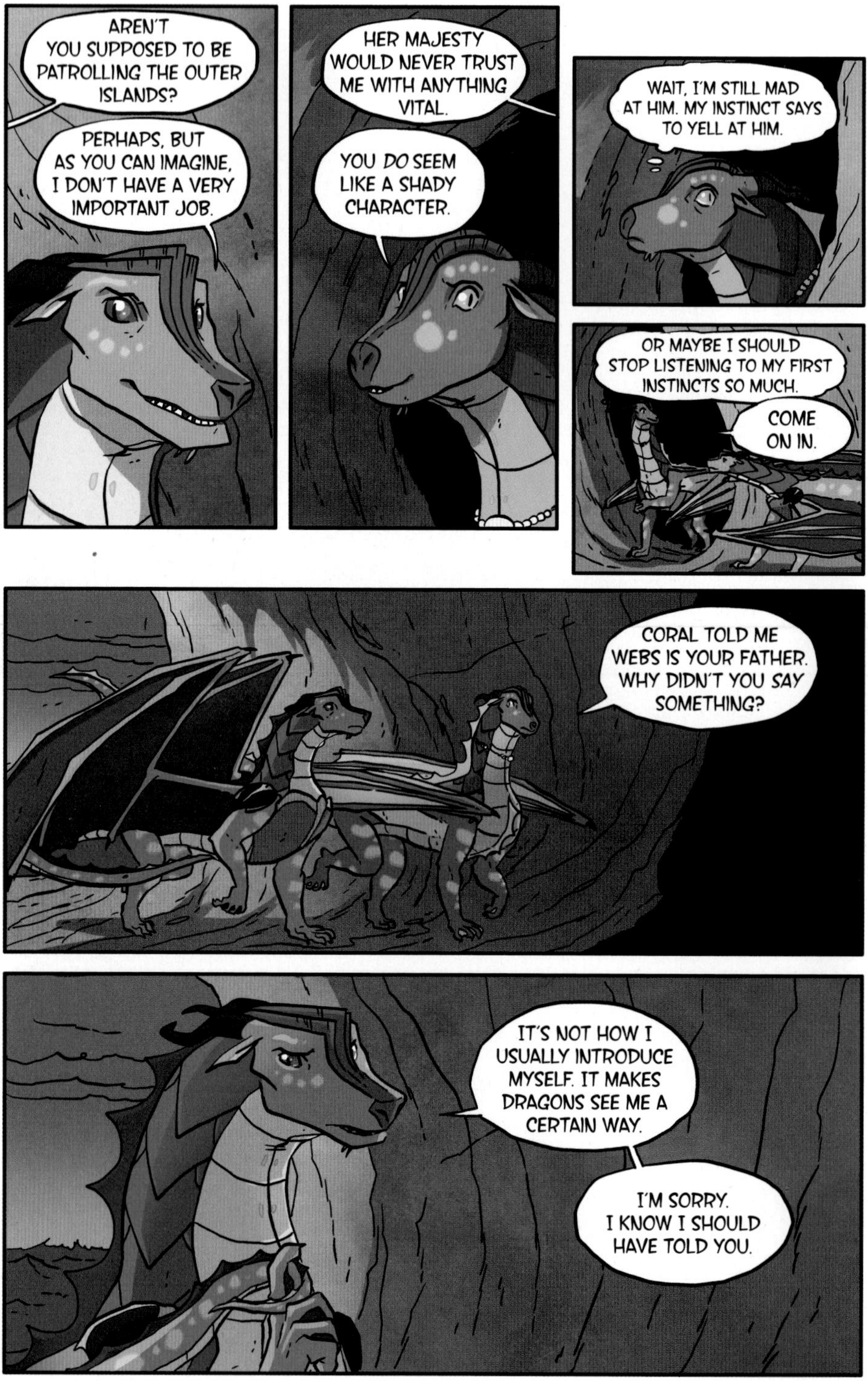
AREN'T YOU SUPPOSED TO BE PATROLLING THE OUTER ISLANDS?
PERHAPS, BUT AS YOU CAN IMAGINE, I DON'T HAVE A VERY IMPORTANT JOB.
HER MAJESTY WOULD NEVER TRUST ME WITH ANYTHING VITAL.
YOU *DO* SEEM LIKE A SHADY CHARACTER.
WAIT, I'M STILL MAD AT HIM. MY INSTINCT SAYS TO YELL AT HIM.
OR MAYBE I SHOULD STOP LISTENING TO MY FIRST INSTINCTS SO MUCH.
COME ON IN.
CORAL TOLD ME WEBS IS YOUR FATHER. WHY DIDN'T YOU *SAY* SOMETHING?
IT'S NOT HOW I USUALLY INTRODUCE MYSELF. IT MAKES DRAGONS SEE ME A CERTAIN WAY.
I'M SORRY. I KNOW I SHOULD HAVE TOLD YOU.

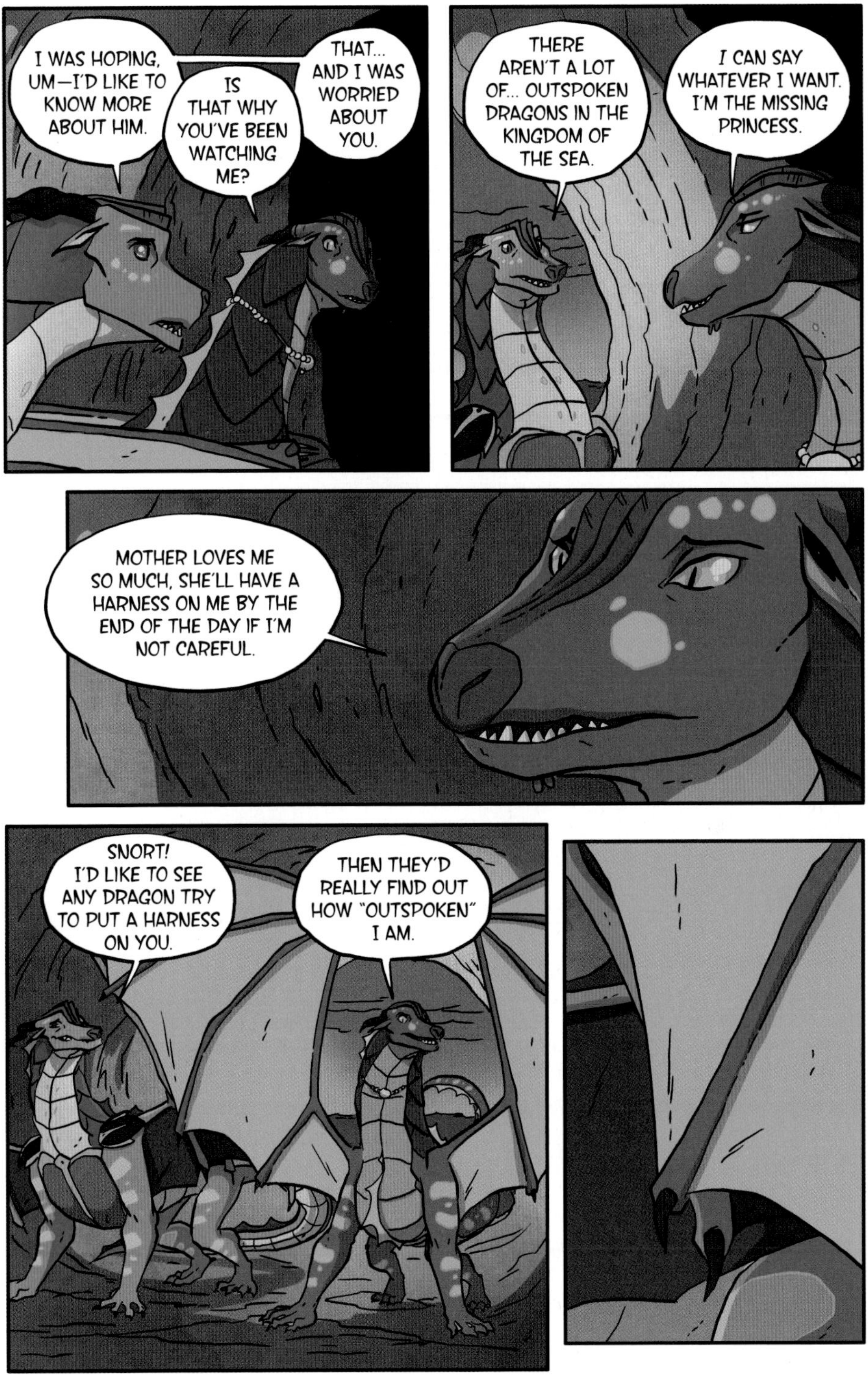
I WAS HOPING, UM—I'D LIKE TO KNOW MORE ABOUT HIM.
IS THAT WHY YOU'VE BEEN WATCHING ME?
THAT... AND I WAS WORRIED ABOUT YOU.
THERE AREN'T A LOT OF... OUTSPOKEN DRAGONS IN THE KINGDOM OF THE SEA.
I CAN SAY WHATEVER I WANT. I'M THE MISSING PRINCESS.
MOTHER LOVES ME SO MUCH, SHE'LL HAVE A HARNESS ON ME BY THE END OF THE DAY IF I'M NOT CAREFUL.
SNORT! I'D LIKE TO SEE ANY DRAGON TRY TO PUT A HARNESS ON YOU.
THEN THEY'D REALLY FIND OUT HOW "OUTSPOKEN" I AM.

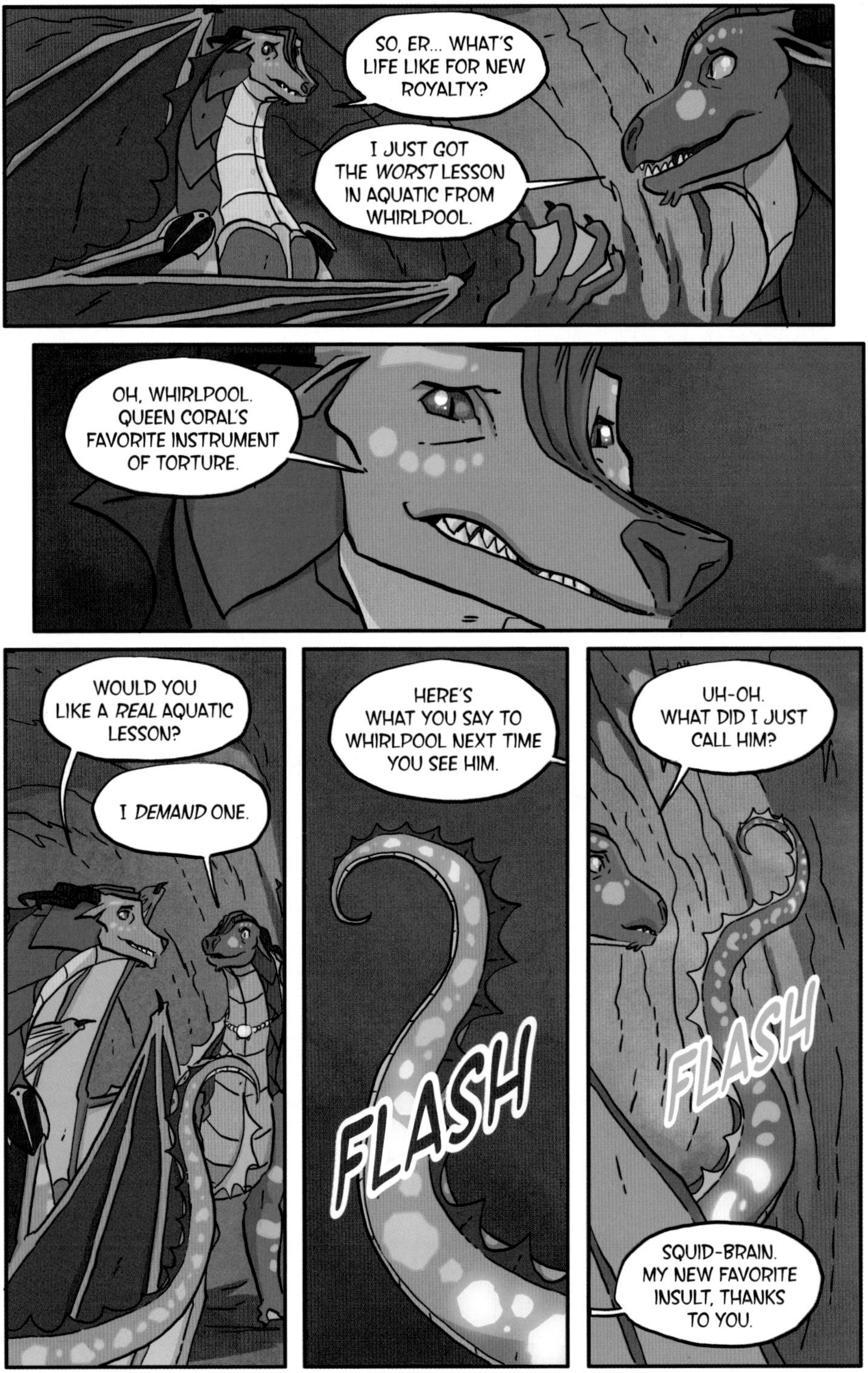
SO, ER... WHAT'S LIFE LIKE FOR NEW ROYALTY?
I JUST GOT THE *WORST* LESSON IN AQUATIC FROM WHIRLPOOL.
OH, WHIRLPOOL. QUEEN CORAL'S FAVORITE INSTRUMENT OF TORTURE.
WOULD YOU LIKE A *REAL* AQUATIC LESSON?
I *DEMAND* ONE.
HERE'S WHAT YOU SAY TO WHIRLPOOL NEXT TIME YOU SEE HIM.
FLASH
UH-OH. WHAT DID I JUST CALL HIM?
FLASH
SQUID-BRAIN. MY NEW FAVORITE INSULT, THANKS TO YOU.

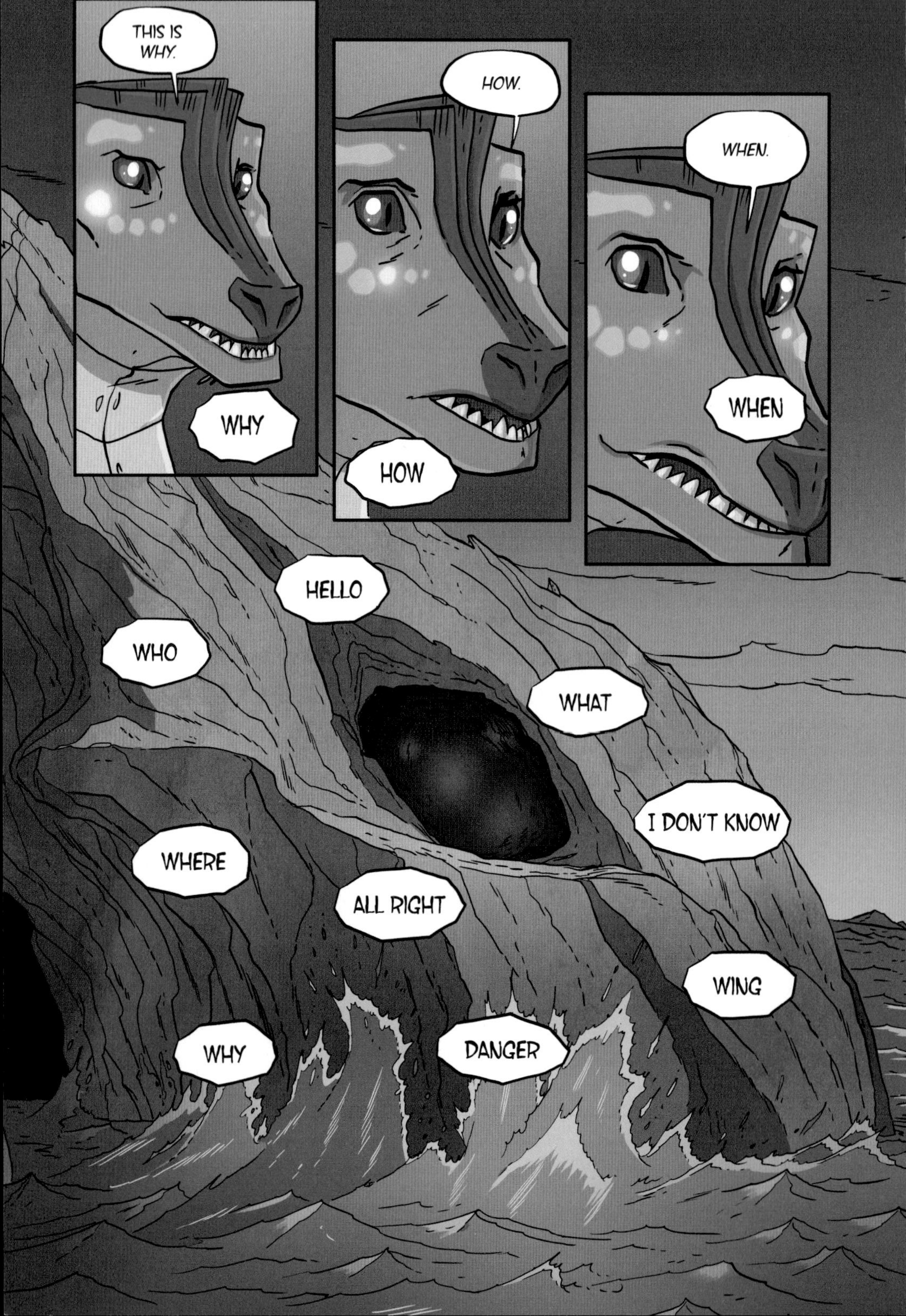
THIS IS WHY.
WHY
HOW.
HOW
WHEN.
WHEN
HELLO
WHO
WHAT
I DON'T KNOW
WHERE
ALL RIGHT
WING
WHY
DANGER

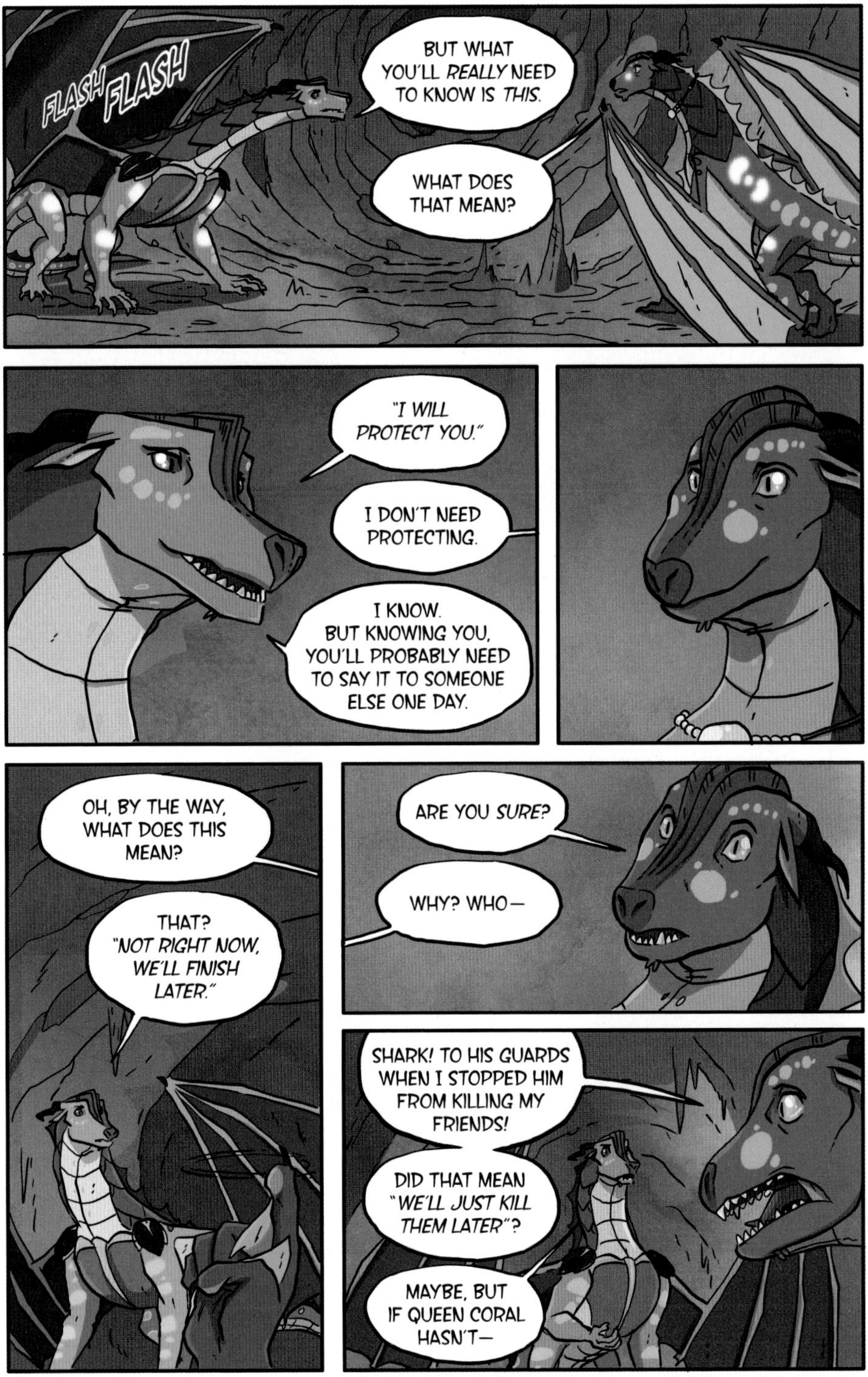
FLASH FLASH
BUT WHAT YOU'LL *REALLY* NEED TO KNOW IS *THIS.*
WHAT DOES THAT MEAN?
"*I WILL PROTECT YOU.*"
I DON'T NEED PROTECTING.
I KNOW. BUT KNOWING YOU, YOU'LL PROBABLY NEED TO SAY IT TO SOMEONE ELSE ONE DAY.
OH, BY THE WAY, WHAT DOES THIS MEAN?
THAT? "*NOT RIGHT NOW, WE'LL FINISH LATER.*"
ARE YOU *SURE?*
WHY? WHO—
SHARK! TO HIS GUARDS WHEN I STOPPED HIM FROM KILLING MY FRIENDS!
DID THAT MEAN "*WE'LL JUST KILL THEM LATER*"?
MAYBE, BUT IF QUEEN CORAL HASN'T—

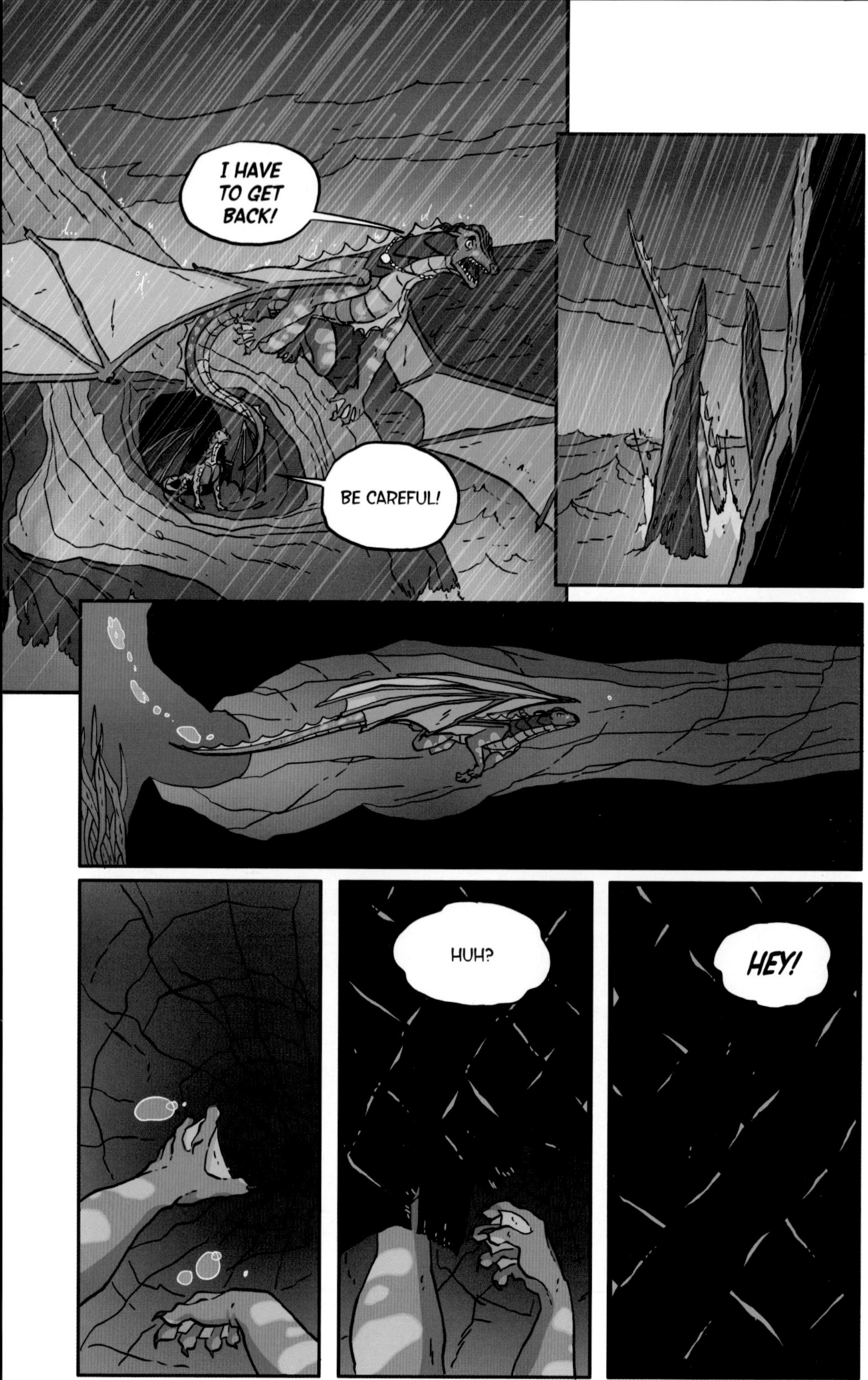
I HAVE TO GET BACK!
BE CAREFUL!
HUH?
HEY!

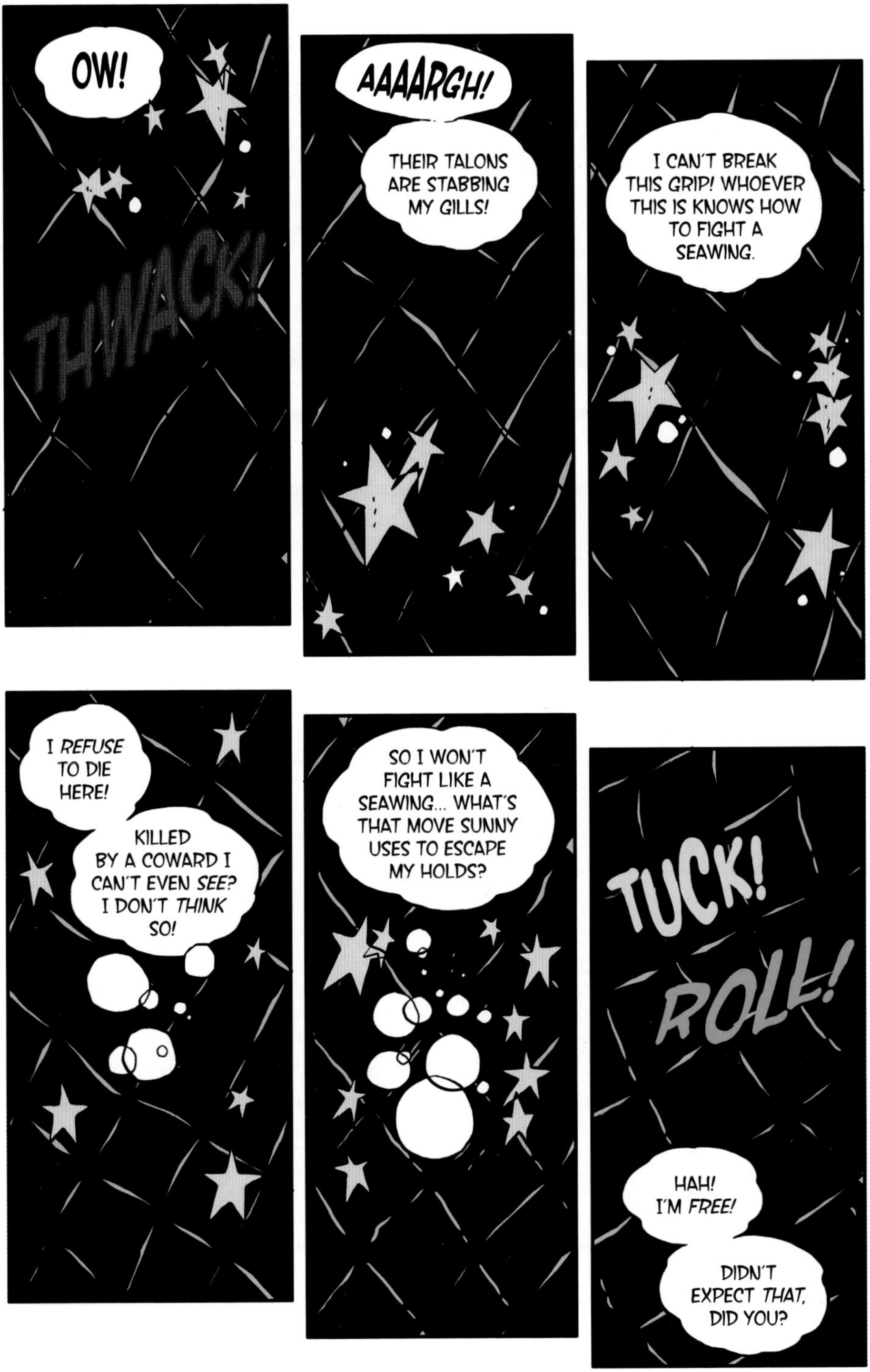
OW!
THWACK!
AAAARGH!
THEIR TALONS ARE STABBING MY GILLS!
I CAN'T BREAK THIS GRIP! WHOEVER THIS IS KNOWS HOW TO FIGHT A SEAWING.
I *REFUSE* TO DIE HERE!
KILLED BY A COWARD I CAN'T EVEN *SEE*? I DON'T *THINK* SO!
SO I WON'T FIGHT LIKE A SEAWING... WHAT'S THAT MOVE SUNNY USES TO ESCAPE MY HOLDS?
TUCK!
ROLL!
HAH! I'M *FREE!*
DIDN'T EXPECT *THAT,* DID YOU?

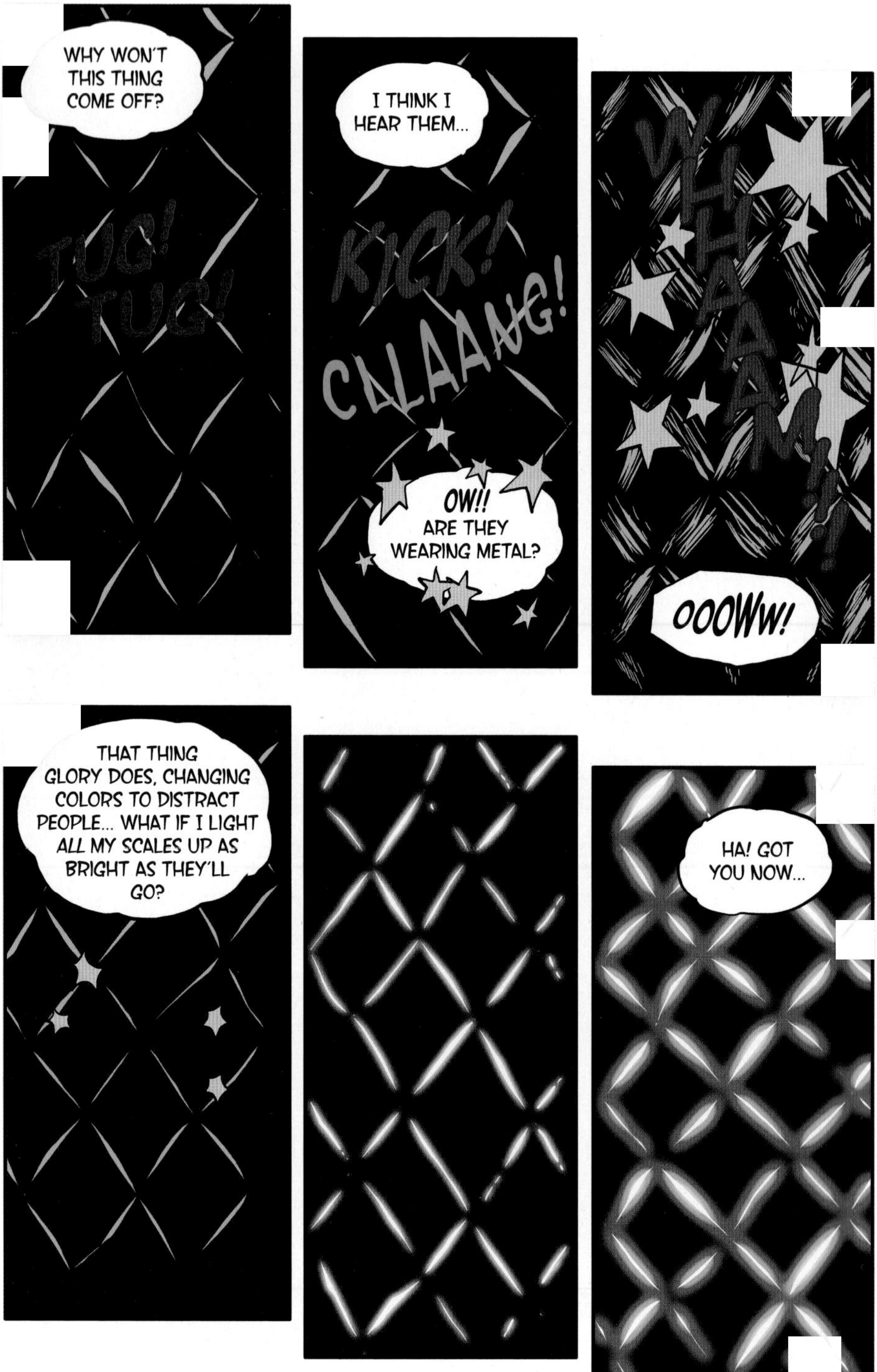
WHY WON'T THIS THING COME OFF?
TUG! TUG!
I THINK I HEAR THEM...
KICK!
CLLAANG!
OW!! ARE THEY WEARING METAL?
WHHAAAM!!!
OOOWW!
THAT THING GLORY DOES, CHANGING COLORS TO DISTRACT PEOPLE... WHAT IF I LIGHT *ALL* MY SCALES UP AS BRIGHT AS THEY'LL GO?
HA! GOT YOU NOW...

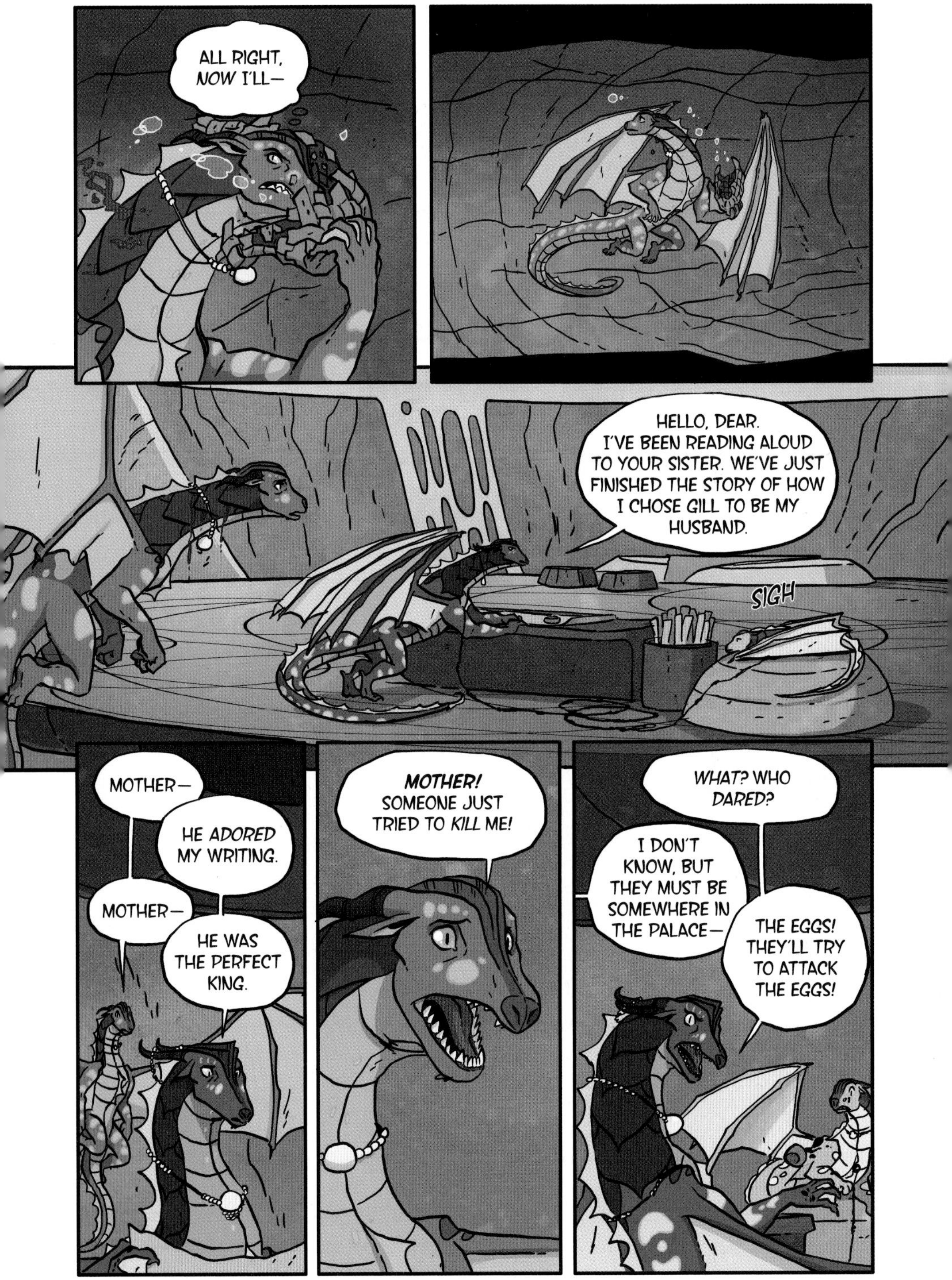

ALL RIGHT, *NOW* I'LL—
HELLO, DEAR. I'VE BEEN READING ALOUD TO YOUR SISTER. WE'VE JUST FINISHED THE STORY OF HOW I CHOSE GILL TO BE MY HUSBAND.
SIGH
MOTHER—
HE *ADORED* MY WRITING.
MOTHER—
HE WAS THE PERFECT KING.
MOTHER! SOMEONE JUST TRIED TO *KILL* ME!
WHAT? WHO DARED?
I DON'T KNOW, BUT THEY MUST BE SOMEWHERE IN THE PALACE—
THE EGGS! THEY'LL TRY TO ATTACK THE EGGS!

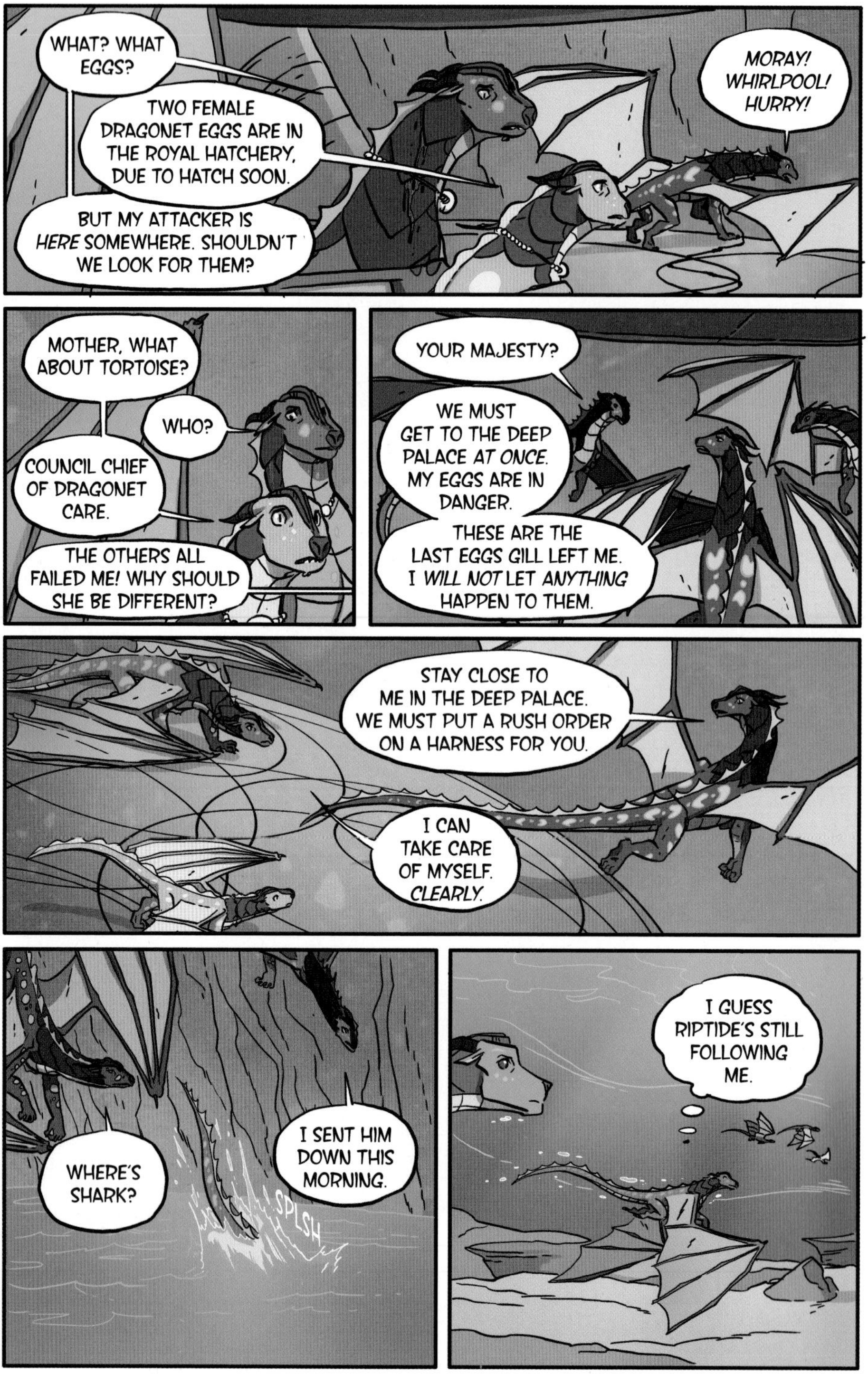
WHAT? WHAT EGGS?
TWO FEMALE DRAGONET EGGS ARE IN THE ROYAL HATCHERY, DUE TO HATCH SOON.
BUT MY ATTACKER IS *HERE* SOMEWHERE. SHOULDN'T WE LOOK FOR THEM?
MORAY! WHIRLPOOL! HURRY!
MOTHER, WHAT ABOUT TORTOISE?
WHO?
COUNCIL CHIEF OF DRAGONET CARE.
THE OTHERS ALL FAILED ME! WHY SHOULD SHE BE DIFFERENT?
YOUR MAJESTY?
WE MUST GET TO THE DEEP PALACE *AT ONCE*. MY EGGS ARE IN DANGER.
THESE ARE THE LAST EGGS GILL LEFT ME. I *WILL NOT* LET *ANYTHING* HAPPEN TO THEM.
STAY CLOSE TO ME IN THE DEEP PALACE. WE MUST PUT A RUSH ORDER ON A HARNESS FOR YOU.
I CAN TAKE CARE OF MYSELF. *CLEARLY.*
WHERE'S SHARK?
I SENT HIM DOWN THIS MORNING.
SPLSH
I GUESS RIPTIDE'S STILL FOLLOWING ME.

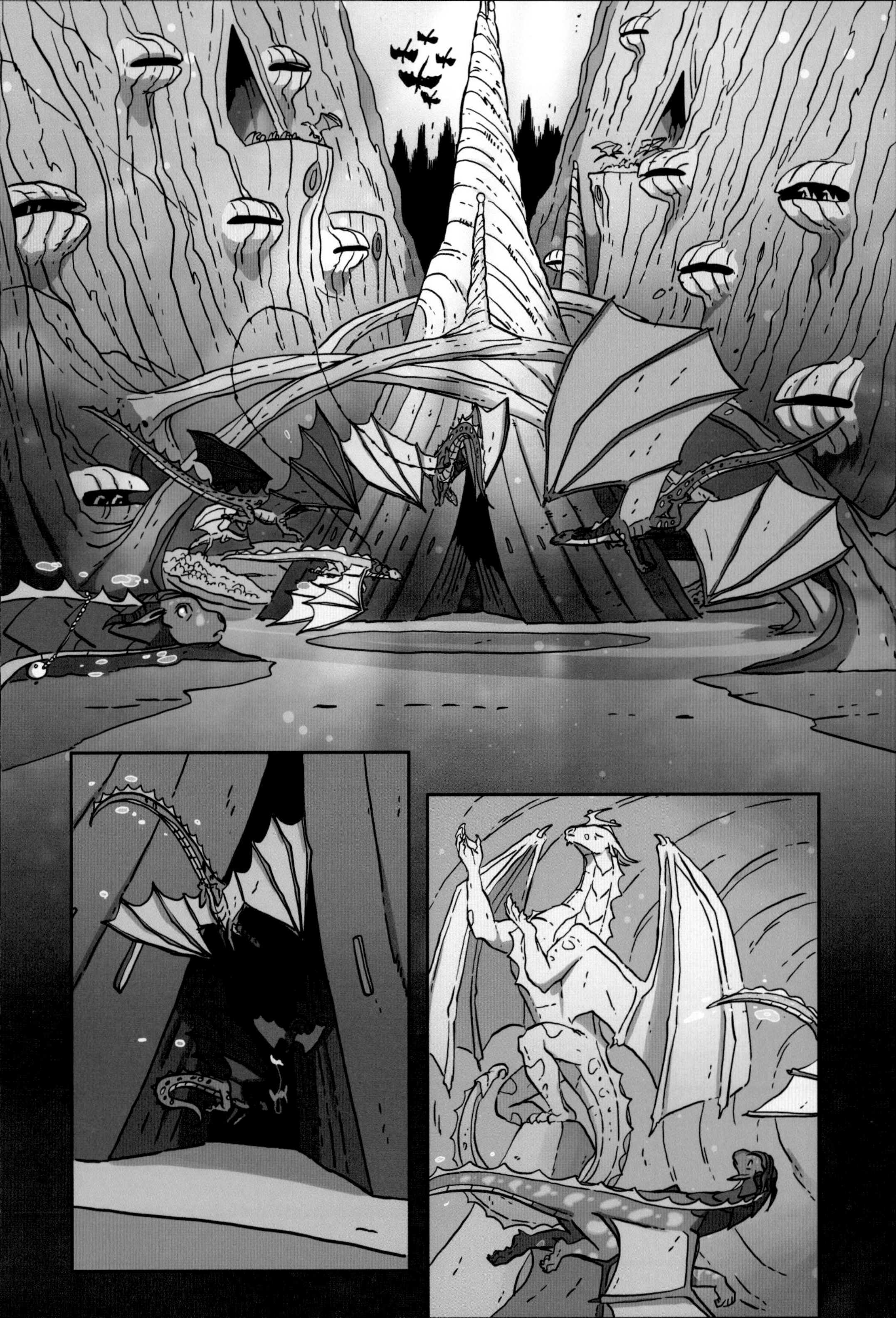

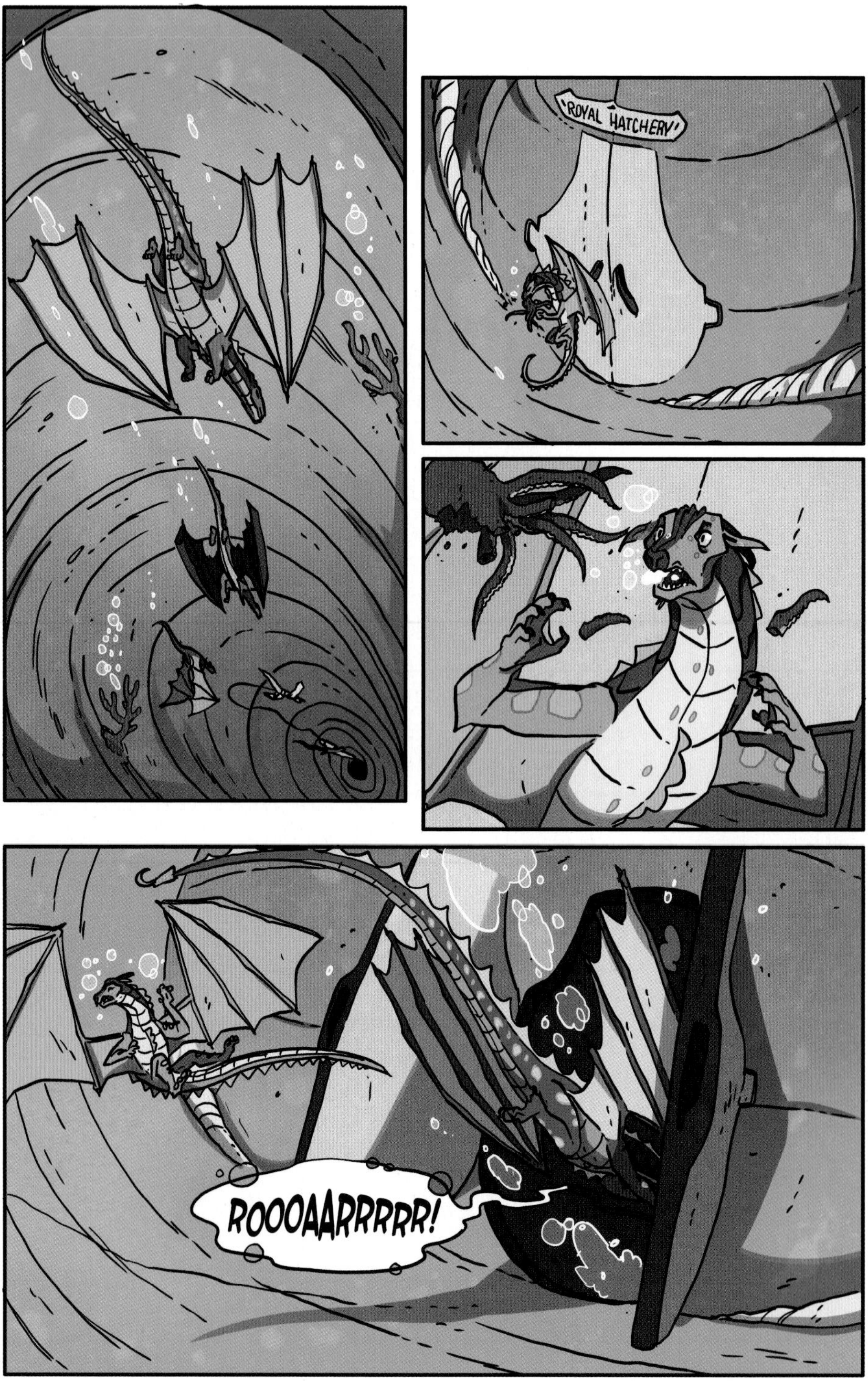
ROYAL HATCHERY
ROOOAARRRRR!

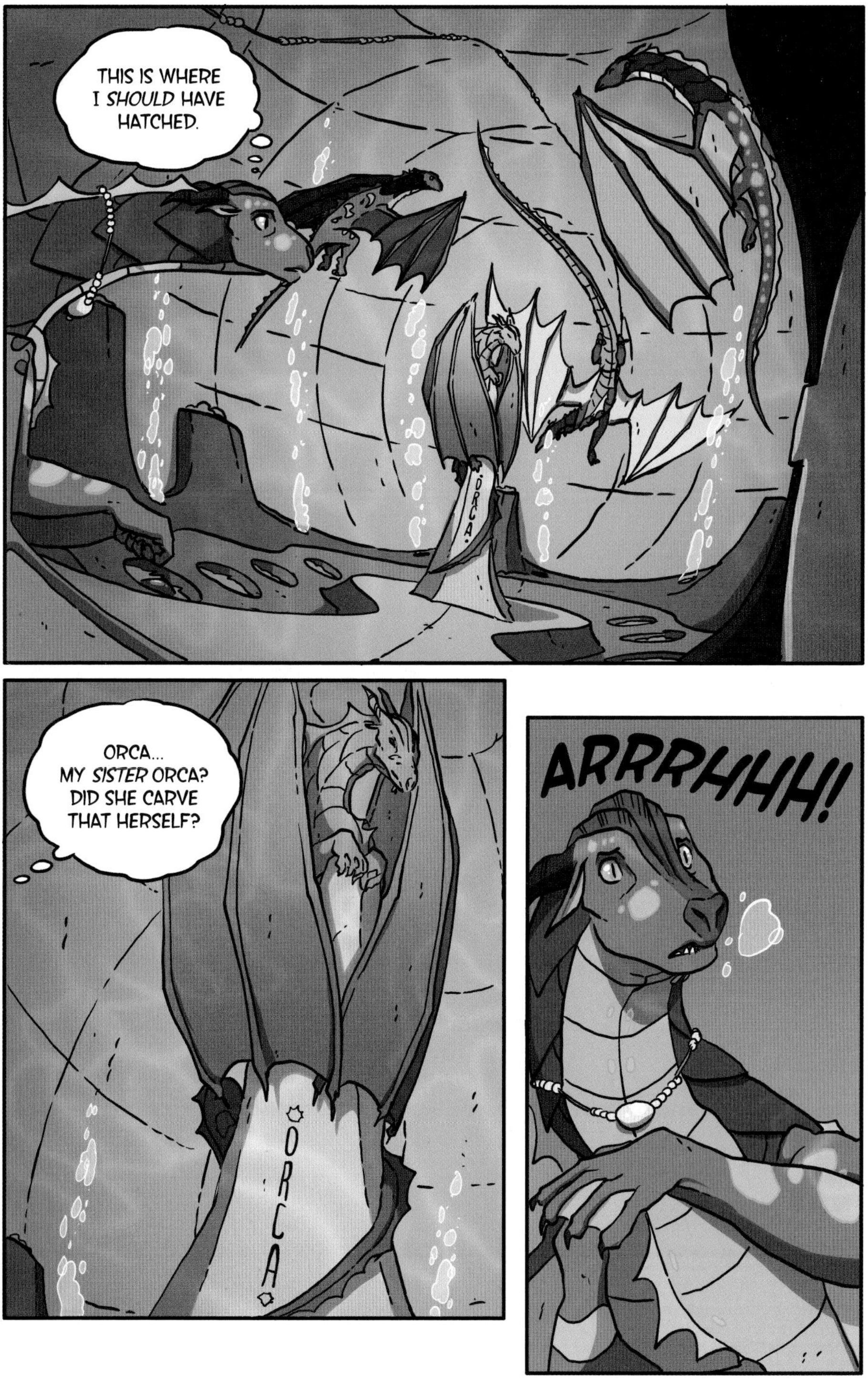
THIS IS WHERE I *SHOULD* HAVE HATCHED.
ORCA
ORCA... MY *SISTER* ORCA? DID SHE CARVE THAT HERSELF?
ORCA
ARRRHHH!

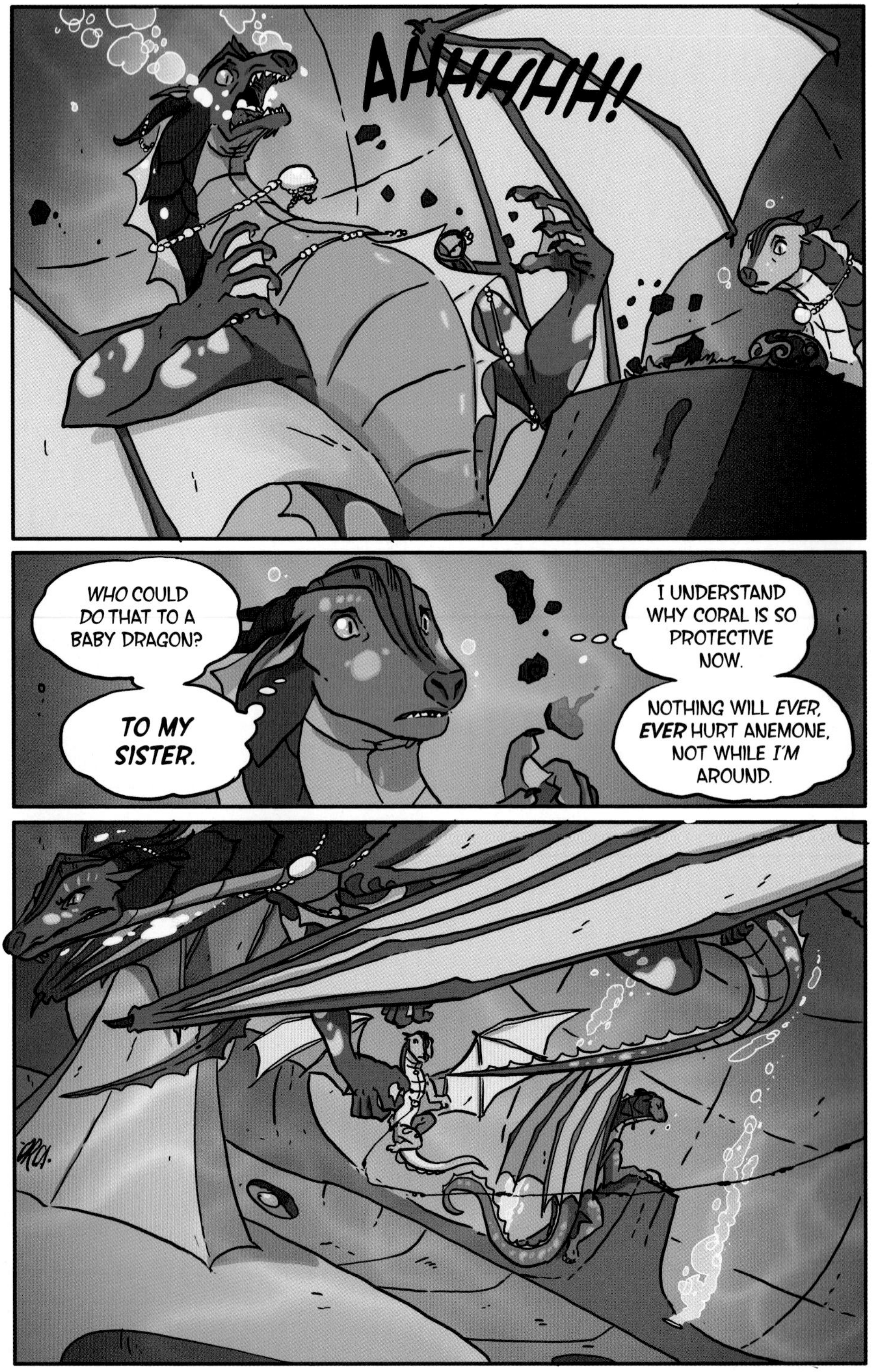
AHHHHHH!
WHO COULD DO THAT TO A BABY DRAGON?
TO MY SISTER.
I UNDERSTAND WHY CORAL IS SO PROTECTIVE NOW.
NOTHING WILL EVER, EVER HURT ANEMONE, NOT WHILE I'M AROUND.

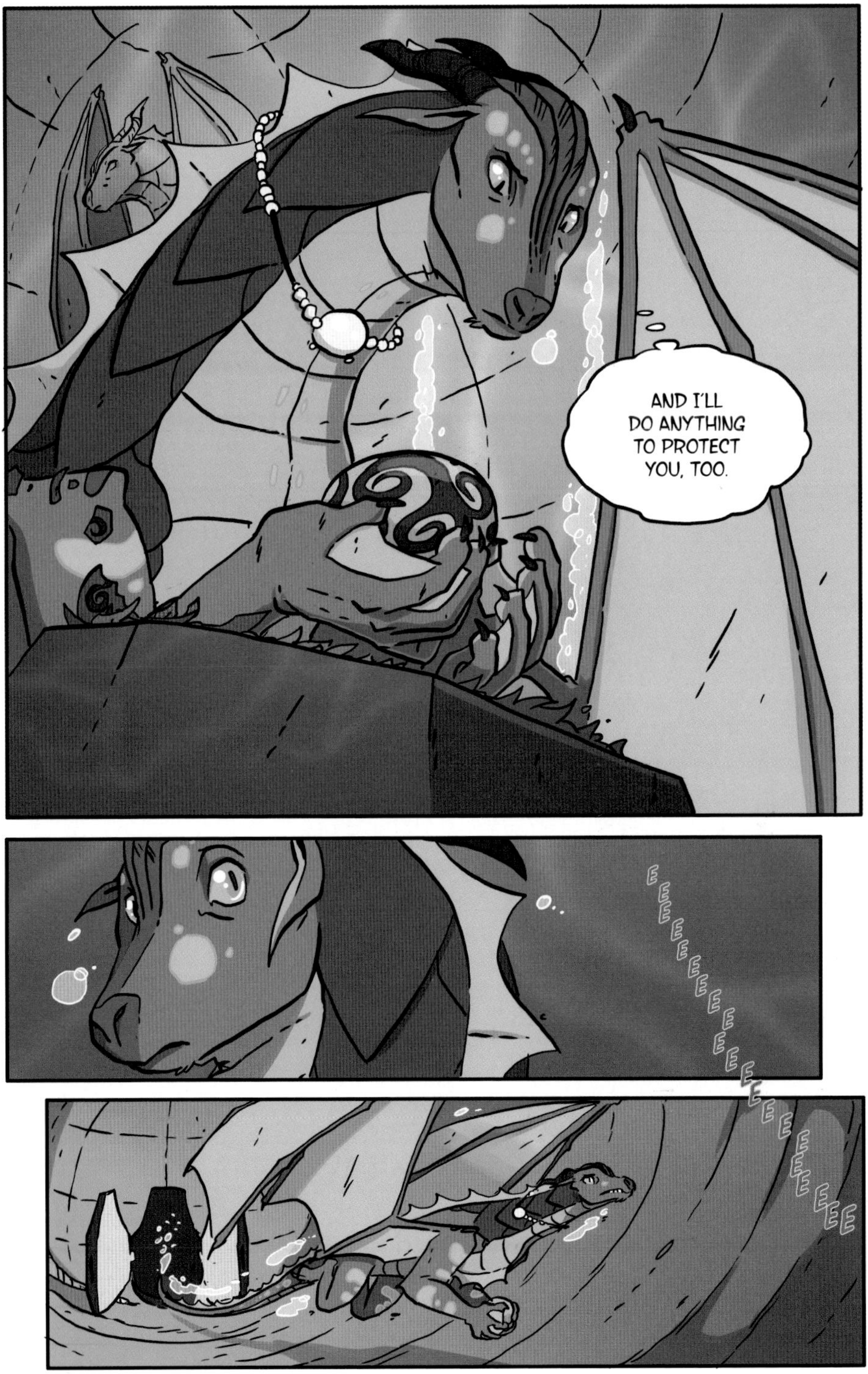
AND I'LL DO ANYTHING TO PROTECT YOU, TOO.
EEEEEEEEEEEEEEEEEEEEE

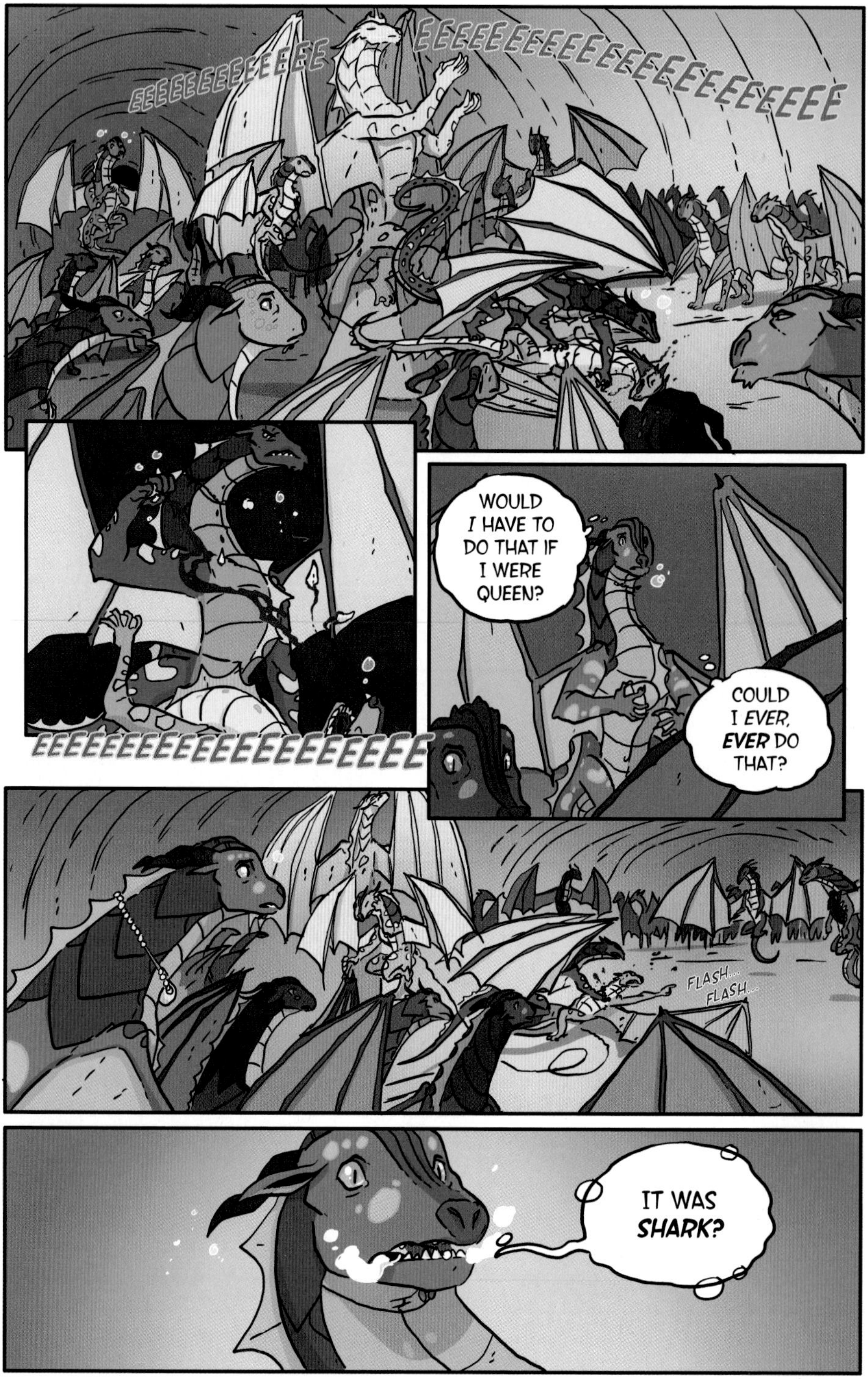
EEEEEEEEEEEEEE
EEEEEEEEEEEEEEEEEEEEEEEEEE
EEEEEEEEEEEEEEEEEEEEEE
WOULD I HAVE TO DO THAT IF I WERE QUEEN?
COULD I *EVER*, ***EVER*** DO THAT?
FLASH... FLASH...
IT WAS **SHARK?**

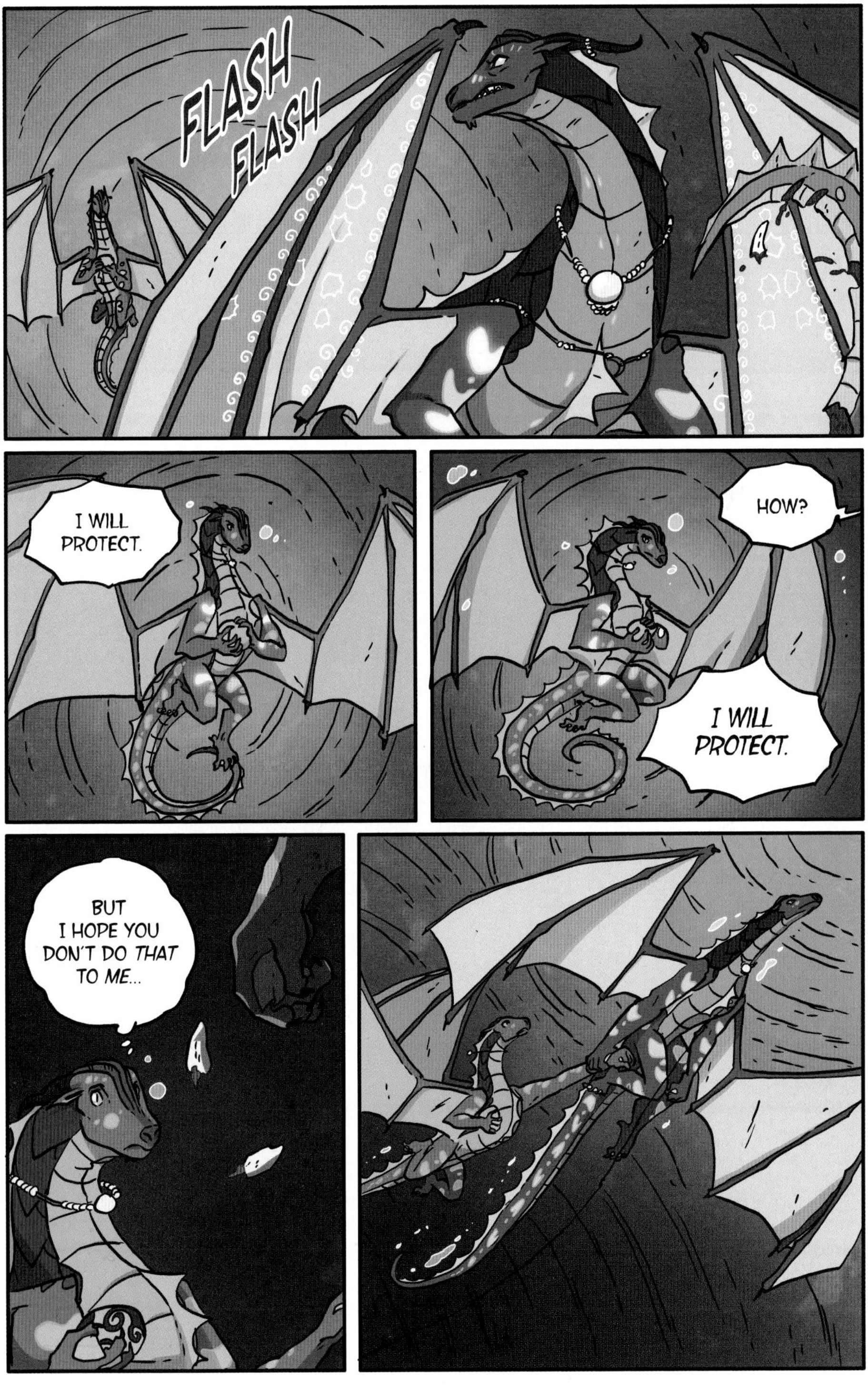
FLASH
FLASH
I WILL PROTECT.
HOW?
I WILL PROTECT.
BUT I HOPE YOU DON'T DO *THAT* TO *ME*...

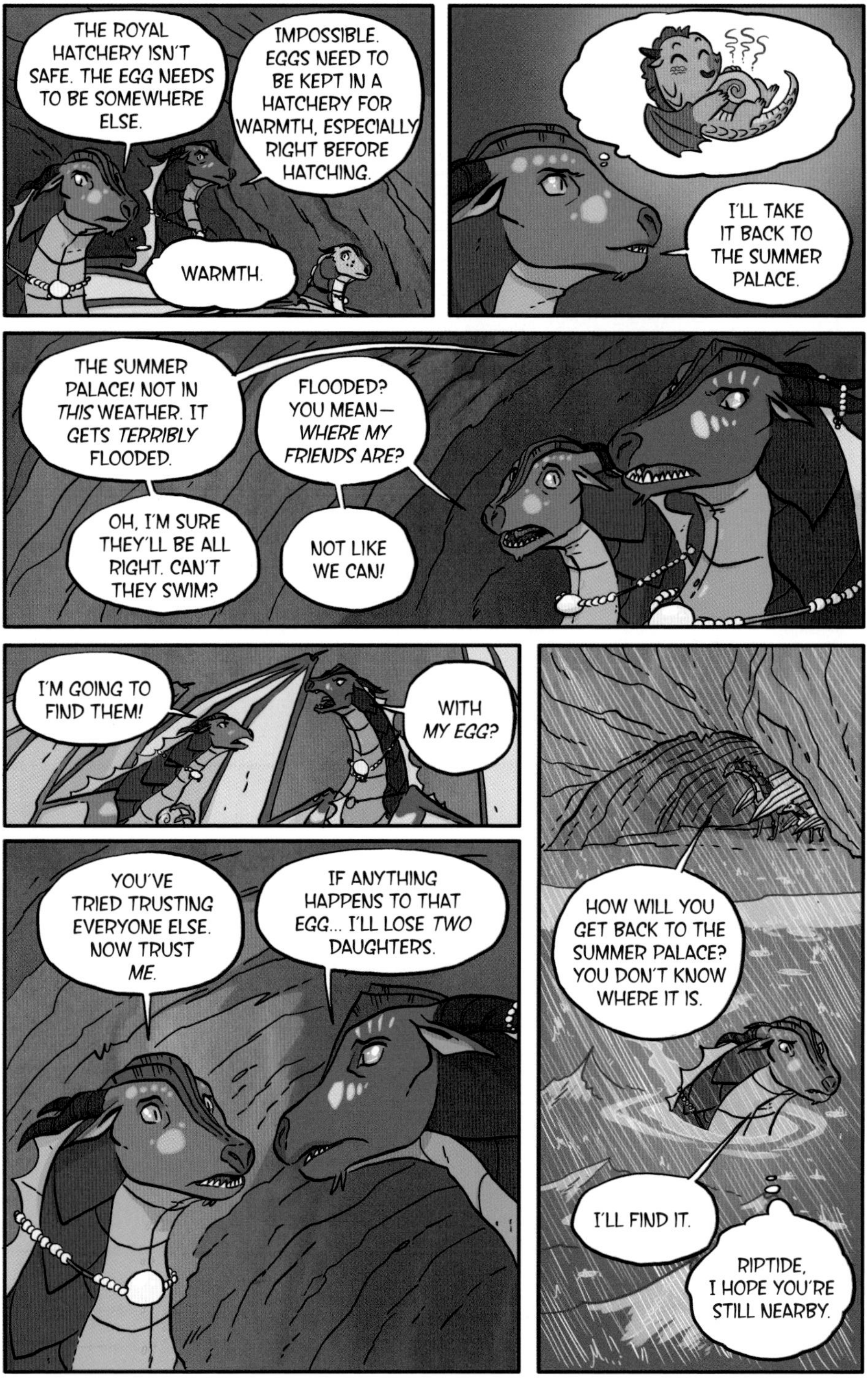
THE ROYAL HATCHERY ISN'T SAFE. THE EGG NEEDS TO BE SOMEWHERE ELSE.
IMPOSSIBLE. EGGS NEED TO BE KEPT IN A HATCHERY FOR WARMTH, ESPECIALLY RIGHT BEFORE HATCHING.
WARMTH.
I'LL TAKE IT BACK TO THE SUMMER PALACE.
THE SUMMER PALACE! NOT IN *THIS* WEATHER. IT GETS *TERRIBLY* FLOODED.
FLOODED? YOU MEAN— *WHERE MY FRIENDS ARE?*
OH, I'M SURE THEY'LL BE ALL RIGHT. CAN'T THEY SWIM?
NOT LIKE WE CAN!
I'M GOING TO FIND THEM!
WITH *MY EGG?*
YOU'VE TRIED TRUSTING EVERYONE ELSE. NOW TRUST *ME.*
IF ANYTHING HAPPENS TO THAT EGG... I'LL LOSE *TWO* DAUGHTERS.
HOW WILL YOU GET BACK TO THE SUMMER PALACE? YOU DON'T KNOW WHERE IT IS.
I'LL FIND IT.
RIPTIDE, I HOPE YOU'RE STILL NEARBY.

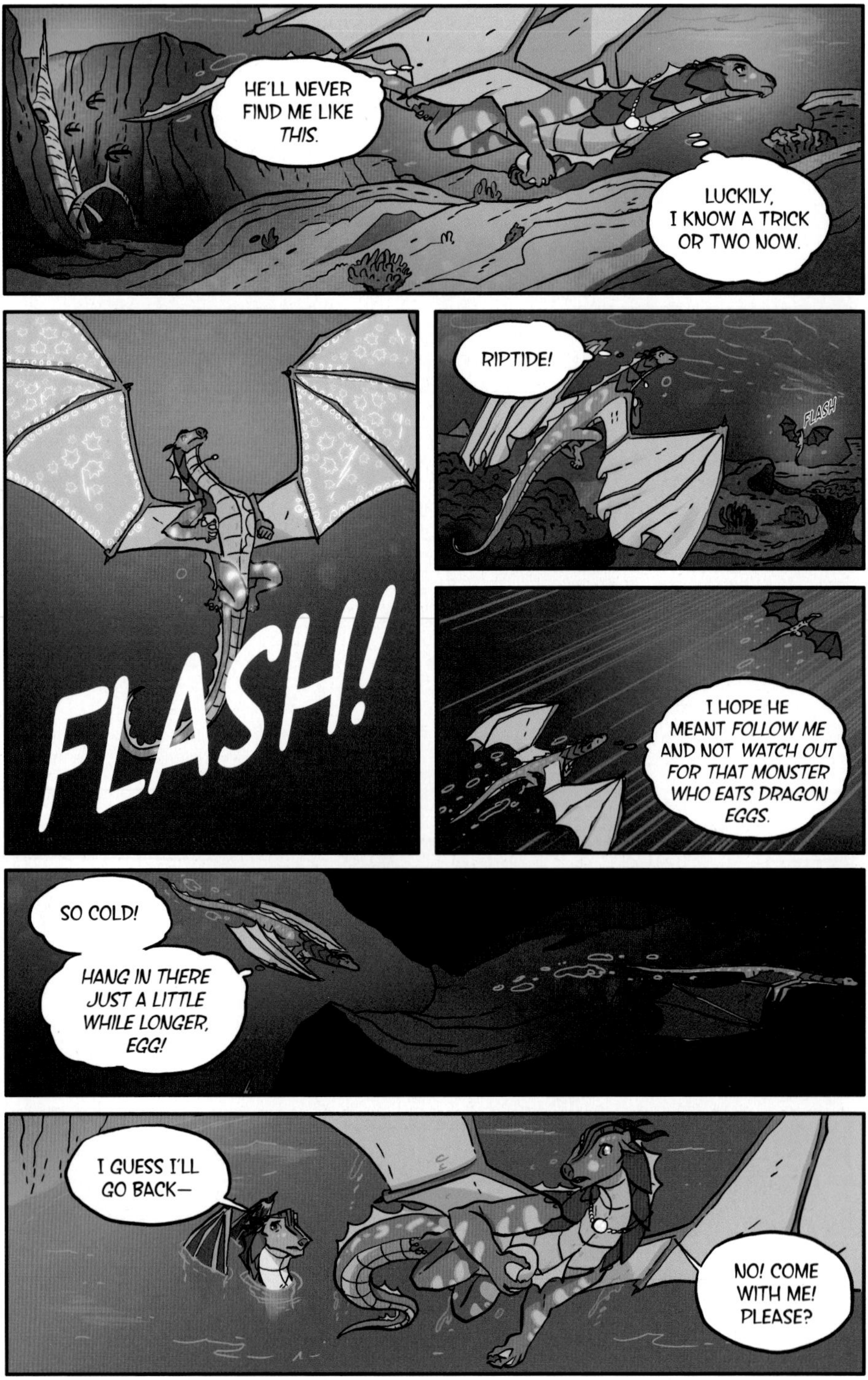
HE'LL NEVER FIND ME LIKE *THIS.*
LUCKILY, I KNOW A TRICK OR TWO NOW.
FLASH!
RIPTIDE!
FLASH
I HOPE HE MEANT *FOLLOW ME* AND NOT *WATCH OUT FOR THAT MONSTER WHO EATS DRAGON EGGS.*
SO COLD!
HANG IN THERE JUST A LITTLE WHILE LONGER, EGG!
I GUESS I'LL GO BACK—
NO! COME WITH ME! PLEASE?

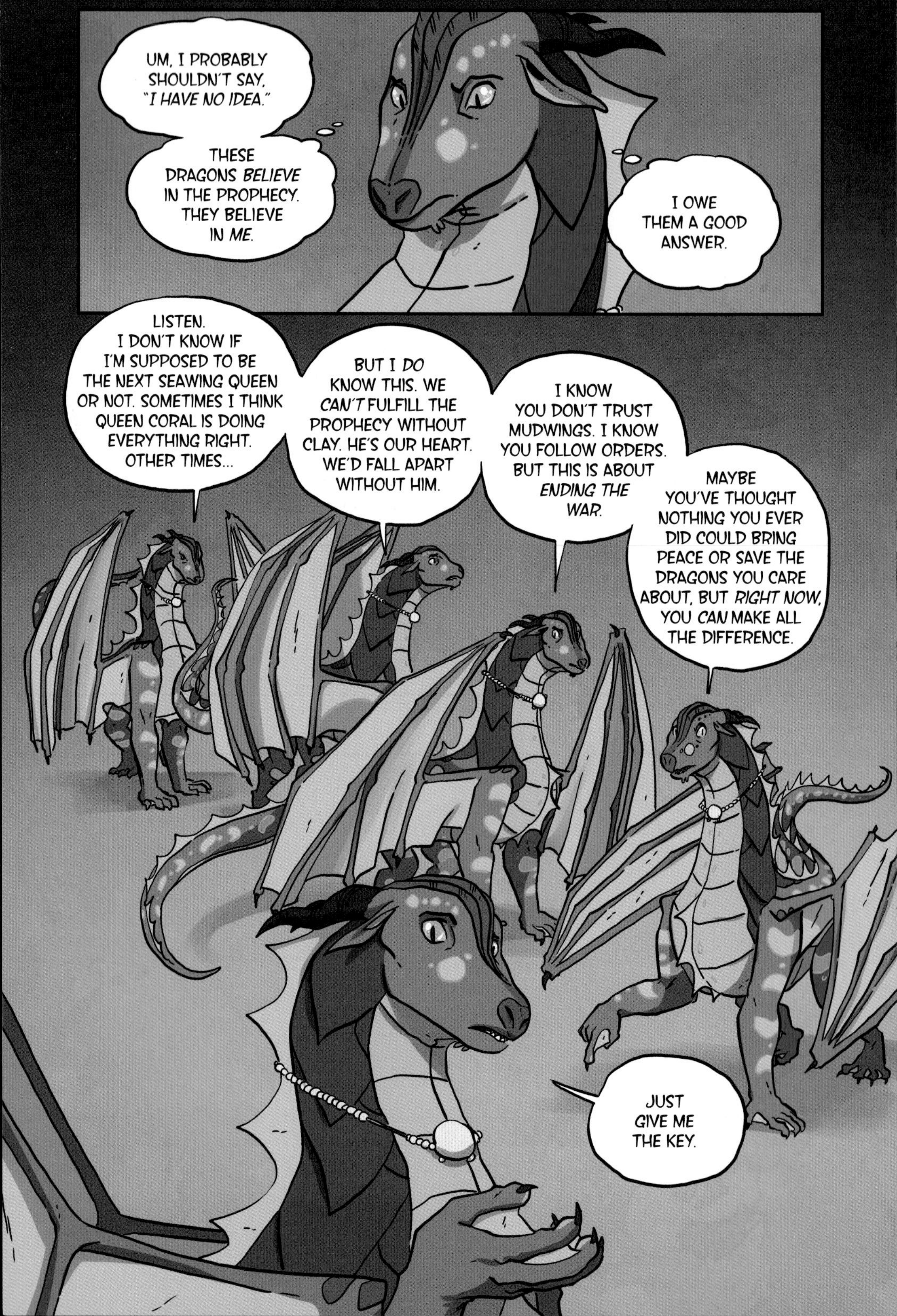
UM, I PROBABLY SHOULDN'T SAY, "*I HAVE NO IDEA.*"
THESE DRAGONS *BELIEVE* IN THE PROPHECY. THEY BELIEVE IN *ME*.
I OWE THEM A GOOD ANSWER.
LISTEN. I DON'T KNOW IF I'M SUPPOSED TO BE THE NEXT SEAWING QUEEN OR NOT. SOMETIMES I THINK QUEEN CORAL IS DOING EVERYTHING RIGHT. OTHER TIMES...
BUT I *DO* KNOW THIS. WE *CAN'T* FULFILL THE PROPHECY WITHOUT CLAY. HE'S OUR HEART. WE'D FALL APART WITHOUT HIM.
I KNOW YOU DON'T TRUST MUDWINGS. I KNOW YOU FOLLOW ORDERS. BUT THIS IS ABOUT *ENDING THE WAR*.
MAYBE YOU'VE THOUGHT NOTHING YOU EVER DID COULD BRING PEACE OR SAVE THE DRAGONS YOU CARE ABOUT, BUT *RIGHT NOW*, YOU *CAN* MAKE ALL THE DIFFERENCE.
JUST GIVE ME THE KEY.

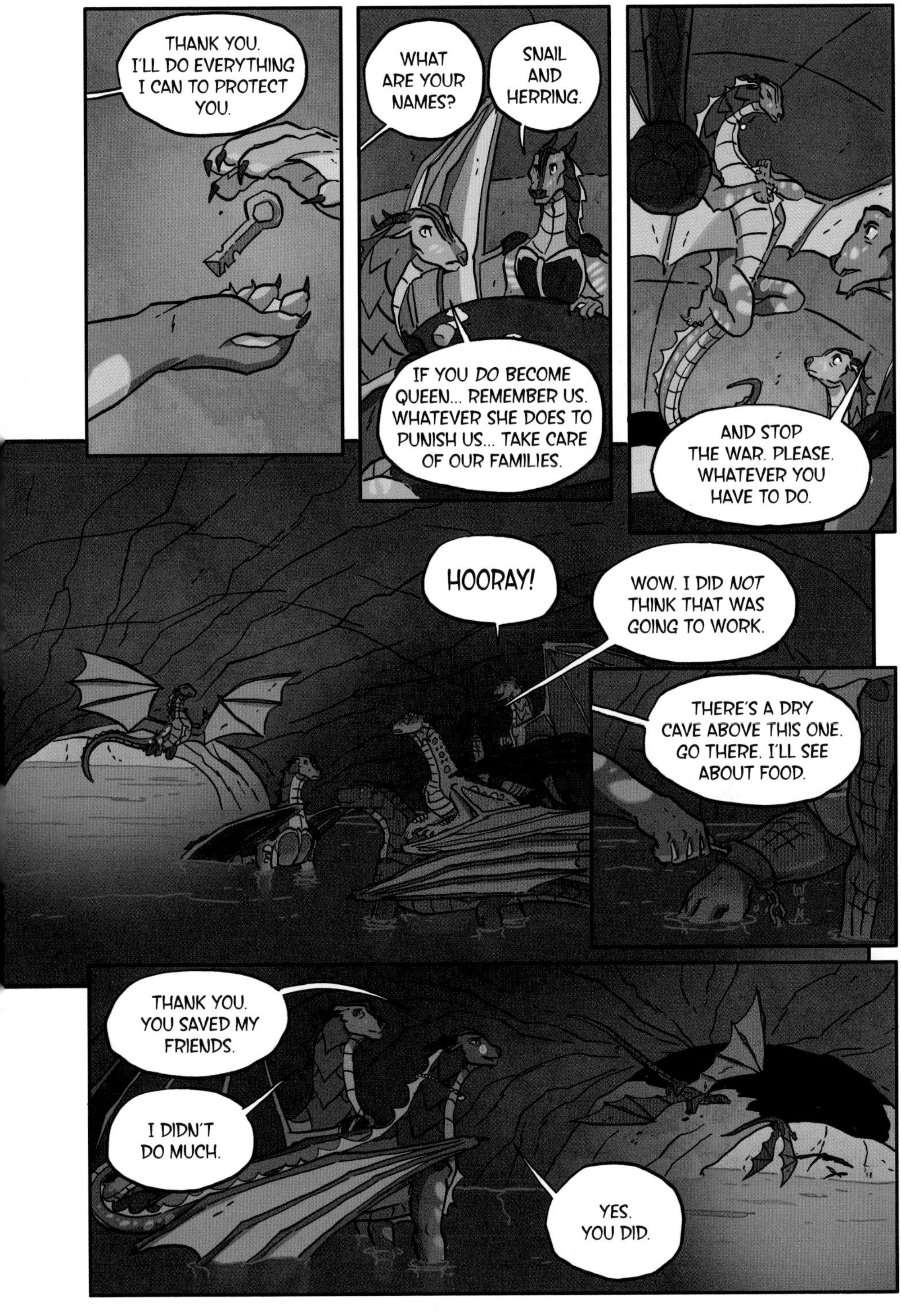
THANK YOU. I'LL DO EVERYTHING I CAN TO PROTECT YOU.
WHAT ARE YOUR NAMES?
SNAIL AND HERRING.
IF YOU *DO* BECOME QUEEN... REMEMBER US. WHATEVER SHE DOES TO PUNISH US... TAKE CARE OF OUR FAMILIES.
AND STOP THE WAR. PLEASE. WHATEVER YOU HAVE TO DO.
HOORAY!
WOW. I DID *NOT* THINK THAT WAS GOING TO WORK.
THERE'S A DRY CAVE ABOVE THIS ONE. GO THERE. I'LL SEE ABOUT FOOD.
THANK YOU. YOU SAVED MY FRIENDS.
I DIDN'T DO MUCH.
YES. YOU DID.

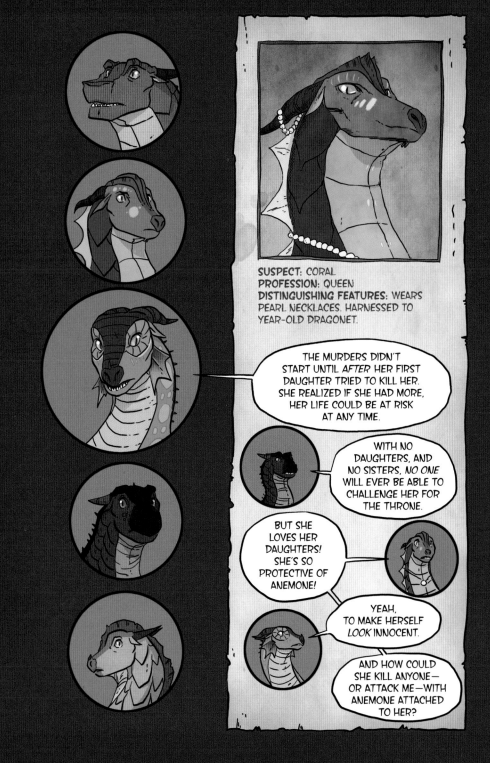

SUSPECT: CORAL
PROFESSION: QUEEN
DISTINGUISHING FEATURES: WEARS
PEARL NECKLACES. HARNESSED TO
YEAR-OLD DRAGONET.

THE MURDERS DIDN'T START UNTIL *AFTER* HER FIRST DAUGHTER TRIED TO KILL HER. SHE REALIZED IF SHE HAD MORE, HER LIFE COULD BE AT RISK AT ANY TIME.

WITH NO DAUGHTERS, AND NO SISTERS, *NO ONE* WILL EVER BE ABLE TO CHALLENGE HER FOR THE THRONE.

BUT SHE LOVES HER DAUGHTERS! SHE'S SO PROTECTIVE OF ANEMONE!

YEAH, TO MAKE HERSELF *LOOK* INNOCENT.

AND HOW COULD SHE KILL ANYONE — OR ATTACK ME — WITH ANEMONE ATTACHED TO HER?

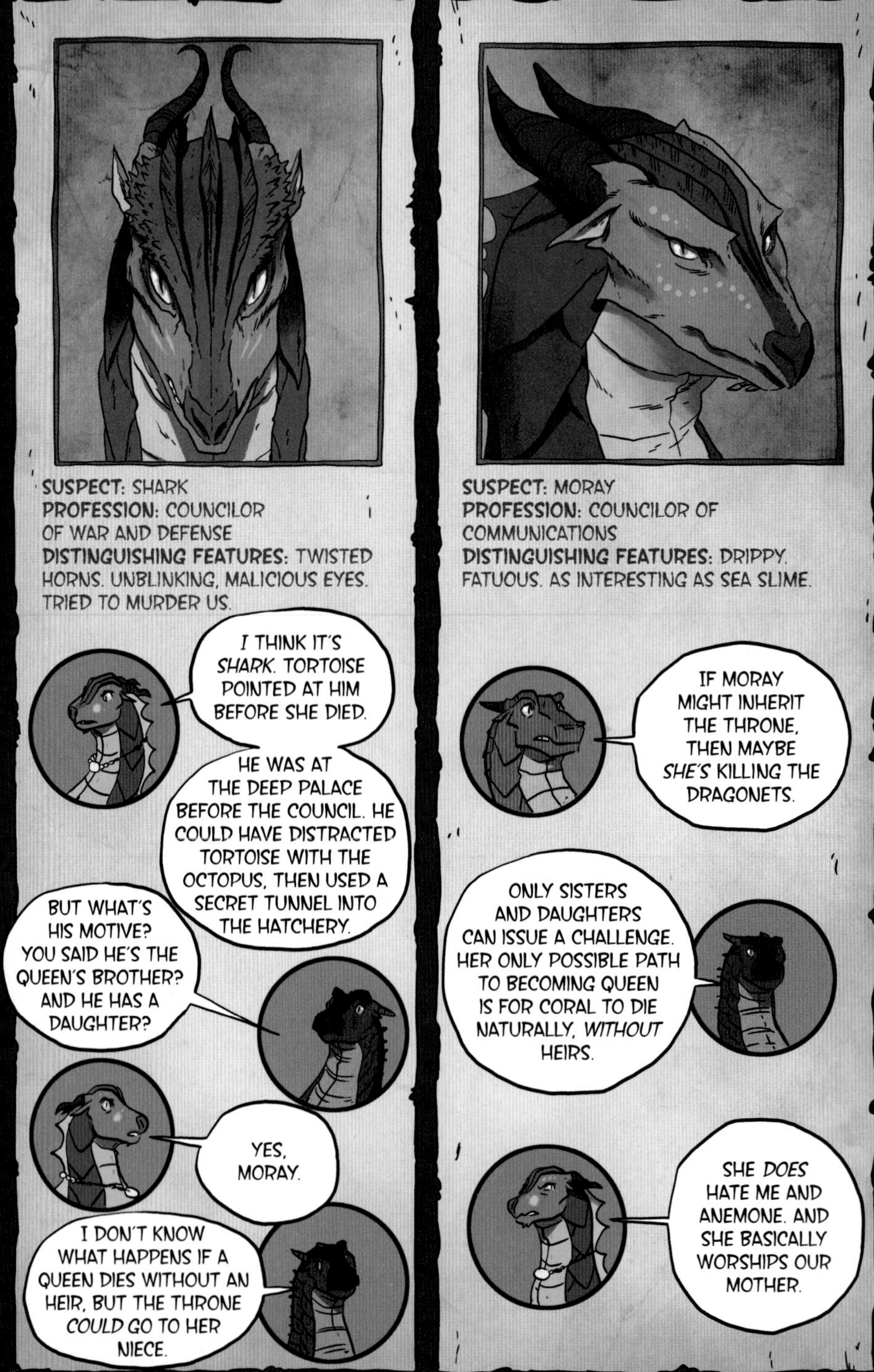

SUSPECT: SHARK
PROFESSION: COUNCILOR
OF WAR AND DEFENSE
DISTINGUISHING FEATURES: TWISTED
HORNS. UNBLINKING, MALICIOUS EYES.
TRIED TO MURDER US.

SUSPECT: MORAY
PROFESSION: COUNCILOR OF
COMMUNICATIONS
DISTINGUISHING FEATURES: DRIPPY.
FATUOUS. AS INTERESTING AS SEA SLIME.

I THINK IT'S *SHARK*. TORTOISE POINTED AT HIM BEFORE SHE DIED.

HE WAS AT THE DEEP PALACE BEFORE THE COUNCIL. HE COULD HAVE DISTRACTED TORTOISE WITH THE OCTOPUS, THEN USED A SECRET TUNNEL INTO THE HATCHERY.

BUT WHAT'S HIS MOTIVE? YOU SAID HE'S THE QUEEN'S BROTHER? AND HE HAS A DAUGHTER?

YES, MORAY.

I DON'T KNOW WHAT HAPPENS IF A QUEEN DIES WITHOUT AN HEIR, BUT THE THRONE *COULD* GO TO HER NIECE.

IF MORAY MIGHT INHERIT THE THRONE, THEN MAYBE *SHE'S* KILLING THE DRAGONETS.

ONLY SISTERS AND DAUGHTERS CAN ISSUE A CHALLENGE. HER ONLY POSSIBLE PATH TO BECOMING QUEEN IS FOR CORAL TO DIE NATURALLY, *WITHOUT* HEIRS.

SHE *DOES* HATE ME AND ANEMONE. AND SHE BASICALLY WORSHIPS OUR MOTHER.

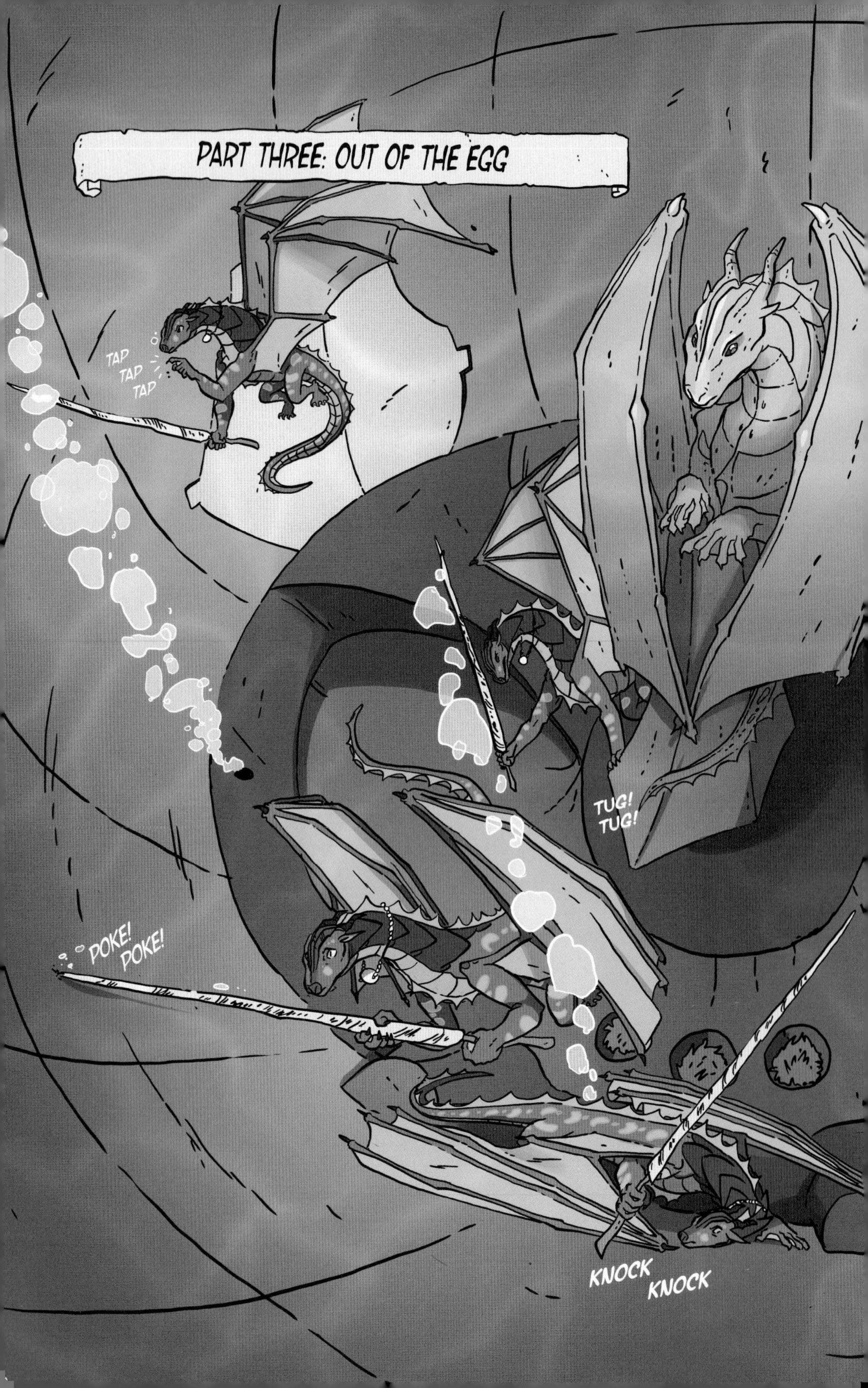
PART THREE: OUT OF THE EGG
TAP TAP TAP
TUG! TUG!
POKE! POKE!
KNOCK KNOCK

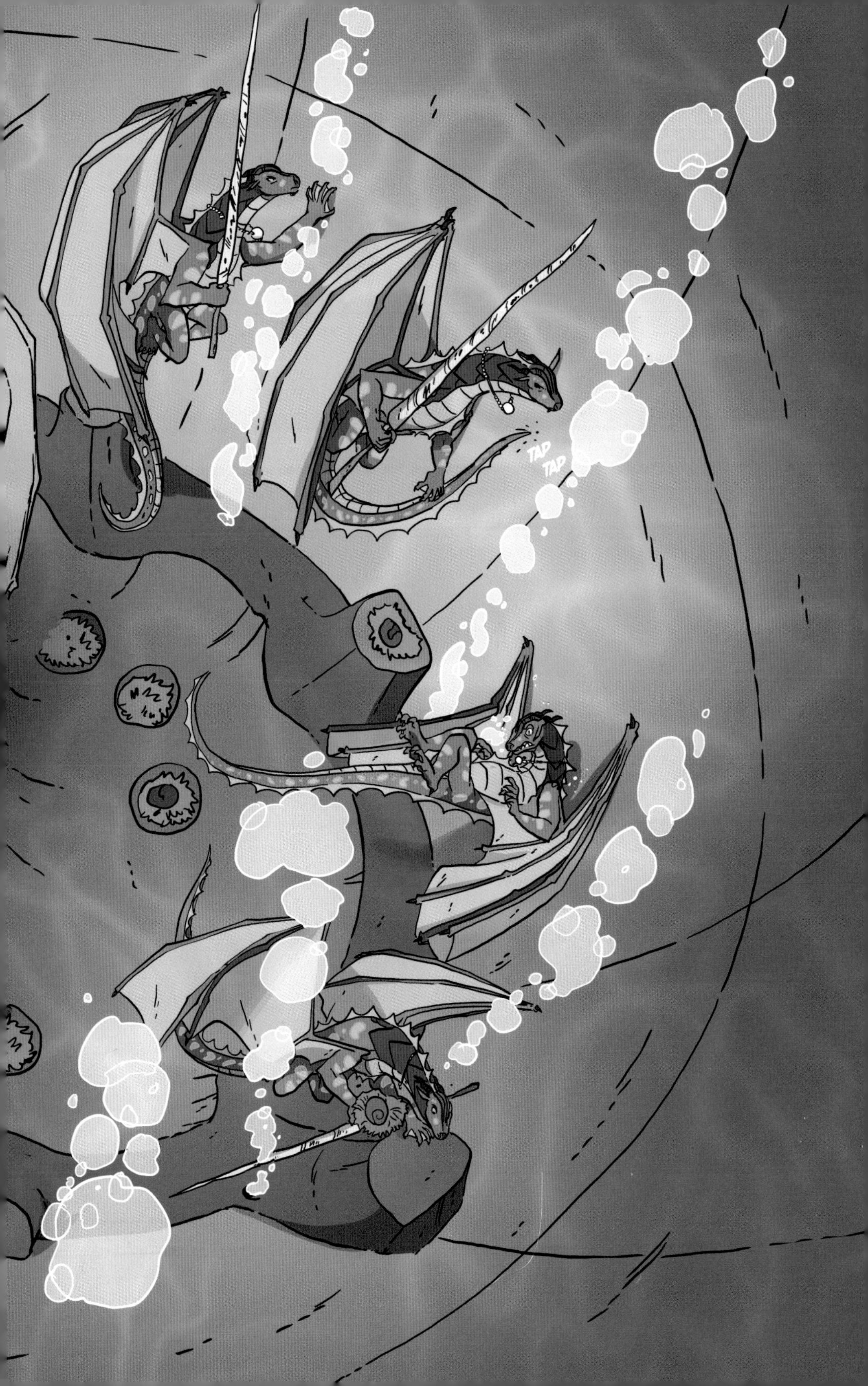
TAP
TAP

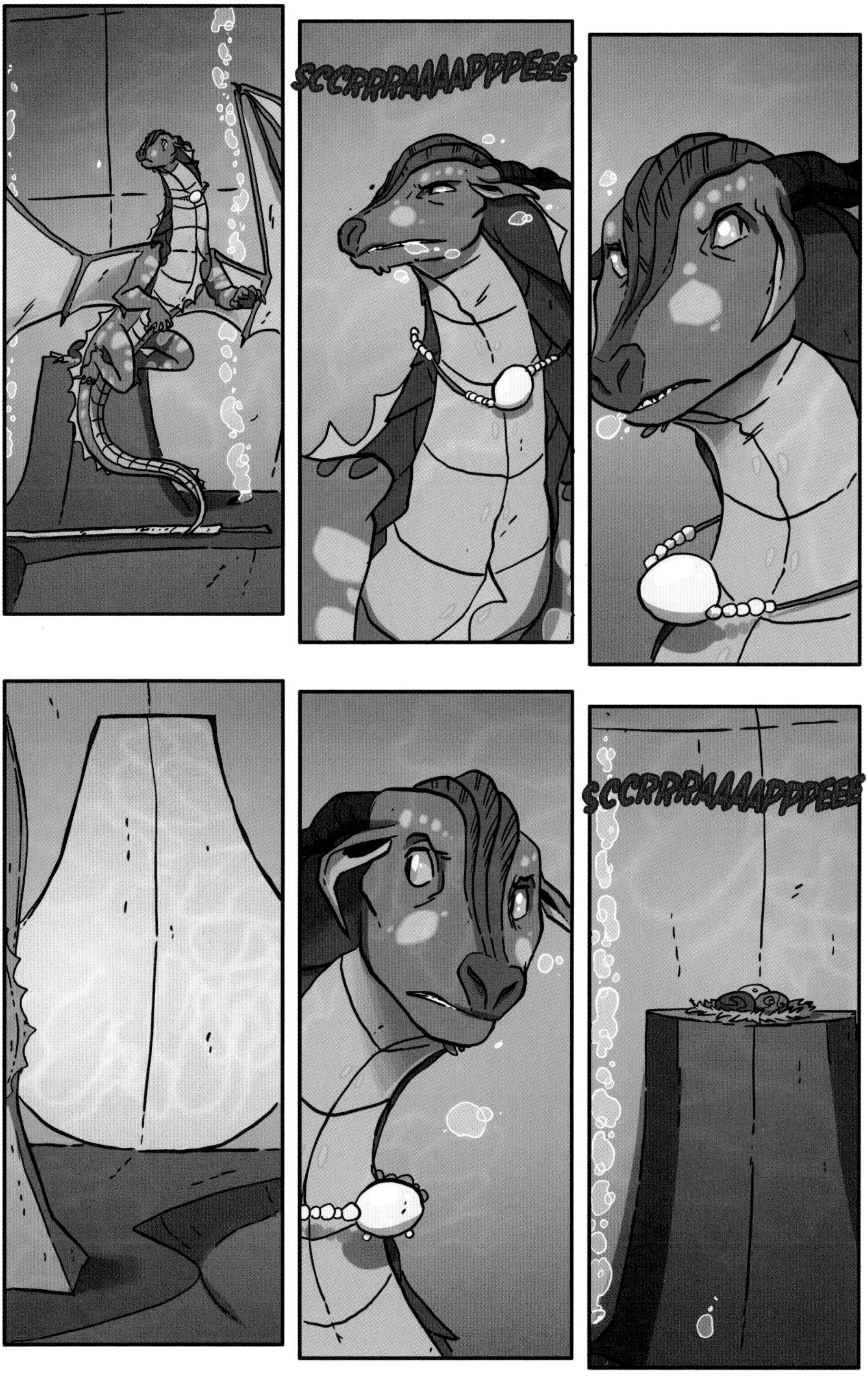
SCCRRRAAAAPPPEEE
SCCRRRAAAAPPPEEE

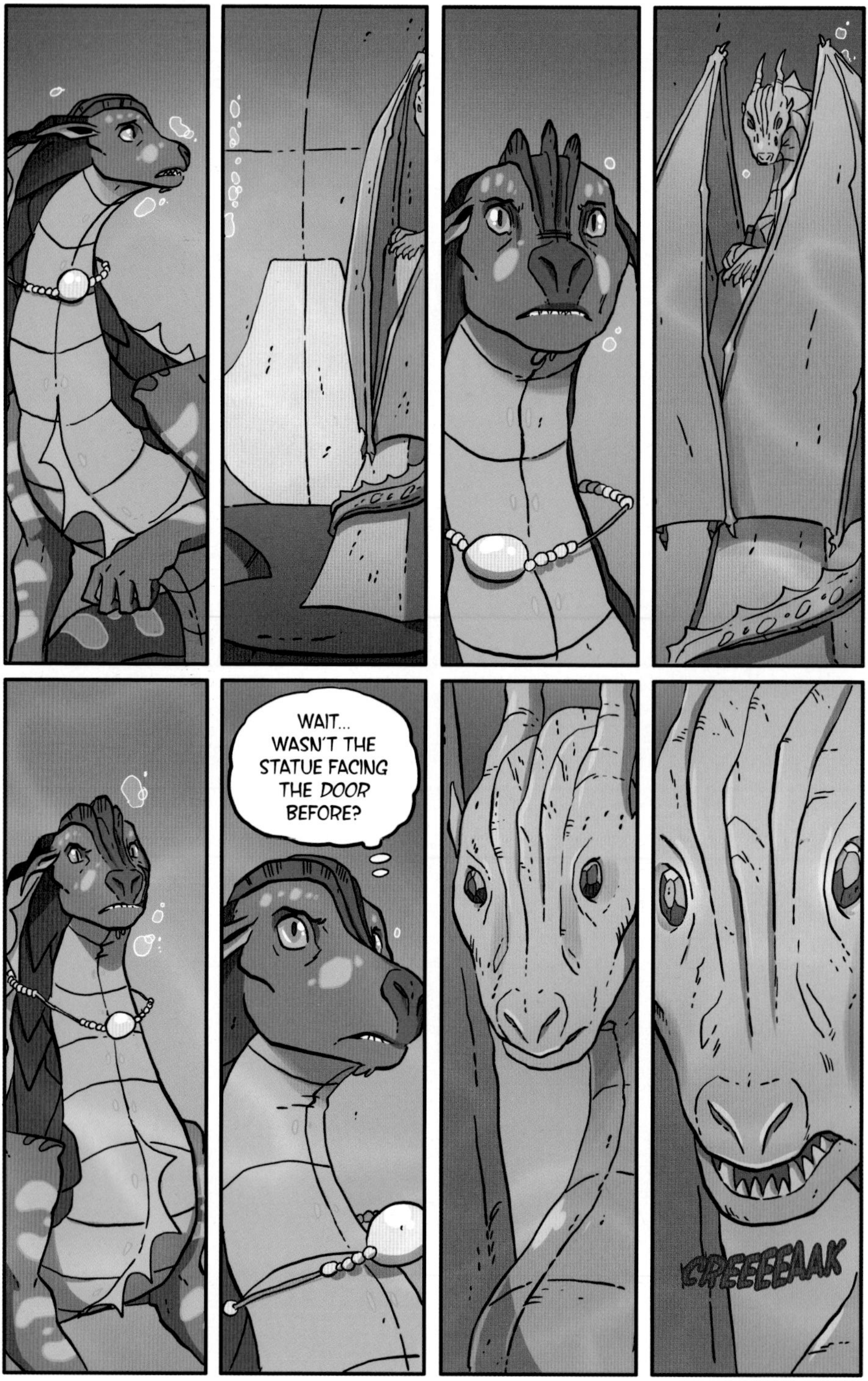
WAIT... WASN'T THE STATUE FACING THE *DOOR* BEFORE?
CREEEEAAK

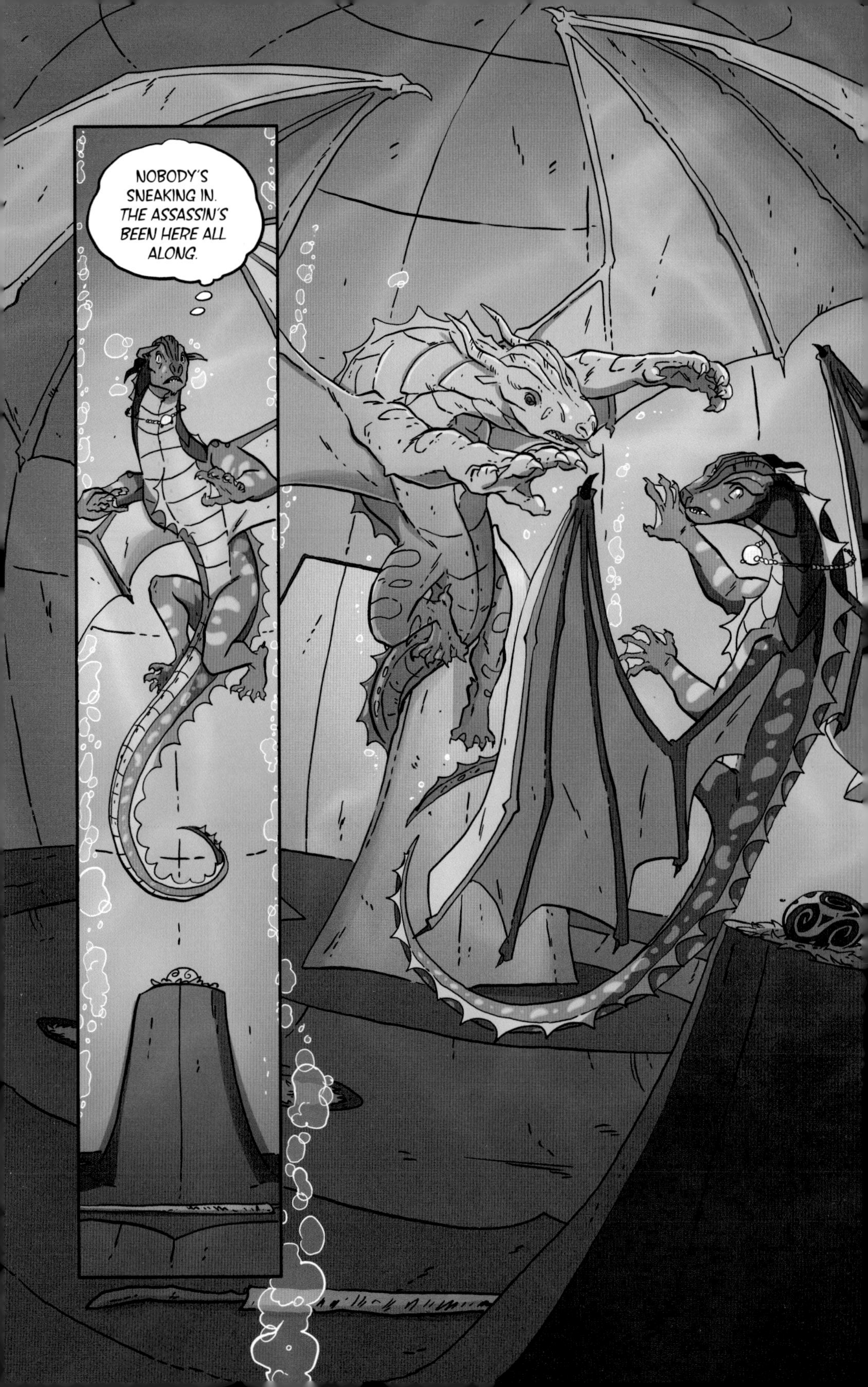
NOBODY'S SNEAKING IN. *THE ASSASSIN'S* BEEN HERE ALL ALONG.

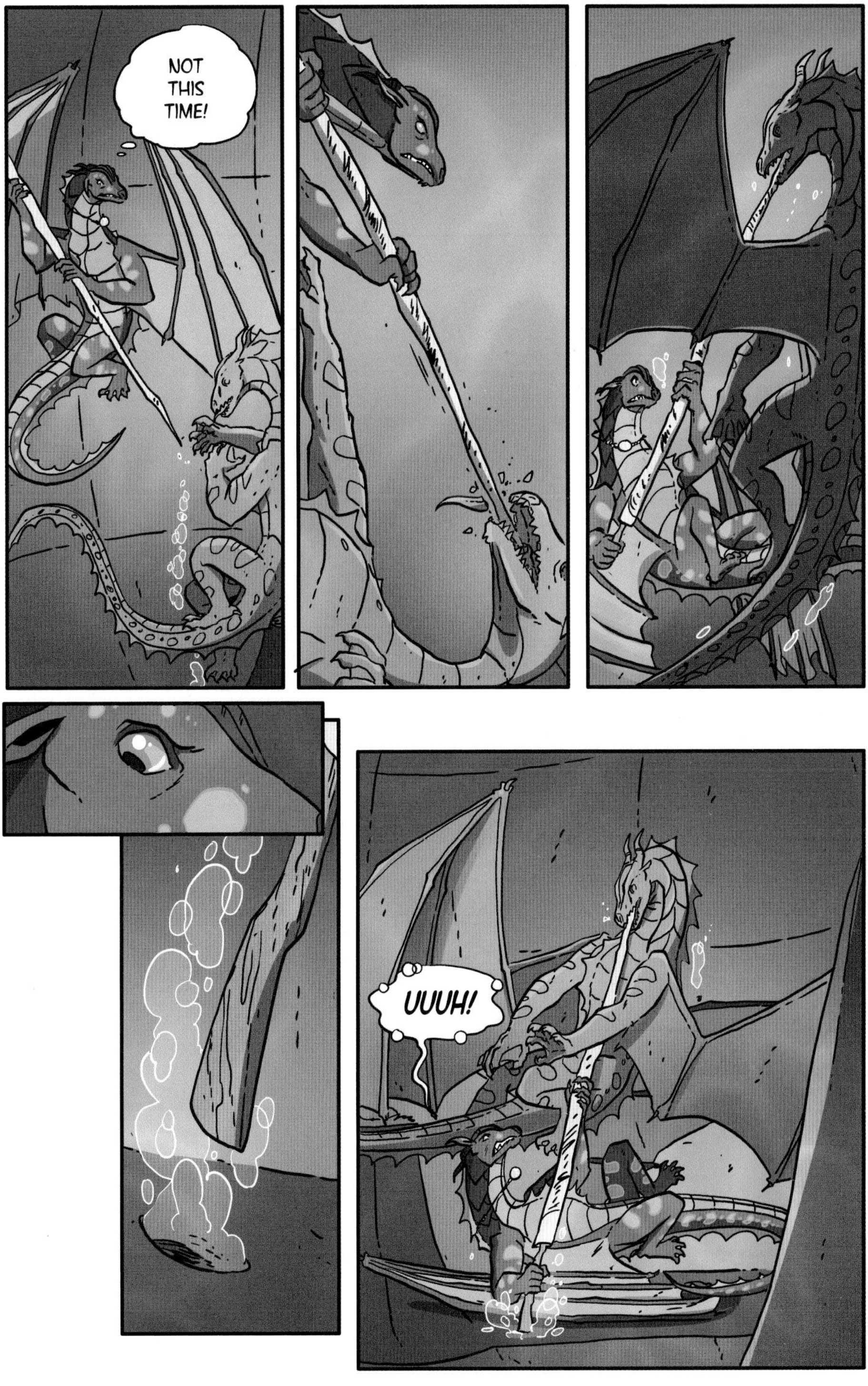
NOT THIS TIME!
UUUH!

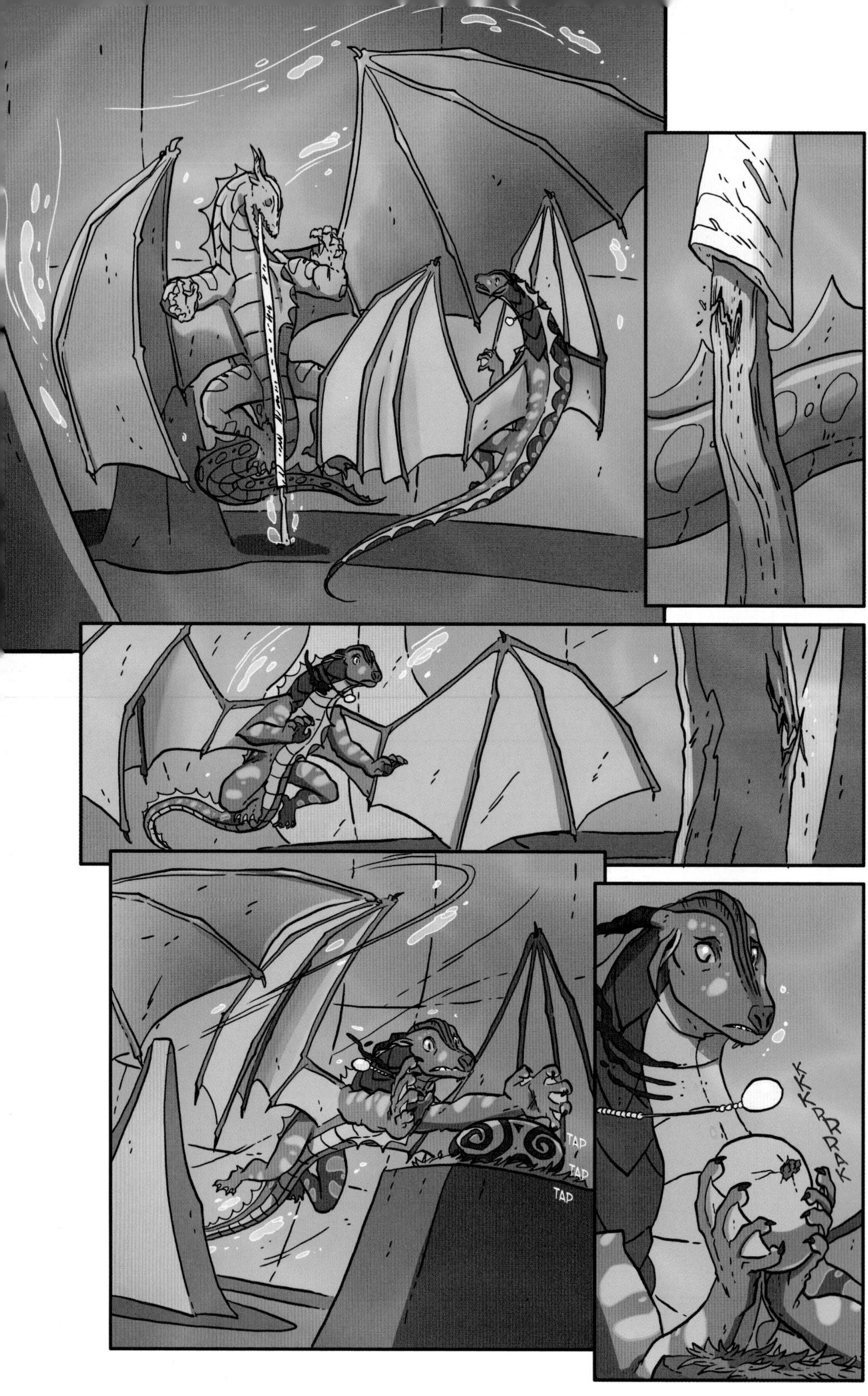
TAP
TAP
TAP
KKKRRRAK

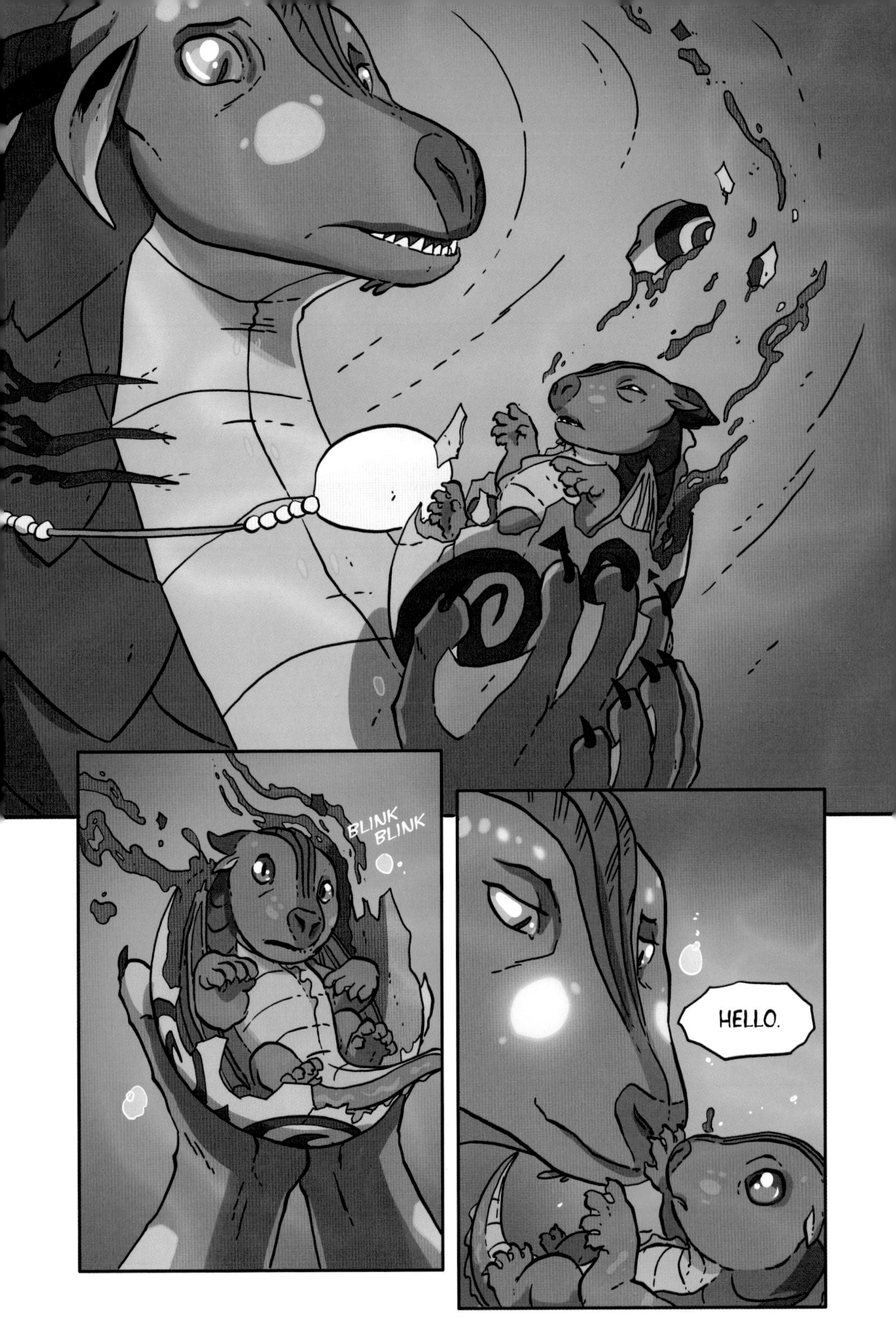
BLINK
BLINK
HELLO.

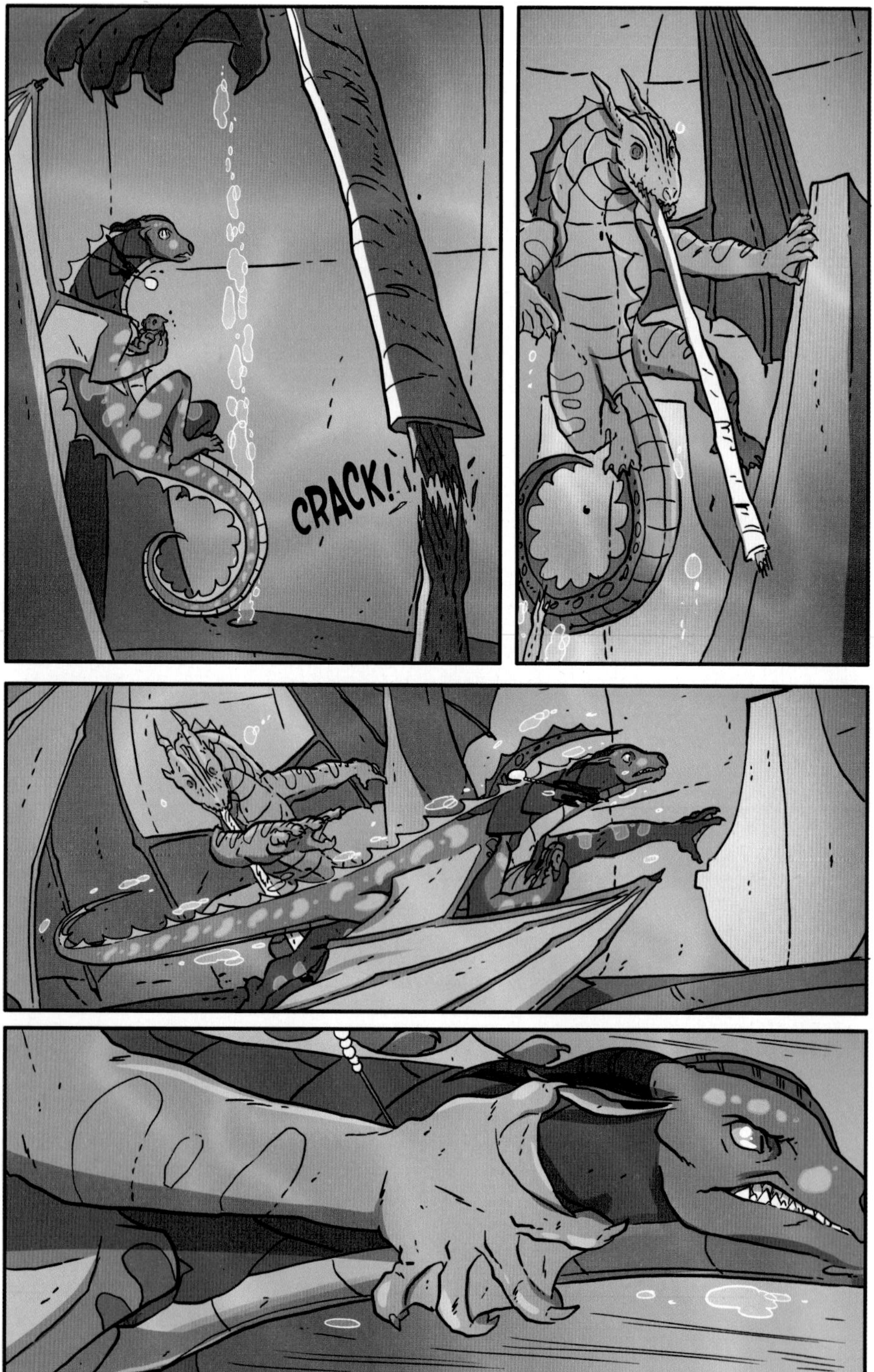
CRACK!

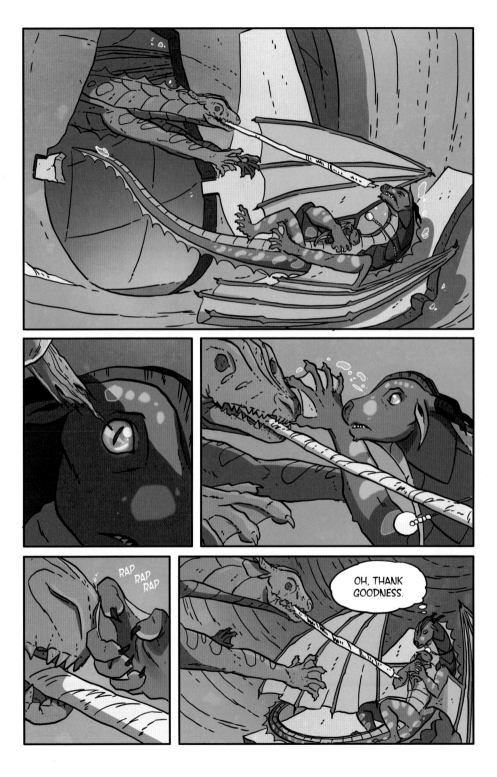

SUSPECT: ORCA
PROFESSION: PRINCESS, SECRET ANIMUS
DISTINGUISHING FEATURES: GREAT AT SCULPTING. DEAD.

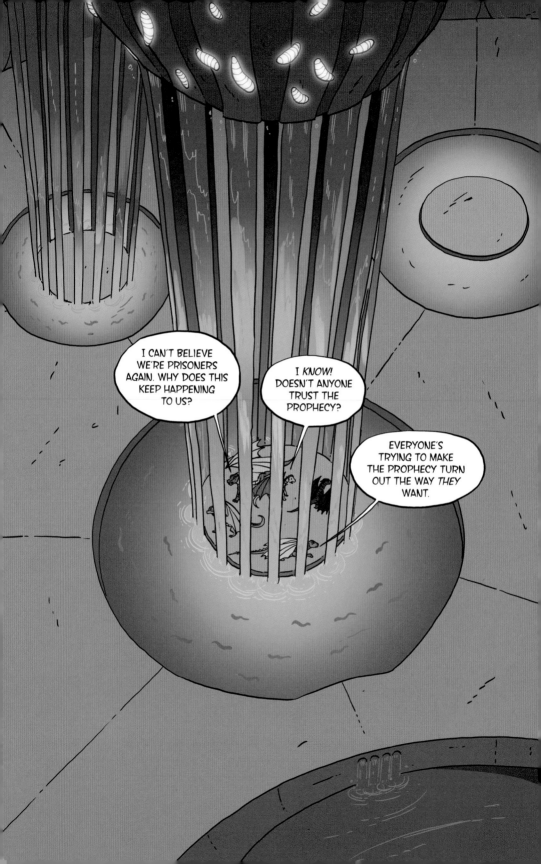

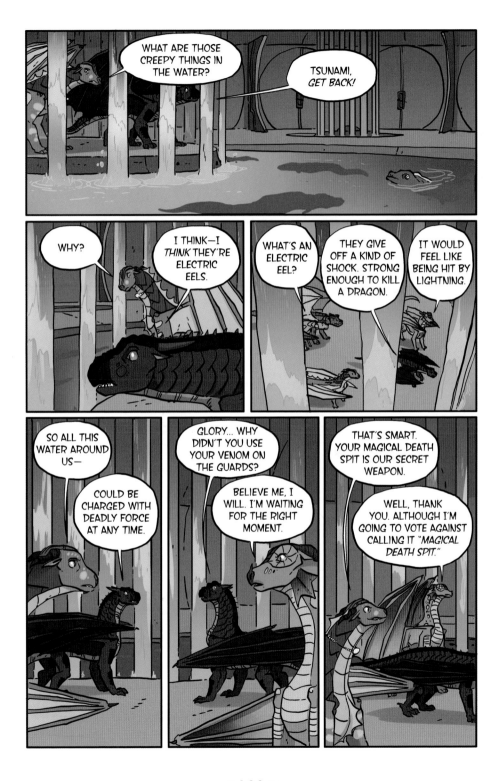

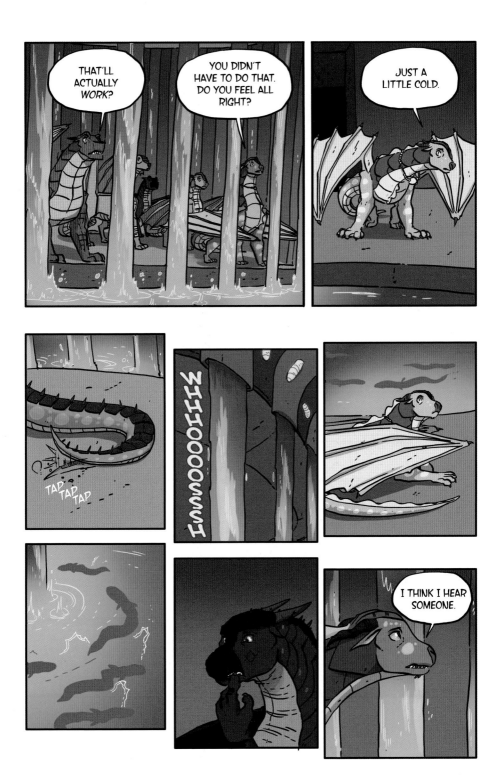

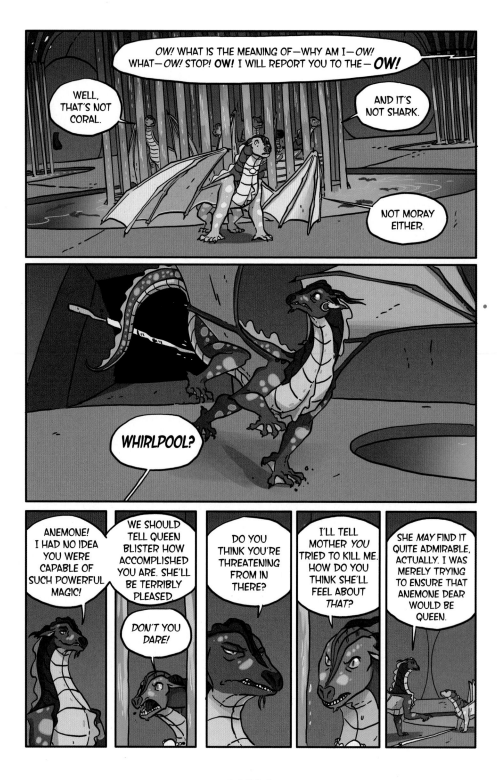

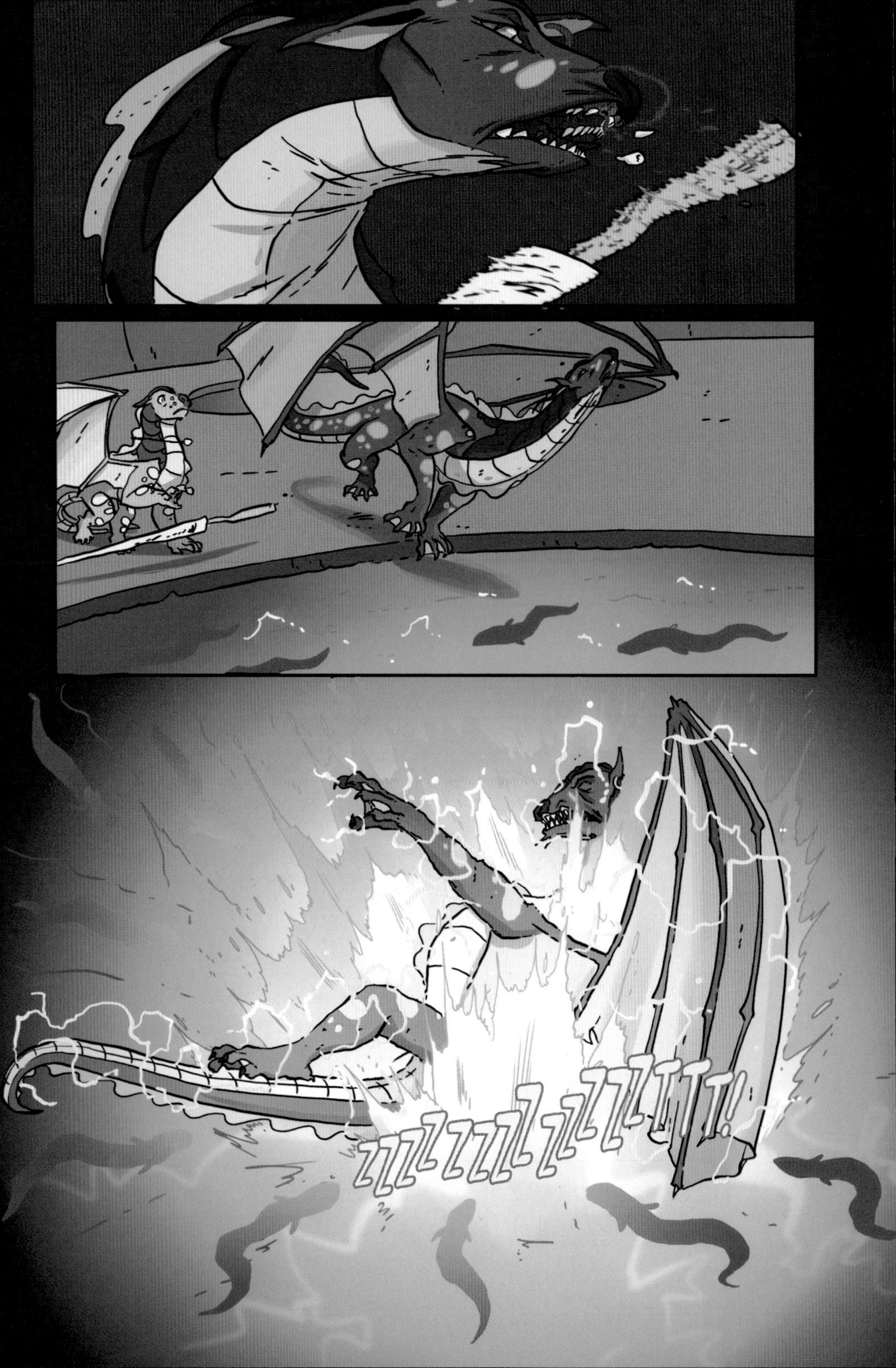
ZZZZZZZZZZZZZZZZTTTT!

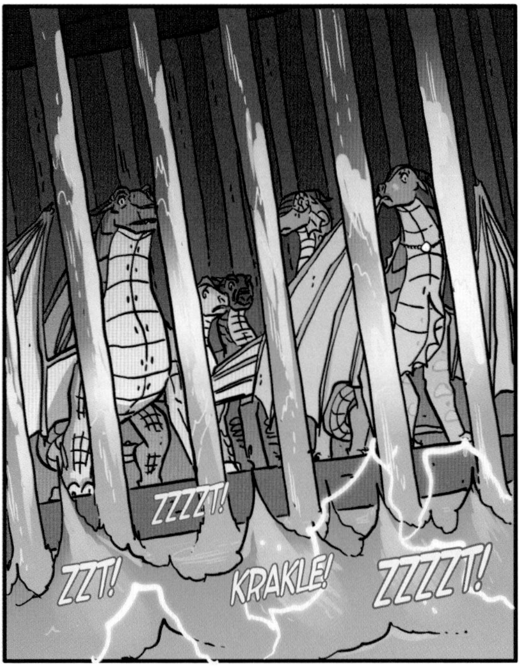
ZZZZT!
ZZT!
KRAKLE!
ZZZZT!

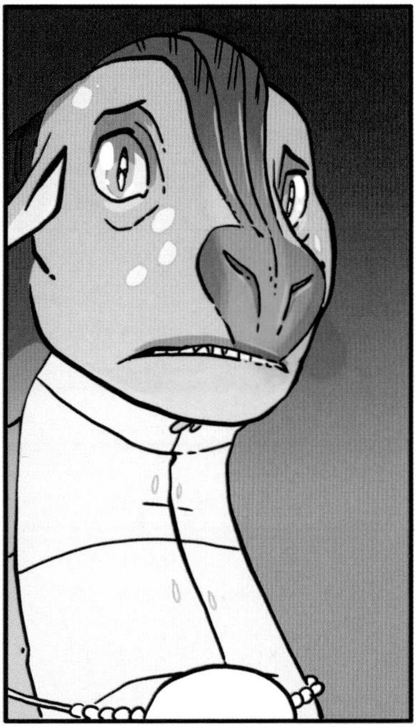

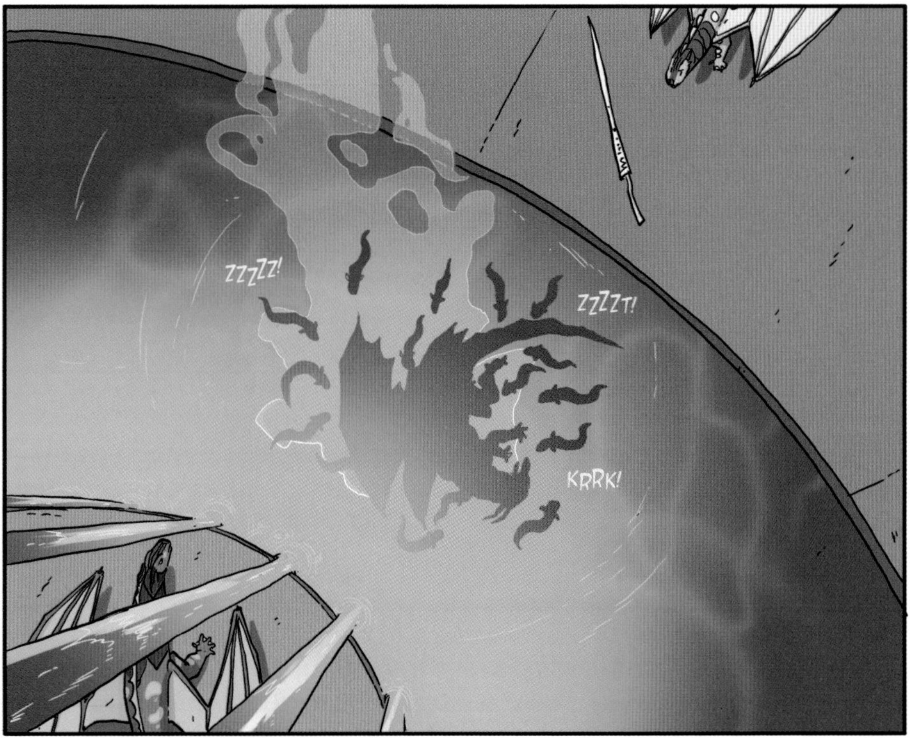
ZZZZZ!
ZZZZT!
KRRK!

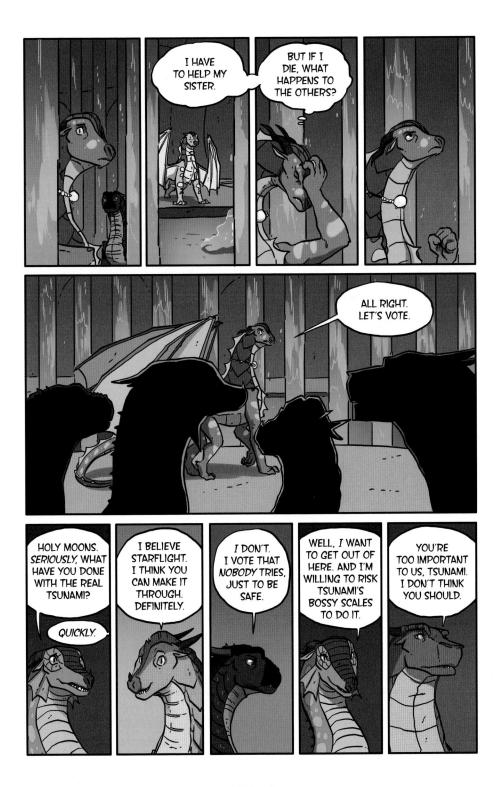

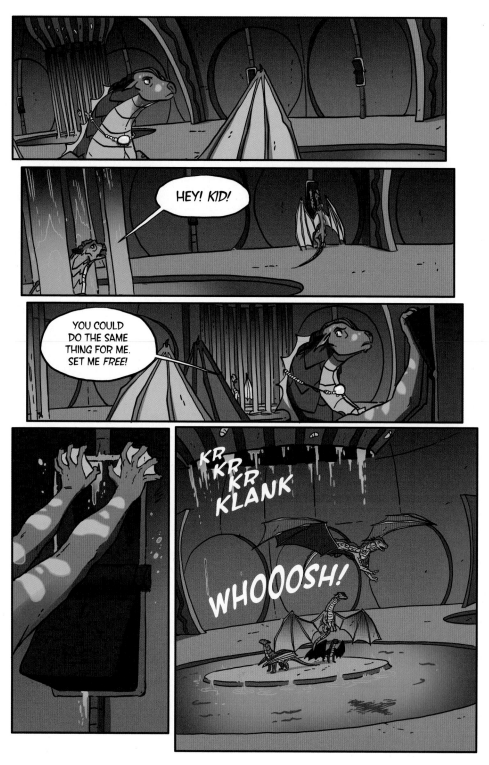

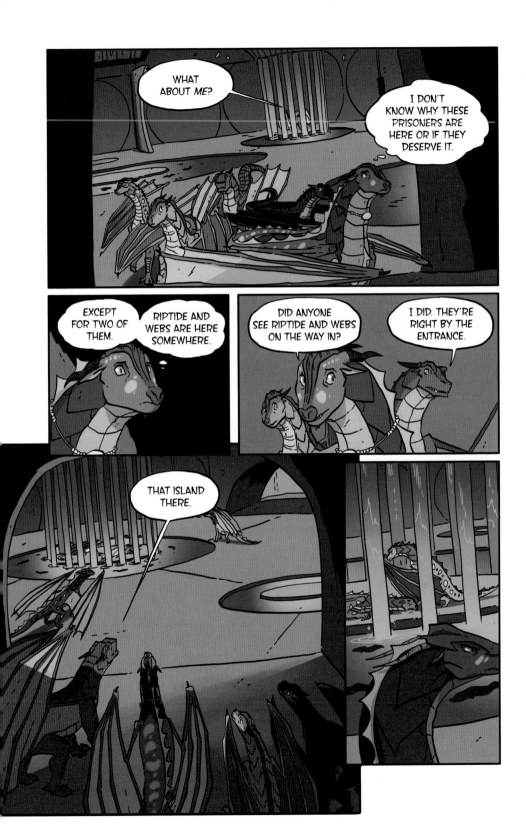

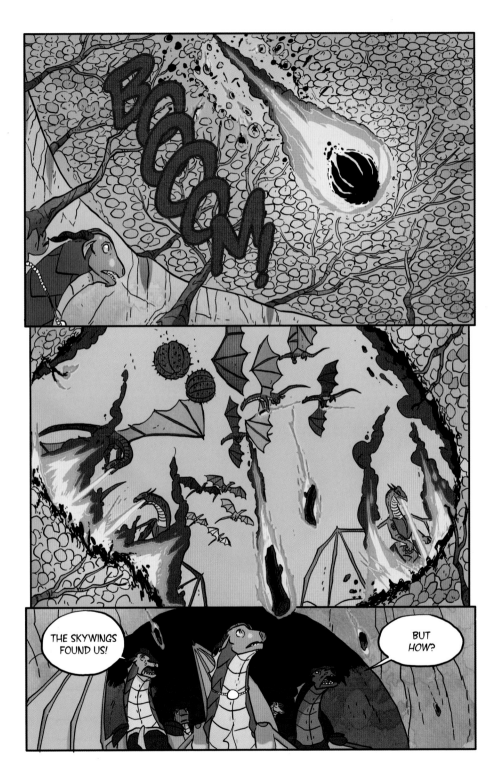

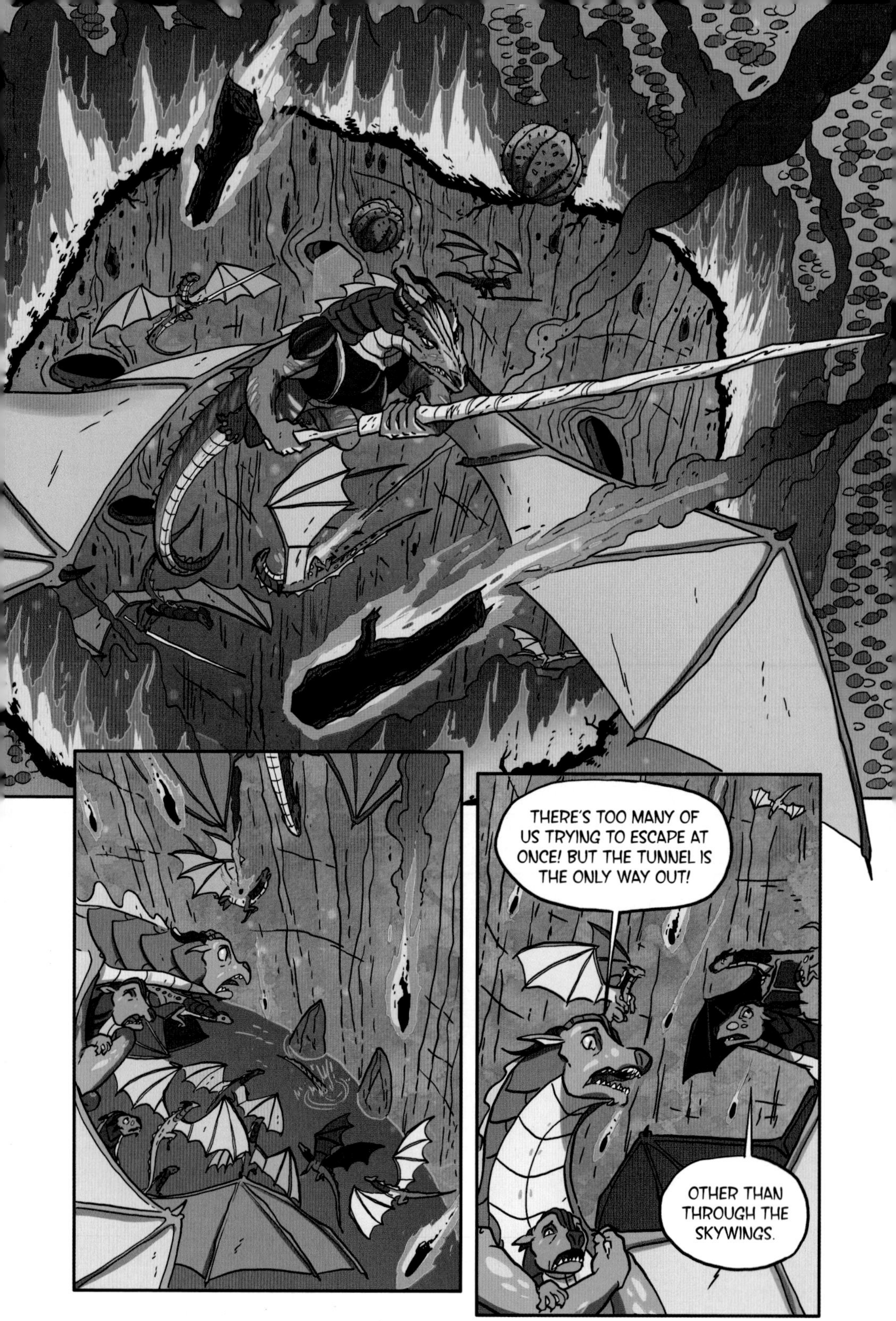
THERE'S TOO MANY OF US TRYING TO ESCAPE AT ONCE! BUT THE TUNNEL IS THE ONLY WAY OUT!
OTHER THAN THROUGH THE SKYWINGS.

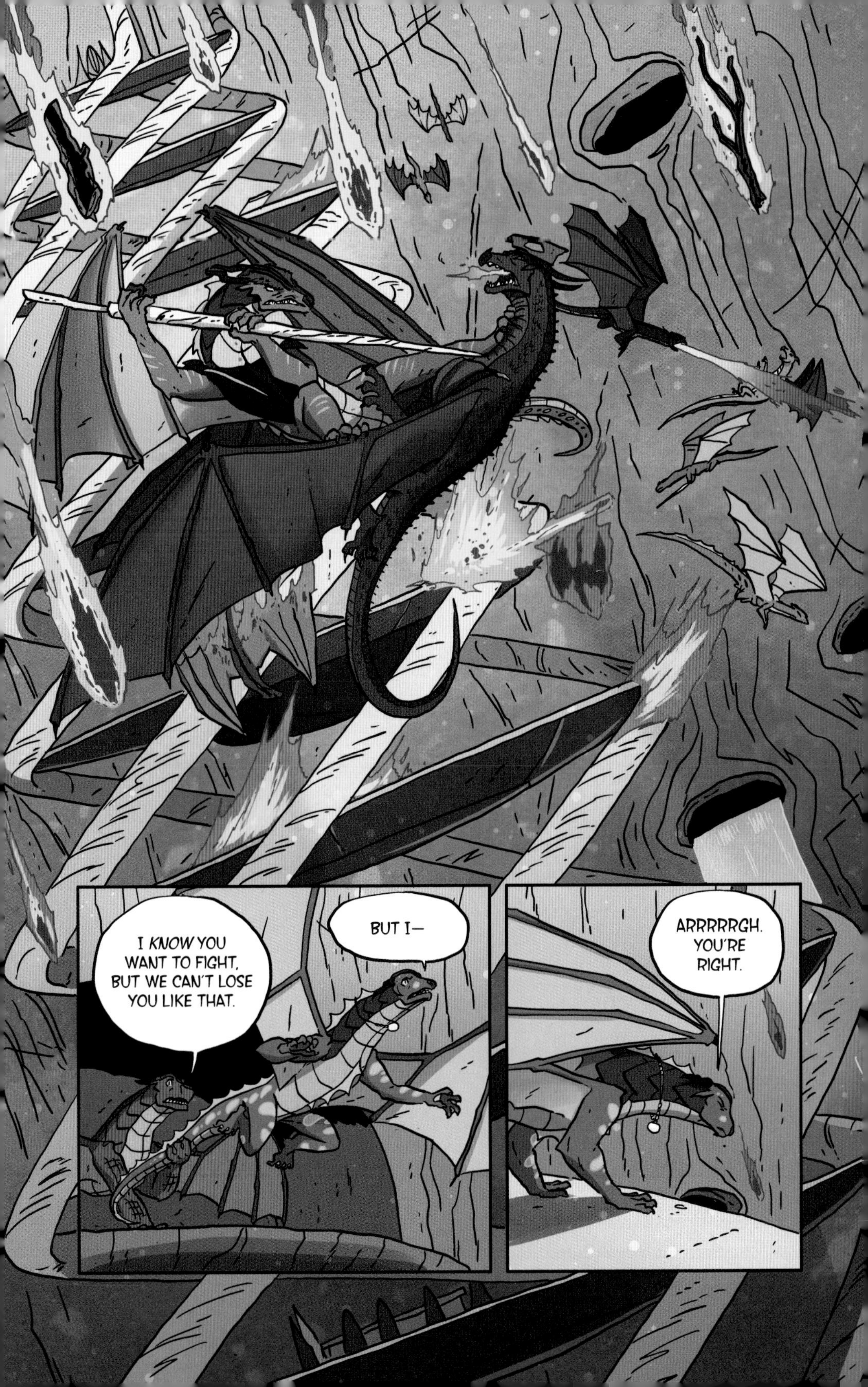
I *KNOW* YOU WANT TO FIGHT, BUT WE CAN'T LOSE YOU LIKE THAT.
BUT I—
ARRRRRGH. YOU'RE RIGHT.

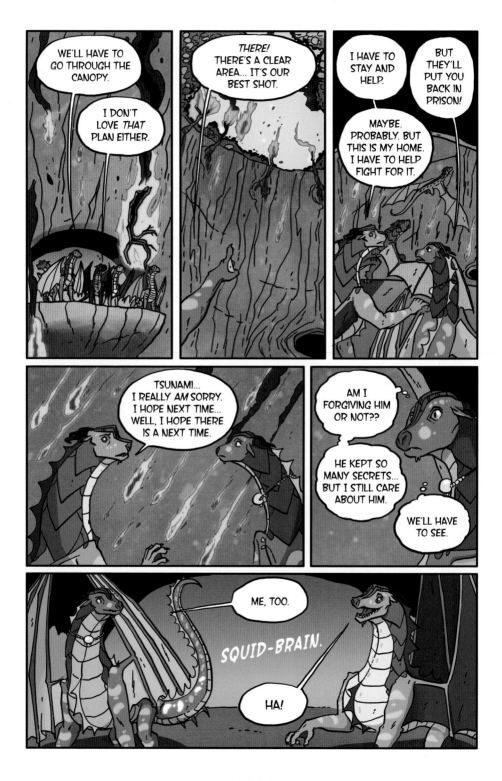

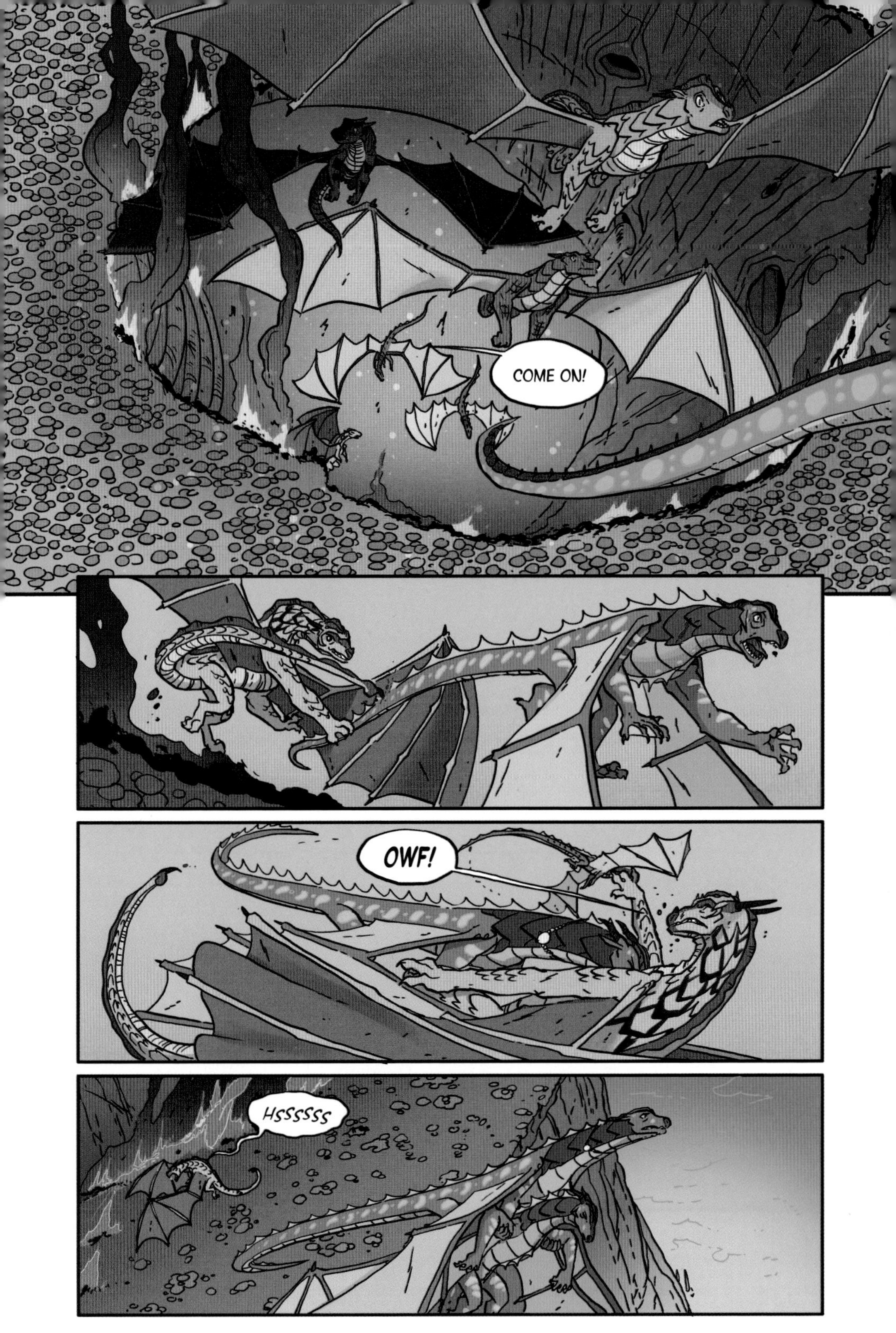
COME ON!
OWF!
HSSSSSS

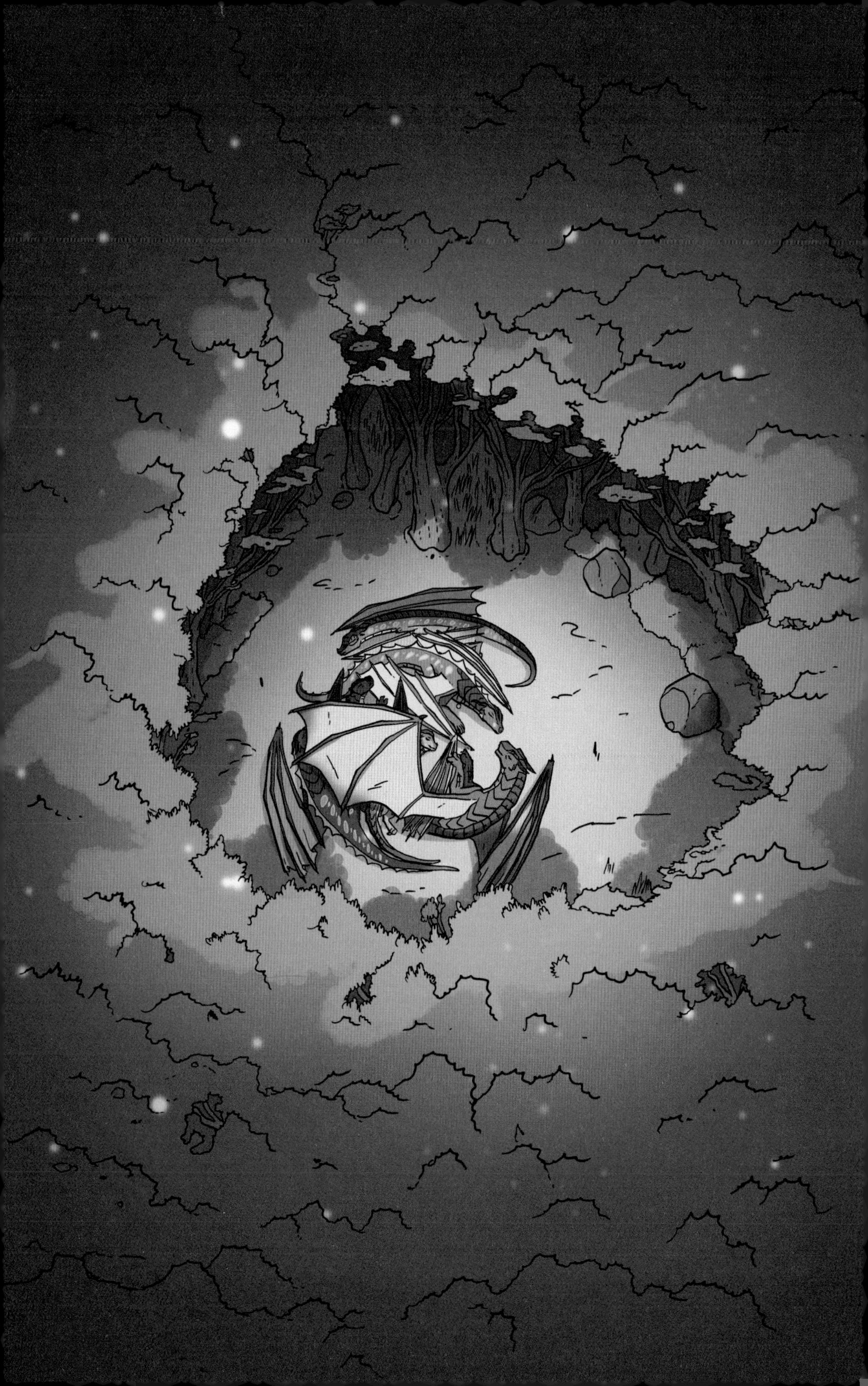

DISCOVER THE EPIC SERIES WHERE IT ALL BEGAN!

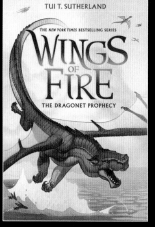

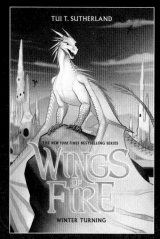